THE SHADOW DECEPTION
THE SHADOW ENFORCER SERIES BOOK TWO

N. M. THORN

The Shadow Deception

By N.M. Thorn

Copyright © 2021 by N.M. Thorn. All rights reserved.

nmthornauthor@gmail.com

This is a work of fiction. Any resemblance to actual persons living or dead, businesses, events, or locales is purely coincidental. Reproduction in whole or part of this publication without express written consent is strictly prohibited.

Cover art design by www.originalbookcoverdesigns.com

Edited by Spirit Editorial

THE SHADOW DECEPTION

THE SHADOW ENFORCER SERIES BOOK 2

N.M. THORN

PROLOGUE

* * *

Semlevo Village, Russia.
The Fall of 1812

WINTER ARRIVED EARLY THAT YEAR. It whistled with frosty winds, rustled with dry foliage and colored the ground white with frost every morning. The trees stood naked, stretching their crooked branches in a silent plea toward the gray sky covered by dark, heavy clouds.

A flock of black birds followed a long string of carts traveling west along the Old Smolensk road, their loud screeches heard for miles around. Day and night, the leftovers of the once powerful *la Grande Armée* of Napoleon Bonaparte moved with their carts, quietly cursing the barbaric wasteland and Russian winter that started at the end of October. Chased by the relentless Russian army and harassed by partisans and Cossacks, they couldn't stop. They couldn't slow down and rest. People, hungry, exhausted and frozen to the bone, barely moved their feet, wrapping dirty rags and torn blankets around their bodies to shield themselves from the chilling breath of early winter.

While the hazy, warmth-deprived sun inched its way toward the horizon, the temperature dropped even lower, and large white flakes of the first snow started to fall from the dark sky. As the army kept moving forward, the dark silhouette of a small village rose before them, but by the time they reached it, the sun was gone, and night wrapped the land in its bone-chilling embrace.

They marched through the village, looking for a place to stop for the night. With locals meeting the starving and weary French soldiers with hostile, rancorous looks, Napoleon chose a small church located in the center of Semlevo village as his shelter for the night.

He wasn't sure how long he sat on one of the benches with his arms folded over his chest, staring at the crucifix mounted above the altar. He didn't pray, but his mind was working on overdrive, going over everything that had happened after his victory in the bloody battle of Borodino. Out of over six hundred thousand men he had when he crossed the border into this unforgiving country, barely thirty thousand were still following him. How did it happen? He kept asking himself this question over and over, but there was no answer.

The front door opened with a loud squeak, bringing the howls of the wind and a blast of the frosty air inside, ripping Napoleon out of his depressing thoughts. Inhaling the scent of the fresh night air, he lifted his head and turned around to find his general, Comte de Ségur, standing in the doorway in the company of a man who looked like one of those Russian peasants he had seen while traveling through the country. Wrapped in a coat and with a fur hat on his head, the man looked like a massive bear next to the refined French Count. The peasant pulled his hat off, displaying a mop of thick, untidy black hair, and bowed low, touching the floor with his hat. However, Napoleon had no doubt—the savage didn't bow to him. He bowed to the altar.

Comte de Ségur crossed himself and made his way toward the bench, lowering himself heavily on it.

"My Emperor," he said, inclining his head, "we need to talk." He threw a quick look at the peasant who remained by the doorway, brushing snowflakes off his wide shoulders.

"I know," replied Napoleon with a long sigh, sending a veiled gaze at his general. "Tell me what brought you here, Comte."

Comte de Ségur leaned forward, lowering his face into his hands, weariness and discomfort lingering over him.

"We're moving too slow," he said after a while, lifting his head to throw a sideways glance at his commander. "All these carts are slowing us down significantly. If we don't speed up..." His hoarse voice trailed off, and he shook his head. "Take your pick, Emperor. Either the Russian army or the Russian winter will eventually destroy us. People are freezing to death, falling off their feet because of disease and starvation."

"I know," repeated Napoleon, pressing his hand over his eyes. "You know what's in those carts, right?"

Comte nodded faintly, his eyes remaining as cold as the weather outside. Napoleon sighed, slamming his fist on the bench. He got up, tucked his hand behind the lapel of his coat and started pacing in front of the altar, muttering something under his breath. Comte didn't stop him, knowing that at times like this, he was better off remaining silent. After a while, Napoleon came to a sharp halt and turned to face the general.

"These carts are filled with all the treasures taken from Moscow," he said quietly, iron notes of resolve in his voice. "The most priceless and rarest pieces—gold, silver, precious stones, ancient armor and weapons, religious artifacts—we need to hide them. Everything less valuable—burn it all. If we can't have it, no one will."

He fell silent, tapping his foot on the floor, a deep frown settling on his features. Throwing a quick glance at the peasant, he leaned forward to be closer to Comte and lowered his voice to a whisper.

"There are other things among all the treasures in one of the carts," he said, his eyes staring at his confidant without blinking. "The kinds of things that cannot be destroyed by fire or any other elements. Yet, we can't leave them here for the Russians to find. These artifacts carry way too much mystical power to leave them in the hands of these barbarians. Not if I can help it. We need to find a safe location to store them and mark it somehow. God willing, we'll return here one day."

"I know, my Emperor. I suspected as much," replied Comte de Ségur. "So, I found the perfect place. Just two kilometers away from this village, there is a lake. Locals call it the Dead Lake or the Black Lake, and they prefer to stay away from it. There are no fish there, and even birds don't nest in the woods around it. Hidden in the depth of a forest and surrounded by swamps, it's not easy to discover. If we dump everything into the black waters of this lake, except for us, no one will ever be able to find it." Comte pointed at the peasant and continued, "This man is willing to show us the way at a hefty price."

Napoleon huffed, shrugging indifferently. "Obviously, we have more gold than we can carry. Pay him twice what he wants and make sure that once we're done, he speaks to no one about it."

He smirked coldly and waved at the peasant to approach. The man covered the distance between them in a few strides and halted, towering a few inches over the Emperor. Napoleon looked up at him, and an expression of displeasure darkened his features.

"He's too tall, de Ségur," he grumbled, folding his arms. "I don't like him."

The man bowed, touching the floor with his hat, and as he

straightened, a dark smirk hid under his thick facial hair.

"My apologies, Your Majesty," he said in perfect French, "but unfortunately, my height is not something I can change."

"But I can," replied Napoleon, moving his finger across his throat. "You speak French?"

"No," the man replied calmly. "I speak magic."

"Magic? I do not believe in such nonsense," Napoleon huffed, but his eyes widened for a heartbeat, the old superstitions of his motherland flashing through his quick mind. "Who are you, and what's your name, peasant?"

"Yakov," replied the man without blinking an eye, his deep voice rumbling through the empty building. "Villagers call me '*chernoknizhnik*' and '*koldun*', which means sorcerer and warlock, but I'm neither. What I am is really not important. What is important is that I can help you hide your treasure, as well as give you a way to recover it later, should the need arise."

Napoleon stared at the man, a touch of respect springing to life in his soul. Then he inclined his head. "If you deliver on your promise, I will pay you as much as you wish," he said, iron tones ringing in his voice. "Do not disappoint me, Yakov, or I will make you shorter. That I can guarantee."

Yakov met Napoleon's burning gaze without blinking, the corners of his lips twitching under the thick mustache. "Get your men ready. We're leaving immediately." He bowed and walked out of the church without waiting for Napoleon's permission to leave.

SURROUNDED by a dense forest and a shallow swamp, Semlevsky Lake wasn't easy to find, but Yakov led them forward with the confidence of a man who had walked this path many times. The ground wobbled under their feet, yet he didn't seem to worry about it, from time-to-time reminding Napoleon and his soldiers to stay behind him and not to stray from the main path. A few times, he raised his hand to halt the procession and squatted, placing his hands on the shaky surface of the swamp, whispering something incoherent. The path was still unsteady, but even the carts with their heavy load made it all the way to the final destination.

It was well past midnight when Napoleon and his men reached the lake. The temperature had dropped even lower, and a thin layer of ice covered the shallows near shore, glistening in the blueish shades of the moonlight. The silence was overwhelming, deadly even—no screeches of night birds, no howls of hungry wolves that roamed these woods in plenty, not even a rustle of wind through the forest.

Yakov approached the lake and stretched out his arms, muttering something under his breath. His words sounded like gibberish, and no matter how much Napoleon strained his hearing, he couldn't understand even one word this unusual man was saying. Yakov's entire body emitted a weak, white glow, and his voice became louder and stronger. Soft whispers rose behind Napoleon as his soldiers started muttering prayers, crossing themselves. The Emperor glared at them over his shoulder, immediately silencing them all.

Suddenly, the surface of the lake lit up with a soft blue light, and a sparkling mist rose above it in the air, rotating slowly in a clockwise motion. Yakov stopped his strange monologue and turned around, his face gray with exhaustion. For a few seconds, he just stood with his hand pressed over his heart, breathing laboriously, unable to say anything. Then he waved at the lake and finally spoke.

"Your Majesty, order your men to unload all your treasures into the lake," Yakov said, his voice hoarse and strained. "I swear, no one will ever find any of it. No one, but you." He smirked darkly and reached under his heavy winter coat, producing a piece of paper.

Napoleon glanced at the paper and frowned, his temper rising. "It's empty. Are you—"

"Not at all," objected the man. "I'm just a little drained after using so much of my energy to grant your wish." He sucked in a large gulp of the frosty night air and brushed his fingertips over the paper. A map of the lake and the surrounding areas materialized on it. He whispered something, and a strange symbol shone in the corner of the paper. "If you ever return here, Emperor, just throw this paper into the water, and you'll find everything that's yours."

"Hmm..." Napoleon carefully took the paper as if it could bite him and peered at it. Then he folded it and placed it into the inside pocket of his coat. "Well... you delivered on your promise, Yakov. I'm a man of honor, and I always keep my word." He waved his hand at the carts. "Take anything you want and as much as you can carry. It's yours."

"My gratitude, Emperor." Yakov inclined his head and headed toward the carts.

As Napoleon watched the man moving heavily toward his treasure, he expected him to walk straight to the cart that held the items he considered mystical. So, when Yakov passed it all without giving it as much as a second look, a spike of disappointment surged through him. Instead, the strange man halted in front of the cart with silver jewelry and religious artifacts—expensive and rare, but not what Napoleon would consider magical. He moved a few boxes out of the way, barely paying any attention to them, and pulled out a small, wooden box.

With the box in his hands, he made his way back to Napoleon, and it seemed that every next step he took came with more effort than the previous. He halted before the Emperor of France, inclining his head in a bow, and showed him the piece he picked.

"This is all I want," he said softly, brushing his fingers over the plain surface of the wood.

"Open it," ordered Napoleon, curiosity taking the best of him.

Yakov didn't object and opened the box. On the bed of black silk, two silver bands shone, reflecting the orange, flickering light of the torch Comte de Ségur was holding. The bigger one had a chain of words in an unfamiliar language engraved along its perimeter. The second one was a plain silver ring that looked like a wedding band. While skillfully crafted, there was seemingly nothing special about them.

"Hmm," Napoleon hummed, shoving his hand beneath the lapel of his coat. "What is it? What's so special about it?"

"For you?" Yakov smirked with a half-shrug. "Nothing. It's just beautiful silver jewelry. But for me, it's a family heirloom."

Napoleon's lips quirked up in an uneven smile. "I do not believe you, peasant. But I gave you my word, and I always keep my promises. As soon as you escort us back to the village, it's yours."

He took the box and closed the lid, passing it to Comte de Ségur. Without giving a second look to Yakov, he turned on his heel and shouted the command for his men to start unloading the priceless treasure into the misty waters of the Dead Lake.

* * *

Semlevsky Lake
Three hours later.

YAKOV SAT at the edge of the lake, staring at its dark, motionless water. The box lay on the ground next to him, his fingers tracing the shape of the lid absentmindedly. Still drained after the extensive use of his magic, he wasn't sure he had enough energy in him to do what needed to be done, but he had no choice.

With a deep sigh, he moved into a kneeling position and

leaned forward, breaking the thin layer of ice with his fingers. Channeling his magic, he sent a small amount of it into the water, and shimmering circles spread over the surface, rushing away from his hand.

"Mavka Kostroma," he whispered, "I summon thee..."

He pulled his hand out, wiping the icy water off his fingers with the side of his coat. For a few long seconds, the lake remained still, but then a soft gust of wind rushed through the area, and the surface rippled, lighting up with a deep, ultramarine glow from within. The water parted, and a young woman stepped out of the lake, lowering herself on a large stone next to Yakov.

Completely naked, the only cover she had was her long, blonde hair. It cascaded down her chest and back, shimmering with slightly green shades. Her large, blue eyes drilled into Yakov, her full, pale lips parting a little, and for a moment, he forgot why he was here, unable to take his eyes off her.

She averted her gaze, breaking their eye contact, and Yakov sucked in a sharp breath, realizing that he just fell victim to a rusalka's charm. Kostroma chuckled, humorous twinkles igniting in her eyes as deep as the lake itself.

"Hello, Yakov," she said, her voice as musical and tender as the song of a bubbling creek. "Long time, no see. What brought you into my domain the second time in a single night, old wizard?"

"Let go of your rusalka's magic. I need your help, Kostroma—"

"Really?" she asked with a thin layer of sarcasm in her voice. "And what might that be?"

Yakov took the box and opened it, showing its contents to the young woman. Her eyes widened, and a shadow of fear crossed her tender face. She reached toward it, but then changed her mind and jerked her hand away.

"Be careful. It's silver," warned Yakov, closing the box.

She nodded, but the tense set of her shoulders told him she knew exactly what was locked inside this plain wooden case.

"Today, I retrieved this box from Napoleon Bonaparte. Luckily, I was in time, and this dangerous man had no idea what he had in his possession," he said quietly. "Tomorrow, I could have been too late to stop another human from discovering the magical properties of this artifact and using it. Since it cannot be destroyed, I need it hidden and well-protected."

"I understand," she said, hatred and disgust distorting her face. "This thing is a magical abomination. It should have never existed in the first place."

"Agreed." Yakov reached into his pocket and produced a tiny, clear crystal. He whispered a few words, and a soft purple glow ignited within it, giving it the resemblance to amethyst. Moving the crystal along the seam of the box, he sealed it completely and offered the box to the rusalka. "It is sealed. Without this crystal, no one can open this box again, but I don't think it's enough. I need you to take it into your kingdom and guard it."

The young woman got up, stepping softly with her bare feet on the frozen land. With trembling hands, she took the box from Yakov and nodded to him.

"You and I are the only people who know about it," said Yakov, rising. "Protect it with your life. No one should ever get their hands on it."

"I'll guard it with my life." The young woman turned around and dove into the lake, disappearing in its dark waters.

Now it's gone forever...

Yakov snapped his fingers and spun around, a dark mist wrapping around him like a shimmering veil. A moment later, the man was gone, and a large white-tailed eagle materialized in his place. With one flap of its enormous wings, the bird rose in the air and disappeared into the dark of night.

CHAPTER 1

~ DAMIAN BLAKE ~

*Somewhere on the outskirts of Phoenix, Arizona
Halloween night...*

A giant orange moon hung low over the horizon. Its bright light made its way between the dusty window shutters, reflecting in the faded mirror above the bar counter, throwing playful flares at the multicolored liquor bottles.

The bar was relatively dark, illuminated only by the LED strip lights installed around the perimeter of the room and an old neon sign above the mirror with the name of the establishment—*The Midnight Shift*. A curtain of cigarette smoke flowed under the low ceiling, and its smell mixed in with the pungent odor of different liquors seemed to be permanently etched into everything.

Fake spider webs, spangled with plastic spiders and other creepy crawlers, hung in every corner. A plastic pumpkin with a wide smile shining with electric light stood at the side of the counter, completing the Halloween decor.

Owned by one of the Phoenix packs, *The Midnight Shift* had recently been declared a sanctuary, allowing all local representatives of the supernatural community to relax and have a drink or two without being concerned for their lives and safety. A powerful turn-away spell placed on the building kept all mundanes untouched by the World of Magic away, and the local human hunters who were well aware of the bar's status normally avoided it. Despite his "professional" status, Damian liked this place and allowed himself to spend a few hours here once in a great while.

Damian twirled an empty shot glass between his fingers, a muscle twitching in his tightly pressed jaw. He reached for his phone just to see a dark screen without any new notifications.

"Come on, Cole," he murmured under his breath. "What's taking you so long?"

He put the phone back in the pocket of his light leather jacket, nibbling on his lip.

"One more?"

Damian glanced at the bartender and nodded, placing the shot glass back on the counter. The man was dressed in an orange, Halloween-themed shirt with a black cat that looked too cute for a person of his size and shape to wear in public. Damian lowered his eyes, the corners of his lips quirking up in a tiny smile. It wasn't only that the bartender was almost as tall as him, but he was also a werewolf, and a picture of a kitty in a pointy witch hat stretched across his overly muscled chest just didn't fit the bill.

The bartender filled another glass with vodka and placed it in front of him. Damian took it, rolling it between his thumb and middle finger.

"Thanks, Kaleb," he said to the werewolf. "Something tells me I may need another one later."

Kaleb flicked his eyebrow at him, and his one-sided smirk exposed a set of sharp, paper-white teeth shining with bluish shades of the LED lights.

"Hey, Damian, slow down." Jamie pushed him on his

shoulder slightly to attract his attention. "Are you sure drinking is a good idea?"

"It takes a lot more for me to get drunk, Jamie," he muttered, emptying the contents of the shot glass into his mouth. "A lot more than a bottle of vodka, let alone two small shot glasses. I may as well be drinking water."

He glanced sideways at the young wizard and smirked. Nervousness shone in Jamie's blue eyes, his fingers folding and unfolding a napkin.

"Listen, Jamie." Damian straightened, turning toward him slightly. "No offense, but you're not ready, man. I've been training you less than three months, which is nothing when it comes to the World of Magic. It takes years to muster your spell casting and even longer to control your magic. Fire magic is supposed to be your strength, but you can barely light a candle."

"Oh, yeah?" said Jamie, his lips forming a stubborn straight line. "And Ace is ready? Your brother has no problem with her following him everywhere."

Damian drew in a long breath and knocked on the counter with an empty shot glass to attract Kaleb's attention. Normally, he didn't mind Ace tagging along with Cole. During the day, she worked at his company, and at night, she attended all his royal meetings and Court gatherings. Even though she was very young as a person and had barely taken off her training wheels as a Destiny Enforcer, the Destiny Council considered her fit to shadow the King of Arizona, so he wasn't going to argue despite his personal reservations. Besides, protecting his brother had always been *his* job, so he never counted on any outside help.

Today, however, his nerves were on edge, and the presence of two young people who barely had any experience with real combat situations just added to his feeling of unease. Cole was in a meeting with the leaders of the largest opposing group of vampires, hoping to find common ground and convince them to join his Court. Knowing this particular faction, Damian had been against this meeting from the get-go, considering it to be as dangerous as it was useless. However, his brother had disagreed, trying to use diplomatic methods first before plunging the state into open warfare.

Kaleb filled another glass with vodka, moving it closer to him. Damian brought it up, inhaling the burning scent of alcohol, and then downed it in one shot. Letting out a harsh breath, he turned back to Jamie.

"I'm not my brother," he said quietly, "and Ace is not my responsibility. But it's my responsibility to support Cole's position in the Vampire Court and make sure the war between different vampire factions is not going to affect the realm of humans. And that's exactly what I'm planning to do. If something goes wrong—"

His cellphone vibrated in his pocket, and he cut himself off, rising. He pulled the phone out and quickly read Cole's message on the screen.

"NO DICE 911"

Turning toward Jamie, he looked down at him and frowned. He wished the young wizard would change his mind and stay back, but there was no power in this world that would have talked him out of going.

"Last chance, Jamie," he said softly, his voice almost pleading. "Please, stay behind, my friend. You still have a lot to learn."

"Theory without practice is useless. Practice makes perfect," retorted Jamie, sounding like a high school student reporting in front of the class. He got up and adjusted his light jacket, checking his pockets.

"And don't forget the most famous one—buy low, sell high," muttered Damian snidely. "Any other quotes you'd like to share?" He reached into his pocket, pulled out his wallet, and threw a few bills on the counter. Stifling a sigh, he headed out of the bar, motioning for Jamie to follow him.

As soon as they stepped out the door, the cool evening air

enveloped him, but Damian ignored the cold, his mind set on getting to his brother as soon as possible. Quickly surveying the area, he grunted. It was Halloween evening and despite the late hour, kids dressed like assorted monsters and superheroes promenaded down the street accompanied by their parents. Laughing, chatting and having fun, they were none the wiser of the terrible territorial war unfolding in the shadows behind the well illuminated and decorated main street.

He turned the corner, leaving the main street behind. Hiding in the shadows, he made sure there was no one watching them. Then he placed his hand on Jamie's shoulder and snapped his fingers, teleporting them closer to the location of the meeting. Since he didn't know what kind of security measures the leaders of the opposing faction had taken, he teleported to a secluded location he'd selected ahead of time—a tiny dark alley located away from any major streets and a safe distance from their final destination.

As soon as they manifested in the alley, he switched to a light run, throwing an occasional glance over his shoulder to make sure Jamie was keeping up with him. Soon, the tiny suburban street turned into a narrow two-lane asphalt road. Curving its way around a few sandy hills, it left the peaceful suburbia on his right side.

The farther they moved, the colder and darker it became, and Damian had no doubt it wasn't just the night desert temperatures that sent shivers down his back. Sharpening his senses, the putrid stench of demonic essence assailed him, but besides the reek of sulfur, he detected some other presence he couldn't identify. Dark and elusive, it seemed vaguely familiar, yet he couldn't put his finger on it.

Damian pressed the back of his hand to his nose and mouth, slowing down to allow Jamie to catch up with him. The young man halted by his side and leaned forward, bracing his arms against his lap to catch his breath.

"For an old man, you sure know how to run," he said, panting. Looking up, he shook his head and straightened, wiping sweat off his forehead. "Why are we here, anyway? Farther, just around this hill..." He waved to the left at the dark silhouette of a mountain, still breathing hard. "It's Camelback mountain... Expensive homes... in the millions..."

"I figured as much. Old vamps and their money," murmured Damian. "This entire area emanates hostility and dark magical energy." He thought for a moment, staring at his young companion, and added, "Be careful. Chances are, once we breach the perimeter, I may not be able to protect you."

Quickly crossing the road, Damian switched to a light jog, following the road circling the hill. A view of a beautiful, contemporary estate perched on a hillside unfolded before him, and he halted again, scanning it with his second sight. It was surrounded by black wrought iron fencing but only from three sides as the back of it was blocked by the hill. Tall double gates were locked, but as far as he could see, no one was guarding the entry, and that just threw a countless number of red flags in his mind.

A thick layer of protective magic lingered around the perimeter of the property, and runes glowing with a deep purple light were inscribed on the fence and the gates, indicating the presence of powerful wards.

I can't break through these wards without triggering some kind of reaction and an alarm. Damian explored the fence as far as he could see but didn't find even a single weak point. He looked up just to realize that he couldn't go over the fence either—a thin net of glowing lines encapsulated the entire estate, crisscrossing and shimmering with purple light like some freakishly large spider web.

"Jamie..." He glanced to the side where Jamie was supposed to be, but he wasn't there. Damian twirled around and found him by the gates. "Jamie, no!" he yelled, but it was too late.

The young wizard reached forward and touched the gates. The wards lit up brighter, responding with a soft, barely noticeable vibration. Seemingly, nothing changed, but Damian knew better. In one swift motion, he grabbed Jamie, pulled him away from the gates and turned him around, shielding him with his body.

"Procedia Amnia!" he shouted the basic protection spell, channeling the elemental energy into his magic to reinforce it. Just as the shield, glowing with a dim yellow light, surrounded them, a powerful surge of dark magical energy exploded outward from somewhere within the property lines. It traveled as fast as a blast wave, lifting clouds of sand and tiny pebbles into the air. Damian growled as the dark energy impacted his shield, his arms shaking with tremendous strain. Jamie bent down, wrapping his arms around his head.

The wave moved a few feet farther and dissipated on its own. Without removing the protective shield, Damian turned around in place, staring at the wards in shock. The lines in the sky and runes over the gates and fences shone brighter than before, the air around them vibrating with a low buzz.

"What the hell was that?" mumbled Jamie, straightening.

"Wards," replied Damian, breathing hard. "You activated the wards that were placed on this property."

"Sorry," whispered the young man, looking as guilty as a dog who had stolen a piece of juicy chicken. "What now?"

"Now, since the element of surprise is no longer an option, we make an entry," replied Damian, channeling as much magic toward his hands as he could. "And we fight. No matter what we find behind this overpriced fence."

"But we don't know what—"

"I don't give a damn. My brother is in there. I'll kill anything that gets in my way." He thrust his arm forward, his body igniting with the bright orange glow of the elemental energy he was wielding, and shouted, *"Exitius!"*

The gates blew up, turning into warped chunks of metal, and the ground shook, the tremors spreading around Damian in rapid succession. He stepped heavily over the threshold created by his magic and looked up, a dark smirk curving his lips. The glowing web of wards was gone, but a cloud of gray particles was slowly rotating above the ground.

"I suggest you run," he hissed at Jamie and moved toward the entrance into the house, following the beautifully paved driveway up the hill.

Even though the driveway lights were still glowing, and the windows of the house were shining with bright, electric lights, the closer he got to the entrance, the darker it became. As the driveway started to curve sharply, multiple shady figures emerged from the night, the hostile vibes of demonic presence unmistakable around them.

Damian didn't slow down. As his daggers materialized in his hands, he cut into the first demon who was close enough for him to reach. A ray of eye-watering white light pierced the demon's body, obliterating the host and the demonic essence before the demon could shimmer out.

"*Igneous,*" yelled Jamie, but instead of a fire blast, a tiny flickering flame ignited in the palm of his hand, making the demon he was facing bark with laugher. The monster swung his hairy arm, aiming at Jamie's face. His massive fist was met by Damian's hand. Wrapping the demon's fist with his fingers, Damian applied some pressure, making the attacker stagger backward.

"Pick someone your own size, asshole," he growled at the demon, squeezing his fingers tighter. Then he turned to Jamie, and his lips curved into a snarl. "Let me show you how it's done, student of mine." Extending his free hand forward, he shouted, "*Ignius Orbus.*"

A fireball crackling with blistering flames materialized in his palm. With lightning speed, he thrust the fireball into the demon's chest and let go. The monster screamed in pain, twirling in place, setting other demons on fire.

"Igneous Amplio!" Damian held out both his hands, and a powerful jet of physical fire erupted from his palms, spraying the remaining monsters. He turned back to Jamie, his chest shuddering with ragged breaths. "That's how it's done, boy."

Jamie nodded, his mouth half-open, his eyes glued to the screaming monsters being devoured by the hungry flames. "But you just killed a bunch of people," he exhaled. "Their souls could have still been inside their—"

"I don't have the luxury of caring about it right now," growled Damian, heading toward the entrance door, but noticing the shock on the young wizard's face, he sighed and added, "It was either them or us. Besides, I can see human souls with my second sight. They had none. Just monsters wearing dead human bodies."

He halted in front of the door and scanned the building inside with his magical sight as far as he could reach. Glancing back at his companion, his lips pulled up into a sneer before he could stop it.

"Now the real fun begins," he whispered, channeling his magic toward his hands. "Vampires. Deadly, clever, merciless. Don't get cute with them, Jamie. Stay back and let me do all the talking."

Instead of blasting the door with his spell, he placed his hand on the lock and whispered, *"Recludius."*

The lock clicked softly, leaving the entrance unprotected. As his daggers materialized in his hands, he pulled his leg back and kicked the door open. The door hit the wall with a thunderous bang, and the sound carried through the enormous marble-adorned lobby, reverberating against the tall ceiling.

As soon as Damian crossed the threshold, something heavy crashed on his shoulders, and a cold, muscled arm wrapped around his neck, squeezing it with the strength of an industrial press. A strong hand forced his head to the side, and before he could react, razor-sharp fangs penetrated his skin.

A wild roar broke from his lips as he grabbed the unfortunate vamp's head and twisted it, ripping it off his shoulders. A shower of gray ashes fell to his feet, and he raised his glowing eyes, his second sight revealing the position of every single vampire in the room.

"Jamie, stay outside," he ordered without looking back, "it's about to get..." He laughed and moved forward, the daggers in his hands blazing.

All the vampires came into motion at the same time, assailing him from every direction. Silent and fast, Damian spun around, his daggers slicing through the vampires' bodies, severing limbs and cutting their heads off, leaving piles of steaming ash behind. The attackers pulled back, shock in their glowing scarlet eyes.

"What happened?" Damian snickered, cocking his head slightly. "Are you done?" The vampires froze in that unnerving way only vampires could, waiting for his next move. "What? Already? No stamina, eh?" He dropped to one knee, placing his hand on the marble floor, and a wild smile crossed his face—the marble was natural. *Got to love these rich undead assholes...*

Rising, he waved his arm, the air around him vibrating with the deadly magic he was channeling. "Well, I barely warmed up, boys."

The vamps hissed, leaping into action once again.

"*Risurgius!*" he yelled, moving forward. He ripped two massive blocks of marble off the floor and blocked both doors, barricading all ways in and out of the lobby.

Damian wasn't moving as fast as the vampires, but he didn't have to. Now that the vampires had no place to hide and no way to escape, he knew he had them exactly where he wanted them. Halting in the middle of the lobby, he allowed the monsters to surround him. As they started to squeeze the circle, he spread his arms, and the floor shook violently, deep fractures marring perfectly polished marble. The vampires hissed like a bunch of wild cats, retreating again.

He clenched his hands into fists and twisted them. The fractures grew wider, spreading farther and farther, pushing the vampires toward the walls. Once they had no more space to run, Damian touched the leather bracelet with his fingers, turning it into a silver bullwhip. He moved around with the fluidity of a dancer, the fractures closing beneath his feet and reopening once he was gone. The whip in his hand cut through the air with a soft whistle, striking vampires with deadly precision. A few seconds later, it was over, the last remains of the attackers slowly dissolving into ashes.

Damian stopped, breathing hard. With his other sight opened, he probed the area ahead but didn't find any vampires or demons. He could still detect some vampiric energy in the building, but it was weak, barely detectable.

"Cole," he breathed out, a feeling of dread settling in the pit of his stomach.

Connecting with the power of Earth once again, he moved the blocks of marble out of the way, allowing Jamie to come in. The young man passed the doorway and halted, observing the lobby with the warped marble floor covered in a thick layer of ash, awe in his eyes.

"I'm afraid to ask," he mumbled. "How many?"

Damian shrugged, wrapping the whip around his wrist, turning it back into the bracelet.

"Sorry. I had no time for math exercises." Motioning for Jamie to follow him, he ran through the dimly lit hallway. With all his senses focused on Cole's dimming presence, he knew exactly where he needed to go. Soon, the hallway came to a dead-end in front of a tall glass door. Without slowing down, he pushed the door open and crossed into a large living area.

Every piece of furniture in the room was either moved,

turned upside down or destroyed. The floor was slippery with blood, covered in ash and dead bodies, undoubtedly demons. At the far end of the room, he saw his brother. Cole lay on the floor, his hands clutching the blade of a sword protruding from his chest. Ace lay next to him, her blood-coated sword on the floor by her side. Her eyes were closed, blood still seeping from a wound on her neck.

"No," moaned Jamie, his grief-infused voice ripping Damian out of his momentary stupor.

Damian crossed the room, dropping to his knees next to his brother. Opening his second sight, he checked Ace and exhaled with relief. She was still alive—barely, but alive. His gaze darted to Cole. He gently unlocked his bloodied fingers and explored the wound.

At his touch, Cole's eyes opened, and his lips twitched slightly, blood dripping from the corner of his mouth. Meeting Damian's gaze, he smiled weakly, his lips forming just two words, *"Brat moi..."*

Brother mine...

CHAPTER 2

~ DAMIAN BLAKE ~

"Hold on, Cole." Damian got up, his hands trembling slightly as he wrapped his fingers tightly around the grip of the sword. "I'm sorry..."

In one sharp movement, he pulled the sword out and threw it on the floor, a loud clatter of metal against the marble tiles catalyzing his boiling fury. Cole growled, his jaws pressed so tightly his teeth squeaked. He pressed his hands tighter to his chest, but the blood didn't stop, trickling between his unbending fingers.

"You're not healing," hissed Damian, his voice shaking with anger and desperation. "Why aren't you healing?"

He glanced at Ace, noticing that the glow of her human soul started to dim down. His eyes darted back to his brother. Cole groaned, and his eyes rolled back, his features distorted by undiluted anguish.

"Dammit!" Damian threw his hands up and dropped to his knees next to Ace. Glancing back at Cole, he muttered apologetically, "I have to help Ace first. If I don't heal her now, she'll be dead in a few minutes."

Cole nodded, large, red drops slipping from the corners of

his eyes, running down his strained, pale face. Suppressing the desire to take care of his brother first, Damian turned back to Ace and quickly explored her body for any visible injuries. Besides the vampire's bite on her neck, she had a few bruises and lacerations on her arms and face, but none of them were lethal.

Taking a deep breath, he connected with the elemental power of Earth and placed his hands over Ace's forehead and chest, slowly circulating the healing energy through her body. In front of his eyes, the cuts closed up and the bruises disappeared, but the bite on her neck remained opened, even though the bleeding slowed down.

"What the hell?" muttered Damian. Leaning down, he explored the bite marks, noticing four puncture wounds instead of two. "Cole, does it—"

He cut himself off, remembering that his brother wasn't in any condition to help him. Turning back to Ace, he opened his other sight and carefully checked the wound on her neck. He could see the presence of vampiric energy, but there was something else there. Dark, menacing, unclean, it lingered over the bite mark, seeping into the wound, entering Ace's bloodstream. He didn't recognize what it was, but it made his blood run cold with the expectation of something terrible.

"What on Earth is that?" he murmured, channeling more of the healing energy through Ace, but no matter what he did, the wound wouldn't heal. He summoned one of his daggers and frowned, staring down at the shining blade in his hand. "If that's not going to work, I'm taking you back to the Destiny Council realm, sweetheart. Now..." His voice wavered, and he swallowed hard. "I'm truly sorry about this."

He pressed the blade to the bite mark on her neck and whispered, *"Illucious..."*

The purifying energy of Creation lit up the weapon, penetrating the wound. Ace screamed, and her body arched like a tightly stretched bow. The dark energy hissed, and its tendrils slithered out of the wound, refusing to give up its territory. Keeping his other sight open, Damian increased the flow of the purifying energy. Ace screamed and thrashed violently, almost knocking the dagger out of his hands.

"Jamie," he yelled, struggling to keep the energy of Creation flowing. "Hold her."

As Jamie grabbed Ace's shoulders, pinning her down with the full weight of his body, Damian pressed the blade to her neck with both hands, channeling all the power he could gather through it. Blood oozed from under the dagger where the blade cut into his palm, but he ignored the pain. The dark energy hissed and slithered, fighting his magic, but little by little, it started to retreat, and a few seconds later, it dissipated in a dark smoke-like wisp.

Ace stopped screaming, and her body relaxed, lying on the floor limply.

"Ace?" Jamie called, gently slapping her cheek. Her eyelashes fluttered, and she cracked her eyelids open, her hand rising to her neck.

"What happened?" she croaked, her voice barely audible.

"That's what I would like to know." Damian let go of his magic and sat back on his heels, wiping sweat off his forehead with the back of his hand. Feeling slightly dizzy, he closed his eyes, taking a deep breath.

Overused my magic... A troubling thought flashed through his mind, but he forced it back. Rising on his knees with a strenuous grunt, he turned toward his brother. The sharp movement made the world around him spin, but he clenched his teeth, focusing on Cole.

"Do you know why you're not healing?" he asked.

Cole nodded and winced. "Silver bullet... in—" He endeavored to lift his hand but had no strength, and it fell to the floor with a dull thud.

"Whoever did this to you..." Damian growled, anger spiraling through him. Channeling his magic once more, he opened his other sight. It wasn't as strong as it normally would be, and this little bit of magic came with an effort, but he could see the soft glow of silver in his brother's chest. "Sorry, it seems I'm dealing in pain today."

"I'm already... in pain. More... less... don't care..." Cole closed his eyes. "Do it."

"Don't move." Damian placed his hand over the area where he'd seen the silver bullet and whispered the spell, *"Transvectum..."*

Cole's eyes flew open, and a howl of pain tore from his bloodied lips, but he managed to remain still, his hands clenched into tight fists at his sides.

"It's okay, it's okay," mumbled Damian, his mind foggy. "It's over now."

He flipped his hand over, unlocking his fingers. A single silver bullet lay in his palm. He held it between his thumb and middle finger, surveying it from every side. In the bright glimmer of electric lights, he noticed barely visible fissures going all around the bullet. Even though he couldn't recognize the symbols, he was positive they were either sigils or runes.

"Do you recognize any of these symbols?" he asked, showing the bullet to Cole.

The vampire shook his head, struggling to sit up. "I've never seen anything like that," he said, giving up on his fruitless attempts. "But something wasn't right here from the very beginning."

"Okay," said Damian, watching the wound on his brother's chest close up and heal. "You can tell me all the details later." He looked around the large room, sharpening his hearing. Seemingly, the house remained empty, but it didn't mean no one was watching them or listening to their conversation. "I'm going to give you some of my blood so you can walk on your own, and after that, we should get the hell out of here as soon as we can."

"I'll give him my blood, Damian," whispered Ace, sitting up with Jamie's help. "You look like you're ready to faint."

"I'm not going to faint," snapped Damian, turning to her. "Healing magic requires a lot of energy, and whatever was done to you required not only healing but also purifying magic. As a Destiny Enforcer, you should know the toll this kind of effort takes on your body." He took a deep breath, suppressing his aggravation. "Don't argue with me, recruit." His eyes flashed from Ace to Jamie. "Both of you. You, Ace, are head over heels for my brother and are already addicted to his bite, which both are in violation of the Destiny Enforcer's code. I don't want to hear about you donating your blood to him anymore. Am I clear?"

"Yes, Commander Blake," Ace mumbled, her ashen face turning a few shades paler.

"And you, Jamie," exhaled Damian but then just waved his hand dismissively. "We'll talk later about your performance today. In the meantime, stand down and help Ace. I don't need to deal with another child being addicted to a vampire's bite."

Jamie's eyes widened, but he had enough common sense to keep his mouth shut. Damian pulled Cole up into a sitting position, supporting him with his shoulder. He moved his bleeding hand closer to his brother's lips and exhaled, feeling lightheadedness sweeping over him.

Cole's icy-cold fingers seized his arm. "I'll make it painless," he whispered, his fangs expanding.

"No," Damian objected, his entire body going rigid. "Make it hurt. Make it as painful as you can." Cole's eyebrows rose, but Damian just shook his head and chuckled weakly. "Come on, little bro. It's kinky even for you. The pleasure of a vampire bite? Thank you, but no, thank you. I don't want to feel like I want to screw my own brother."

Jamie snorted, unsuccessfully trying to suppress his laughter, and Ace bit her lip, looking anywhere but at him.

"As you wish," said Cole and sunk his fangs into Damian's arm.

Damian drew in a short breath and jerked involuntarily as the sharp sting of pain spiked through him. The heavy copper odor touched his senses, and he held his breath, looking down. But as his blood gathered and spilled from under his brother's fangs, he swallowed and turned away, dizziness assailing him with new strength. A few seconds later, Cole let go and closed his eyes, shifting slightly to rest his back against Damian's chest.

"Thank you." He ran his hand over his face, trying to wipe the blood off but only making it worse by smearing it all over his cheeks. "Give me one minute, and I'll be ready to go."

Damian looked down at his arm where Cole had bitten him—two small, bleeding holes. He'd seen the marks left by vampire bites many times. It was always two deep puncture wounds left by their long fangs. Depending on how much force a vampire had applied, sometimes he could see the imprints of their regular teeth. But never had he seen a vampire bite with more than two puncture wounds. Upirs left deeper holes in their victims' flesh and their fangs were spread wider. But it had always been two. His eyes darted to Ace's neck, but the mark of the vampire bite was gone, healed by his magic.

Cole is right... Something is seriously wrong here...

* * *

A FEW MINUTES LATER, they walked out of the house. As he suspected, the building stood abandoned, and their passage through the property was uneventful. Ace moved slowly, weakened by the blood loss and the healing magic, and Jamie had to nearly carry her all the way to Cole's car that was parked on the opposite side of the driveway.

"Jamie," said Cole, handing him the keys to his car, "can you please take Ace home? Damian and I don't need a car."

"Whoa," exhaled Jamie, his blue eyes lighting up with excitement. "Seriously, man? I can drive this..." His voice melted into silence as his fingers trailed over the streamlined body of the silver *Lamborghini Huracan Spyder*. "Six hundred ten CV, V10 engine, two hundred miles per hour... Dude, it's a dream..."

"Yup," murmured Cole, snickering. "It's a dream. Two hundred miles per hour in combination with thirty-five miles per hour speed limit. Do try not to get any speeding tickets." He turned to Damian and shrugged. "Why do I feel as if I'm giving matches to a child?"

"Because you are," muttered Damian, switching his attention to Jamie. "I expect to see you in Paradise Manor for training tomorrow after you're done with your shift at the library, Jamie. Don't be late." He turned to Ace, giving her a quick once-over. "Ace, you are taking the day off tomorrow."

"But Commander Blake—," she started to object, but he made an impatient gesture with his hand, and she fell silent, averting her gaze.

"You do as I say," he said dryly, "or I'll have to have a personal chat with Commander Moore, which I'm sure you're not going to appreciate."

"No, my lord," she whispered, looking guilty. "Please, don't do it."

"Damian—," started Cole, but Damian's scorching stare silenced him.

"Ace, you will remain at home for at least twenty-four hours. I will shadow my brother in your absence. As an owner of the company, Cole will give you a paid day off. Am I right, Mr. Adams?"

"Yes, sir, Commander Jackass," replied Cole, sarcasm overflowing his voice. "Oops, did I say it out loud? I meant to say, yes, my lord."

Ace giggled, pressing her hand to her mouth, and Damian looked heavenward with a heavy sigh.

"And Ace, no more bleeding for Cole. Am I clear?" asked Damian, frowning. "You're addicted already. You have to get clean or your career as a Destiny Enforcer will end with a dishonorable discharge. Trust me, you're not going to like the consequences."

Ace nodded, her face turning a flaming shade of red. Jamie helped her sit down in the passenger seat and made himself comfortable in the driver's seat, beaming with exaltation. Damian waited until they drove away, watching the silver car disappear into the darkness. Then he placed his hand on Cole's shoulder and snapped his fingers, teleporting them to the entrance door of Paradise Manor.

Letting go of his brother's shoulder, Damian swayed and lowered himself down, hiding his face in his hands. Cole sat down next to him.

"You okay?" he asked, touching Damian's elbow.

"I'm fine. Drained," replied Damian. "Nothing a good night's sleep can't fix."

"You were right," said Cole, staring into the dark desert. "I shouldn't have gone for peaceful negotiations. It never works with assholes like that."

"I'm not sure about that," objected Damian, lifting his head. "Something is not right. You said it yourself." He glanced at the puncture wounds on his arm and frowned.

"Do you want me to heal you?" asked Cole, tones of remorse in his voice. "You don't have to drink my blood for—"

"No," Damian interrupted him, shaking head. "This doesn't bother me. The bite that I healed on Ace's neck does." He turned slightly toward Cole. "Have you ever seen a vampire or an upir with more than two fangs?"

"What?" Cole's eyes widened, his eyebrows climbing up.

"No. Never. It's always two fangs. Upirs have bigger fangs and wider space between them." He rolled his eyes. "Big mouths."

Shivers ran down Damian's back, raising goosebumps on his arms. "There were four puncture wounds on her neck, Cole," he said quietly. "What the hell are we dealing with? Who attacked you?"

Cole gave a barely visible shake, leaning forward as he rested his elbows on his lap. "It all started as usual when the leaders of the two vampire factions gathered for territorial negotiations," he started, his gaze going out of focus for a moment. "But at the same time, something wasn't right. It was something on the level of intuition, you know? I can't even point out exactly when all hell broke loose. It was so sudden—"

He stopped talking abruptly, staring at Damian with wide-open eyes.

"Nikolai, what is it?" asked Damian.

"Dima, I have no idea how the fight started or why," whispered Cole, his face losing all color. "I don't... I can't remember anything. Everything is a blur. One moment we were just talking. Even though it wasn't a friendly conversation, but no one was drawing swords. The next moment, we were at each other's throats. For no reason, as far as I can recall. The next thing I remember is you and Jamie coming in."

Damian was about to ask Cole another question when the door behind them opened with a slight squeak. He turned around and found River standing in the doorway, Gypsy peeking from behind her leg, a feline smirk on her face.

"Hello, boys," said River dryly, folding her arms. "How long are you planning to sit here? It's a cold night. Get inside." She raised her hand to stop Damian from interrupting her and pursed her lips. "I know, I know—immortal supernatural cop and an immortal vampire. Catching a cold is not an issue for you two. I know and I don't give a damn. Get your asses up and inside the house."

"Yes, ma'am," Cole and Damian said at the same time and exchanged a quick look, getting up.

"Heel. Roll over. What good boys you are." Gypsy snickered. Swaying her bushy tail, she strolled around River as if she owned the place.

As they walked inside, River grabbed their arms and pushed them toward the mirror. "Look at you! Both of you!" she yelled, throwing her hands up, tones of desperation breaking through to the surface. "You look like someone put you through a grinder! Blood and gore!"

Damian glanced into the mirror and couldn't help but snicker. Zerkalitsa, the spirit of the mirror, made some amendments to their reflections by adding a pair of little red horns to Cole's head and placing tiny, fluffy, Cupid-like wings behind his back. Cole snorted and pressed his hand over his mouth, trying to stifle his laughter unsuccessfully.

"Ugh!" River threw her hands up again. "Cut it out, Zerkalitsa. I'm not joking with these thousand-year-old juvenile delinquents! Just look at them!" As the wings and the horns disappeared, River turned to Cole. "You, go to your room and take a nice, long shower. You'll probably need a full bottle of soap to get rid of all this blood and God knows what else. You both are like the troublemaking, little brothers I never wanted."

"Yes, ma'am," replied Cole, raising his hand to his temple in a military-like salute. "Am I grounded?" He sounded absolutely serious, grave even, but wild twinkles of laughter were dancing in his eyes.

She ignored him and snapped toward Damian. As her eyes halted on the bleeding wounds on his neck and arms, she sighed reproachfully. "Do you need stitches?"

"No, thank you," replied Damian, warmth accumulating in his chest. "I'll be fine. I just need a shower and a few hours of rest, if possible."

She nodded and placed her hands on her hips. "Sometimes...

No, most of the time, I'm afraid to ask what you two are doing at night, and why, more often than not, you come home bleeding." She stared at her reflection in the mirror. "I'm a police detective. So, please, go to your rooms, lick your wounds quietly and tell me nothing." She pursed her lips, shaking her head. "Plausible deniability."

Damian smiled warmly at her. "I swear none of this blood is human," he said softly.

She reached up, her fingers lingering over the bleeding bite marks on his neck. "If any of this blood is yours or Cole's, it's human to me."

She turned around and headed out of the foyer.

CHAPTER 3

~ DAMIAN BLAKE ~

The run through the forest seemed endless. With every branch aiming to hit him in his face and every root trying to trip him, Damian couldn't understand how his own element could be working against him. A noise produced by heavy footsteps—a lot louder and duller than any human could produce—sounded behind him, and he was terrified to look back.

He tried to connect with the energy of Earth but couldn't find it. It felt as if the entire spectrum of elemental powers was drained from this world, leaving him weakened, gasping for breath. He tried to connect with his magic but found none. The steps were getting closer, and he could almost feel the hot, foul breath of a monster on the back of his neck.

He didn't need to look back. He knew what was after him. Staring straight forward, he saw the edge of the forest, a bright white light shining between the thick trunks. A shadowy figure —a stark silhouette against the blinding whiteness—appeared out of nowhere. Damian couldn't see the man's face. He had no idea who he was, but for some reason, he looked familiar. All he had to do was take one more step closer, and he'd see his face.

A giant, hairy beast jumped in front of him, making him skid to an abrupt halt. Damian reached for his daggers, but for the first time since he became a Destiny Enforcer, they didn't obey his mental command. A massive hairy paw with long claws plummeted down on him, tearing the left side of his face.

As the pain twisted his insides, he pressed his hands to his mangled face, blood streaming down his cheek, dripping to his chest. The beast roared and swung its paw again. Damian moved to avoid the next impact, but his feet sank into the ground, thin, thorny vines wrapping around his legs. He screamed and started to fall backward.

* * *

HE WOKE up and jolted upright, almost falling off the bed. Breathing hard, he looked around, barely recognizing his surroundings. The shrill ring of his cellphone made him flinch. He grabbed the device, nearly dropping it, and stared at the screen, recognizing River's photo.

"Hello," he answered the call, his vocal cords painfully sore.

"Damian?" River's voice sounded troubled. "Did I wake you up?"

She took a pause, obviously waiting for his response, but he couldn't say a word.

"Sorry," she continued after a moment, speaking a little faster than normal. "Yesterday, you looked like you could use some rest, and I didn't want to wake you up, but I sort of have no choice. I called Cole first. He didn't answer my call but texted back that he was in a meeting, promising to call me as soon as he could."

She fell silent again, and he could hear people talking somewhere in the background.

"It's okay, River," he managed to say, rubbing the back of his neck. "I wasn't sleeping..."

"You humans have no idea how to sleep properly. You should learn

from us, cats. Up to twenty hours of sweet, blissful sleep a day—every day. Hee-aaa-ven," purred Gypsy, trotting into the room. *"Anyway, what was it? A nightmare? Did a monster under your bed bite you? I could hear you screaming all the way from the kitchen."*

Damian glowered at the cat, mouthing, "Shut up."

"I need your expertise," continued River. "I'm at a crime scene, and I think you should see the victim. It could be your jurisdiction."

"Text me the address," replied Damian, rising. "I'll be there in thirty minutes."

He hung up the phone and headed toward the bathroom but then halted by the doorway and turned to Gypsy.

"Gypsy, if you hear me scream in my sleep again..." he started to say, but as the images of his last nightmare flashed before his eyes, his throat constricted, and he fell silent, a painful smirk curving his lips. "Anyway, if you hear me scream, wake me up."

"Do I look like an alarm clock to you?" grumbled the cat, jumping on top of the bed stand. She stretched and made a few circles in place for good measure before lying down and curling into a ball. Lifting her head, she pinned Damian with her round, emerald eyes and added, *"Fine, I'll wake you up. Maybe you are a Sasquatch, but you are my Sasquatch, and no one except me has the right to bite you."*

* * *

Twenty minutes later, he walked out of the shower, toweled himself dry and quickly got dressed. He read the address one more time before putting the cellphone in his pocket. He knew the location well, so teleporting there wasn't a problem.

It was a small gas station on the outskirts of Blue Creek, next to the entrance to the freeway leading to Phoenix. Right behind the plaza, there was an old, half-demolished warehouse. At some point, it belonged to a large construction company, but since it relocated to Phoenix, no one had rented the building, and now it stood dark and empty, which was exactly what Damian needed.

He snapped his fingers and vanished from Paradise Manor, manifesting behind the warehouse a moment later. Quickly surveying the area, he made sure that no one had seen him and circled around the building, heading toward the gas station.

A large area of the plaza next to the store was isolated by yellow police tape, and a few men in police uniforms secured the perimeter, stopping the crowd of onlookers from entering the crime scene. Damian put his dark sunglasses on and opened his other sight, scanning the area. At first glance, he didn't notice anything out of the ordinary, and he started to wonder why River had decided her case had a supernatural origin.

He made his way through the crowd and stopped in front of the yellow line, searching for River. Since he couldn't see her, he approached a young man in a police uniform who stood in front of the yellow line observing the onlookers.

"Excuse me, sir," said Damian calmly. "I'm here to see Detective Evans. Can you please call her?"

The policeman observed him with interest, his eyes moving up and down Damian's body as if sizing him up. Then he shrugged and pressed a button on his mic, turning his back toward Damian.

"Detective Evans," he said quietly, taking a few steps toward the crime scene. "There is a man here waiting for you next to the store. Should I let him through?"

Before he finished speaking, Damian saw River heading toward them. She walked briskly, the flaps of her unbuttoned trench coat blowing in the wind. Waving at the policeman, she ordered, "Jason, let him through. He's with me."

With a tiny smirk on her lips, she watched Damian double up to pass under the police line even though Jason pulled it up for him. She led him toward the crime scene, giving him quick instructions about maintaining the scene's integrity, minimizing contamination, and preserving physical evidence. He barely listened to her instructions, hundreds of thoughts rushing through his mind.

"Here you go," said River, coming to a halt, gesturing for Damian to look. "Her name is Sarah Mitchell. She used to own the local flower shop next to the library." She sighed, for a brief moment looking away from the victim. "She was killed approximately an hour ago. After the autopsy is done, we'll know the exact time of death. The wound on her neck suggests an animal attack, and don't get me wrong, I know the desert is full of mountain lions, gray foxes, and coyotes, but I just don't see wild animals attacking people in broad daylight. This is why I called you. Something doesn't smell right."

He glanced down and frowned. The victim—a woman in her middle to late forties—lay sprawled on the asphalt. Her neck had been ripped to shreds by something resembling sharp fangs of what could have been a large dog or a wolf, and her chest and arms were covered in brown spots of dried blood.

Damian squatted next to her and quickly surveyed the area. Once he was sure none of the responding officers or investigators were looking at him, he took his glasses off, looking up at River.

"River, can you please make sure no one comes close to me," he whispered.

She nodded, and he channeled his power, opening his other sight. Carefully, he moved his hand over the wound on the victim's neck and sucked in a sharp breath, pulling his hand back. Even though the presence of the vampiric energy wasn't strong, he identified it right away.

Besides that, he detected a barely noticeable residue of some other magical energy he couldn't recognize. It felt oddly familiar, but just like in the house where Cole had the meeting with the leaders of the opposing vampire faction, he couldn't put his finger on what it was. The answer lingered somewhere on the outskirts of his mind, but no matter how hard he chased it, he couldn't catch it.

There was also something off about the victim herself. While there was nothing special about her appearance—she looked like any suburban soccer mom—there was something about her that made him do a double-take. Scanning her with his second sight, he frowned. She was dead, so even if she was mundane, her body would no longer be emitting the energy of a human soul. Yet there was a strange, weak glow about her. Even though it was dwindling down, he could still see it.

As realization dawned on him, he glanced up at River, his chest tight with worry. "Perun almighty, you were right. It is my jurisdiction," he whispered, scrambling to his feet. He pressed his hand over his mouth while searching for his cellphone with his other hand. "No good... this is not something we need now..."

Pulling his cellphone out of his pocket, Damian dialed Cole's phone number, but as his call went straight into his voice mail, he groaned and swore under his breath. Opening the messages, he started to type, searching the screen for every letter.

"CALL ME BACK NOW! YOU HAVE A MUCH BIGGER ISSUE THAN THE VAMPIRE OPPOSITION."

"I really don't like the sound of that," muttered River, frowning. "You better explain yourself, soldier."

"River—," he started to say, but was interrupted by a howl of despair that made the small hairs on the back of his neck rise.

"Let me through!" A man was fighting against two policemen who were struggling to hold him behind the yellow tape. "This is my wife! My Sarah..." His voice turned into a painful sob which slowly morphed into a low, feral growl. His eyes lit up with a dangerous orange light, and Damian knew if he didn't do something at once, it would be too late a heartbeat later.

"Let him through!" he yelled, sprinting toward the police

line.

Reaching the yellow tape before River, Damian grabbed Jason and the second police officer, yanking both of them away from the man. Then he put his sunglasses on and placed his hand on the man's shoulder, allowing some of his magical energy to wash over him.

"Sir, you need to calm down," he said firmly, watching the orange glow in the man's eyes slowly dissipate, and added in a whisper, so only the man with his supernatural hearing could hear him, "Stay calm... You must control your true nature. You don't want to expose the World of Magic in front of all these humans."

The man raised his eyes at Damian, and his face turned ashen. "My lord," he whispered, making a move to kneel, but Damian held him up.

"Stop it," he whispered, his fingers digging into the man's shoulder. "I know you respect me, but there is no need to kneel." He smiled, hoping his smile was friendly enough to calm him down. "Please, follow me, and no matter what you see next, you can't allow yourself to transform. If you do, I will have no choice but to fulfill my duty. Do you understand me, sir?"

"Yes, my lord."

"The name is Damian Blake," said Damian, turning around to meet River's troubled gaze. He waved at her, making a quick introduction. "This is Detective Evans."

"I'm Craig Mitchell. Sarah is... was..." His voice shook, breaking. Tears gathered in his brown eyes, threatening to spill, but he pressed the heels of his hands to his eyes, forcing them back, and two deep wrinkles materialized between his bushy eyebrows. A moment later, he lowered his arms, meeting River's calm gaze. "Can I see her, Detective?"

River nodded, motioning for him to follow her. As they approached the dead woman, Craig froze in place, and the air around him shimmered. Damian channeled his magic, getting ready to do whatever he had to do to stop a purebred werewolf from a full transformation in front of human witnesses. Werewolves weren't known for their patience and self-control, so Damian was pleasantly surprised when Craig took a deep breath, suppressing his emotions.

He turned to Damian, looking up at him, his gaze deadly still. "Who did it?" he asked, a dangerous growl accompanying his words. Throwing a quick glance over his shoulder at River, he added in a hoarse whisper, "Was it a vamp attack?"

"I don't know," replied Damian honestly. "Detective Evans summoned me here because she suspected the case was supernatural."

"Oh?" The werewolf glanced at River with renewed interest. "She is touched?"

"Exposed," replied Damian. "Anyway, I can detect the presence of vampiric essence, but it's not pure. There is something else here."

"Bloodsucking motherfuckers," growled Craig, spitting out one word at a time. A dangerous orange light ignited in his eyes, and the air around him shimmered again like a desert mirage. "It's time we put these disgusting leeches back in their place."

"Craig, you need to calm down." Damian frowned, taking a step closer to him. "We already have tension in the Arizona Vampire Court. We don't need to add a conflict between the werewolves and vampires—"

Craig laughed, his voice filled with bitterness. "You're too late for that, Enforcer," he said, shaking his head. "My wife wasn't the first werewolf killed by a vampire in the last month. Ask the detective here."

Damian turned to River, his limbs filled with led. "River, do you have any other cases of... um... animal attacks in Blue Creek or Phoenix?"

River frowned, approaching them. "Why?"

"Are there more cases like this?" asked Damian, pointing at

the dead woman. "It's important, River."

She nodded. "One case in Blue Creek about a week ago, and another one in Phoenix," she replied.

"Dammit..." he cursed quietly, frowning. "I wish you'd told me that earlier." Turning to the werewolf, he put his hand on his shoulder. "Craig, I'm deeply sorry for your loss, but I have to ask you to keep the situation with your wife's murder down and let me do my job. As I mentioned, the situation in the state is unstable already because of internal conflict in the Vampire Court. I can't allow the tension to escalate. It's my job to preserve the secrecy of the World of Magic at any cost." He gave a pointed stare to the werewolf and repeated. "At *any* cost. I mean it."

Craig glanced down at his wife's bloodied body, and a tortured expression of undiluted grief darkened his face. He pressed his hand to his mouth, his dark eyebrows lowering over his glassy eyes, deep creases cutting across his forehead.

"How am I supposed to keep it down?" he whispered, his voice sounding so hoarse Damian could barely make out his words. "Please tell me, how am I supposed to explain Sarah's death to my pack? Besides..." Craig smirked darkly, averting his gaze. "You're too late, Lord Enforcer. The daughter of one of the Phoenix Alphas was killed by a vampire. Hawk is an honorable man, but it's his baby girl. I can't even imagine..." He cringed visibly, tears gathering in his eyes. "He's not going to let it go, and I can't blame him. The war has started already, and there is no way back. You can't stop it now."

"God damn it all!" growled Damian, burying his hands into his hair. He stilled for a moment, his mind working on overdrive. "How can I find Hawk?"

"You're not serious," muttered Craig, staring at him in shock. "Destiny Enforcer or not, Hawk's pack will tear you limb from limb if you ask them to stand down without avenging their own."

"I'll take my chances," replied Damian calmly.

Once Craig had given him directions to Hawk's ranch, he thanked the werewolf and once more expressed his condolences, promising to bring the person who murdered his wife to justice personally.

Pulling River aside, he halted by the side of the building and fell silent, staring at the cracks in the asphalt.

"I understand it's bad," said River, touching his arm. "But how bad is it?"

"It's beyond dangerous, River," he said quietly, throwing a careful glance around. "As far as we know, all the victims are werewolves, but we can't be sure—killed vampires don't leave bodies behind. If I don't stop this confrontation, humans will start dying, too. It's not the first war between different supernatural clans that I've witnessed, and every time there are human casualties. Besides, Cole as the King of the Arizona Vampire Court may end up on the receiving end of the local Alphas' anger."

He raked his fingers through his hair, covering the left side of his face, and exhaled a ragged breath.

"With the exception of my brother, I don't have warm feelings toward vampires," he said at length, "but something tells me this time, they're innocent in the deaths of these werewolves. I don't know how I'm going to prove it, but I must find a way."

"Can I do anything to help?" asked River gently.

Damian shook his head, staring at the dark warehouse. "Just do your job, Detective, and be careful. Warn Jesse, too. I know he's no longer your partner, but since he has been exposed to the World of Magic, it would be a good idea to make sure he's not going to get in the middle of this mess."

"I'll talk to him," replied River, wincing. "What are you going to do? How do you even deal with something as huge and dangerous as this?"

"One step at the time, like in that elephant joke for kids," he replied, a tired smile ghosting his lips. "How do you eat an elephant?"

"How?" asked River, gazing up at him with curiosity.

"One bite at a time." He shoved his hands in his pockets, staring over River's head at the gray wall of the shop. "I'll talk to Cole first, and then I'm going to find Hawk and see if I can stop the war between the vamps and the werewolves. After that is taken care of, I'll see what my next step should be." He glanced down at her, reading all the concern in her light eyes, and for a moment, his chest tightened with warmth and worry about her. "I'll have to leave for a short while, River. Keep an eye on Cole for me, would you?"

"Didn't you mean the other way around?" She chuckled, shaking her head.

A lopsided grin split Damian's face. "This royal troublemaker better be guarding you with his immortal life," he muttered. "But if you haven't noticed yet, Cole is stupidly brave and has no instinct of self-preservation. Someone needs to be his voice of reason while I'm gone."

"I'll do my best." River smiled back at him. "But you know how your brother is. For someone who's been dead for centuries, he sure is full of life—a force of nature."

"He's a force, alright." Damian sighed and pulled out his phone. "I have to go, River. If everything goes well, I'll be back in a few hours. But if my negotiations with Hawk take longer, don't worry. I'll be fine."

Giving her a quick wave goodbye, Damian headed toward the abandoned warehouse. He dialed Cole's phone number and pressed the device to his ear. The phone beeped a few times, and the call went to his brother's voicemail.

Oh, come on, Cole, answer your goddamn phone! Isn't it the reason you have it?

CHAPTER 4

~ COLE ADAMS ~

The text message Cole received from Damian sent his thoughts into a wild frenzy, and he couldn't wait for the meeting to be over. When he finally walked out of the conference room, he had to practically force himself not to run. A soft beep alerted him that he had a new voice mail, and the pit of his stomach fell. Even without looking at the notification, he was positive the message was from his brother.

Cole walked into his office and closed the door before making his way to his chair. He pressed the play button and stilled, listening to his brother's deep, calm voice.

"Cole, we have a serious problem. River can give you all the legal details, but to make it short, vampires are killing werewolves. We are facing a war. You must find the vampires responsible—whether they are your subjects or the opposition. I am on my way to Phoenix to speak with Hawk, the Alpha. His daughter is one of the victims, so the conversation is not going to be easy, but I must find a way to get through to him. We must stop this situation before it escalates into a full-blown supernatural mayhem. Hopefully, I won't be long, but keep an eye on River. And Cole..." Damian took a short pause. "It could be about the power succession in the Arizona Vampire Court, but something tells me it's not the case. Watch your back, brother."

Cole listened to Damian's message one more time and threw the phone on the desk. Leaning back, he crossed his hands on his stomach and closed his eyes, processing everything that had happened in the last few weeks, trying to isolate some kind of pattern that would shed some light on the latest events.

A few minutes later, he opened his eyes and grabbed his phone. After a quick search, he dialed the phone number of his righthand man, Luciano.

"Luciano," he said once the vampire answered the call, relief spreading through him. "I know it's a little unusual, but I need to speak with you immediately. It's urgent."

"Yes, Your Majesty, I'm at your service," replied the old vampire, but the tones of surprise laced his deep voice. "Where would you like to meet?"

"I'm at the *InvictusGame* corporate office," replied Cole, his fingers fidgeting with a pen. "How soon can you be here?"

"It's daytime, my lord," replied Luciano, "so I have to use a car, which will slow me down significantly. Give me thirty minutes, and I'll be with you."

* * *

EXACTLY THIRTY MINUTES LATER, his executive assistant called to let him know that Luciano Di Angelo was here to see him, and before he could hang up the phone, Luciano walked into his office. Dressed in a black business suit and a tie, he looked like a banker, and his business-like appearance put a smile on Cole's face.

The ancient vampire hated modern clothes, and preferred to stay away from the outside world, most of the time remaining in his large home, coming out only at night for a tranquil walk in the desert. Even though he fully supported Cole's direction toward peaceful co-existence with humans, he favored solitude and a nocturnal lifestyle.

"Luciano," said Cole, rising. "I know you don't like to travel during daylight, and I appreciate you coming to meet with me right away."

"But of course, my liege." Luciano bowed ceremoniously, keeping his glowing eyes down.

Cole glanced at the large windows facing the company floor, glad that he had closed all the blinds before Luciano came in.

"Don't bow, Luciano," he said, gesturing for him to sit down. "I called you not as your king. I need to speak with a trusted friend." He stopped talking, exploring Luciano's impassive face. "My maker has been gone for a while, and no matter what I do, I can't find him. Without Ruslan, you're the only person in the entire court I trust."

For a heartbeat, Luciano's features softened, and the corners of his mouth lifted just a little, the scarlet glow slowly leaving his eyes.

"If you can't find Ruslan, it means he doesn't want to be found," replied the ancient vampire with a light flick of his wrist. "I'm sure you'd feel if your maker was dead."

"I know that." Cole pinched the bridge of his nose, trying to focus. "I just wish he were here now." He lowered his hand and met Luciano's steady gaze. "I'm glad I have you. I need your help, my friend."

"And your powerful brother?" Luciano arched his brow, tilting his head.

"Damian?" Cole smiled. "He always supports me, Luciano. He's my stronghold, and I trust him with my life. At the moment, however, he's conducting an investigation, and it's in our best interest to help him. You'll understand as soon as I explain the situation."

"Tell me what troubles you, my child." Luciano leaned back in his chair, crossing his legs at the knee.

"A few things. I'll start with the easiest one." Cole grabbed a piece of paper and a pen and drew four dots. "Do you know what could leave a mark like this on the neck of a victim?"

Leaning forward, Luciano took the paper out of Cole's hands and peered at it. "Are you sure?" he asked without taking his eyes off the drawing.

Cole nodded. "Yes, I am sure. The bite marks were deep—deeper than vampire's or upir's fangs would have left, and the victim was drained of nearly all blood."

"Hmm." Luciano placed the paper on the desk and rubbed his forehead. "Where did you see something like this?"

"During my meeting with the leaders of the opposition," replied Cole. As briefly as he could, he described everything that had happened the night before. "What bothers me the most is that I don't remember how the fight had started and why. Everything is a blur, and I can't..."

His voice trailed off as he tried to focus on the events of that night. The images, blurry and shady, appeared in his mind, but no matter how hard he tried, he couldn't bring them to focus, as if something was blocking them. With a soft groan, he massaged his temples.

"I can't remember anything, Luciano," he whispered, leaning forward. "I was wounded. Someone shot me with a silver bullet and put a sword through my chest, and I have no idea how it happened."

"Peculiar," mumbled Luciano, readjusting a cufflink on his shirt. He thought for a brief moment, his gaze going out of focus. "Have you ever heard of volkolaks?"

Cole nodded. "I've never seen one, but from what I recall, it's something like a werewolf but a lot stronger and bigger. Do you think we're dealing with a volkolak?"

"No and no." Luciano pursed his lips, a troubled look in his deep eyes. "No, volkolaks are nothing like werewolves. I think our friendly Arizona lycanthropes would get offended if they heard you say that. And no, I don't think we're dealing with a volkolak."

"Then why did you ask?"

"Let me explain," continued Luciano. "Unlike werewolves, volkolaks are not created by a random bite. Also, one cannot be born a volkolak. Only a powerful sorcerer can create volkolaks by cursing a man with a dark spell. Until recently, I thought only humans could be turned into a volkolak. I was wrong."

A sad smile crossed his face, and he glanced at the piece of paper with a picture of four dots.

"Anyway, besides volkolaks, there is one more creature born of dark magic. If volkolaks resembles werewolves, this second creature resembles"—he arched his eyebrow, twirling his wrist—"well, us. It resembles vampires and upirs, but it's a lot stronger, faster and more powerful than even the oldest of us. I'm talking about wurdulaks."

"You can't be serious," mumbled Cole, staring at the old vampire with widened eyes. "I thought they were nothing but a Slavic bedtime story."

Luciano chuckled. "No matter how old you are, there is always something to learn, isn't there?" He tapped his index finger on the paper. "The only vampire-type being that leaves four puncture wounds is a wurdulak. There are no others as far as I know. But it's not the wurdulak itself you need to worry about."

"What do you mean?"

"I mean, you must find out who conjured it because this person controls the monster. Not every witch or wizard has the power to wield such dark magic..." His voice faded, and his lips parted, exposing his long fangs. "Unfortunately, I have no idea which branch of dark magic can work this kind of spell. If your brother doesn't know either, you'll have to find someone else to ask."

"Thank you, my friend. I think I know the right person to

ask this question." Cole inclined his head and continued, "There is one more thing I wanted to talk to you about. And this topic is a lot more complicated and dangerous."

"More dangerous than a wurdulak roaming the streets of Phoenix and getting involved in the affairs of the Arizona Vampire Court?" Luciano smirked, his downward angled eyes shining with sadness.

"Possibly," replied Cole. "The answer to your question would depend on who controls the monster and why." He rubbed his forehead, gathering his thoughts. "Luciano, a few werewolves were killed in Blue Creek and Phoenix. Seemingly, they were killed by vampires. I don't know who these vampires are. They could've been my subjects or belonged to the opposition, or they could've been rogue. I don't know. No matter what, we must stop them."

Cole got up and walked to the window facing the public golf course. Spreading the blinds, he peeked outside, squinting at the bright sunlight.

"As we speak, my brother is trying to negotiate with werewolves to stop the war," he continued. "Even if he succeeds—which knowing the werewolves' explosive nature, I sincerely doubt that—if we don't find those responsible and don't stop the killings, the war will be unavoidable." He took a pause, searching the green of the golf course absentmindedly. "If you know anything or even suspect anyone, please tell me."

Luciano chuckled, and there was something so cold and menacing about this short burst of laughter that it sent shivers down Cole's back. He spun around just in time to see Luciano rising. His eyes were glowing a sinister red—a lot brighter than a normal vampire's eyes should've glowed. A tiny purple rune appeared on his forehead. It lingered over his pale skin for a brief moment and then dissipated. Luciano's smile grew wider, exposing his fully expanded fangs.

"Oh, shit," mumbled Cole, staggering back until he hit the window.

The old vampire growled and bolted toward him, his arms outstretched, his fingers elongating into razor-sharp claws. Moving at the fastest speed he could muster, Cole darted to the side just in time to avoid Luciano's strike.

Quickly assessing the situation, Cole jumped on top of the desk, and as Luciano followed him, he met him with a quick front kick, his instep impacting his opponent's chin and sending him flying back. Something cracked, and Luciano cried out, his hand clasping at his chin. Knowing that the reprieve was temporary, Cole zoomed toward the door, hoping to take the fight outside the company, but before he reached it, Luciano was already on him.

He seized Cole's long hair at the back of his head and slammed his forehead against the wall by the door, breaking his nose. Bright white light exploded in Cole's vision as a blinding pain spiked through his brain and blood gushed from his nose.

Pressing him flat against the wall with the full weight of his body, the old vamp hissed into his ear, "You're too young to fight someone as old as me and live to tell the tale, little King. I'll kill you, and then I'll find your little human pet and kill her, too. I don't need to worry about your ogre of a brother. The dumb werewolves will take care of him for me."

Cole pushed against the wall, realizing with horror that Luciano was right—he was too slow and too weak to fight a vampire who was almost two thousand years older than him.

"Luciano, what are you doing?" he groaned, struggling against his vice-like grip, but it was equivalent to pushing against a concrete wall. "You're my friend. You're my father's friend. It's not you... Whatever was done to you, you must fight it."

For a moment, Luciano's hand shook, and his grip lightened up. "Cole? What's going on? Why am I..." His voice wavered and changed into a feral growl. He laughed again, the dark and malignant sound of his laughter chilling Cole to the bone.

However, this short moment of weakness was enough for Cole to twist out of Luciano's hold, leaving a few strands of his hair in his fist. With a speed he didn't expect from himself, he crossed the room toward the wooden coat rack standing in the corner with his trench coat hanging from it. Just as he reached it, a heavy thud behind him made him flinch and glance back. Luciano crouched on top of the desk like a predator ready to pounce, his eyes burning with a sinister red glow.

Cole grabbed the coat rack and slammed it against the wall, breaking it. Luciano leaped off the desk, aiming to push Cole into the corner. With no place or time to run, Cole spun around and ducked to the side as much as he could, but he wasn't fast enough. Luciano's fist connected with his jaw. Cole's head jerked back, hitting the wall hard.

For a heartbeat, the room swam around him, and the metallic taste of blood filled his mouth, but he managed to hold on to the piece of the broken rack. Luciano's claw-like fingers wrapped around his right wrist, pinning it to the wall above his head. His other hand seized Cole's neck, his unnaturally red eyes burning just inches away from Cole's. With a strenuous groan, Cole struggled fruitlessly against his assailant.

"Stop fighting, boy," growled Luciano, squeezing his wrist stronger to make him drop the piece of wood. "You can't win. You don't have what it takes to kill someone like me. I can rip your head off your shoulders with one hand."

Luciano's fingers dug deeper into Cole's throat, nearly tearing it apart. Blood gushed from under his claws, coloring Cole's white shirt scarlet. Cole moaned and unlocked his fingers, dropping the piece of wood. A burst of maniacal laughter erupted from Luciano's lips, and his eyes shone brighter, the purple rune igniting on his forehead again.

Cole caught the falling piece of the rack with his left hand

and thrust its sharp end into Luciano's chest, moving it forward and up with all the strength he had left in his body. The old vampire gasped and staggered a step back, both his hands wrapping around the wooden stake protruding from his chest, but Cole didn't let go.

"Missed the heart, imbecile," growled the old vampire, his face contorted by pain and anger.

"I didn't," whispered Cole, staring down at the only vampire in his Court he'd trusted for years. "Please, Luciano..." He swallowed painfully, his torn throat constricted with the inevitability of what he had to do. "Fight it, my friend. It's some kind of spell. You can fight it. I don't want to kill you."

For a split second, the purple rune over Luciano's forehead dimmed down, and the red glow in his eyes subsided.

"Cole, my boy... my King," whispered Luciano, blood gathering in his eyes, "I can't fight it. Kill me or I *will* kill you, and I won't be able to live with that. Do it before—" His voice cut off, and his face tensed as he fought the effects of the dark spell. The rune shone brighter as the spell took him over again.

No, Luciano... please...

Crumbling inside, Cole screamed and pushed the wooden stake through Luciano's heart. The old vampire cried out and dropped to his knees. The rune vanished. His eyes turned to their normal color, and his lips twitched in a pained smile.

"Thank you..." Luciano's last words touched Cole's hearing, and the ancient vampire turned into a pile of gray ash, falling to the floor in soft flakes. Something metallic hit the carpeted floor with a soft thud and rolled away, catching the reflection of the electric lights.

Cole dropped the stake and flinched as it hit the Berber carpet with a dull thump. His arms hung limply along his sides as he stared at the ash, unable to wrap his mind around everything that had just happened. A tiny light flare attracted his attention. Feeling hollow inside, he stepped over the ashes and lowered to one knee, staring at a small metallic disk. It wasn't bigger than a dime, and the rune he had seen glowing on Luciano's forehead was inscribed on it.

He didn't touch it. Instead, he got up and headed back to his desk. Opening one of the drawers, Cole shuffled through its contents until he found a small iron box in a thick leather binding. He grabbed the box and a pen and walked back to the metal disk. Lowering to one knee, he opened the box and placed it next to the disk. Using the pen, he moved the disk inside the box and closed it.

Luciano, I swear I'll find who did this to you...

CHAPTER 5

~ COLE ADAMS ~

Cole walked back to his desk and leaned forward, bracing his fists against its cold surface. Anger boiled inside him, ready to spill, and he needed a few seconds to calm down and get his tangled thoughts in order. He had to get to the bottom of this. He owed it to Luciano and to the rest of the vampires of his Court who trusted him. But most of all—he owed it to his brother who stood by his side no matter what, risking his safety to help him.

As he looked down, a deep shudder ran through him. His wounds had healed, but his hands were covered in brown and red stains. His white shirt was soaked through on his chest and stomach, and he was sure his face was smeared with blood, too. He couldn't walk through his company looking like a serial killer on the loose.

Noticing his trench coat lying in the corner, he walked around the desk and grabbed it, shaking pieces of wood off of it. He put it on, adjusted the scabbard with the sword under it and buttoned it up, covering his bloodied shirt and suit as much as he could. He realized that the coat couldn't hide his face, but at this point, there was nothing he could do.

Cole put his hands into the pockets of his coat and lowered his head, allowing his long hair to cover most of his face. Ignoring the shocked looks of his employees, he ran across the company and out the door, not slowing down until he reached his car and dropped into the driver's seat.

He pressed the start button and put his hands on the steering wheel, squeezing it until the leather squeaked under his deadly grip. As he entered the freeway, heading toward Scottsdale, he dialed Ace's phone number. She answered right away.

"Cole?" Her voice sounded troubled. "Is everything okay?"

"No," he replied.

"What happe—"

"I don't have time to explain," he cut her off. "I need you to go to my office as soon as you can." He fell silent for a moment, thinking about the best way to express himself. "I had a... fight in my office. It's a bit of mess there, and if someone sees it..."

"Got it," said Ace. "I'm leaving right now, and I'll take care of everything."

"Thank you. I'll call Mackenzie and tell her you're doing private work per my request, using my PC."

"Cole, are you okay? Are you hurt? You don't sound like yourself."

He chuckled bitterly. "I'm a goddamn vamp, Ace," he said, staring straight ahead at the gathering traffic. "If I'm still talking to you while driving my car, I'm fine. I can't get hurt. I'm either alive, or I'm a pile of ashes. There is no in-between."

For a moment, the phone went silent, and Cole thought Ace had hung up on him, realizing how abrupt he sounded talking to her.

"That's not true. You're a vampire, but it doesn't mean you're soulless. The pain of one's soul could be a lot worse than any physical pain." Her voice was quiet and raspy as she spoke again. "Judging by the way you speak right now, I know you're hurt. I know you well enough, Cole. I've been shadowing you for a while."

He slammed his hand on the steering wheel, cursing quietly. "I'm sorry, Ace," he said through gritted teeth. "You're right. I'm not okay. I'm far from it, but I can't talk about it now. I'll call you as soon as I can."

He hung up the phone and dialed his assistant, giving her all the instructions about his office and his schedule for the day. Then he took the exit toward Scottsdale and shortly after, parked his car in a small plaza at the edge of town. Putting his darkest sunglasses on, he raised the collar of his trench coat, stepped out of the car and ran toward a small bookstore.

Even though on the outside it looked just like any other mom and pop shop, the store was a front for one of the most powerful magical organizations—the Wardens Order. Any information related to the World of Magic and different supernatural communities, forbidden spells or deadly incantations—the Wardens had it. However, receiving permission to access their libraries and archives wasn't a simple task.

Cole took the flap of his coat and wrapped it around the handle before turning it. After previous visits to the shop, he had learned his lesson—the door handle was silver-plated. He pushed the door open but didn't walk in, cursing silently at the overly cautious, vampire-hating human Warden who owned the store.

"Aaron?" he called, peeking inside. "Mr. Cooper, this is Cole Adams. I'm going to come in. Please disarm your anti—" He cut himself off, remembering that this store was opened for everybody, humans included. "I don't need any silver jewelry, just your books."

A soft click sounded somewhere inside, and the door swung open all the way. Aaron Cooper stood in the doorway, his left hand resting on the head of a large Doberman Pinscher. Tilting his head slightly, he readjusted his glasses, and a cold smirk stretched his thin lips as he observed Cole's blood-stained face.

"Mr. Adams," he said, his high-pitched voice ringing with tones of sarcasm. "Should I bow and call you Your Majesty, perhaps?"

Cole sighed. The human Warden didn't have warm feelings toward vampires, and he couldn't blame him, but he hoped that since they worked together successfully in the past, Aaron would have lightened up toward him at least a little.

"That won't be necessary, Mr. Cooper," he said softly. "You know I wouldn't come here if I didn't have a really good reason. Please let me in."

Muttering something under his breath, Aaron grabbed the dog's collar, gesturing for him to come in. As Cole crossed the threshold, the dog sniffed him and lowered its head, his fangs exposed in a snarl.

Aaron folded his arms, staring at him. "I hope it's not human blood on your face and hands, Mr. Adams."

"No," replied Cole, feeling empty inside. "Vampire blood. Most of it is mine."

"Uh-huh." He pursed his lips, his entire demeanor exuding a vibe of mistrust. "I would like to know what kind of emergency brought you here this time, looking like that, Mr. Adams?" he asked dryly.

"A war, Mr. Cooper," replied Cole, struggling to keep his cool. "I need to speak with Master Warden Luc de la Crosse as soon as possible."

"For someone who's been undead for centuries, it's always a matter of life and death with you, isn't it?" Aaron reached into the pocket of his thick cardigan and produced a cellphone. "If you're talking about the conflict between different vampire factions, we already know about that, and personally, I don't give a damn. As far as I'm concerned, you can all go ahead and kill each other. Good riddance." He waved his hand dismissively.

"No, Mr. Cooper," objected Cole, stifling a sigh. "I'm talking about the kind of war that would lead to hundreds of human casualties if we don't prevent it." He stopped talking and threw his hands up. "I understand you don't like vampires, but what do you have against me personally? I've been nothing but respectful to you. Why can't you show me the same courtesy?"

Aaron gave him a frosty once-over and didn't reply but dialed a phone number, lifting the device to his ear.

"Master de la Crosse," he said, going around Cole to lock the front door and shut down the open sign. "I have Cole Adams here." He stopped talking, listening to his boss. "Yes, my lord, he's alone, and he demands an audience with you. He said it's urgent."

Before he hung up the phone, a portal opened behind him, and a young man dressed in a black shirt and pants walked out, halting in front of Cole. His hazel eyes moved from Cole's face to his hands, and his mouth opened, shock reflected on his handsome features.

"Cole, what happened?" he asked with a heavy French accent, approaching him.

"I was forced to kill Luciano Di Angelo. This is one of the reasons I am here," replied Cole, but as much as he tried to keep calm, his voice shook. "Can we speak privately?"

"Of course, *mon ami.*" Luc de la Crosse gestured for him to follow and headed toward the small room at the back of the shop. Opening the door, he allowed Cole to pass first but stopped Aaron before he could walk inside. Reaching in his pocket, he pulled out his wallet and gave him a twenty-dollar bill. "I'm sorry, I shouldn't be asking you something like this, but can you please go to the store next to yours and buy a plain black shirt." He gave Cole a quick once-over and added, "Make it size large."

Aaron groaned but took the money and walked out of the shop. Luc de la Crosse turned to Cole and pointed at the small door on the left.

"Perhaps you'd like to clean up first?" he asked.

"Thank you."

Cole took his trench coat off, hanging it over the back of a chair. As Luc glanced at him, he didn't comment on his appearance, but his hand went up to his mouth. Cole smirked bitterly and turned on his heels, heading into the restroom. Once he closed the door, he approached the mirror and stared at his reflection, which looked like something out of a horror movie, unable to make a move.

Making an effort, he took his jacket, shirt and tie off, throwing everything on the floor. Moving like a robot, he scrubbed his skin, removing all traces of blood. As he stared at the dirty brown water running down the drain, resentment spiraled through him, spiking anger and determination. He ripped a few pieces of paper towel, dried his face, chest and arms the best he could, and walked out of the restroom, grabbing his destroyed clothes on the way out.

By the time he was done, Aaron was back, sitting on a chair next to Luc, a black T-shirt lying on the table in front of him. The older man looked up at Cole, and his jaw dropped.

"I always wondered if vampires need to work out to build that"—Aaron moved his hand up and down, pointing at Cole's torso—"Mr. Universe style body. Or is it a package deal—fangs, immortality, six-pack, martial arts skills? BOGO." He pushed the shirt toward him. "This is for you. Please, do me a favor and cover all that before I drown in self-pity."

Cole's eyebrows climbed up and despite the gloom he felt at the moment, he couldn't help but chuckle.

"This is the way I looked when I was turned," he said, taking the shirt and putting it on. "Now that my brother is here, I do some workouts with him, mostly for his sake. I'm entitled to have some fun, you know? It's a chance to relax and unwind for me. As far as the martial arts and swordsmanship, this has nothing to do with what I am—I have to work for it, training every day, just like my brother or any human who practices martial arts."

He sat down across from Luc and Aaron, sobering up. As briefly as he could, he told them everything he found out from Damian and Luciano. For a while, both Wardens sat in silence, looking dumbstruck.

"Damian went to meet with the head of the Phoenix pack whose daughter was killed," added Cole. "I haven't heard from him yet."

Luc leaned back in his chair, his fingers brushing over his well-groomed mustache. "O' Lord, protect us all with your divine light," he whispered, and the sound of his voice sent chills down Cole's back.

"Master de la Crosse, I don't understand why you look so alarmed. This won't be the first conflict between werewolves and vamps," said Aaron, throwing a veiled look at Cole. "It seems like these two groups of monsters can't stand each other and are always at war. We stopped them the last time, and we can do it again."

"You don't understand, Aaron," replied Cole, his fingers gripping the edge of the table. "I'm going to run an investigation in my Court just to make sure, but I'm almost a hundred percent positive it's a waste of time—none of my vampires killed these werewolves. At least, not willingly. It was either the work of a wurdulak, or they were controlled somehow. Just like Luciano was..."

"You don't know that," huffed Aaron, leaning forward. "Besides, it could've been your opposition trying to ignite the war to take over the Court. Did you think about that, Your Majesty?" He filled the last two words with so much contempt that Cole flinched.

"It's possible, Aaron." Cole smirked, twisting the ring on the middle finger of his right hand. "But it's very unlikely. I think we have a much bigger issue than just another conflict between two supernatural groups."

"You—," started Aaron, rising, but Luc raised his hand, stopping him.

"Aaron, stop attacking Cole," said the Master Warden, his voice slightly above a whisper. "I know you hate vampires, but God knows he is not our enemy." He crossed himself, a deep frown settling on his youthful face. "Cole, Luciano was right. Wurdulak is the only vampire-like creature of magic that leaves four puncture wounds on the necks of their victims. Everything he said makes perfect sense, however, what happened after... Are you sure Luciano was controlled? Are you positive he didn't betray you? With the unstable situation in the Arizona Vampire Court, nothing would surprise me."

"No," growled Cole, his hands clenching into fists of their own accord. "Luciano would never betray me. Never!"

He slammed his fist on the table, but then bit his lip and looked away. Luc and Aaron exchanged a quick look but didn't say anything, allowing Cole to continue.

"Luciano wasn't just my righthand man. He was my friend, my maker's friend and brother in arms. The bonds of friendship between my father and Luciano were stronger than blood, more powerful than any dark magic. They carried it through thousands of years, and Luciano had been by my side from the moment Ruslan turned me," said Cole, composing himself. "He would never do anything to jeopardize my safety. He was controlled by some kind of malicious spell, and it had to be extremely powerful dark magic."

Rising, he shoved his hand in the pocket of his pants and pulled out the small iron box where he had stored the metal disk he found after Luciano's death. Turning to Luc, he added, "Master Warden, you know that it's not easy to control vampires. But to control a vampire as ancient as Luciano, it has to be someone extremely skilled in the Dark Arts."

He put the box on the table and pushed it toward Luc. The Master Warden caught the box and opened it, peering inside.

"Oh, Lord," Luc exhaled, raising his eyes at Cole. "Cole, please tell me you didn't touch this disk."

Cole shook his head. "No, my lord, I didn't," he replied. "I suspected this disc was connected to the dark spell that controlled Luciano, similar to the way witches use hex bags for curses." He pointed at the box. "The box is made of cold iron and built to contain cursed objects."

Luc de la Crosse whispered a quick spell, moving his fingers over the box without touching it. A ray of purple light burst out of the disk, and as Cole looked up, he gasped, rising. The rune he'd seen earlier on Luciano's forehead was glowing brightly on the ceiling, projected by the disk.

"This rune," he whispered, pointing up. "What is it?"

The Master Warden got up slowly, his head upturned as his widened eyes explored the rune. "This is bad news, *mon ami*," he whispered absentmindedly. "I need to do more research, but I believe we're dealing with a necromancer. An extremely powerful one."

"No..." Cole staggered back, fear coiling in the pit of his stomach. "It can't be. I thought necromancy was outlawed by the Destiny Council and all practitioners were imprisoned years ago."

"Not all," said Luc. He closed the iron box, and the rune vanished from the ceiling. "When is Commander Blake coming back?"

"I don't know," replied Cole. "Either later on today or tomorrow."

"He needs to know. Call him as soon as you can," muttered Luc, taking the box. "I'm going back to Paris. I need to discuss the situation with the Grand Master of the Order." He thought for a moment, nibbling on his lip. "If indeed we're dealing with a necromancer powerful enough to conjure wurdulaks and control an ancient vampire, you're not safe, Cole. None of the undead are safe."

Luc waved his hand, opening a portal, but before he walked through it, he stilled, rubbing the back of his neck.

"Cole, you can't go back to your home or your company," he said, twirling the box in his hands. "From here, I want you to drive straight to Paradise Manor. The left wing of the building is protected by powerful wards and spells. Whoever this necromancer is, even they won't be able to break through. You should be safe there. I'll talk to Commander Blake as soon as he comes back to Blue Creek, and we'll find a way to protect your subjects."

"I understand," replied Cole, "but I can't put myself on lockdown while the Court is hanging in the balance, and we're on a brink of war with the werewolves which may spill into the realm of humans, exposing the World of Magic. I can't hide, Luc. I must keep fighting. No matter how hard or how dangerous it gets, I must do what's right. What kind of King would I be if I—"

"You'd be an alive King," objected Luc de la Crosse dryly. "Live today to fight tomorrow, Cole. Do as I say. I'm not asking you. I command you in the name of the Destiny Council. If you don't obey, we'll lock you in a Destiny Council holding facility, and you're not going to see your Court until all this is over. It's better to have an imprisoned King than one controlled by a necromancer."

Cole frowned but pressed his fist to his chest, inclining his head. "As you wish, Master Warden."

CHAPTER 6

~ DAMIAN BLAKE ~

Since Damian wasn't familiar with the location of Hawk's residence, he couldn't teleport there, so he had no choice but to drive. From the warehouse, he teleported directly to Cole's house and headed to his garage.

He entered the security code, using a small keypad located next to the entrance, and the door rolled up, giving him access to a spacious six-car garage. Shaking his head, Damian walked inside, flipping the light switch on. It wasn't the first time he visited Cole's garage. However, every time he was here, he couldn't help but wonder why his brother needed so many vehicles, especially since he was a vampire and could move a lot faster than any car in his arsenal.

Damian walked toward the large white Mercedes G-Class SUV and opened the door, getting into the driver's seat. It was the only car his brother owned that he felt comfortable driving. Cole had offered to transfer the title to him, but since Damian never cared to own a car, he just dismissed that idea, promising Cole that if he ever needed a vehicle, he'd borrow it.

Starting the engine, he peered at the touchscreen. "Dammit...

How do you use it?" he muttered, scratching the back of his head. "Where the hell is that GPS-thingy..."

It took him a few minutes to find the navigation system and figure out how to enter the address. Once done, he drove the SUV out of the garage, pressed the button on the built-in remote to lower the door, and started on his way to Hawk's residence.

* * *

FOLLOWING THE GPS INSTRUCTIONS, Damian drove through the desert, wondering if the crazy machine was taking him on a wild-goose chase. The brownish-yellow land, covered in dry patches of grass, thorny bushes and towering Saguaro cacti, appeared to be endless and no matter how much he sharpened his human and supernatural senses, he couldn't detect any presence of life.

"In five hundred yards, turn left," demanded the GPS.

"Left where?" grumbled Damian, staring out the window. "There is nothing there."

"Turn left now," said the GPS flatly.

"Fine. Stubborn..."

He swung the vehicle to the left, taking a small byroad. After a short drive, he noticed a white fence surrounding a large piece of land with a small farmhouse visible in the distance. He parked the SUV by the gates and walked out, carefully surveying the area. Even though he didn't notice any people, he could hear the sound of some kind of power tools or machinery working at the far end of the property, and that told him that at least some members of the pack were home.

Damian approached the gate, ready to push it open, when a slight fluctuation in the magical energy field touched his senses. He pulled his hand back and opened his other sight, scanning the gates and the fence around the farm.

"Holy shit," he muttered, observing a set of runes glowing with brilliant white light. The thin lines of wards stretched along the fence as far as he could see, and a barely visible net of glowing white lines encapsulated the entire property rising high in the air. "These wards were cast by a god..." He moved his hand over the shiny white lines without touching them and shook his head. "Not only by a god, but also by a Child of Fire or the Great Salamander himself. Perun almighty... Who the hell are these people?"

"Who wants to know?"

Damian spun around to see a young man no older than eighteen standing before him with his arms folded across his chest. Dressed in washed out blue jeans and a shirt, he was tall and muscled, but his body still had the youthful slenderness of a teen. As far as Damian could see, he was unarmed, but that didn't mean he wasn't dangerous. The unmistakable energy signature of a lycanthrope surrounded him like a thick cloud, yet it was too weak to belong to a purebred werewolf.

"Hello," said Damian, trying to sound as friendly as he could, extending his hand. "My name is Damian Blake, and I need to see your Alpha."

"You do, don't yah?" The young man glanced at Damian's hand but didn't shake it, his eyes lingering on it for a moment too long. Instead, he cocked his head slightly, and an arrogant smirk stretched his lips. "First, you're gonna tell me why you are here and what you want with Hawk. And then, I'll decide what to do with you next."

"I'm sorry. The reason I'm here I can only discuss with the Alpha," replied Damian calmly. Getting in a confrontation with one of the members of the pack wasn't going to help his cause. But as much as he was determined to keep it nice and peaceful, the young werewolf was getting under his skin.

The young man laughed. "How does a little human like you know what an Alpha is?"

"I read a lot of Urban Fantasy," replied Damian, unable to hide the amusement in his voice. He took a step closer to the obnoxious teenager, towering at least half a foot over him. "You're going to go to your Alpha now and let him know that the little human needs to speak with him. Am I clear, young man?"

The young werewolf staggered back, and for a split second, his eyes widened, but then he raised his hand and twirled his wrist, a derisive smirk splitting his face. A soft whistling sound touched Damian's hearing, and he turned around in the direction of the noise a moment too late. As something sharp penetrated his skin, he hissed and jerked his hand up to his neck involuntarily. Feeling a cold and slippery object under his fingers, he seized it and pulled it out, staring at a tiny dart lying in the palm of his hand.

The world spun in a slow and nauseating manner, and he dropped the dart, rubbing his forehead. He didn't remember falling, and he didn't feel when he hit the ground. All he felt was two more stings, and suddenly, the teenager's boots were right next to his face. He wanted to move, but his limbs were too heavy, his body refusing to obey the commands of his mind. His eyelids closed, and the darkness embraced him.

THE ACRID SMELL of burned wood, smoke and dust invaded his nostrils, breaking through the heavy cover of the darkness, and the memory of what had happened spiked through his fogged mind. As Damian regained his consciousness, he jerked, hitting his head against something hard. He groaned and moved his hand up to rub his head, just to realize that his hands were bound behind his back. He cracked his eyelids open, squinting at the bright rectangle of light.

"Holy shit! I shot him with three doses of horse tranquilizer, and he's already up!"

Damian heard a youthful voice somewhere above him and blinked a few times, struggling to adjust his blurry vision. He was sitting on the floor of a small smithy. The forge was cold, and it looked like no one had used it for a while. The corner of his mouth lifted into an uneven smirk as he assessed his restraints. Thick ropes wrapped around his torso and arms, tying him to an anvil. His wrists were also bound with a rope. However, as thick as the restraints were, they weren't going to hold him for longer than a few seconds if he decided to break free.

Three young people—two men and a woman, who had barely transitioned from their childhood to adolescence—stood in front of him, staring at him with unconcealed curiosity. All three were werewolves, but none of them were purebred.

"Now that you had your fun, please fetch your Alpha," Damian said, regarding them calmly. "It's urgent, and I don't have time to play games."

The young woman tittered, shaking her head. "I don't think you're in a position to give commands."

"I'm always in a position to command," objected Damian, frowning. As much as he didn't want to fight with these baby-wolves, he had no time to spare. "You have one minute to summon Hawk. You don't have to untie me if it makes you feel safer."

"And what will you do if we don't, little human?" asked the same young man he had met at the gates.

"Trust me, you don't want to know," growled Damian, enhancing his voice with his magic just a little. "Do it! Now!"

As his deep voice rolled through the smithy, reverberating against the walls, the teens flinched, and the younger of the two boys ran out of the building. A few seconds later, the sound of heavy footsteps reached Damian's ears, and a powerful wave of magical energy characteristic to a purebred werewolf assailed his magical senses. A moment later, an older man walked inside the smithy and halted in front of Damian, holding a rifle trained at him.

Even though he wasn't tall, he had the wide chest and muscled arms of a man who got used to working with his hands without shying away from hard physical labor. An old scar disfigured the left side of his face, running from the middle of his cheek down to his neck. Deep wrinkles settled around his tightly pressed mouth, and his thick eyebrows gathered over the golden eyes of a predator as he carefully observed Damian.

After a moment, he sighed and lowered his rifle, staring at the young werewolves reproachfully.

"Have I taught you nothing in the last few years?" he asked them, his raspy voice carrying notes of bitterness. "Who do you think this man is?"

"A human pet of some disgusting vamp," offered the older teen, anger making his voice waver.

Damian's jaw dropped, but he said nothing, allowing the Alpha to continue.

"First of all, not human. He's extremely skilled at hiding his true nature. Even I can't detect any magic in him. But what did I teach you about a werewolf's intuition?" asked Hawk, shaking his head.

"It's very powerful, and we must always listen to our intuition," said the younger boy.

"And what does it tell you when you look at this man?" asked Hawk, sounding like a patient first-grade teacher.

The young werewolves exchanged bewildered looks and shrugged.

"Damn, kids..." Hawk threw his hands up, tones of disappointment clear in his voice. "Second, why would you even think he belongs to a vamp? Do you see any bite marks on his arms or neck?"

"No... but he reeks of one," the girl suggested tentatively.

"Oh shit," mumbled Damian, stifling laughter. "And I thought I took a good, long shower this morning."

The Alpha's eyes darted from the kids to Damian, and for the first time, a spark of humor reflected in his gaze. He inclined his head in a respectful bow.

"My lord, I apologize for my kids' disrespectful behavior. I know you came in peace. They were stupid enough"—he threw a scorching glare at the three teens—"to take you across the wards, and if you wanted war, they would be dead by now," he said softly. "I don't know what you are, but for the sake of the lessons they need to learn, could you please demonstrate your true nature to these juvenile jackasses? In a safe way, of course."

"Are you sure?" asked Damian, checking the space available in the smithy.

"Please, proceed, my lord." Hawk inclined his head, pushing the young members of his pack toward the walls. "They must understand that in the World of Magic things are never what they appear to be."

"As you wish." Damian took a deep breath and channeled his magic, connecting with the elemental energy of the Earth. As the energy of his element traveled to his eyes, he knew they lit up with a bright orange light, and he allowed his magic to take him over, making the ground tremble a little for added effect. A brilliant white light emitted by his body filled the dark smithy, illuminating every corner. The ropes restraining him fell, turning into dust, and he rose to his feet, taking a step away from the anvil.

A deep shudder ran through him as he reveled in the feeling of his full power surging through him. Throwing his head back, he roared and spread his arms wide, his black wings opening to the full extent behind his back.

Hawk's eyes widened, and he dropped to one knee, pressing

his fist to his chest. The teens followed his move, staring at him in awe.

"Lord Enforcer," the Alpha exhaled, inclining his head. "How can I be of service?"

Damian folded his wings and let go of his magic, taking his human form. "Please, don't kneel, sir," he said, touching Hawk's shoulder. "I came here because I need your help. Is there a place we could speak in private?"

Hawk got up, unease reflecting on his weather-beaten face. "Not the first time I hear this kind of preamble," he muttered, frowning. "Usually, it means nothing good. Especially when it comes from a Destiny Enforcer." He turned to his teens and gestured for them to get up. "I hope that was a lesson for you. Assaulting a Destiny Enforcer can be the last thing you do in your lives." He glowered at the teens, watching them squirm under his heavy stare, but then waved his hand dismissively. "You can leave now."

As the young werewolves bowed to Damian and their pack master and left the smithy, Hawk gestured at the door. "Walk with me, Lord Enforcer. Tell me what brought you here."

CHAPTER 7

~ DAMIAN BLAKE ~

Hawk slowly walked across the property, leading Damian around the machine shop. The door was open, and a loud banging accompanied by the hissing noise of lifts was coming through the doorway. The smell of motor oil, grease and gasoline hung in the air, overpowering the scents of the afternoon desert. Hawk glanced at the shop, a wistful smile touching his lips as he waved at one of the men working inside.

Turning to Damian, he gave him a quick once-over. "I always wanted to know," he said, moving toward a small bench next to the fence behind the machine shop. "How do Destiny Enforcers manage to keep their shirts in one piece when they open their wings?"

Damian glanced at him, wondering if the Alpha was joking, but since Hawk looked dead serious, he answered, "I have to cast a spell on all my shirts and jackets. I hate these damn things. I never use them, except for those rare occasions when some werewolf Alpha asks me to intimidate his wild teenagers."

Hawk chuckled, shaking his head. "You're alright, kid," he muttered, but Damian wasn't sure if he said it to him or to himself. "I've met a few of your kind before. Most of them were self-important assholes. You don't strike me as such."

"Thank you, I guess?"

The Alpha lowered on the bench and tapped the space next to him, inviting Damian to sit down. "So, what's your human name, Lord Enforcer?" he asked, staring into the desert, his gaze veiled with sadness. "Sorry, but I'm not a big fan of all these courtly procedures and medieval manners of the World of Magic."

"Neither am I," replied Damian, offering Hawk his hand. "My name is Damian Blake. You can call me Damian, sir."

"Drop that 'sir' part, Damian. You're probably a few centuries older than me." He shook his hand, but his face turned hard as he leaned back, folding his arms over his chest. "The kids were right though, you know?"

"About?"

"You stink of the undead," replied the Alpha, his golden eyes turning darker. "Why is that?"

Damian exhaled, looking at Hawk sideways. Even though on the outside Hawk appeared calm, Damian could sense his grief and internal turmoil, and he wasn't sure how to approach the sensitive subject. Making a split-second decision, he chose to stick to the truth, believing that Hawk deserved his honesty.

"My brother is a vampire," he said, shifting slightly to face the Alpha. "It's his essence you smell on me."

Hawk's eyes rounded, his eyebrows climbing up. "You don't say," he mumbled. "The Destiny Enforcer has a brother who's a vamp." He shook his head, pursing his lips. "The joke is on you, kid. One day you may have to put cuffs on your own brother, you know."

"It'll never happen," replied Damian, cringing inwardly at the thought. "My brother is a good man."

"I'm sure he's a vegetarian," murmured Hawk with a cold smirk.

"My brother's name is Cole Adams." Damian met Hawk's gaze without blinking.

Hawk got up, moving slowly as if his limbs were filled with lead. "The new King of the Arizona Vampire Court is your brother?" he hissed. The air around him shimmered, and the werewolf stiffened, visibly fighting to get his anger under control.

"This is the reason I am here, sir," said Damian.

"Are you here to beg for your brother's life, Enforcer?" the Alpha growled, his eyes igniting with a bright orange light as his fangs elongated. "If yes, then you wasted your time by coming here! The vamps started this war, but I swear, I'm going to finish it."

"No, sir. I don't beg." Damian gestured at the bench, inviting Hawk to sit down. "If you give me a chance to explain, you'll see I have no need to plead for my brother's safety."

For a few seconds, Hawk stood, glowering down at Damian, but then he grunted and sat back down. "Fine," he muttered. "Go ahead. Explain."

"Earlier today, detective Evans summoned me to a crime scene in Blue Creek," started Damian. "One more werewolf was killed by a vampire, or so it seemed. But once I examined the victim and the scene of the crime, I detected a strange magical energy residue which made me think that things were not what they appeared to be. I don't believe vampires killed those werewolves. I believe there is a third party who's trying to ignite a war between two large supernatural groups in Arizona. I don't know who that is or what their motives are, but if you help me, I swear I will find out and bring them to justice. I'm here to ask you to hold the werewolves from retaliating just long enough for me to do my job."

"What makes you think there is someone else?" Hawk wasn't sarcastic, but the vibe of mistrust and antagonism surrounding the old Alpha was too prominent for Damian not to notice it.

He couldn't blame him knowing that his only daughter had been killed recently, presumably by a vampire.

"Intuition. Isn't it what you teach your young ones—to always trust your intuition?" replied Damian. "Centuries of swimming up to my eyeballs in supernatural shit without my full power and magic has taught me a few things."

Hawk raised his face, his gaze lingering on the scar on Damian's face a moment too long, and for a heartbeat, Damian felt as if the old Alpha was reading his soul.

"Ruby was my only daughter," Hawk said after a while. "She was beautiful, kind and..." His voice shook and trailed away, undiluted anguish overflowing his words. He sat, motionless and silent, his face a mask of pain. Finally, he pressed his fingers to his eyes and leaned back, taking in shallow breaths. "A rogue vamp took her from me... and you're asking me to stand down?"

"No, sir," objected Damian. "I'm asking you to give me a chance to find the person who's truly responsible for Ruby's death."

Hawk didn't reply right away, and when he spoke again, his voice was barely audible. "And what if it is your brother who's responsible for her death? What would you do then, Enforcer? Would you put the Destiny Cuffs on him? Would you fulfill your duty, killing your brother in the process?"

Damian shuddered, swallowing with an effort. The Destiny Cuffs were designed to strip any magical or elemental being of their magic, draining them completely and effectively turning them into humans. Since the only thing that sustained a vampire's life was their vampiric essence, which was nothing but pure magical energy, the lightest touch of the Destiny Cuffs to their skin would kill them instantly.

Rising heavily, Damian extended his right hand. As his dagger materialized in his palm, he took one knee before the Alpha, placing the tip of his blade to the ground.

"Hawk, I don't bow, and I kneel before no one. But right

now, I'm kneeling before you so I can swear my oath to you." Damian squeezed the pommel of his dagger, looking up at the old werewolf. "I swear I will find those responsible for Ruby's death and bring them to justice." He bowed his head, a deep crease materializing between his eyebrows. "If it is Cole who killed your daughter, I swear, I'll put the Destiny Cuffs on his wrists myself."

Hawk looked away from him, his hand clutching at his throat as if suddenly he had a hard time breathing. "Your brother is a vampire," he said in disbelief. "How can you be so positive in his innocence? How can you trust him so... blindly?"

Damian got up, and his dagger vanished. Lowering on the bench next to Hawk, he leaned forward, propping his elbows on his lap. "Because I believe that discord in the Vampire Court and the war between the vampires and werewolves are driven by the same individuals. Because despite Cole being undead, he's more human than some people I've known throughout my life." He straightened, turning to the Alpha. "Because he's my blood, and even though he's a vampire and I'm a Destiny Enforcer, we stand together. Always."

"A Destiny Enforcer works with a vamp. And here I thought I'd seen it all by now." Hawk smiled, and there was something in his eyes that gave Damian a spark of hope, but then the Alpha set his lips into a straight line, shaking his head. "I'm afraid you're asking me something I'm not sure I can deliver. Even if I can hold back my own pack and a few more packs whose Alphas would listen to me, there are others who don't care about anything I say."

"I understand, but what if—," Damian started to say when the loud ring of his cellphone interrupted him. Throwing an apologetic glance at Hawk, he got up and pulled the phone out. As he checked the screen, he saw Cole's photo and pressed the green button, answering the call. "It's my brother. I'm sorry, I have to take his call."

Hawk nodded, giving him a dismissive flick of his wrist.

"Cole, finally," Damian exhaled with relief. "Did you receive my message? Are you okay?"

"I'm fine, more or less," replied Cole.

"What happened?"

"I'll tell you later. There are more important things you need to know," said Cole, and the engine roared in the background as he started his car. "I just met with Luc de la Crosse. You were right."

"About?" asked Damian, glancing at Hawk.

"Everything," replied Cole. "Someone is playing a dangerous game in our backyard, and we need to find them before they unleash a full-blown supernatural storm on our state." Cole stopped talking, and Damian heard a loud thud as his brother slammed his hand on something. "When we find this person"—Cole's voice came through as a low growl—"I'll tear them limb from limb with my bare hands."

"Cole, what happened?" asked Damian, unease spreading through him.

"I'll tell you everything when I see you in person," replied Cole, his voice flat. "Did you speak with the Alpha?"

"I'm with Hawk right now," said Damian, giving a curt nod to the Alpha. "I'm going to put you on speaker. Do you mind telling both of us everything the Master Warden told you?"

"Go ahead."

Damian switched his phone to speaker and turned to Hawk. "This is my brother, Cole Adams," he introduced, lowering on the bench. "He just met with Master Warden Luc de la Crosse, and he has some information for us."

"A vampire had a meeting with a Master of the Wardens Order. I never thought I'd live to see the day when any representatives of the Destiny Council would deal with vampires," muttered the old Alpha, shaking his head. "For them, the only good vampire is a dead one. At least, it used to be that way."

"It still is, sir," said Cole, his voice sounding sad even through the speakerphone. "However, the Master Warden understands the gravity of the situation and is willing to work with me to resolve the issue."

"Your brother sounds like one of those corporate sharks," Hawk whispered, giving Damian an arched stare.

Damian almost choked, trying to stifle his laughter. "You know Cole is a vampire," he managed to say. "Whispering doesn't help. He can hear you."

"Oh, shit," muttered Hawk, scratching the back of his head. "So, what did the Master Warden tell you, Mr. Adams?" He cleared his throat and added not without a layer of sarcasm in his words, "Am I supposed to address you as Your Majesty, by the way?"

"No, sir," replied Cole quietly. "You can call me Cole. I am not a proponent of keeping up the medieval traditions in the midst of the twenty-first century."

"Okay, Cole, what do you have for us?" Despite sounding calm, Hawk clenched his jaw and frowned slightly, his every move betraying just how much he hated the idea of speaking with a vampire, even over the phone.

"I'll make it short," continued Cole. "Luc de la Crosse suspects that we have a powerful necromancer working in Arizona."

"How powerful? Did Luc give you a name?" asked Damian, his blood running cold at the realization of the danger his brother was in.

"Powerful enough to conjure wurdulaks," growled Cole. "All those werewolves... they weren't killed by vampires. They were murdered by wurdulaks!"

He all but screamed the last words, anger and despair loud and clear in his voice, and Damian couldn't help but wonder what made his normally composed brother lose his temper. The line went silent for a moment, only the continuous noise of the engine coming through.

"Damian, that night when I met with the leaders of the opposing faction," Cole continued at length, "I think we were all under that necromancer's control. I can't be sure, of course, but that would explain why I can't remember anything that happened after the confrontation started."

"Cole, where are you? I'm coming to get you," said Damian, rising. "You're not safe. Necromancers can control anything without a heartbeat."

"I know," murmured Cole. The ticking of a turn signal sounded too loud to Damian's overly strained hearing as a pregnant pause hung between them. "I'm almost at Paradise Manor. I have orders from the Master Warden to remain there until further notice."

There was so much bitterness in his brother's voice that Damian cringed inwardly.

"Hawk, are you there?" asked Cole. The sound of the engine disappeared, and complete silence stretched across the line.

"I'm here, Cole," replied the Alpha quietly, and for the first time, he didn't sound like he wanted to take the phone and smash it against the biggest rock he could find in his backyard.

"I'm truly sorry for your loss, sir. I'm sorry for all the werewolves who fell victim to this monster," he said softly. "Now that you know what we're dealing with, can my brother and I count on your support?"

Hawk clenched his teeth, his cheek disfigured by a scar twitching from a nervous tic. "You have my support, King," he replied, his fingers clenching into massive fists, his fingernails elongating into claws.

"Thank you," said Cole. "Dima, I'm at Paradise Manor. I'll see you soon."

Damian hung up the phone and turned to the Alpha. "I have to go. I need to get in touch with Luc de la Crosse as soon as possible and start searching for this necromancer. The sooner I find him or her, the safer we all will be."

Hawk nodded, rising. "What's your phone number?" he asked, gesturing at the device Damian held in his hand. "I'll get in touch with you as soon as I talk to the local pack masters. I can't promise you that everyone will believe me, but I'll do my best."

"That's all I can ask for," replied Damian. He gave the Alpha his phone number and offered his hand to him. As the old werewolf squeezed his hand, he smiled. "Say hello to your teen-wolves. I still wonder why they called a man of my height *a little human*, even if they thought I had no magic."

Hawk snorted, rolling his eyes. "Don't even get me started." He turned around and headed toward the machine shop but halted after a few steps and glanced at Damian over his shoulder. "For a Destiny Enforcer, you're alright, kid. I hope we can get together for a cup of coffee after all this mess is over."

"I have a feeling after all this is over, I will need something stronger than coffee," replied Damian, chuckling.

"You got it! Drinks are on me." The Alpha waved his hand and resumed his walk.

Damian turned around and moved across the property toward his car. As he reached the fence, he opened his other sight and check the wards placed around the werewolves' ranch with curiosity.

"I should have asked Hawk about that," he muttered, opening the gates. "I wonder which god placed such powerful wards, and why they were needed in the first place." Promising himself to find out more about Hawk and his pack, he unlocked the car and sat down on the driver's seat, starting the engine.

Driving back toward the main road, he dialed Ace's phone number.

"Commander Blake?" Ace's voice sounded surprised and troubled at the same time.

"Hi, Ace," he said, poking at the touchscreen to set up the GPS. "Where are you now?"

"Just left the office and on my way back to Blue Creek," she replied. "Cole asked me to take care of the mess in his..." Her voice trailed, sounding like the voice of a person who had said something they weren't supposed to say.

"He called me earlier," said Damian, recalling the way his brother sounded on the phone. At first, he wanted to ask Ace what Cole asked her to do but then changed his mind. "Ace, Cole is at Paradise Manor. The Master Warden ordered him to stay within the protected area until the investigation is over. I need you to go there and stay with him. I'll be home soon, but I can't be there twenty-four-seven, and I need you to keep an eye on things while I'm not around. I don't want Cole to be alone even at night."

"Yes, my lord," she replied, tones of excitement coming through the line. "I'm about five minutes away from Paradise Manor."

"Ace," he growled warningly, clenching his jaw. "Remember what I told you. Cole is your charge. You're shadowing and guarding him. Your service doesn't include bodily fluids exchange, and it definitely doesn't include blood donations. Am I clear?"

"Yes, my lord," she replied. "Clear as day."

He hung up the phone, shaking his head. "It's like giving a bone to a dog and asking him not to eat it. If Moore ever finds out about her extracurricular activities, she's not gonna be a happy camper."

CHAPTER 8

~ COLE ADAMS ~

River was still at work, and the house stood dark and empty. Cole walked through the hallway without turning the light on. With his sharp vision, he didn't need it to find his bedroom. He opened the door and walked inside, closing it with a soft thud. For a moment, he stood in the middle of the room, his arms dangling limply alongside his body.

Then he headed toward the bed and collapsed on top without taking his shoes and trench coat off. It took a lot for him to feel tired, but right now, he felt exhausted to the point where he could barely move. Somewhere deep inside, he realized it wasn't physical exhaustion. It was his mind refusing to process everything that had happened in the last twenty-four hours. Grief, scorching anger and a dreadful feeling of his own helplessness blended into one overwhelming concoction within him, driving him to the wall.

He pulled a pillow to his chest and curled himself around it, closing his eyes. But just when he allowed himself to relax, the doorbell rang, its jarring sound making him groan and wrap his arms around his head. The bell rang again, and he sat up, lowering his feet to the floor. Slowly, he made his way through the hallway into the foyer and opened the door to see Ace standing with her hand up, ready to ring the bell again.

She glanced up at him, and her mouth dropped open. Without saying another word, she seized his wrist and pulled him after her, heading back to his room. Once inside, she kicked the door shut and let go of him, placing her hands on her hips.

"I just came from your office," she announced. "It looked like something out of a cheap thriller movie, or as if a stampede of rhinos rampaged through it." She gave him another once-over and added, "And you look like all those rhinos ran over you. Do you want to tell me what's up with that?"

"No." Cole lowered to the bed, dropping his head. He didn't want to offend her, but talking about him killing his best friend who had stood by his side for over a thousand years wasn't going to make anyone feel better.

Ace approached him and threaded her fingers through his entangled, blood-splattered curls. He leaned forward, resting his forehead against her stomach, but she took his chin with her fingers, raising his face.

"Do me a favor, Cole. Get up." She nudged him up, and he didn't resist. Putting her hands under the lapels of his coat, she took it off and tilted her head a little, staring at the T-shirt he was wearing. "Not your style, is it?"

"No... but walking around covered in blood is also not my style." He sighed, looking out the window. "Why are you here, Ace? I'm okay. I just need a few minutes of peace."

"Commander Blake ordered me to shadow you in his absence," she replied, sounding all business. "You have blood in your hair and on your neck, by the way." Ignoring his less than warm welcome, she unbuckled his belt and unbuttoned the waistband of his pants. He flinched from the sound of the zipper but again didn't resist, allowing his pants to fall to the floor. Then he bent down and took his shoes off. As he straightened, she tugged at his shirt. "Take it off."

He lifted his arms and grabbed the collar of the shirt, pulling it off, all his moves torturously slow and heavy.

"Shower, now!" she commanded, pointing at the bathroom.

Cole turned on his heels and headed into the bathroom without any objections. He felt too drained to argue with her. Even more so, he didn't want to speak about what had happened. So, he opened the shower, took his underwear off and stepped under the cool water without waiting for it to warm up. Leaning his back against the wall, he bowed his head to his chest and folded his arms, allowing the water to wash over his hair and run down his chest.

He wasn't sure how long he stood like this, but when he felt a gentle touch to his arm, he flinched and opened his eyes. Ace stood in front of him, water plastering her black hair to her bare shoulders. Without her masculine boots and black clothes, she looked smaller and more delicate than usual. His lips parted as he gazed down at her, his mind getting fogged with desire for a heartbeat. Gathering his thoughts, he grunted and looked away from her.

"Ace, what are you doing here?" he asked, realizing how hoarse his voice sounded. "Damian should be back soon, and he's not going to be happy to see you like this. I thought he made it clear—"

"He made clear what?" she asked, her finger trailing down his chest, barely touching his icy skin. "That I can't be with you because you are my charge? It's my problem. Not his." She tilted her head, staring at him with a playful smirk. "What are you afraid of, Your Majesty? That your big brother will put you across his knee and spank you a few times for disobedience?" She tittered, her fingers moving down his stomach, making his muscles contract under her touch. "Or maybe that's what you want, huh?" She moved her hand over his hip, cupping his backside. "I can do it too, you know. It would be a lot sexier though."

He groaned and stepped to the side, away from her touch.

"Damian is right, Ace," he whispered, holding his hands down to cover himself. "If your Commander finds out, you'll be in a world of trouble, and I don't want to see you suffer. He is also right about your addiction to the pleasure of the vampire bite. I can't do it to you—"

"I don't need you to bite me to feel the pleasure of your... um... company, royal dumbass," she whispered, pinning him against the wall with her hand. Her other hand slipped down under his crossed arms, cupping his groin. He hissed, closing his eyes, and as she started to stroke him gently, he tilted his head back, resting it against the slippery tiles. Too tired to resist, he let go, allowing her to have her way with him.

* * *

Cole wasn't sure how much time had passed. He didn't care. All he needed was a few minutes of oblivion and peace, and Ace gave it to him. Probably noticing his state, she didn't ask any more questions, her hands gently toweling his body dry. Once she was done, he walked out of the shower and headed toward his closet to get dressed.

"Cole, what's going on? I knocked, but no one answered, and your door was unlocked..."

Damian's voice sounded behind him, and he spun around, coming face to face with his brother. An expression of concern on his face got replaced with that of shock as his eyes darted from Cole to Ace who was hopping on one foot in the doorway, struggling to pull her tight jeans over her damp skin. His golden-brown eyes darkened, and his face hardened.

"Ace, did you disobey my direct order?" Damian asked quietly.

He sounded flat and emotionless, but the iron tones of a Destiny Enforcer Commander were unmistakable in his voice.

Cole took a step closer, but Damian's eyes darted to him, pinning him in place.

"Get dressed, Cole," he growled, pointing at the closet.

Damian made his way to Ace who finally managed to put her pants and shirt on and stood with her head bowed down. He seized her arm and pulled her toward the exit.

"I'm trying to protect my brother and you, Ace," he muttered, his fingers digging deeper into her arm, undoubtedly leaving some bruising. "But you're fighting me every step of the way. Don't you get it? You put in a precarious situation not only yourself but also Cole." He threw his hands up. "He's a vampire, goddammit! It means he is blacklisted by the Destiny Council by default. Didn't Moore teach you anything at all?"

She didn't fight him, and the haunted look in her large eyes told Cole that she recognized the truth in Damian's words but stubbornly refused to acknowledge it. Damian halted by the exit and pushed the door open.

"Do you want him to get blamed for seducing an inexperienced recruit?" He pointed at Cole. "And for getting you addicted to a vampire's bite?" Damian stopped talking and shook his head, frowning. "If Moore finds out that Cole is my brother, he will throw you under the bus just to hurt me." He glanced back at Cole, a pained expression crossing his face. "I'm sorry, brother, but whatever you two have must stop."

"Dima, let's—," Cole started to say, but Damian grunted, his jaw tightening, and Cole fell silent, quickly deciding against his original idea.

"I'll deal with you in a minute," promised Damian, and Cole cringed inwardly, feeling like a teenager caught watching porn.

Turning back to Ace, Damian pushed her out of the room. "Go to the living room and stay there until I summon you. I still need you to shadow and protect my brother, but in a professional manner. With your clothes on, preferably."

"Yes, Commander Blake," she whispered, a blush creeping up to her cheeks.

As she bowed to him, Damian grunted and turned away from her, shutting the door in her face. Moving heavily, he walked to the bed and lowered himself, massaging the side of his neck. Cole grabbed a pair of track pants out of his closet and put them on. He didn't bother with a shirt and sat down on the floor, leaning his back against the wall so he could face Damian.

"Don't you think you were a little harsh with her?" he asked with reproach, examining his brother's face.

"No, I don't." Damian leaned forward, staring at him from under his uneven black hair.

"But Damian—"

"You can't be with her. Period. It will get you killed and her..." He bit his lip, burning Cole with his golden eyes. "I don't even know what Moore will do if he finds out. She's breaking every rule in the book. I've been doing this job for centuries, and trust me, it's impossible for a Destiny Enforcer to have personal attachments. I learned that the hard way."

"What do you mean—the hard way?"

"I don't want to talk about it."

"Why not? A long time ago, we had no secrets between us. You're no longer *no one*, but you still refuse to tell me anything." Cole dropped his hands in his lap, shaking his head. "Besides, just because something happened to you, it doesn't mean Ace will—"

"This conversation is over," Damian snapped, cutting the air with his hand. "We have a bigger problem to discuss."

Realizing that this discussion was going nowhere fast, Cole changed the subject. "The Master Warden put me on house arrest," he said, stretching his long legs in front of him. "I can't just sit here and do nothing."

Damian raised his face and glanced at him. "Luc is right," he said, his voice getting softer. "Until we find this necromancer, you can't leave Paradise Manor."

"Dima, I have to feed. I don't need a lot of blood to sustain my energy, but I can't go on without feeding for a long period of time. The thirst will turn me into a monster," he said, averting his gaze. Talking about feeding with Damian wasn't something he was comfortable with, and right now, he felt like a cornered animal with no way out. "I need to go home. I have a few blood bags stored there in case of emergency."

"I know you need to feed." A sad smile appeared on Damian's face, quickly dwindling down. He got up and crossed the room, lowering to the floor next to him. "I'll send Ace to your house to bring everything here. In the meantime, you can have mine."

"Dima, I can't... Last night I was hurt, and I had no choice but to feed on you... but I can't do it again. I should have fed when I got home, but I didn't think this would happen. I'm sorry..." He looked away, struggling to suppress the rising thirst. His brother was too close. He could hear his heartbeat, the sound of blood pumping through his veins, and it was hard for him in his condition not to react. "I'll be fine. Let's focus on finding the necromancer so I can get back to a normal life."

"Define normal." Damian looked at him sideways and tapped him on the shoulder, rising. "I'll be right back."

He walked out of the room and came back a few seconds later with an empty plastic cup in his hand. Lowering to the floor in front of Cole, he extended his arm, and one of his blazing daggers materialized in his hand.

"Damian, no," Cole gasped, grabbing his wrist a moment too late.

In one sharp move, his brother cut his arm with his dagger and moved the cup under the incision, collecting the blood. He locked and unlocked his fingers a few times, increasing the flow. Cole hissed as the copper scent of blood invaded his nostrils, igniting his thirst with renewed strength. His fangs expanded despite the effort he put in to control his nature, and he pressed his hand over his mouth, staring at his brother with widened eyes. A few seconds later, the bleeding started to slow down, and Damian offered the cup with blood to him.

"Feed," he said softly, and there was neither judgment nor disgust in his voice, just warmth. As Cole took the cup, Damian pressed his hand over the bleeding incision and turned around to rest his back against the wall, closing his eyes. "Feed, I'm not watching you."

Cole brought the cup to his lips, and as the warm blood rushed down his throat, pacifying his relentless thirst, he finally relaxed.

"I was in love once." His brother's soft voice reached his ears, and he opened his eyes, glancing at him over the rim of his cup. Damian stared straight ahead, a tortured expression on his tense face. "She was a witch—a good witch, one of the Romani people. I loved her so much, Cole... I was willing to give up everything just to be with her." He stopped talking, his fingers rubbing the edge of his leather bracelet.

"What happened?" Cole put the empty cup on the floor and turned in his direction slightly.

"I killed her," whispered Damian. He took a deep breath and exhaled slowly, throwing a veiled gaze at him. "Not directly, of course. But if she hadn't been with me, who knows, she could have still been alive. Gypsy witches have long lives." He bit his lip and pulled his legs to his chest, folding his arms atop his bent knees. "They were after me... the monsters, you know... They tore her apart in front of my eyes, and with my full power of a Destiny Enforcer, I couldn't do anything to protect her." His voice turned into a hoarse whisper, and he dropped his head. "I hate rules, but there are some rules that are placed there for a good reason. A Destiny Enforcer cannot have personal attachments. Period. I fell in love, and by doing so, I drew a bullseye on her back."

"When did it happen?" Cole stared at his brother, chills running down his back.

"Hundreds of years ago. The Carpathian Mountains, fifteenth century." Damian shrugged. "I learned my lesson. Never again."

"Five hundred years ago?" whispered Cole, horrified. "And you still carry this burden? Jesus Christ, brother! How can you live like this?"

"When it just happened, I couldn't," replied Damian after a momentary pause. "This is why I demanded to be discharged. Assuming the *no one* status was the only way they agreed to let me go. I've been alone ever since."

"You haven't been with a woman since then?"

"I didn't say that." Damian smirked. "Of course, I have. I'm not a monk. I just don't allow myself to get attached. Besides, have you seen my back? What do you think happens when I undress?"

"I can't imagine living like this..."

"I don't see a Queen on your arm either, little brother?" Damian raised his eyebrows, tilting his head.

"A long story," murmured Cole. His mind went back to his toxic relationship with the late Queen Roxana, and he shuddered. "Anyway, what's your plan, big bro? I know you have something up your sleeve."

"I wear a tank top, if you didn't notice," Damian murmured snidely.

"Ha-ha." Cole rolled his eyes. "What's the next step? I can't stay here, imprisoned forever. I have a business to run and a Court to rule."

"I hope to hear from Luc de la Crosse soon." Damian got up, straightening his jeans. "Well, first, I'm going to send Ace to your house to bring some blood bags for you." He headed toward the door and halted there with his hand on the handle. "After that, I'm going to go to a bar."

"To a bar," Cole parroted in disbelief. "Vodka is exactly what we need to find a necromancer. Why didn't I think about that? Drink yourself to death, and the necromancer will be right there to take care of you."

"Lighten up on your sarcasm, little bro." Damian chuckled, but somehow laughter left his gaze as tense and uneasy as before, making Cole wonder if his brother knew how to let go and relax even for a moment. "I'm going to *The Midnight Shift*. It's a sanctuary. All sorts of supernatural creeps—including yours truly—gather there. Someone may have heard something. So, stay here and keep up your level of sarcasm while I do my job, Dracula Junior."

"Doofus," murmured Cole, snickering.

Damian waved his hand and walked out of the room.

Cole made his way to the door and closed it, placing his hand against its cold surface. "Watch your back, brother mine..."

CHAPTER 9

~ DAMIAN BLAKE ~

Damian turned around at the soft thud of the closed door and placed his palm against it. "For once, Cole, please listen to me and do as I say," he whispered, a weight settling on his heart.

He made his way to the living room and stopped in the doorway, observing a peaceful view that didn't match the gathering supernatural storm outside of the walls of Paradise Manor. While deep in the conversation with his brother, he hadn't heard when Jamie had arrived, and now the young man was sparring with Ace in the limited space between the couch and the big-screen TV. It seemed like Ace had the upper hand since Jamie was sprawled on the floor, and she had her knee planted against his chest, her fist lingering a few inches away from his face.

Jamie didn't fight her even though Damian could see a few ways he could have easily turned the situation around. Instead, he gazed up at her with googly eyes, his cheeks slightly flushed.

Oh, brother... Damian rolled his eyes. *That's all I need... A friggin' love triangle in the making.*

"Young love," purred Gypsy, stretching her paws, her emerald eyes overflowing with more sarcasm than her tiny body could hold. She made a gagging noise as if she was ready to cough out a hairball. *"Damian, please do something before I throw up."*

Damian gave her a heavy stare and cleared his throat to attract their attention. That worked like a charm. Ace jumped to her feet and spun around. As soon as she saw him, she gasped and dropped to one knee, pressing her fist to her chest. Jamie scrambled into a sitting position, grinning sheepishly at him.

"Get up, Ace," Damian grumbled, folding his arms over his chest. "You disobey my direct orders, so stop kneeling and pretending that you respect me as a Commander. I have neither the time nor the desire to deal with that. After all, you're reporting to Commander Moore. Not to me."

She got up and opened her mouth to say something, embarrassment overflowing her brown eyes. "I'm sorry, Commander Blake. I truly am, but when it comes to Cole, I can't—"

"I don't want to hear any of your excuses." He raised his hand, interrupting her. "If you want to help Cole, I need you to go to Brown's estate and bring his blood bags here. I'm sure you know where he keeps them."

"Yes, my lord," she replied.

"Go now and take Jamie with you. Once you get the blood, come back to Paradise Manor and stay here until I return," he added with a sigh. "From now on, no one goes anywhere alone. With the unrest in the Vampire Court and the tension between the vampires and werewolves, the left wing of Paradise Manor is probably the safest place in the entire state."

Jamie got up. With all mirth gone from his eyes, the young man looked serious and alert, reminding him of the Guardians Order guard he once was.

"Damian, I should be going with you," he said softly. "I know I'm not skilled enough as a wizard, but I'm learning, and I'm still a trained guard. I know how to do my job."

Damian sighed, nibbling on his lip. "I know that, Jamie. And

I appreciate the offer, but until I finish the investigation, I'm better off on my own."

Jamie nodded and dropped his head, disappointment surrounding him like a heavy cloak. "I understand."

"The truth is, I need you here, Jamie," continued Damian, placing his hand on the young man's shoulder. "My brother is in a lot more danger than anyone else in our small circle, and his life and safety mean a lot more to me than my own. I need you to be *his* guard. Please stay here with Ace. I'd feel so much better if I knew he was well protected. I'll give you all the details when I return, but right now, I just need you to trust me and do as I say."

"I trust you, Damian," replied Jamie with a reproachful half-shrug. "I always have."

"Good," said Damian. "Then can I count on you as the Guardian to protect the King of the Arizona Vampire Court?"

Jamie lowered to one knee. "Yes, my lord. With my life."

Cringing inwardly at the salutation and all the kneeling, Damian looked from Jamie to Ace. "Ace, can I count on you to fulfill your duty as a Destiny Enforcer? From this moment forward, can I trust you to obey my commands?"

"Yes, my lord," replied Ace, lowering to one knee with her fist over her heart. "I'm yours to command."

Yeah, right... She's mine to command as long as she's not in Cole's bedroom. Damian suppressed the desire to roll his eyes. "Perfect, I count on both of you to do your jobs," he said, observing them. Then he turned around and headed out of the room. Halting in the doorway, he glanced at them over his shoulder, and an uneven smirk turned the corner of his mouth up. "Stop kneeling and just do your friggin' jobs. That's all I need from you."

Perun Almighty, why are you punishing me by turning me into a glorified babysitter?

He marched through the hallway and pushed the entrance

door open, almost running into River. She gasped and hopped back, her hand reaching for her gun holster automatically.

"Damian," she exhaled with relief as she recognized him. "Sorry. I'm too jumpy lately. Did you find Hawk? Did you talk to him?"

"Yes, I did," he replied. In a few words, he gave her the gist of the situation. "The Master Warden ordered my brother to remain in Paradise Manor until the situation with the necromancer is resolved. With all the spells and wards the Guardians Mages placed on the left wing of your estate, it's become an impenetrable magical fortress. Ace and Jamie are going to guard Cole when I'm not around. I hope you don't mind that."

"Whoa," she exhaled. "I guess the situation is a lot worse than we initially thought."

"You can say that. Cole is undead, and that puts him in more danger than any of us. Any skilled necromancer can control a vampire, turning him into his mindless slave. Cole is an ancient vampire which makes him extremely powerful and dangerous, and if you add on top the fact that he's the King of the Arizona Court... Well, you get the picture. We can't allow for this to happen."

"Of course, Cole can stay here for as long as he wants to," she replied with a dismissive wave of her hand. "He is with you all the time anyway, and to be honest, I love having both of you around. It's your home, too, you know. You're my family."

Her simple words took his breath away, and for a heartbeat, he couldn't say anything. Reaching for her hand, Damian took it and brought it up to his lips, gently kissing her knuckles.

"Thank you, River," he said finally, letting her hand go. "I'll be home late tonight. Don't wait for me and don't worry. I'll be all right."

"Do you have your phone?" she asked, giving him an arched stare.

"Yes." He reached into his pocket and showed her the device.

"Is it charged?"

"Eh..." Damian unlocked the phone, looked at the upper right corner of the screen and scratched the back of his head, a guilty smile playing on his lips. "Thirty percent?"

River sighed and smiled reproachfully. "When it comes to technology, you're obsolete."

"What can I tell you," he started, laughter rising in his chest. "When I was your age, we were—"

"*Communicating via smoke signals and drums?*" Gypsy chimed in snidely, approaching River and rubbing her furry side against her leg.

"Just go already, caveman, and be careful." River laughed, waving her hands at him. "The necromancer is not going to find himself."

"Like owner, like cat." He chuckled and snapped his fingers, vanishing from Paradise Manor.

* * *

D‌AMIAN MATERIALIZED IN THE DARK, empty alley behind a vacant building that used to be occupied by a department store before it went out of business. He sped through the empty plaza onto the well-lit main street, following it to *The Midnight Shift*. Before entering, he quickly scanned the street, but since he didn't detect anything alarming, he pushed the door open and walked inside.

Despite the hour, the bar was unusually empty. Two small groups of people sat at the tables by the windows, drinking their beers and chatting quietly. Damian sharpened his senses and quickly checked them, verifying that one of the groups was demons and the other was werewolves. He crossed the room and sat down at the bar as he always did.

The Halloween decorations were gone, and when Kaleb showed up behind the counter, he was dressed in his usual black

T-shirt with the name of a hard-rock band printed on it and a black leather vest. Glancing at him, Damian smirked—he almost wished he could see this giant werewolf dressed in the cute orange shirt with a black kitty on it again.

"Hey, Damian." A friendly smile crossed Kaleb's face as he reached for a bottle of vodka. "The usual?"

Damian nodded, turning slightly to rest his elbow on the counter. Kaleb placed a white napkin in front of him and put a shot glass on top of it, filling it up with vodka. Damian lifted the glass, turning it slightly between his thumb and middle finger, and jerked his chin at the empty seating area.

"Slow today?" he asked as Kaleb leaned forward, propping his elbows on the counter.

"Not surprising." The werewolf reached under the counter and produced a cigarette case. Pulling one of the cigarettes out, he offered it to Damian.

"Thanks, I don't smoke."

"Do you mind if I do?" Damian shook his head no, and Kaleb continued as he lit up his cigarette, "I get all sorts of supernatural clientele here, but most of them are demons, werewolves and vamps. Since vamps are at war with my kind..." He shrugged, taking a drag off of his cigarette.

"What is your pack's position on this situation?" asked Damian casually. He lifted his glass slightly, observing the bartender over the rim. "Are you with Hawk and his pack?"

Kaleb didn't reply right away. He exhaled the smoke, blowing it to the side, away from Damian, and waved his hand to dispel it. "Earlier today, Hawk spoke to all local Alphas," he said, tapping the end of his cigarette into the ashtray. "Something about giving a chance to the new King of the Arizona Court to prove the innocence of his subjects." He shrugged, staring at his visitors with narrowed eyes. "Something about a Master of the Dark Arts controlling the undead."

"What do you think personally?" asked Damian. He swallowed the content of the shot glass in one gulp and exhaled, placing the empty glass on top of the napkin.

"What do I think?" Kaleb straightened. "I believe him, but who cares what I think? The question is what other Alphas think."

"And?"

"Those who have always been supporting Hawk are onboard. Others are not. The usual." He took another drag and stubbed his cigarette into the ashtray. "It's bad all around, man. No matter what happens, the new King of the Vampire Court is screwed. Unless he can find this Master of the Dark Arts and kill him, the war is unavoidable as far as I can see."

Dammit... Damian turned to Kaleb, meeting his dark eyes. "I hope it's not going to happen."

Kaleb smirked and cocked his head a little. "And whose side are you on, Damian? I've heard rumors among the undead. They call you the Shadow Slayer. Is that what you are? A vampire slayer?" He leaned slightly closer, raising his eyebrows. "Sorry, I didn't catch your supernatural identity."

"I stand with Hawk. The werewolves should give a chance to the new King to prove his innocence." Damian chuckled and flicked his wrist indifferently. "As far as my supernatural identity, you didn't catch it because I never gave it to you."

"That's why this is a sanctuary, handsome." Damian heard a soft female voice on his left and snapped around. A young woman—a werewolf, judging by her energy signature—sat on a tall barstool with her legs crossed at the knee, a smile as sweet as the scent of her perfume playing on her full lips. "No one will ever demand to know what you truly are." She turned to Kaleb, offering him a smile just as sugary. "Kaleb, darling, would you please refresh it for our mysterious friend." She tapped her finger with a long, red nail on the edge of Damian's shot glass. "And give me whatever his poison is."

Kaleb pushed away from the counter, looking heavenward,

but then put two empty shot glasses on the counter and filled them with vodka.

The woman turned back to Damian, lifting her glass. "Cheers." She clicked her glass with Damian's, even though he didn't lift it, and took a small sip, wrinkling her nose. "So, what's your name, handsome?"

Kaleb leaned down, resting his forearms on the bar, and whispered into the woman's ear, but loud enough for Damian to hear, "Mila, leave our mutual friend alone." He glanced at Damian, a smirk showing off his perfect teeth. "If you didn't notice, he's not that into you."

Damian smirked and picked up the shot glass, but put it down and got up, slowly turning toward the exit. A barely noticeable wave of magical energy touched his senses, and he held his breath, recognizing the same energy signature he had detected on the murdered werewolf and around the bite on Ace's neck. Shivers ran down his spine, making the small hairs on the back of his neck stand on end.

"Kaleb," he said urgently, turning toward the bartender, "something is coming. I'm not sure what it is, but I'm positive it's coming here, and it's up to no good. You need to get all werewolves out, including yourself."

"This place is a sanctuary. We're safe here," said Mila with a shrug.

Damian glanced at her, frowning. "I don't think these particular individuals care about observing the laws of the World of Magic, sweetheart." He nodded to the bartender. "Kaleb, now!"

Kaleb lifted the flip-up countertop and grabbed Mila's elbow, leading her toward the small backdoor behind the bar. Then he approached the visitors and spoke with them in hushed tones. A few minutes later, the bar was empty, only Kaleb and Damian remaining in the inside.

"Kaleb, you need to go, too," said Damian, gesturing at the backdoor.

"How do you know this person is after the werewolves?" asked Kaleb.

Damian frowned. "I recognize the energy signature. Kaleb, they're getting closer. I can feel their dark presence growing stronger. You need to go now."

"No." The bartender folded his muscled arms, staring at Damian calmly. "You don't look like you're planning to go, and I'm not leaving you alone to face whatever is coming."

Damn, a werewolf in shining armor... Wrong timing to display chivalry.

Damian was about to object when the door exploded inward, hitting the wall with a loud bang, and the rectangle of light emitted by the streetlights got blocked by three large silhouettes towering in the doorway.

CHAPTER 10

~ DAMIAN BLAKE ~

The three men, all of them tall and brawny, walked inside and halted, their eyes glowing with a bright, red light. They completely ignored Damian's presence, staring only at Kaleb.

Kaleb and Damian exchanged a look, and the werewolf's mouth twisted in a grim smirk. The air around him shimmered slightly as he partially transformed—a sure sign of purebred werewolves who could transform at any time of the month and could stop their transformation halfway.

"Three vampires walked into the bar," he growled, throwing a sideways glance at Damian.

"Is this some kind of joke?" Damian snickered, carefully channeling his magic toward his hands. He didn't want to display his full power, preferring to maintain his supernatural identity a secret if it were possible.

The men hissed and stepped forward, their moves fast and fluid as if they were gliding without touching the floor. Their mouths opened, a thin web of saliva stretching between their unnaturally wide jaws. Their cuspids and lateral incisors elongated, turning into a terrifying set of four sharp fangs.

Suddenly, the amount of dark energy they were emitting doubled, and they vanished.

Damian pushed Kaleb behind, shielding him with his body. Opening his other sight, he shouted, *"Moderius!"*

Even though his spell slowed them down a little, the attackers still moved extremely fast, but now Damian could at least see them clearly enough to follow their steps. At his mental command, his daggers materialized in his hands, and he swung his arms in cross-motion, slicing the chest of the man closest to him. Dark, thick blood gushed out of the wound, filling the air with its nauseating reek. An earsplitting cry of pain—a high-pitched screech that seemed to be unfit for a man of his size—erupted from the man's malformed mouth, and he hopped back. Staring down at the two deep cuts crossing his chest, a horrifying smirk stretched his lips too wide for human anatomy as the wounds started to close almost immediately.

Damian spun around, his deadly blades reaching the other two attackers. As the monsters staggered away from him, clasping their bleeding wounds with their deformed fingers, he regrouped, pulling back. He knew the injuries he inflicted weren't deadly, but they were enough to slow them down and give him a moment to speak with Kaleb.

"Kaleb," he hissed without taking his eyes off the three monsters, "I need you to step behind the counter and close your eyes."

"What?"

"Do as I say if you want to live," hissed Damian, speaking fast. "These are not vampires. They're wurdulaks. You can't kill them with a sword, or a gun, or your claws. Do as I say—"

As all three wurdulaks leaped into motion again, he cut himself off and channeled his magic, entwining it with his elemental power. Conjuring a protection shield around himself, he stepped forward, allowing the monsters to surround him. They attacked all at once, their claws tearing at his shield, pushing him back with the sheer amount of strength they had in their magically enhanced bodies. He grunted but managed to withhold their attack, throwing a quick glance over his shoulder to make sure Kaleb took cover.

Since the werewolf was no longer behind him, Damian smirked darkly and extended his hands forward.

"Ventius," he muttered, and a powerful blast of wind spread all around him, pushing the wurdulaks away.

The walls trembled, and the bottles on the shelves behind the bar counter jingled. Some of them fell off and dropped to the floor, crashing against the tiles with a loud crunching noise. As the expensive liquor turned into splinters of glass and puddles of liquid, the acrid odor of alcohol rose in the air.

The wurdulaks hissed, an earsplitting sound piercing Damian's heightened hearing. They moved closer, hissing louder, their eyes glowing brighter in the darkness of the room. Feeling slightly disoriented, Damian staggered backward until he hit the counter with his back. As his control of his magic wavered, his daggers vanished, and his shield dropped. One of the monsters reached him and swung his claws, leaving deep bleeding gashes on his upper arm. The pain rushed through Damian's body, eliciting a torturous groan out of him, but it also sent a burst of adrenalin through his system, clearing his fogged mind.

As all three monsters jumped atop him, sinking their fangs into his flesh, slicing his body with their sharp claws, he dropped to his knees and summoned his daggers again. A terrible fury boiled up in him, fueled by the unbearable pain, and he rose to his feet, surrendering himself to the full power of the Destiny Enforcer. The wings opened up behind his back, throwing the monsters off of him. His entire body lit up with a blinding white light, and two rays of pure magical energy escaped his blades.

He slashed his daggers through the air, and every time their light touched the monsters, a burning wound appeared on their bodies. The wurdulaks screamed and rushed forward, ignoring their injuries. Damian sidestepped one of them and swung his dagger, decapitating the monster. As the wurdulak's head rolled off his shoulder, hitting the floor with a dull thud, Damian thrust the blade through his heart.

"*Illucious,*" he hissed, and the wurdulak's body disintegrated, turning into a pile of ash.

Spinning around, he met the second monster with a powerful punch, and as the wurdulak fell to the floor, he pinned him to the ground with his knee and pierced his heart with the blade, calling to the energy of Creation. Damian didn't need to look to know that it worked, but as he straightened, he saw the last wurdulak vaulting over the counter.

Kaleb's low growl and the high-pitched shrill of the wurdulak sounded behind the counter. With a light flap of his wings, Damian rose in the air and landed softly on the countertop just in time to see the fully transformed werewolf embraced in a deadly struggle with the undead monster. Since the wurdulak was on top, Damian seized his neck and yanked him off Kaleb, raising him in the air. With all his strength, he propelled the monster down, smashing the wurdulak's face and chest against the hard tiles. Before he could recover, Damian forced his blade between his ribs, summoning the light of Creation.

As the last wurdulak turned into ashes, Damian got up to his feet and let go of his magic, his chest rising and falling with laborious breaths. Kaleb transformed back into his human form, his shredded and torn clothes barely concealing his body covered in bleeding lacerations, bite marks and bruises.

Ignoring his state of undress, Kaleb reached under the counter and grabbed his cigarette case. Then he made his way around and lowered down to the floor with a pained groan. He opened the box and pulled out a cigarette, his fingers shaking slightly either from pain or from leftover adrenaline still surging through his body. Patting his hips where his pockets used to be, he threw his hands up.

"Dammit, my lighter is gone," he muttered, aggravation in his voice.

Damian sat down next to him, leaning his back against the counter. "*Ignius*," he whispered, channeling a small amount of magic. As a tiny flame ignited on the tip of his thumb, he moved his hand closer to Kaleb. The werewolf smirked and ignited his cigarette, taking a drag off of it as he leaned back.

"What the fuck was that?" he growled, exhaling a thick cloud of smoke. "I've never seen a vamp moving or fighting like that." He pulled his legs up and hissed in pain, turning his hip a little to see four deep bleeding lacerations on his thigh left by the wurdulak's claws. "Dammit... I've never seen anything like that."

"Don't move," said Damian with a tired smirk.

He connected with the elemental power of Earth and placed his hand over Kaleb's forehead, circulating healing energy through him. Kaleb drew in a sharp breath and closed his eyes. A few seconds later, the bleeding stopped, and the cuts and lacerations closed. Damian removed his hand and sat back, exhaustion settling in his shoulders. Being a Child of Earth, the healing energy came with the package. He didn't have to use magic and spells, but even though it was a part of his nature, healing always took a lot of his strength.

"Thank you," murmured Kaleb, opening his eyes. "You didn't have to. Healing magic takes a lot of work, and I'm a werewolf. I heal, you know... Not as fast as vamps, of course, but I would have been back to normal by this time tomorrow."

"I know."

"You're also bleeding," pointed out Kaleb, puffing his cigarette. "Can you heal yourself?"

Damian nodded. "Yeah, I can, but I'm not going to. I need to preserve my strength in case this is not over yet. I'm fine."

Kaleb took another drag and closed his eyes. "So, what was it?"

"That, my friend, were the monsters who killed all those werewolves," replied Damian, stretching his legs, his entire body buzzing with exhaustion. "The new King of the Arizona Court was right. His vampires are innocent in all this. Now that you've seen it with your own eyes, I hope you'll speak up in his favor."

"I'll try. I don't know how much weight my words carry, but I'll do my best." Kaleb stubbed his cigarette onto the floor. "Listen, Damian, it's only the two of us here, so it's between us. You've been coming to my bar for a while, and all this time, I thought you were one of those human hunters or slayers. I could never detect even an ounce of magic in you. What are you, man? You have magic and elemental power, but what's with the wings? And the way you fight..." He raked his fingers through the thick mane of his hair, an awkward smile gracing his face. "Truth is, I've never seen wurdulaks, but I don't think I've ever seen a being of magic like you either."

Damian glanced at him briefly but then looked away, his fingers tracing the edge of his bracelet absentmindedly. "Consider yourself lucky," he said quietly. "Trust me, you don't want to meet someone like me ever again." Catching Kaleb's shocked gaze, he tapped his shoulder. "Don't worry, I come to your bar when I'm off duty, to relax and unwind."

"I need something stronger than a cigarette," mumbled Kaleb. He got up and walked around the bar. Placing two shot glasses on the counter, he found a bottle of vodka that survived the fight and filled the glasses to the brim. Damian scrambled to his feet and picked up a tall barstool, positioning it closer to the counter. As he sat down, his wounds responded with sharp pain, and he winced, clasping his torn shoulder.

"Thank God you were here," muttered Kaleb, raising his glass. "We all would've been dead if not for you. I owe you, man. If there is anything I can do to repay you, let me know."

Damian downed his vodka in one gulp and exhaled a ragged breath, pressing the back of his hand to his mouth.

"Actually, there is," he said at length, raising his eyes at the werewolf. "Unlike vampires, wurdulaks are conjured by dark magic—usually by a forbidden branch of the Dark Arts called necromancy. So, I'm looking for a necromancer powerful enough to cast this kind of incantation. Your bar is a sanctuary, so you see all kinds of supernatural... um... beings here. Do you know of anyone like this?"

"Supernatural beings?" Kaleb chuckled and leaned forward, bracing his forearms against the counter. "Is that your way of saying supernatural scum?"

"I'm sure some of your clientele are scum." Damian propped his elbow on the bar top, running his index finger over the rim of the glass. "Far from all, though."

"Agreed. The beauty of a sanctuary—no judgment zone," muttered Kaleb. He thought for a moment, furrowing his brow, and then added, "I don't know anyone with such skills. But I may know someone who can point you in the right direction." He grabbed a napkin and a pen and quickly wrote down an address, offering the paper to Damian. "He's a small-time wizard with less than average magical skills, but his ability to skim and manipulate are unmatched." He smirked and waved his hand carelessly. "He does some potion-making and divination to make a few bucks here and there. Charlatan, you know? Skimming unsuspecting humans." Kaleb rolled his eyes. "It's his connections that you want. If there is a powerful player in this community, he will know who it is no matter how secretive and careful this person is."

Damian glanced at the address, frowning. The wizard's place of residence was in Blue Creek, and he wondered if Sam knew about him. "What's his name?" he asked, folding the napkin and placing it in his pocket.

"He goes by Az," replied Kaleb, straightening. "I'm sure it's not his real name, but that's all I know."

"Thanks," replied Damian, rising. "Something tells me Az's services are not going to be cheap, but I have to start somewhere." He looked around, carefully checking the area with his second sight as far as he could reach. "Do you mind if I teleport directly out of your bar? I'm covered in blood and too tired to walk around."

"There is no one here." Kaleb shrugged nonchalantly, his eyes taking in his partially destroyed establishment. "Knock yourself out. I have to stay and clean up this mess."

Damian shook Kaleb's hand and snapped his fingers, vanishing from the bar.

* * *

PARADISE MANOR STOOD DARK, only porch lights illuminating the entrance. Gloomy shadows gathered in every corner where the electric lights or the glimmer of the moon couldn't reach, spooking them away. Damian glanced at his wristwatch, realizing that it was a lot later than he thought. He unlocked the door and tiptoed his way through the hallway toward his room.

"Psst..."

He heard River's voice coming from the kitchen and turned around, halting in the doorway. Dressed in her pajama pants and a tank top, she sat at the table, her hands wrapped around a cup of tea. Her long hair wasn't tied in a ponytail and fell over her shoulders and chest in messy, copper strands.

"Come here, Damian," she said, patting the chair next to her, her eyes alight with relief.

"River, what are you doing up so late?" he asked, lowering onto the chair with a groan as his battered body responded to his move with sharp spikes of pain and soreness. "It's past midnight."

"Couldn't sleep." She shrugged nonchalantly and got up, heading toward the refrigerator. "Hungry?"

A faint smile touched his lips. "Probably. I'm too tired to feel hunger."

"Sorry, I'm not the best cook in the world, but you have to eat something," she said, taking a box with Chinese takeout. "When I have to cook, I make a reservation or order takeout."

She put some fried rice and chicken on a plate and placed everything in the microwave. Once it beeped, she pulled the plate out and put it in front of Damian.

"Eat, soldier," she said, giving him a fork. "I already know how you function. Most likely you haven't eaten since morning." She thought for a moment and added, "Assuming you had breakfast, that is."

"Thank you," Damian said, warmth filling his chest. "One day, I promise, I'll cook for you."

He'd never had anyone take care of him, not even when he was a child. As an adult, he led the kind of life that didn't allow him to settle down or to have any kind of personal attachments. Since he moved to Paradise Manor, his life had changed drastically—he had found his brother, had a roof over his head, and most importantly, he was surrounded by people who actually cared about him.

Even though it had been a few months, he never took anything for granted, quietly enjoying his new lifestyle while always waiting for the other shoe to drop. The World of Magic was cruel, and he knew that everything he had right now could have been easily taken away from him the next moment.

"Are you going to heal that?" she asked, sitting down as she pointed at the wound on his upper arm. "Do you need me to take care of it for you?"

"No, it's okay. It looks worse than it feels," he replied, throwing a quick glance at the welts on his arm. The bleeding had stopped, but the cuts looked grisly, and his skin was covered in brown stains of dried out blood. "I'll heal. I just need to take a shower and get some rest. Not necessarily in that order."

"I can heal you, Dima." Damian snapped around to see his brother stand barefoot in the doorway, his eyes glowing slightly. Dressed in silky pajama pants and a T-shirt, with his long curls in disarray, he looked like he had just gotten out of bed. Cole closed his eyes and when he opened them again, they were back to their normal color. "With all that 'walking-dead' vibe you're giving off, I don't think you have what it takes to perform any self-healing."

Cole headed toward the table, pulled a chair out and sat down across from him. His fangs expanded as he brought his wrist to his lips, ready to bite, but Damian grabbed his arm, stopping him.

"Thanks, Cole," he said, throwing a veiled glance at River as he gave a soft squeeze to his brother's wrist. "Freshly brewed vampire blood is not on my menu today."

River gasped, her eyes darting from Cole to Damian. "He wants you to drink his blood?" she asked, grimacing.

Cole chuckled. "Vampire blood has healing properties," he explained, lowering his arm onto the table. "Besides, with everything that's going on, I want to create a blood bond with this doofus. Since he doesn't know how to use his phone to call for help when he's in trouble"—Cole waved his hand at Damian's blood-covered arm—"at least I would know when he's in distress."

"That's all I need—a vampire in my head," muttered Damian, rolling his eyes. He quickly finished his food and got up, walking toward the kitchen sink. He washed the plate, dried it and put it inside a cabinet. Turning around, he leaned his back against the counter, folding his arms across his chest.

"At least you'd have something in your head." Gypsy jumped on the kitchen counter soundlessly and rubbed her head against his elbow.

Damian drew in a deep breath, shaking his head at the sarcastic feline, and picked her up, allowing her to settle in his arms.

"I wouldn't want you around me anyway," he objected softly. "Not until I find this necromancer." He told River and Cole everything that happened at *The Midnight Shift*. "Tomorrow, I'm going to visit this Az and see what gives."

"I'm coming with you," said Cole in a no-nonsense voice. "You are not going anywhere alone."

"Sure thing, Cole." Damian turned half-way to face his brother, sarcasm overflowing his words. "You come with me, so I can deliver you directly into the hands of a man who can turn you into a mindless slave. Sounds like an awesome plan."

Cole dropped his head, biting his lip, and Damian stifled a sigh, realizing how hard it must have been on him to stay behind doing nothing while his brother was fighting the fight for him. Cole got used to living his life at its fullest, despite him being a vampire, and laughing in the face of danger came natural to him.

"It's temporary, Cole. Just be patient," Damian added softer and switched the subject. "Where are your bodyguards, anyway?"

"Bodyguards?" Cole snorted. "River set up rooms for them, and they're doing what bodyguards of their caliber are supposed to be doing—sleeping. I think if something happens, I'll be the one protecting their bodies."

"That was always the idea, anyway." Damian smirked with a slight shake of his head. "I want those kids in Paradise Manor behind all the protective magic. Don't get me wrong, Ace is a capable fighter, but she's too young as a person and too inexperienced as an Enforcer. As far as Jamie..." He sighed. "He's a good man, but he has a lot to learn, and I actually want to teach him."

"Well, on that note, boys, I'm going to go and see if I can get some sleep. Unlike you, I'm not immortal, so sleep is not optional for me," said River, rising, stretching her arms.

She ruffled Cole's hair as if he were her ten-year-old brother, eliciting a soft growl out of him and a chuckle out of Damian. As she approached Damian, Gypsy jumped off his arms, settling by his side on the counter. River's eyes halted on the ugly wound on his arm, and she raised her hand, her fingers lingering over his damaged skin without touching it.

"Dima, can we speak tomorrow morning, before I leave for work," she asked, her voice a little raspy.

She glanced up at him, lowering her hand on his forearm. He tensed at her touch and gently pulled away.

"Of course. I should be awake by then, but if I am not, just wake me up."

She nodded, averting her gaze, sadness darkening her azure eyes, and he cursed himself inwardly for inadvertently hurting her. Taking her hand, he squeezed it gently, giving her a shy smile.

"Good night, River... and thank you," he said softly, placing all his gratitude into these simple words.

"Good night, boys." She smiled like nothing had happened and walked out the door, giving a dismissive wave of her hand.

As soon as she was gone, Cole leaned back in his chair and folded his arms, staring at Damian with reproach.

"Wow, that was really smooth, big bro," he murmured, shaking his head. "Centuries later, you still have no idea how to make a lady happy."

"Learn from your brother, Sasquatch," chimed in Gypsy, jumping off the counter to the floor. *"His purr is almost as perfect as mine."*

"Shut up, both of you," grumbled Damian, making Cole snicker.

"Even Gypsy knows I'm right." He bent down, scratching the cat between her ears. "Good kitty." Then he sobered up and sighed. "Dima, you know River likes you, right?"

"And it's a big problem," snapped Damian, pushing away from the counter. "I'm a friggin' Destiny Enforcer. Again!" A spike of anger rushed through him but quickly subsided, leaving him hollow on the inside. "I can't do it, Cole. It's not safe for me and her."

"River is a big girl, Damian. And she's been exposed to the World of Magic," he objected frostily. "If you like her at all, don't you think she deserves to know the truth and make her own choices? Free will and all?"

"Okay, this is where this conversation is over. Between the pain of my wounds and you being a pain in my neck, I choose the wounds. At least I can go and perform some healing magic." Damian threw his hands up and headed toward the exit, shaking his head.

"Good talk, big bro," Cole yelled after him, tones of humor in his voice.

Damian cursed quietly at his brother's undying sarcasm and left the room.

CHAPTER 11

~ DAMIAN BLAKE ~

Damian woke up with a start and jolted upright, sweat running down his face. He looked around and blinked a few times at the rays of morning sun bursting through the open window. He took a deep breath and dropped his head, leaning forward slightly as he tried to calm down.

He had already forgotten the last time he had a peaceful rest. Since Mara showed him the vision of the mysterious man at the edge of the forest, who according to the goddess of Nightmares was responsible for his failure and death of his beloved, he couldn't sleep. Every time he closed his eyes, even just for a few minutes, the same vision played in his mind over and over, until he would wake up screaming.

"I need to speak with Magnus about this," he mumbled, wiping the sweat off his forehead. "I need to know who that man is. For more reasons than one..."

He exhaled a ragged breath and sat up, lowering his feet to the floor. A soft knock made him flinch and snap his head. Opening his second sight, he scanned the area around and sighed with relief—the soft golden glow of a human's soul outside his door reminded him that River wanted to speak with him in the morning.

"Come in," he yelled, raking his fingers through his hair to pull it over the left side of his face.

River cracked the door open and looked inside before entering. She made her way to a chair and sat down, crossing her legs at the knee.

"Did I wake you up?" she asked.

"I wish you did, but no, you didn't," he replied, rubbing his cheeks, feeling the roughness of his stubble under his fingers.

She nodded, readjusting her high ponytail on the back of her head. "Are you still planning to approach this man, Az, today?"

"Yes. I need to clean up and get dressed, and then I'll be on my way," replied Damian, his voice sharper and more strained than he intended. "The sooner I find this necromancer, the faster we can go back to our normal lives. Besides, if I don't do it soon, even Hawk won't be able to stop the werewolves from killing the vampires. I can't have it. Cole's rule of the Arizona Court must be stabilized by any means necessary, and the current situation doesn't do him any favors."

"By any means necessary, huh?" huffed River, pursing her lips. "With whom am I speaking, Damian? The Destiny Enforcer Commander or my friend?"

Damian grunted, stifling a sigh. "Both. I'm your friend, River, and your friendship means a lot to me, but just like you, I have my duties and obligations, and I can't ignore them." He frowned, pinching the bridge of his nose, and added, sounding softer, "I know you cooked up something in your head. Go ahead, I'm listening."

A hurt expression crossed her face, but it disappeared so fast that he wasn't sure it wasn't a figment of his imagination.

"I want you to wait," she said in that no-nonsense tone he got used to hearing from her when she was around other cops. "I need a couple of hours."

"What for?"

"From what I understand, you know nothing about this Az. You don't even know his real name," she said dryly, iron tones ringing in her voice. "You're going alone, without any backup, and I don't want you flying blind. Give me two hours to run at least a basic background check and see what I can find on him."

A reproachful smile touched Damian's lips, and he tilted his head slightly. "Can your background check tell me what kind of magic he wields or his supernatural identity?" She didn't reply, remaining still with her lips pressed into a stubborn line. "That's all I need to know, River. I don't care if he ran a few red lights or was arrested for possession of an illegal substance."

"Be that as it may," said River, rising. She didn't raise her voice but lifted her eyebrows just a little, and that told Damian she wasn't going to give up. "Can you give me just two goddamn hours? Cole is not going to lose his throne in a hundred-twenty minutes." She approached him, gazing down into his eyes and added, gently touching his shoulder. "I understand you don't care, but it would make me feel a lot better if I knew with whom you're meeting and where. Last night, when I saw you all banged up, bleeding, your arm mutilated..." Her voice wavered, and she looked out the window, a light breeze coming through it playing with her hair. "I'm glad you can self-heal almost any injury, but don't tell me you weren't in pain..."

"River," he said and cleared his throat, realizing how hoarse his voice sounded. "You have no idea how much—" He cut himself off and rubbed his forehead awkwardly. "Thank you. I'll wait for your call." He took the napkin with Az's address on it and gave it to River.

She snapped a picture of the address with her phone and tapped his shoulder, winking at him. "Much better, soldier." She headed toward the exit, but then halted by the door and turned around. "Eat before you leave. I left breakfast for you in the microwave. Just press the start button."

Before he could say anything, she walked out the door, leaving him alone. For a few seconds, he gaped at the closed door, massaging his arm absentmindedly. Even though he had healed all his injuries yesterday, he still felt sore, and the lack of restful sleep for a prolonged period of time left him drained and slightly disoriented. After a while, he got up and headed to the bathroom.

* * *

An hour later, Damian left Paradise Manor and started on his way to Sam's shop located in downtown Blue Creek. November started with temperatures cooler than normal, and without the scorching Arizona sun blasting from the unblemished sky, his walk was easy and enjoyable.

A small brass bell rang above his head as he pushed the door open and walked inside the shop. The store was as clean and organized as ever, new tools hanging on the display, reflecting the rays of the morning sun coming through the window. A slight scent of cleaning chemicals hung in the air, entwining with the smell of lacquers, paints and wood.

Sam sat behind the counter with his usual newspaper in his hands. At the sound of the bell, he raised his eyes and glanced at him, his hard features warming up a little. Without any rush, he folded the newspaper and placed it on the counter, arching his eyebrows at Damian.

"Well, hello there," he said, rising to offer his hand to Damian. "I didn't expect you to show up today."

Damian shook his hand, staring at him with surprise. "Why is that?"

"River called me." Sam waved his hand, lowering back on his stool. "She's running a background check on the local fortuneteller, and since he resides in Blue Creek, she wondered if I knew anything"—he twirled his wrist with a half-shrug

—"unnatural about him." His stare became heavier, and he leaned forward, rising slightly. "You know she's worried about you, kid. More than she should."

"I know," replied Damian calmly. "I told her that she shouldn't worry about me. I'm an immortal Child of Earth. I can't die, and if I get hurt, I can always self-heal. There is no reason to worry."

"Yeah," Sam huffed, gazing heavenward. "Your stupidity seems to be just as undying as you are. You're what? Like a thousand years old or so? And you still can't see beyond your ego. Yes, you can't die, but she can."

"Sam—," started Damian, but the old hunter raised his hand, wagging his finger at him.

"You put my little girl in danger, and I swear, I'll find a way to kill an immortal Child of Earth." Sam glanced back at his newspaper, but then slammed his hand on it, frustration emanating from him. "This is exactly what I didn't want to happen. To be honest, if I knew you were a friggin' Destiny Enforcer, I would never get you involved in the first place. You have more supernatural assholes who have a grudge against you than hairs in that black mane on your head. Just being next to you is already dangerous for her." He shook his head, crestfallen. "I spent my life trying to protect her from the World of Magic. Now, she is exposed, and there is no way back."

Damian dropped his head, swallowing hard. "I'm sorry, Sam. You're right. I have orders to remain in Paradise Manor, but I'll talk to my superior and move out tomorrow."

Sam took a deep breath and exhaled with a soft groan, a muscle playing in his tightly pressed jaw. "Don't do it, kid. I shouldn't have said that to you. It's not your fault. You actually saved her life, and for that, I'm eternally grateful." He glanced out the window and added, "I know you'd never let anything happen to her. Besides, she loves having you and that crazy brother of yours around. At least she is not alone in that giant, empty house. So, yeah... don't listen to an overprotective old man."

Damian smiled tiredly, leaning forward slightly. "So, do you know anything of any use about Az?"

Sam shrugged. "Nothing special, at least on the surface, and I don't think River will find anything on him either. He is..." He thought for a moment, rubbing his chin. "He's one of those psychics, you know? He has a little shop where he sells some magical bullshit and pretends to be clairvoyant, and he lives in the back of his shop. I think he's just a charlatan who preys on people who don't know any better." He fell silent, his fingers playing with a set of keys lying on the counter. "Unlike you, I can't see the flow of magical energy, but I think he's not touched by the World of Magic. I'm not sure he is even exposed to it." He shrugged again, opening his arms slightly. "Like I said—a plain and simple charlatan. A slippery fellow, if you ask me."

"Thank you, Sam," said Damian. "I guess I have to go and check him out. Let's see if he has the information I need."

"Don't hold your breath," muttered Sam, throwing the key on the counter. "Even if he has what you need, he's not going to give it to you without getting something in return."

"I figured as much—" The loud ring of his cellphone interrupted him, and he straightened, pulling the phone out of his pocket. River's smiling face appeared on the display and he swiped his finger across the screen, answering the call and placing it on the speaker. "River, hi, I'm here with your father. Did you find out anything interesting?"

"Nothing special," she said, her voice sounding distant across the line. "You were right."

"What did you say?" Damian chuckled. "Could you please repeat those last three words?"

River snorted. "Oh, shut up, smartass." A loud clicking sounded on the other side of the line as she typed something on her computer. "Anyway, this man is squeaky clean—your regular, red-blood American taxpayer. His real name is Azul Moreno, so Az is his real name, a shorter version of it. He moved to Blue Creek about forty years ago and opened his psychic business right away. You know how popular all that was in the seventies and eighties."

Damian nodded. Sam chortled, amused, and tapped him on his shoulder. "River, our elderly friend here just nodded, in case you couldn't hear that."

River laughed quietly.

"He should be pretty old, assuming he's a human," said Damian, throwing a killer-stare at Sam. Then he arched his brow at the hunter and added with an evil smirk, "At least Sam's age."

"Who're you calling old, kid? I'm not old. I'm a vintage model, and compared to you, I'm a spring chicken." Sam snorted, leaning his back against the shelf behind the counter.

Damian heard a soft thud on the other side of the line and River spoke to someone, her voice muffled as she probably covered the receiver of her phone. A male voice answered her, and another thud of a closed door announced that the man left the room.

"Sorry," said River, sounding clear now. "I have to go. Damian, be careful out there, and if you need my help, call me."

She hung up, and Damian put his phone in his back pocket. Then he said his goodbyes to Sam and left the store, heading in the direction of the address Kaleb had given him. Once he reached a place where no one could see him, he snapped his fingers and vanished.

CHAPTER 12

~ DAMIAN BLAKE ~

It'd been a few months since Damian moved to Blue Creek. The town was relatively small, and he had made a point to explore every single neighborhood, carefully searching different areas for the presence of the supernatural. Walking for hours from one street to the next, he had committed to memory the plan of the town, discovering abandoned buildings and obscured places suitable as teleportation points for him.

One of these points was located only a couple of houses away from the address Kaleb had given him. It was an old house, half-demolished by time and an unkind desert climate. Its roof had partially caved in, and the glass of the windows had been gone for years. Its walls had lost whatever paint they used to have, and now they were gray and dirty, standing out like a sore thumb among the other well taken care of houses in the neighborhood.

Jamie had told Damian that the last owners of this house passed away in some tragic accident about ten years ago, and since that time, no one wanted to buy it, whispering about strange lights and sounds coming from the place. Despite the efforts of the local Real Estate agents, the rumors of it being haunted spread wider, turning every potential buyer away from the property.

Once Damian flagged this place as a potential teleportation point, he had checked it for any paranormal presence but found none. However, he detected a barely noticeable residue of some magical energy. It was so light and vague, he couldn't identify its origin and decided not to worry about it, at least for now.

Damian manifested inside the house, in the middle of what once had been a large living area. Now it was half-demolished, like the rest of the building, and covered in dirty strings of spider webs. He headed to the window facing the main street and made sure no one was watching the house. Then he crossed the living room toward the door and walked outside, putting his dark sunglasses on.

Since Az's place was only a few yards away, he opened his other sight and carefully scanned the area around. His intuition whispered in his mind, suggesting that despite everything Sam, River and Kaleb had told him, Az couldn't be a regular human. However, he didn't discover any presence of magical energy around the house or even in a few blocks' radius.

If Az was a real psychic, he would emit at least some energy of his magic, but since Damian couldn't discover anything supernatural, the only thing that made sense was that he was nothing more than a human charlatan.

Not the first one, and definitely not the last, thought Damian, walking slowly toward Az's house.

In his experience, ninety-nine percent of all people who claimed to be psychics or have extrasensory abilities lied, entertaining their clientele with cheap parlor tricks and sound effects to entice them to open their wallets willingly. Most of them were harmless, but some of them fed on people in distress, exploiting their grief and desperate situations. When their actions became too malicious, the local authorities, inconspicuously encouraged by the Destiny Enforcers, had to step in. Luckily, something like that didn't happen too often.

Just to be on the safe side, Damian completely suppressed his magical energy signature before reaching Az's home. He halted and observed the house once more before crossing into the property. It was a small, one-story building with a tiled roof and a tiny front yard decorated by a few spiky representatives of the local flora. Except for the window display, it looked like the rest of the houses in the neighborhood.

The window was decorated with a large neon sign, stating 'Psychic Reading by Az, the Great and Powerful. Mystical Astrology, Palmistry, Potions, and Divination. Walk-ins Welcome'.

"Isn't that swell," muttered Damian, shaking his head. "The Great and Powerful, my ass..."

The 'Open' sign in the window on the other side of the entrance was off, but he didn't care. He crossed the front yard, walked up the steps, and raised his hand to knock on the door but then changed his mind. Placing his palm against the rough wooden surface, he sharpened his senses. Since he still couldn't detect anything out of the ordinary, he took a deep breath and knocked.

Damian waited a few seconds, but the door remained closed, so he knocked again. After a short while, a soft shuffling noise sounded inside, and the door cracked open just a little with the chain remaining locked.

"I'm closed," a slightly raspy voice of a person who had just woken up sounded through the opening. "Come back in an hour... no, make it two."

"I would love to," said Damian, smirking, "but I think we should talk now. It's urgent."

"Trust me, your destiny is not going to change if I read it two hours later." A grunt of displeasure followed by a jingle of the dropped chain reached Damian's ears, and the door finally swung open.

Damian looked down, and his jaw dropped. A tiny, scrawny man stood in front of him, barely reaching his chest. His gray hair, soft and wispy like the white tuft of a dandelion, surrounded his narrow face covered in a multitude of wrinkles. A pair of round glasses with thick lenses sat on the bridge of his slightly upturned nose, making his gray eyes look unnaturally large. He was dressed in striped pajama pants and a long robe thrown over his bare torso.

He tilted his head back, taking in Damian's appearance, and his lips stretched into a tightlipped smile which completed his resemblance to a tiny, gray mouse. Stepping aside, he gestured for Damian to come in.

"Well, you woke me up already, young man," he said, stifling a yawn. "Come in then. Tell me what's so urgent."

Damian crossed the threshold and wrinkled his nose at the overpowering reek of incense and scented candles. The small entrance hall was separated from the living area by a beaded bamboo curtain, which chimed softly as Az pulled it apart to let him proceed. The living area was a spacious room decorated in the best traditions of fortuneteller's stereotypes, with a heavy inclination toward the Disco era. Crystal balls, Tarot decks, multicolored crystals, burning candles, large books in thick, leather bindings—you name it, it was here.

A small, round table covered with a dark, velvety tablecloth was positioned in the center of the room, and four chairs surrounded it. Making tiny, shuffling steps, Az made his way to the table and sat down, gesturing at the chair across from him. Damian pulled the chair out and lowered himself on it, observing the room with interest.

"So, what can I help you with?" asked Az, his steel eyes staring at him through the thick lenses of his glasses without blinking. "Are you looking for a reading, or do you already know your destiny? Do you need to make a connection with someone behind the veil? Or maybe you need a love potion?"

He spoke slowly, in a monotonous, droning voice, and Damian was positive he had repeated this speech more than a hundred times before. But then Az cocked his head, giving him a quick once-over, and his lips formed a smile that made his eyes crinkle at the corners.

"Ehh..." he hummed. "I don't think you need any of this crap. A strapping lad like you doesn't need any potions. So, what are you looking for, young man? Let's see if I can help you with whatever troubles you."

Damian tilted his head a little, meeting Az's slightly humorous gaze calmly. "I'm looking for someone, and I wondered if you could give me an idea of where I could find this individual."

"Oh?" Az's eyebrows climbed up, and he pulled away just a little. "That's quite an unusual request, but I'll do my best to help you, Mister—" His voice rose at the end, and he fell silent, expecting Damian to introduce himself.

"Damian."

"Damian," repeated Az, observing him with sarcastic twinkles in his eyes. "Is it like Beyonce? Or do you have additional parts to your name?"

"Aren't you clairvoyant?" Damian smirked, arching his brow wryly, but then changed his mind and introduced himself, offering Az his hand. "Damian Blake, sir. Nice to meet you."

The old man took Damian's hand, his thin, bony fingers squeezing it stronger than he expected, and to his shock, Damian detected a faint wave of magical energy rushing through him as Az checked him out.

Holy shit, thought Damian, putting extra effort into completely shadowing his own magical energy. *The old man may not be a fraud after all. Then what is he? A psychic? A wizard?*

"Damian Blake," said the old man with an appreciative nod.

"I've heard of you, young man." His wide smile exposed a set of perfectly straight, white teeth, too white and straight for his age. "The Shadow Slayer... in my modest home, wow! You're a legend. At least among the undead. I think since you moved to Blue Creek, every vamp is shaking in their pants." He laughed, his high-pitched laughter unexpectedly contagious, and Damian couldn't help but smile back. "Well, it's an honor to meet you." His laughter dwindled into a friendly smile, and he sat back down. "So, what can I do for you, Damian?"

"I'm looking for a necromancer," replied Damian straight, observing Az's reaction. "Do you know of anyone who is into the Dark Arts, especially necromancy?"

Az coughed and cleared his throat, averting his gaze modestly. "Well..." His voice disappeared into silence, his fingers fidgeting with the edge of the tablecloth.

"I understand your hesitation," continued Damian, "but I need to find this person, and if you know anything about their whereabouts, please let me know. It's important."

A light blush colored the old man's cheeks, and he finally raised his face, meeting Damian's eyes. "Well, when I was younger, I fiddled with the Dark Arts a little," he mumbled, a guilty grin splitting his face, and then waved his hand with a small shake of his head. "Necromancy included. Stupid, I know." He rolled his eyes and chuckled nervously. "The Destiny Council taught me a good lesson. Never again."

"Necromancy is a forbidden branch of magic." Damian observed the old man with new interest. "I'm surprised the Destiny Council let you off their hook."

"Yeah, me too." Az chuckled again, nervousness making his eyes shine brighter. "I guess that was because I was no threat. My skills with magic were extremely limited, and to be honest, I'm not that powerful and gifted as a wizard at all. With age, I learned to accept my limitations. So, I do the best I can with what I have." He waved his hand around the shop.

"The necromancer I'm looking for is skilled and powerful enough to wield this dark branch of magic to its full potency," said Damian. "Do you know anyone who fits that description?"

"Damian, you sound like a good man, and you do a great job as the slayer, keeping the vamps at their best behavior." Az frowned, pursing his thin lips. "But you're asking for trouble, my friend. Nothing good can come out from dealing with someone like this. Take an old wizard's word for it—the Destiny Council prison is not the kind of place where you want to spend the rest of your life."

"I know," replied Damian quietly. "But if I don't find this person, the consequences would be a lot worse." He thought for a moment and decided to err on the side of caution. "Sorry, sir, I can't give you all the details. Do you know any powerful necromancers in the area?"

Az fell silent and leaned back, chewing on his lip, a vibe of unease spreading around him. "Not in Arizona," he said after a while. "But I used to know someone with this level of skill in California." He ran his fingers through his soft hair, making it fluff up even more. "It's been years since I've heard from him, and I can't guarantee the Destiny Council hasn't put him where he belongs." Az visibly shuddered. "A terrifying individual he is, if you ask me. Extremely powerful and truly scary."

"What's his name? How do I find him?"

"I have no idea," replied Az with a shrug. "Years ago, he was going by JB, but he used to change his legal name every few years. I don't even know if he's still in California, or in the human realm for that matter."

Damian frowned, rubbing the edge of his bracelet absentmindedly. It was never easy to find a person who didn't want to be found, especially if this person was a powerful Master of the Dark Arts. Dark wizards weren't famous for upholding the rules of the World of Magic, and that made them almost limitless in what they could do.

"You're a wizard with psychic abilities, Az," he said at length. "Can't you scry for him?"

Az chuckled, his agitation visibly growing with every next question Damian asked. "I can scry, but it's not as easy as it sounds." He glanced around the room as if searching for something, but then waved his hand, giving up. "To scry I need to have something that belongs to the person I'm looking for." He shrugged apologetically. "Sorry, but I don't have anything of his."

Dammit. Another dead-end. Damian got up, offering his hand to the old wizard. "Sorry, I woke you up and wasted your time."

Az got up, his eyes lingering on Damian's hand as he rubbed his chin thoughtfully. "Hold on, Damian. There is something we can try, but I'm not sure you'd be willing to do it." He gestured at the chair again, motioning for Damian to sit down. "There is one object that used to belong to JB. The object itself has no magical properties, but if you could get your hands on it, it would be enough for me to scry."

Damian sat down. "What is this object, and how can I find it?"

"How do you feel about grand theft?"

"Excuse me?" Damian raised his eyebrows, staring at Az in shock.

"It's quite a story, you know." A sly smirk crossed Az's face as he leaned forward, resting his elbows atop the table. "The object in question is a dagger—"

"Wait... what?" Damian tensed, his mind immediately on high alert. "What kind of dagger? A ritual athame?" He huffed, shaking his head, a wave of mistrust rising within him. "Let me get this straight. You want me to steal some kind of mystical weapon that used to belong to some terrifying Master of the Dark Arts and give it to you—a wizard with unknown affiliations?" He laughed and got up, crossing his arms. "Not gonna happen."

"Jesus! Relax, slayer." Az rolled his eyes and readjusted his thick eyeglasses with the tip of his index finger. "First of all, I already told you—the dagger has no magical properties whatsoever. It's expensive because it's an antique weapon dated back to the seventeenth century, but as far as magic goes—it's a piece of metal."

He pursed his lips, tapping his fingers on the tabletop. "Second," he continued, "even if it was a powerful athame, I don't have the kind of magic and skills to use it for anything other than what we discussed." He thought for a moment and added with a dismissive jerk of his hand. "You can keep the dagger at all times. You can take it home after we're done for all I care. I will need it only for a few minutes while I cast the spell, and you can stay and watch me as I'm doing it." He threw his hands up, pursing his lips. "Jeez, man... not everyone's out to get you, you know? Lighten up."

Damian frowned, thousands of thoughts and possible worst-case scenarios surfacing in his mind. If the dagger indeed had some magical properties, he would sense it as soon as he touched it. As much as he needed to find the necromancer, placing a dangerous weapon in the hands of a shady wizard wasn't something he was willing to do. However, if the dagger wasn't magical, then there was no harm in giving it to Az.

Except for the breaking and entering part... He rubbed his forehead, feeling cold sweat under his fingers. *Damn... what could possibly go wrong with that idea...*

Az threw his hands up. "I'm trying to help you, young man, and I'm not even asking anything in return, which is quite unusual for me. It's a business, you know, and I like to get paid for my services. If I knew where JB keeps his toothbrush, I would send you to get that. But unfortunately, this dagger is the only object I know of that used to belong to him."

"How do you know about this dagger in the first place?" asked Damian.

"Like I said," Az continued, readjusting his position slightly. His robe opened up, exposing his skinny, caved-in chest, and he quickly covered it, wrapping the robe tighter around himself. "It's a funny story."

Damian lowered onto his chair and stretched his legs, crossing them at the ankle. "I'm ready to be entertained," he murmured, staring calmly at the wizard.

"There is a rich private collector in... um... Carefree, I think. I'll have to look up the address," started Az, his eyes lighting up with the excitement of a person who loved telling long stories. "If you meet him, you will think there is nothing special about him. As untouched of a human as it gets—doesn't believe in anything he can't see with his own eyes or touch with his grubby hands."

Az chuckled, flicking his eyebrow at Damian as if asking him to join in on the joke, but Damian just nodded, gesturing for him to proceed.

"However," continued Az, "there are two things about him that are interesting. First"—he raised his fist and extended his index finger—"he has the most amazing collection of antique weapons. Knives, swords, daggers, stars, mazes—you name it, he has it. Of course, he has no idea that some of his blades are actually magical."

"And what is the second thing?" asked Damian.

"The second..." Az snickered. "He-he-he-he... He's a Mexican drug lord, or at least I think he is. Police raided his place a few times, but except for his extensive collection, they found nothing of interest." He thought for a moment and then added, "Well, maybe he's not a drug lord, but he's definitely a Mexican mobster of a sort."

"Uh-huh," murmured Damian. "So, you want me to break into the house of some rich Mexican mobster. If he is so obscenely rich and has criminal affiliations, don't you think his place will be guarded by state-of-the-art tech as well as people?

Being shot at from various automatic weapons doesn't sound like my type of fun."

"But of course, his house is protected, and every piece in his collection is secured as well. I never said it wasn't. It's up to you, slayer." Az shrugged. "Do you want to find your necromancer or not? You steal the dagger, bring it here, and I'll scry for your Dark wizard."

"How do you know the dagger is in the collection, and how can you be sure it used to belong to the necromancer?" asked Damian.

"Back in the day, when I just met JB, I saw this dagger in his house." He fell silent, thinking. "Many times, as a matter of fact. It's the kind of piece that is hard to mistake for anything else."

Az got up and walked out of the living area. He returned with a small laptop, placed it on the table, and opened it. He typed something in and turned the computer around so Damian could see the screen. Then he got up and walked around the table.

"This is the accounting software I use for my business," he explained.

"Business? What business?" Damian looked up at him, shocked.

"Well, you know. All this..." Az waved his hand toward the neon signs on his front window.

"Fortune-telling is a legit business nowadays?"

"No, of course not." Az chuckled, all but rolling his eyes. "But psychic consultant or spiritual advisor are legal terms. So, I am a psychic consultant entrepreneur. I have a registered LLC, and I pay my taxes every year." He pointed at the screen. "Anyway, here is the list of all my invoices to one Ricardo Torres. As you can see, I was invited to quite a few of his parties to perform Tarot card readings and palmistry services to entertain his guests." He clicked around the screen, opening one invoice after another.

"I'm in the wrong line of business," muttered Damian under his breath, staring at the numbers on Az's invoices.

"I've seen Ricardo's collection quite a few times. He's so proud of it, he shows it to all his guests. The first time I laid my eyes on that dagger, I recognized it right away," Az continued, his eyes turning slightly off focus as if he were lost in his memories. "Its pommel is shaped like an eagle's head, and the eyes of the bird are made of black cat's eye scapolite. Easy to identify. I have no idea how it ended up in Ricardo's collection, but it is displayed without a glass case, positioned on a pedestal." His fingers brushed over his cheeks, rubbing his silvery stubble. "JB was quite attached to it... sentimental value or something like that."

Az sighed and grabbed a small, pink notepad and a pen. Quickly, he scribbled the name and the address and tore the page out, handing it to Damian.

"Here you go, Shadow Slayer," he said, the corners of his wide mouth lifting in a tiny smile. "You want to find your Dark wizard? This is the only way I can help you." He shrugged, scratching the back of his head. "Unless you want to seek help elsewhere, of course."

Damian got up and placed the piece of paper in his pocket. "Thank you, Az. Let me think about it."

"Take your time." The old wizard chuckled in his nervous manner, directing him toward the exit. "Like I said when you knocked on my door—your destiny is not going to change if I read it in a few hours or even days."

CHAPTER 13

~ DAMIAN BLAKE ~

After leaving Az's house, Damian didn't return home right away, but instead walked all the way to the Blue Creek police department building and dialed River's phone number, pacing in front of the entrance. The call went to her voicemail, and he hung up, thinking that he shouldn't have come here during working hours.

A light touch to his shoulder made him flinch and turn around. Jason, the young police officer he had met at the crime scene yesterday stood in front of him. His attentive eyes moved up and down Damian's body, and a friendly smile lit up his round face.

"You're Damian Blake, Detective Evans' consultant?" he asked, offering his hand for a handshake.

"Yes, sir," replied Damian, shaking his hand.

"Are you here for Detective Evans?"

"Yes, but I think I missed her." Damian glanced at the small, one-story building, wondering if River was inside or somewhere out, working a case. "Do you know if she's here?"

He nodded and motioned at the building. "Let's go. I'll find her for you."

Jason left Damian in the small lobby and disappeared behind a door, leaving him to his thoughts. The lobby was empty with the exception of a young woman in a police uniform sitting behind the counter with a book in her hand, separated from the rest of the world by thick glass.

Damian lowered himself onto a chair, his mind circling back to his conversation with Az. He didn't believe even for a moment that Az was a trustworthy good supernatural Samaritan who was willing to help him out of the goodness of his heart. People like him didn't do anything without some kind of a hidden agenda. However, no matter how much he twisted and turned, he couldn't see anything that would explain his behavior.

"Damian... Is everything okay?" River's voice sounded next to him, breaking his train of thought, and he snapped his head up.

"Yes, everything is fine," he replied, rising. "I was wondering if you could help me with something." He chuckled and scratched his head, cringing inwardly at his own awkwardness. "But then I realized that the police station is probably not the best place to discuss this. I should wait until you come home."

She frowned, her eyes halting on his face, and then glanced at her wristwatch. Seizing his elbow, she pulled him outside and headed across the parking lot. She stopped in front of an unmarked Dodge Charger and reached into her pocket for the remote.

"Get in," she ordered in a no-nonsense voice, her full lips curving in a lopsided grin as she stared at him across the top of the vehicle. "Yeah, I know. You don't like cars, especially sedans. Tough shit. I'm not walking. Get in, soldier."

"Yes, ma'am." Damian gave her a military salute, stifling laughter, and lowered himself to the passenger seat.

She drove her car across downtown and parked it in front of a tiny restaurant. Damian had seen this place many times but had never actually stopped by to try their food. He stepped out of the car and followed River toward the building, opening the door for her. She stilled for a moment, giving him a surprised glance, but said nothing and walked inside.

The place was just as small inside as it looked on the outside. Decorated in the old-west style, just like the majority of establishments in downtown Blue Creek, it had black and white pictures of people in cowboy hats, views of the desert, and a few old guns decorating the walls. The six booths located along both walls were occupied, but one small table at the back of the restaurant by the window was free, and River headed toward it.

A young woman in a T-shirt with the restaurant's logo on it smiled and waved at her. "Detective, I kept your favorite table open for you," she announced. Grabbing two menus and two sets of utensils, she walked around the counter and stopped by the table, staring at Damian with unconcealed curiosity. "Do you need a few minutes?"

"River, do you know what you want?" asked Damian, bending the corner of the menu booklet without even realizing he was doing it. "I'm not that hungry, to be honest."

River scolded him with a heavy gaze but didn't reply and turned toward the waitress. "My usual and make it two, please. Whether he likes it or not, he's going to eat."

Once the young woman was gone, River switched her attention to Damian.

"Dima, what happened?" she asked, gently touching his hand, her fingers barely brushing over his knuckles. "I know something is off, so start talking."

He looked down at the wrinkled menu, biting his lip. "Nothing yet," he replied at length. In so many words, he described his meeting with Az, explaining some of the details related to the rules of the World of Magic as he went.

River listened to him without interrupting, her face void of emotions, and when he finished, she remained silent for a while, shaking her head. The waitress brought their order, placing the plates before each of them and walked away, leaving the receipt on the table.

"Eat, Damian. You're a giant man, but lately, you've been running on fumes," she said softly, her eyes down on her food. "You can't keep doing it. With all your magic and power, your body is still human, and one day you'll collapse. I understand that the weight of responsibility is on your shoulders, but you need to take care of yourself. You barely eat and sleep, and even if you fall asleep, you wake up in the middle of the night screaming... Your room is next to mine. I can hear you."

He exhaled with a soft groan and took one of the French fries from his plate, twirling it between his thumb and index fingers. "I know. I'm sorry. I'll find a way to control these... nightmares," he replied, biting on it.

"Don't apologize. Not your fault."

For a while, they ate in silence, each deep in their own thoughts.

"I have to find a way to get this dagger, River," said Damian, pushing the plate to the side.

"You realize you're discussing a robbery with a police detective?" River's lips twitched in a tiny smile, sadness gathering in her bright eyes, dimming their warm light.

"I do," replied Damian, "but you're also my friend—one of the very few people I actually trust."

River nodded, staring somewhere at his chest. "Are you sure this is the right thing to do?" she asked after a short pause. "This Az doesn't strike me like the kind of fella you can trust."

"And I don't," replied Damian with a half-shrug. "But unfortunately, he is my only lead. I know it can be a trap or some kind of deception, but I have to do something, and so far, no one else can provide any information. Besides, by attacking the sanctuary, this necromancer broke one of the most sacred laws of the World of Magic. By doing that, he made it my direct responsibility as a

Destiny Enforcer to find him and bring him to justice, so I have no choice but to move forward with the investigation." He glanced out the window, troubling thoughts racing through his mind. "If I didn't know any better, I would say he wants me to go after him. It's like he's challenging me to find him, and that troubles me more than any kind of backhanded agendas Az may have."

She opened her mouth to object but snapped it shut as Damian's phone rang loudly in his pocket. He got up and pulled it out, reading Hawk's name on the screen. He raised his finger, asking River to give him a moment, and answered the call, sitting back down.

"Damian?" The Alpha's voice sounded tense across the line.

"Hi, Hawk," said Damian, unease twisting his insides into a tight knot.

"I spoke with the rest of the Alphas," continued Hawk. "Just like I expected—those who have always supported me throughout the years took my side. But a few pack masters with whom I'd never seen eye to eye didn't care to listen to reason. Even after Kaleb told them about the attack on the sanctuary, they didn't want to hear anything, hungry for revenge. I can't hold them back, kid. No one can. Your brother better be watching his back twenty-four-seven. They're coming for him."

He sighed. Something cracked on the other side, and the noise of heavy machinery invaded the line.

"Thank you, Hawk," said Damian. "You did what you could."

"What are you going to do?" the old Alpha asked, some warmth coloring his tensed voice. "You are a Destiny Enforcer, and whoever this asshole is, he broke the sanctuary law. From what I understand, that makes things a lot more complicated for you. Not only do you need to guard your brother, but also, it's your direct responsibility to find this monster and cuff him. Am I right?"

"Yes."

Hawk sighed, muttering something incoherent that sounded a lot like a colorful set of profanities. "You have your hands full, kid," he said finally. "If there is anything I can do to help, let me know. Also—" He cut himself off and grunted like a person who was about to say something he would most likely regret later. "If you need me to protect your brother, bring him to my ranch. I have some serious wards placed on the property. I doubt a necromancer, no matter how powerful he or she is, can break my protective magic."

"Thank you, Hawk," said Damian, the corners of his mouth lifting as an image of Hawk cursing at the idea of a vampire living in his ranch house surfaced in his mind. "Right now, Cole is safe, but if something changes in our situation, I may have to take you up on your offer. Your wards are quite potent. I believe they were cast by a god and a Child of Fire?"

"Oh, yeah," replied Hawk, tones of pride in his voice. "Originally, my wards and protection spells had been placed by a god of the Celtic Otherworld, and later on they were reinforced by an elf and the Great Salamander himself. So, yeah... If you and your brother need help, I offer both of you my packs' protection."

"I greatly appreciate it, my friend," said Damian.

"Well, keep me posted, kid, and good luck."

Hawk hung up, and Damian put his phone on the table, turning back to face River. She looked away, unease imprinted on her tender features, but then moved her plate aside and leaned forward.

"Give me the name and address of the collector," she said quietly. Damian pulled out the piece of paper, offering it to her. She took it and snapped a photo of the address with her phone, pursing her lips. "Carefree is not my jurisdiction, but I'll see what I can dig out."

"Thank you." Damian got up and reached for his wallet.

Glancing at the receipt, he placed three ten-dollar bills on the small tray to cover the cost of both meals and the tip.

"I can pay for myself," said River, looking at him with reproach.

"I never said you couldn't." Damian flashed her a wide grin and headed toward the exit, ignoring her protests. "I'll see you later at home."

* * *

THE REST OF THE DAY, Damian spent discussing the details of the upcoming heist with Cole, Jamie and Ace. He needed to know the layout of the property and the floor plans of the house. He was positive that between Cole and Ace, discovering any information, even the one hidden in the darkest corners of the world wide web, wasn't a problem. Jamie promised to see if there was anything about Ricardo in his father's archives. All the research had to be done inconspicuously and fast, so going the standard routes like visiting the municipality archives wasn't an option.

River came back late at night, and the information she brought didn't really shed much light on who Ricardo Torres truly was. She confirmed Az's story, stating that the Carefree Police Department had indeed checked him a few times and even kept his house under surveillance for a while. However, they had found nothing incriminating.

Ricardo Torres owned an absolutely legit construction company and a large chain of Real Estate offices. He started his business by flipping houses, and with time, it grew into a serious venture with seven-digit annual revenue reports. On the surface, Ricardo looked like a lawful taxpayer, but a few visits from some shady individuals as well as a few anonymous tips triggered the interest of the local police department. Nevertheless, none of the suspicions were confirmed, and since collecting antiques wasn't a crime, the police had to back off.

Listening to everything River had to say, Damian shuffled absentmindedly through the reports she had brought. While some information she had was helpful, the state of Ricardo's business affairs was of little interest to him. Unfortunately, the intelligence he truly needed couldn't have been found in police archives, or any human organization for that matter.

River also had no idea if Ricardo had any affiliations with Mexican criminal organizations. Based on the information she had received from the Carefree Police Department, she thought it was highly unlikely, but she didn't discount the possibility completely. River confirmed that the house was protected by a state-of-the-art security system, installed by one of the most reliable companies in Arizona. It had a gated entry with a twenty-four-seven guard on duty, security cameras covering every square inch of the property and the inside of the house, as well as motion sensors and heat detectors.

It was well past midnight when they finally finished the discussion, ready to start preparations early in the morning.

Damian walked into his room but stilled for a moment as Cole's voice reached his ears. His brother spoke with River in hushed tones, and then the sound of their laughter rang through the hallway, carried by the strange acoustics of this house. He smiled faintly, thinking that it was nice to hear them having a little fun in the middle of this supernatural doom and gloom.

Once all this is over, I'm going to climb up to the attic and see if I can find out what causes this mysterious sound effect.

Quietly closing his door, Damian walked to the bed and lowered heavily on it, massaging his stiff shoulders. He glanced toward the bathroom and sighed, forcing himself back to his feet. It didn't take him long to clean up and change into his pajama pants. Making his way to the window, he pushed it open and inhaled the cold night air infused with the scents of the desert. His chest ached with the desire to walk outside and fall asleep under the open sky with his bare back pressed against the cold earth.

Cars and planes, houses and especially high-rises weren't something he enjoyed, but sleeping in the middle of the desert also wasn't a good idea. So, he settled for the open window and lay down on the bed. Pulling one of the pillows to his chest, he turned to his side and wrapped his arms around it, closing his eyes. As his exhausted body took over, he fell asleep almost immediately, his racing mind surrendering to the loving embrace of oblivion.

He woke up in the middle of the night and blinked sleepily, rubbing his eyes as he tried to understand what had ripped him out of his peaceful slumber. It was especially annoying because lately, it hardly ever happened that he actually slept without some kind of nightmare tormenting his mind. With a low groan, he sat up and opened his second sight, scanning Paradise Manor as far as he could reach, but except for the energy signature of the Guardians' protective magic placed over the left wing of the property, he could detect nothing.

Pain, dull and nagging, built up somewhere behind his eyes, and he groaned, lowering his head in his hands.

"Fuck..." he exhaled as the realization dawned on him. Magnus was summoning him. While the Head of the Destiny Council used a light summoning spell, Damian knew that ignoring the summons, no matter how gentle they were, wasn't a good idea. The light headache would soon become stronger, quickly morphing into a terrible migraine, and increasing with every passing second until he wouldn't be able to tolerate it.

Rising, he channeled some of his magic and drew a dimly glowing rune on the wall between the bed and the window. Touching it, he infused it with the soft, orange glow of his magical energy and then brushed his fingers over the rune of the Shadow Enforcer on his shoulder, whispering a quick spell. Both runes lit up brighter, and the air in front of the wall shimmered with a brilliant white light. When the light dissipated, an oval communication window unfolded before him. Magnus stood on the other side of the window, looking as impeccable as ever in his long white robe.

"Commander Blake," he said, his voice sounding too loud in the sleepy silence of the house.

Damian winced, massaging his temples as the headache of the summoning spell started to subside. "Magnus," he muttered, slightly inclining his head. "It's three in the morning..."

"You're not working a nine-to-five job, Commander," objected Magnus dryly, "and your responsibilities don't stop at sunset."

"I know. I'm sorry, sir. It just—" He cut himself off and exhaled, rubbing his forehead. "I'm a little tired. It was the first night in a long while since I was able to sleep."

"Oh?" The blazing light in Magnus' eyes dimmed down, and a shadow of concern crossed his face. "Tell me what's going on, Commander."

Damian stepped closer to the communication window and lowered his voice as if that could give him more privacy. "Can we speak off the record, my lord?"

Magnus glanced around and whispered something with a slight flick of his wrist. Once the room behind him filled with a soft yellow glimmer of a cloaking spell, he turned back to face Damian. "Speak freely, my child. It's just the two of us here. What troubles you?"

"A few months ago, when I fought Mara and Morok," started Damian, "the goddess of Nightmares showed me a vision—"

"You realize you can't trust anything Mara says or shows, right?" asked Magnus, reproach in his voice. "You're old and experienced enough to know how the ancient gods work."

"You're right," agreed Damian. He took another step closer and braced his hands on either side of the window, dropping his head. "Maybe it's just my intuition, but something tells me she showed me the truth."

"About?"

"Vita—the only woman I have ever loved," he whispered without raising his eyes. Talking about his personal life had never come easy to him. Talking about it with the Head of the Destiny Council was even harder. "The fight I lost..."

He slammed his hand against the edge of the window and bit his lip, the painful memory forever engraved in his mind. Since Magnus didn't interrupt him, he continued.

"Mara told me it wasn't my fault, and by showing me this vision, she proved her point. I don't think she lied." He raised his eyes, meeting Magnus' troubled gaze. "I saw it, Magnus. If you remember that moment... right before I summoned you. There was a man there. I don't remember seeing him during the fight, but at the time, I was hurt and..." He grunted, looking away for a moment before continuing. "In the vision, I couldn't see him clearly either—just a glowing white outline in the darkness of the forest, but somehow his appearance felt so familiar..." He exhaled, pressing the heels of his hands to his eyes. "And now, every time I close my eyes for a few minutes, I see this vision over and over again, but with an added layer of nightmarish monsters and horrors. I already forgot when I had a good night's rest."

"Dmitri, my child, you must protect your mind," said Magnus, stressing the word 'must'. "You're a trained Destiny Enforcer with hundreds of years of experience under your belt. You know how to shield your mind from any outside intrusion." Magnus' voice faded, and he frowned. "Unless for some reason you don't want to block these visions?"

Damian dropped his head and clenched his jaw, recognizing the truth in Magnus' words. "I don't know," he exhaled, his voice so hoarse he could barely recognize it. "Mara was right, I think. To stop it once and for all, I need to find this man, if he exists, that is." He glanced up and found Magnus staring at him with a warning in his unnerving silvery eyes. Damian shook his head and added quietly, "It's not about vengeance, Magnus. I swear... At least, not entirely. I need closure, you know? After hundreds of years, I need to understand what happened that day. This is the only way I can finally move on."

"Oh, my boy," Magnus whispered, running his fingers over the surface of the communication window as if he were trying to touch Damian's face. "I didn't realize you were still blaming yourself for what happened. No one should carry this kind of burden through so many years." He stopped talking, a pained look settling on his features. "I'm going to visit the archives and see if I can find anything on that old case to help you. However, I do believe Mara is manipulating you. She's in the wind now and who knows, she could be reaching out to you psychically since she was able to get access to your mind once already. Guard your mind, Dmitri." He cleared his throat and squared his shoulders, seemingly becoming taller. "It's an order, Commander. You must do it."

"Yes, my lord." Damian took in a long breath and smiled faintly. "I don't think there is a lot of sleep in my foreseeable future, anyway."

"And that brings us to the reason for my late-night summons," chimed in Magnus. "You have a sanctuary law violation on your territory, Commander. I need you to take care of the situation as soon as possible and deliver the responsible party to the Destiny Council holding facility."

"I'm working on it," replied Damian. "I was in *The Midnight Shift* when it happened. The sanctuary was attacked by wurdulaks."

"Excuse me?" Magnus' voice was nothing more than a hoarse whisper.

"Yes, sir. I have a rogue necromancer on my hands." Damian reported on everything that had happened in the last few weeks, omitting just some personal details related to his brother.

"Impossible." Magnus frowned, his eyes blazing so brightly, Damian had to look away.

"I also thought it was impossible. Until I had to fight the wurdulaks myself, that is," he objected quietly. "Can I count on your support in case my heist fails, and I get detained by the local human authorities?"

"Don't fail, Commander," the Head of the Destiny Council snapped icily, but Damian just smirked, knowing perfectly well, Magnus' aggravation wasn't directed at him. "I hate doing clean up jobs, so I may let you experience the pleasures of human incarceration."

"Been there, done that." Damian laughed, but then bowed and pressed his fist to his chest in an overly exaggerated manner. "Yes, my lord. Your wish is my command. I won't fail."

"Keep it up, keep it up..." Magnus shook his head, but humorous twinkles danced in his silvery eyes. "You will show me proper respect, Dmitri, when the time comes." His gaze shifted, and a warm smile tugged at his lips. "In the old days, I used to love it about you..."

"There was something you actually liked about me?" Damian lifted a shoulder in a half-shrug. "All I remember is you chastising me for being reckless, or for breaking a chain of command, or for having poor manners."

"You used to have this uncanny ability to make jokes and laugh, no matter how tough the situation was," replied Magnus, ignoring his last statement. "Your team used to love that about you, too... What happened to that man?"

Damian swallowed, barely meeting Magnus's gaze. "He became *no one*, my lord."

"Keep an eye on that royal brother of yours," said Magnus, switching the subject. "From what I see, you will have angry lycanthropes knocking on the door of Paradise Manor in no time."

"I'll guard him with my life," replied Damian.

After his conversation with Hawk, Damian knew it was only a matter of time before the werewolves would launch a full-force attack against anything without a heartbeat. The only way to stop them was to find the responsible party, so he had to do whatever he could to make it happen as soon as possible. And if that included breaking and entering into some rich collector's home, so be it. He would do a lot more to keep his brother safe.

"That's what I'm afraid of," muttered Magnus, pinning Damian with a heavy gaze. "Keep me updated, Commander." The Head of the Destiny Council snapped his fingers, and the communication window closed.

CHAPTER 14

~ DAMIAN BLAKE ~

A full week passed before Cole, Ace and Jamie announced that they had gathered all the information they could about Ricardo Torres and his collection. Now, Damian had the blueprints of the house, the layout of the property, and he knew the types of security devices installed inside the building and around the gate area. He even had pictures of the room with Ricardo's collectibles.

Apparently, Ricardo was quite the social butterfly who loved a good party with enough alcohol to fill his sizable swimming pool. He didn't spare expenses on entertaining his rich and often famous guests and would do pretty much anything for his young and beautiful female visitors. So quite a few selfies with sensual poses, duck faces, and round eyes adorned with a generous layer of mascara had shown up on different social media sites with his collection in the background. In fact, there had been so many of them taken at different angles, that Ace could point out almost every single motion and heat detector installed around the perimeter of the room.

Damian couldn't help but wonder if Ricardo was truly so careless exposing his collection to everyone who cared to see it or if there was more to his security measures than met the eye—figuratively and literally speaking. However, with the situation getting worse with every passing day, he did not have the luxury of spending more time on research. With new murder cases popping up all over the Greater Phoenix area almost every day, all police precincts were on high alert, searching for a possible serial killer, or a vicious animal, or God knows what. All in all, they had no clue what was killing people and how to find them.

River and Jesse were the only two cops who knew what was truly going on and what kind of monster stood behind the homicidal spree. Every day, when River came home, she was so destroyed and exhausted that Damian was ready to just walk into Ricardo's house without any preparations and take the dagger by brute magical force, exposing the World of Magic and breaking all the laws and rules at his own risk.

It was early morning when Damian walked into the kitchen and prepared a cup of coffee for himself. River had been called to work in the middle of the night again, and that only added to his decision to move forward with his mission as soon as possible. Taking a quick sip of his coffee, he unfolded the blueprints and maps on the table, looking over everything one more time. After a few seconds, he sat down and wrapped his hands around the cup, enjoying the heat. He had no doubt his magic wasn't enough to make him completely invisible.

Ricardo made sure that his collection was well protected. The sensors of the passive motion detectors were visible on all the photos taken inside the room where he held his collection, and the security cameras covered every square inch of the house and the surrounding property. Damian bit his lip, looking at the blueprint where Ace had marked the security devices she could identify. If his concealment spell could hide him from the security cameras, it couldn't conceal his infrared heat signature.

"You can't do it on your own, Mr. I-work-alone."

Damian raised his eyes to see his brother standing in the

doorway. A soft smile touched Cole's lips as he headed toward him, his bare feet stepping absolutely soundlessly on the tiled floor. All his life, Damian had destroyed vampires without remorse, without mercy. If they hunted and killed humans, he hunted and killed them. It had been simple until he found his brother, and the irony of that wasn't lost on him.

Cole approached him and leaned forward, bracing his hands against the table as he observed the blueprints. His long curls fell over his face, and he straightened, tucking the stubborn strands behind his ears.

"The expression on your face tells me you are planning to do it tonight," said Cole, perching himself on the edge of the counter.

"Ace said Ricardo is supposed to be out on some socialite party in Paradise Valley tonight," replied Damian, taking a sip of his coffee. "I'm sure he's going to have plenty of security guards on the property, but it's probably the best chance I have. Besides, I can't wait any longer. Hawk called me last night, and the situation is escalating a lot faster than I expected..." His voice trailed off, and he exhaled, staring out the window. "Cole, the werewolves are actively hunting your subjects. They are searching for you, and sooner or later, they'll find out where you are."

"I'm coming with you," said Cole, folding his arms across his chest.

"Cole, I can't take you with me," objected Damian, knowing ahead of time it was a waste of breath. "If something goes wrong, and I get captured, the Destiny Council will cover for me. As much as Magnus hates the idea of getting involved in the affairs of the human realm, he will clean up after his personal Shadow Enforcer. But if you get captured..." Damian shook his head.

"Then let's make sure we don't get captured." Cole flashed him a wide grin, pushing away from the counter. "That's the reason I want to come with you. I don't have as much knowledge of magic as you do, but from what I know, your concealment spell is not going to hide you from the passive motion detectors. Your heat signature will give you away."

He placed his hand against Damian's bare arm, making him jerk aside. The vampire chuckled.

"Hey! Your hands are—" As Damian glanced up at his brother, understanding dawned on him.

"I rest my case," Cole announced, his winning smile growing wider. "I don't have a heat signature. I don't breathe, and I can move absolutely soundlessly. Also, I can keep still for a long period of time or move extremely slowly. I have all the skills I need to trick the motion detectors."

"Cole," said Damian, almost pleading with his brother. "Even though we know quite a bit about Ricardo and his property, we still don't know everything, and I'm going there, relying solely on my magic. My plan has more holes than a spaghetti strainer, but I have no choice. It's my obligation to find and detain the necromancer." He exhaled, rubbing his unshaven chin. "Despite the necessity behind my actions, if I expose the World of Magic, I will be punished according to the law. Severely, I must say. I can't let you—"

"Try to stop me," Cole snapped, interrupting him.

"But Cole—"

"This discussion is over," announced Cole, imitating Damian's voice almost to perfection.

"Good talk, little bro." Damian snorted, shaking his head.

Cole rolled his eyes and leaned over the blueprints, pointing at the area indicating the gates. "Look," he said, "there will be a guard here, and I can easily take care of him if you take care of the camera."

"Wait." Damian frowned. "You're not planning to kill humans, are you?"

"As tempting as it sounds, no," quipped Cole, gazing heavenward. "I don't need him dead. I need him... um... obedient. I'll make sure he opens the gate for us willingly, and we'll walk through it. I will ask, but I'm sure the guards serving in the gatehouse won't know how to shut down the security system inside the house, so the rest will be up to you and your magic. As soon as we reach the area covered by the motion detectors, I'll have to leave you behind and go alone. Once I get the dagger, you teleport us back home." He shrugged, a boyish grin splitting his face. "Easy."

"Jeez, Cole," muttered Damian, half-turning to his brother. "You're always too optimistic and too fast to act without thinking things through. Nothing is ever as simple as it seems to be."

"And you read too much into everything. Sometimes you have to let go and make a leap of faith," said Cole, but then sighed and added, "Your glass is always half-empty."

"What can I tell you, I need a refill. I got dehydrated," murmured Damian, his mind racing through all possible ways of preventing Cole from going with him. Since he couldn't find anything that would work, he threw his hands up, surrendering. "Fine. You can come with me, but we do things my way."

"Fine..." Cole snickered and tapped Damian's shoulder with his icy hand. "We'll see... Doofus."

"Dracula Junior."

"What could be better than an early morning compliment exchange between two brothers?" Jamie's voice, filled with sarcasm, sounded from his left, and Damian turned around. The young man stood in the doorway, leaning his shoulder against the frame. Ace stood next to him with an uneven smirk on her face.

"We're coming with you," she said in a no-nonsense tone, folding her arms.

Damian glanced at Cole, and they both said, "No!" at the same time.

"Dang," murmured Jamie. "At least there is something these two agree on."

It was close to midnight when Damian teleported with Cole to a point he had selected a few days ago. A vacant lot with a real estate sign planted in front of it stood far enough from any houses. Obscured by the darkness of the night, this location was relatively safe, and even if some unfortunate human saw them appear from thin air, there was always Cole with his vampire glamor.

Damian wasn't a big proponent of using any kind of magic that messed around with people's minds, but needs must, and Cole's glamor was less invasive to humans than his own oblivion spells. Besides, anything would be better than exposing another innocent soul to the World of Magic.

Ricardo's house was only a couple of blocks away, and Damian headed toward it, carefully observing the area and checking the surroundings for any supernatural presence.

"Hey, Damian." Cole fell into step, throwing a sideways glance filled with humorous twinkles at him.

Damian met his brother's eyes and winced inwardly, knowing Cole was up to something, wondering if remaining silent was his safest bet.

"What's up?" he asked carefully, stifling a sigh.

"I had an interesting conversation with River a few days ago," Cole started, amusement in his deep voice.

"About?"

"Well, she asked me if you were"—he twirled his hand, a wide grin on his face—"you know..."

"No, I don't know."

"Well... playing for the other side," explained Cole, barely containing his laughter.

"What?" Damian halted, flabbergasted. "And what did you tell her?"

"I told her that of course you're not," replied Cole, blinking with innocence in his baby-blues. "I said you were playing for both sides."

"I'm going to kill you," muttered Damian, resuming his walk. "Or better yet, I'm going to throw you to the angry werewolves myself."

"No, you're not," objected Cole, laughing quietly.

"Unfortunately, you're right—I'm not," grumbled Damian. "I have no idea how I survived all these years without you being a giant pain in my neck."

Cole tapped Damian's shoulder, his smile melting away. "On the serious side, Dima, she did ask me this question." He fell silent for a moment, staring straight ahead. "I told her no, you're not gay, but you have a thousand-years-long past. I asked her to be patient with you and give you a chance."

Damian glanced at his brother, his chest tightening with worry. "Let's focus on the mission," he said, his voice sounding too hoarse even to his own ears. "We're almost there."

They took a narrow two-lane asphalt road leading up the Carefree hills toward a luxury estate located at the very top. The building was positioned on a large piece of land, at least five acres, and surrounded by the Sonoran Desert, which provided a breathtaking view as well as perfect privacy.

Tall, privacy fencing enclosed the house, but as far as Damian could see, there wasn't any kind of magical protection around the property line. Quietly, they approached a small gatehouse, and Damian peeked over, trying to locate a security camera. He found it right away—a small, modern device attached to a pole next to the gates. He held out his hand, and a low-voltage energy ball materialized in his palm. It rotated slowly, crackling and spreading around tiny electrical discharges. He touched it with his fingers, whispering a spell, and a ray of pure magical energy erupted from it, blinding the camera.

Cole stepped forward, leaving Damian behind in the shadows. He raised a finger to his lips, glancing over his shoulder at his brother, and wild sparkles of humor ignited in his eyes. Then he approached the door, knocked on it and took a step back. The door swung open right away, and a giant man in the gray uniform of a security guard stared down at Cole, his face a stone mask. For a heartbeat, the vampire looked at him with his eyes widened as he took in the height of the man, but then he got over the initial shock and flashed him a friendly smile.

"Excuse me. I know it's a little late..." He chuckled, a vibe of awkward discomfort lingering around him, and Damian smirked, thinking that his brother should have been an actor. "I'm here visiting my girlfriend, and we had a heated argument..." He chuckled again, rubbing the back of his neck. "So, I was stupid enough to storm out of the house in the middle of the night and"—he shrugged guiltily—"I'm a little lost. Can you please show me the direction to Cave Creek?"

"Cave Creek?" the guard parroted, stepping closer to Cole.

Judging by the height difference, the man was at list six-foot-six and next to him, in his black track pants and a tight T-shirt, the vampire looked like a young, slim teenager.

"Yes, Cave Creek," repeated Cole, raising his gaze at the giant.

As soon as their eyes locked, the vampiric energy rose around Cole, and his eyes lit up with a bright scarlet glow. The guard froze, and his jaw slacked.

"That's it, look at me..." purred Cole, gently directing him back into the gatehouse while keeping their eye contact. He said something else, but his voice was so soft, it was lost in the whisper of the midnight breeze, and Damian couldn't hear him.

"How can I help you, sir?" asked the guard, his gaze dazed, his features slacked and emotionless.

"Mr. Torres is expecting my visit," Cole said louder. "Please, open the gate for me."

"Right away, sir," replied the guard flatly. He pressed a button, and the gate started to slide softly to the side. "Is there anything else I can do for you, sir?"

"Yes, you can shut down all security systems in the estate," replied Cole, staring at the guard without blinking.

The guard flinched, and his body tensed. "I'm sorry, sir. Mr. Torres is the only person who can do that."

Cole walked up into the gatehouse and pressed on the guard's shoulder, forcing him to sit down. Leaning forward, he lowered his face within inches from the man's. The vampire's eyes lit up brighter, and his voice became the dangerous purr of a wild feline as he spoke again.

"You spent all night in this gatehouse. No one came in or out, and you didn't see anyone. Don't leave your station until you're released off duty. Am I clear?"

"Yes, sir," replied the guard, his wide-open eyes fixed on Cole's.

"Good boy," murmured Cole. His vampiric energy leveled down, turning his eyes their normal blue.

He stepped out of the gatehouse and gestured for Damian to follow him through the gate. As Damian walked out of the shadows, the guard looked straight through him as if he were invisible and turned away. Damian moved under the camera and squeezed his fist, making the energy ball dissipate.

"*Oprimenta Amnia*," he whispered and waved his hand, placing a light cloaking spell over himself and his brother. "Okay, Cole, we are invisible to the cameras and humans now."

"Great," whispered Cole. He pointed at the brightly lit entrance into the house at the end of a long driveway, paved with multicolored cobblestones. The entrance was partially obscured by elaborately placed decorative rocks and tall saguaro cacti. "Can you teleport us there?"

Damian placed his hand on Cole's shoulder, ready to snap his fingers when he heard a raspy, cracked voice somewhere above him and froze in place, checking the area.

"Oh, yeah. Oh, yeah... Ehhhhh... Here goes... heeeereee gooooeees.... a night of entertainment with two jackasses landing in the middle of a pond surrounded by thorny cacti."

"What are you doing?" hissed Cole, grabbing Damian's elbow.

"One sec, Cole." Damian spun around, and to his shock, he saw a small magpie sitting on a leaf of a decorative palm tree at the edge of the driveway, its beady black eyes staring at him with amusement. Glowering at the bird, he folded his arms and asked, "What pond? What are you talking about?"

The bird turned its head, looking around, and since there was no one else there, it stared back at Damian, its beak open.

"Ehh... Are you talking to me, giant?" the magpie asked, and added without waiting for his response, "Oh, yeah. I'm the only one here, so yeah... you are talking to me. How cool is that, dude, eh? You are a Kid of Earth. Oh, hell no. No, not the Kid, they call it the Child of Earth, right? Oh, yeah, oh, yeah, finally I can speak with someone who has a brain slightly bigger than that of a snail—"

"Stop it," hissed Damian. "Tell me about the pond. Where is it located?"

"Ehhhh, yeah-yeah, the pond..." The magpie waved its wing toward the house. "You know when Ricardo bought this house, he was like, yeah... I love Arizona, but you know what? There is just not enough water here. Yeah, dudes, install a pond for me. And the construction dudes were like, sure, why not, and how many would you like? And Ricardo was—"

"Tell me where this goddamn pond is located, or I swear to God, I will pluck every single feather out of your wings one by one," growled Damian, taking a step closer to the chatty bird. Cole snorted, and Damian threw a scorching glance at him, making him snort louder.

"Alright-alright-alright." The magpie flew down and landed on Damian's shoulder. *"Chill, dude. You see those two saguaro cacti by the entrance? The one that looks like a man with two arms up?"*

"Yeah, I see it," hissed Damian, his patience running dangerously thin.

"Well, forget about this one then," the bird chattered at an incredible speed. *"This is not the one you need. Look at the next one. Yeah... the one that looks like a man with two giant arms up and a tiny-small pe—"* The magpie made a sound that resembled laughter. *"Well, yeah... dude.. you want that one. If you go to the left of it, that is where the pond is, grampus. So, don't go there. Aim to the right. How are your aiming skills?"*

"I understand you're talking to this magpie," murmured Cole. "What I don't understand is how the bird can see us through your cloaking spell."

"Animals," whispered Damian. "Their vision is not like ours. It can be compared to my other sight. They can see magical and elemental energy, as well as the objects hidden by cloaking spells." He placed his hand on his brother's shoulder. "Are you ready?"

"Let's get it done." Cole took a step closer to Damian, sending a curious gaze at the bird sitting on his shoulder.

"Here goes," Damian exhaled and snapped his fingers.

THEY MANIFESTED in front of the entrance into the building next to a large artificial pond surrounded by Echinocereus cacti and decorative rocks. Damian scanned the area with his other sight, and since he didn't notice anything that looked remotely like wards or protection spells, he walked up the steps and covered the security pad located next to the entrance with his hand, channeling some of his magic through it. Something clicked, and the light switched from red to green.

Then he placed his hand on the door handle and whispered, *"Recludius..."*

The lock clicked, and Damian cracked the door open without walking inside. He quickly scanned the house for the presence of human souls but didn't find anyone there. His intuition twitched, suggesting something wasn't right. He frowned, pushing the negative thoughts out of his mind. Time was working against him, and he couldn't delay anymore.

Turning to his brother, he whispered, "Cole, I don't think there is anyone in the house. No guards, no live-in help... Something is not right."

"Or something is exactly right." Cole winked at him, but a shadow of concern crossed his features.

Damian grunted, biting his lip. "Just be careful." He sighed and opened the door wider. "The collection is in the large hall at the end of the hallway on the right. Hopefully, Ace is right and there are no motion detectors in the lobby and anywhere in the hallways, otherwise, we're screwed."

The magpie leaned forward, its long black tail rising, and pecked Damian on his cheek. *"Hey, Kid... dammit, I mean Child of Earth, can a little birdie tag along? It's fun... yeah... what you two are doing... please-please-please..."*

"No!" snapped Damian in a low hiss. "I need to focus on the mission. I don't need a bird's voice screeching in my head."

"Screeching?! How dare you? I don't screech. I vocalize in a musical and euphonious manner. Luh-luh-luh-luh-la-la-la-la-laaaaa...." The bird hopped in place and moved its wing across the beak. *"My beak is sealed."*

"It better be," grumbled Damian, carefully passing through the doorway with the magpie still nestled on his shoulder.

He stepped into a large lobby—glass and marble—and stilled, taking in his surroundings while scanning for the presence of magic. Despite the late hour and the absence of the house owner and staff, the lobby was well lit with electric lights.

Two beautifully crafted staircases positioned at either side of the area led to the second floor. A tall arched window effectively decorated by curtains presented a gorgeous view of the desert. A white grand piano, surrounded by a few leather sofas, took the center of the floor, and a large, crystal chandelier hung from the ceiling right above it.

Damian motioned for Cole to follow him and crossed the lobby toward the wide hallway on his right. He walked slowly and as soundlessly as he could, keeping his second sight open, but just like in the lobby, he couldn't detect any presence of magical energy. Everything was quiet and unremarkably human.

The hallway opened into a small hall. One of the walls was made entirely out of glass, presenting a view of the desert and mountains. The entire space of the other two walls was decorated by different weapons—crossed swords, shields, and daggers. By the looks of them, all the weapons were modern and presented no monetary value, used as décor only. Four security cameras were installed at the four corners of the hall, but as far as Damian could see, there weren't any motion or heat detectors here.

The wide doorway on the wall across from the entrance led into a large windowless space. Multiple shelves with different weapons and artifacts were positioned inside, protected by thick glass cases. A few marble pedestals were arranged across the floor, each of them holding a single dagger, illuminated by a thin chain of LED lights installed around the perimeter of the base. To Damian's unease, he noticed that the items on pedestals weren't enclosed in glass, confirming the statement Az had made earlier, and even with his other sight, he couldn't see any other methods of protection.

Cole halted at Damian's side and pointed toward the room and up at a few motion detectors and cameras of the security systems. Damian nodded, confirming that he had registered the mundane security devices as well. Cole leaned closer to him and whispered so quietly that only Damian with his sharp hearing could make out his words.

"I see the dagger," he said. "Not under a glass, and there are no laser beams around it either. I would sense them. I'm good to go."

"Cole, wait," hissed Damian, grabbing his brother's arm, his fingers clenching it stronger than he intended. "It's too easy."

Cole turned, staring at his brother with reproach. "Since when is easy bad?"

"Don't you think if something seems too good to be true, it most likely is?"

Cole tilted his head, a sad smile curving his lips. "Dima, I'm reckless, but I'm not an idiot. I know you're right," he whispered, his lips barely moving. "But do we have a choice? Do you see any other options?"

Damian frowned, slowly shaking his head, his chest numb with dread. He let go of his brother's arm and dropped his head.

"If something goes wrong, you can still teleport us out of here," Cole whispered and slowly moved toward the entrance into the collection room. He halted by the doorway, looking from left to right, carefully exploring everything in the room. Then he glanced over his shoulder at Damian and smiled before crossing the threshold.

Cole moved slowly, stepping weightlessly and soundlessly on the shiny, tiled floor, but every step he took sent a jolt of anxiety down Damian's spine.

"Ohhhhh... The suspense is killing me... he'll be fiiineee..." breathed out the magpie, its voice clear in Damian's mind, and he swallowed hard, raising his hand to pet the bird's wings.

Damian glanced up, quickly checking all the motion detectors he could see from where he stood, but none of them seemed to react to Cole's presence. He exhaled, just now realizing he had been holding his breath since the moment Cole crossed the threshold.

Cole halted by a pedestal at the far end of the room and sent a quick glance to Damian, slowly raising his hand. He froze, for a heartbeat remaining completely still, but then he carefully moved his hand in front of the pedestal, checking it from different angles. Once satisfied with his observations, he reached into his pocket and pulled something out. Bringing both hands up, he wrapped his fingers around the hilt of the dagger and froze again, checking the sensors.

A drop of cold sweat ran down Damian's face as he watched his brother, and he held his breath again, terrified to make the tiniest move. Cole's face tensed, and his vampiric essence rose around him, igniting his eyes with a bright scarlet light. In one fluid motion, Cole lifted the dagger and replaced it with something he was holding in his other hand. The change was so subtle and so immediate that neither Cole nor Damian could react.

With a thunderous bang, thick metal bars dropped from the ceiling, blocking the only exit out of the collection room. A soft, continuous hiss invaded Damian's hearing. He screamed his brother's name at the same time as a terrible howl of pain erupted from Cole's lips. His fingers unlocked, and the dagger fell to the floor with a loud clunk. Cole collapsed, his body convulsing like from a seizure, and bleeding ulcers spread around the exposed skin of his face and arms.

"Cole!" Damian didn't hear himself screaming as he reached the metal bars. He channeled all the magic he could gather and shouted, *"Exitius!"*

CHAPTER 15

~ DAMIAN BLAKE ~

A mighty wave of magical energy impacted the metal bars. Normally, this spell would turn any door into scraps of metal or a pile of splinters, but the bars separating Damian from his brother barely bent inward, withholding the powerful attack. Cole screamed, large drops of blood sliding from his wide-open scarlet eyes. His body arched, and his fingers turned into claws, his fangs expanding to their full length. A heartbeat later, his muscles relaxed, and he fell to the floor, his glowing eyes fixed on Damian's, silently pleading for help.

Blind fury mixed in with suffocating fear blended into one explosive concoction within him. Damian seized the bars and connected with his element, surrendering to the power of Earth. The muscles on his arms and shoulders bulged, a thick vein pulsing in his neck. Using his physical strength, he combined it with his elemental power and applied the pressure on the bars, trying to spread them apart. The entire house shook under the assault of his power, but the bars didn't budge, and for a split second, he felt as though the shining metal was absorbing his magical energy, draining him. He jerked his hands away, noticing the red blemishes on his palms resembling first-degree burns.

"Dima, stop!" Cole screamed, his voice infused with torment beyond anything any person—human or a vampire—could handle. "It... reacts... ahhh... to your magic..." He cried out again, his entire body convulsing uncontrollably.

"What reacts?" Damian yelled, slamming his fist into the bars separating them. "What is it, Cole?"

"I'll check it!" The magpie flew between the bars and started on its way toward Cole, but after a few flaps of its wings, the bird made a sharp U-turn and flew back, its black eyes filled with horror, its beak wide open. *"There is no oxygen there! Silver is everywhere! I can't breathe!"* It zoomed between the bars, dropped to the floor and flopped to its back, its tiny white chest rising and falling with strained breaths.

As a toxic wave of panic enveloped Damian, the adrenalin rushed through his system, sending his heart into a wild overdrive. His training kicked in, and he let go of the bars, taking a step back. To think clearly, he needed to calm down. Closing his eyes, he dropped his arms and took a few deep breaths, getting his anxiety and panic under control. He let go of his elemental power and magic, carefully suppressing them. As soon as he did that, Cole's body relaxed, his eyes rolled back, and he blacked out, blood still slipping from under his tightly shut eyelids.

"On your knees! Hands behind your head!"

A loud voice sounded behind Damian, and he spun around with his hands clenched into fists, a feral growl rumbling in his chest. At least ten men—most likely guards—stood around him, their weapons trained at his chest. They were dressed in what appeared to be military tactical uniforms, but strange vests covered their chests. They were too thin to be bulletproof, and their surface shimmered with bluish sparkles, reflecting the electrical light. The weapons they held also weren't something Damian had expected. While two of the guards had guns pointed at his head, the rest of them held strange weapons the likes of which he had never seen before. They looked like spears, but their long spearheads, made of some silvery metal-like material, were split into two at the end.

One of the men stepped closer and thrust his spear into Damian's chest. He didn't put a lot of force behind it, and the sharp ends of the spearhead barely penetrated his skin, but a wave of weakness rushed through him, making his stomach heave. Damian seized the spear with his hand and took a tiny step forward, leaning heavier on it, anger spiraling through him. The guard didn't expect it. His eyes widened in unmistakable shock, and he pulled back slightly, still holding the spear at Damian's chest.

"Lower your weapons and let my friend go," Damian growled, his voice deep with unadulterated hatred. "Or I swear to all the gods I know, I will kill every single one of you and take this house apart brick by brick."

The men exchanged a quick look and burst out laughing. Two more stepped closer, holding their spears at the ready. "On your knees, freak," commanded one of them, pointing at the floor before him.

Damian's body locked up with rage and despite his effort to control his power and magic, tremors spread through the floor. In response, Cole howled in pain, his fingers scratching spasmodically at the polished tiles.

"Everyone, stand down." A deep male voice sounded behind the group of men. It was filled with the kind of authority that comes only with years of experience of giving orders and a habit of having every single one of them obeyed, no questions asked. The men lowered their weapons and spread apart, allowing the newcomer to come forward.

He made his way between his guards and halted a few steps away from Damian, observing him with interest in his dark-brown eyes. He was at least six feet tall and moved with a confident swagger bordering on arrogance. He didn't look more than thirty years old, but after the display of power he had over these men and the unmistakable vibe of authority he gave off, Damian wondered if he was older.

The man's large eyes under long, black eyelashes swept through the room, and his sensual, full lips twitched into a frosty smile under his mustache, dimpling his cheeks covered in a stylishly trimmed stubble. In his hands, he held a box made of either lead or iron, or some kind of mix of both. The lid was tightly closed, but he held one hand over it, ready to flip it open. Cocking his head slightly, he raised his dark eyebrows.

"What a gorgeous specimen you are, aren't you?" he muttered under his breath. Although his looks suggested Hispanic heritage, he spoke in perfect English without any accent. "As much as I would like to see you in action, I don't think you'll be killing anyone today. Unless you want to murder your vampire-pet, that is." He jerked his chin toward Cole and waved his hand slightly as if dismissing the matter. "Let's be civil, shall we? Get down to your knees, and we'll call it a day. I'm a lover, not a fighter, you know." He smiled, his smile almost playful, despite the situation. "I would much rather settle the situation in a peaceful, business-like manner without the need to apply physical force, but if you don't comply with my orders, you'll leave me no choice."

Damian stared down at him, focusing on suppressing his magic and elemental power. "No," he said softly.

The man pursed his lips, shaking his head, looking almost crestfallen. Then he seized the lid of the box and cracked it opened. A wave of magical energy escaped through the opening, impacting Damian straight in his chest. He grunted and staggered backward until his back hit the bars. Overwhelming weakness spread through him, making his knees shake, but he grasped the bars behind his back and remained standing, ignoring the pain in his burning palms.

A deep shudder ran through Damian as he recognized the malignant energy signature of the artifact hidden within the box, and the blood froze in his veins as with painful clarity, he realized how hopeless his situation truly was. The so-called gray stones could bring any being of magic or elemental power to their knees, no matter how powerful they were. Even gods weren't immune to their toxic magic, and depending on the size of the stone, it could drain them completely, making them weak and helpless against those holding the artifact.

"Impressive," exhaled the man, staring at Damian in awe. He took a couple of steps closer and opened the box slightly wider.

As the next wave of weakness overwhelmed him, Damian dropped to his knees and leaned forward, wrapping his arms around himself as his stomach twisted with nausea. Struggling to breathe, he raised his eyes at the man holding the box.

"Much better..." The man leaned down and seized Damian's hair, tilting his head backward. As his eyes halted on the scar cutting across Damian's left cheek, he frowned and waved at one of his guards. "This is quite a landmark here." He followed the shape of the scar with his finger, eliciting a growl of anger out of Damian. "Find out who he is and what his supernatural identity is. He should be easy to identify with this beauty."

The man let go of Damian's hair and straightened, gesturing for one of his guards to approach. "Check the vamp," he said icily. "I want to know if he's worth anything or if we need to put him out of his misery."

Damian groaned, making an effort to look over his shoulder at his brother. Even this tiny movement came with a serious effort, sending the next wave of nausea through him, and he moaned softly, his own defenselessness crushing and suffocating him. The guard left the hall, and a few seconds later, he walked into the collection room through a tiny door Damian hadn't noticed before, wearing a respirator mask.

He approached Cole and yanked his head backward, prying

his jaws open. His fingers quickly checked the vampire's fangs and then moved down to his arms and chest, probing his muscles. The guard's moves were so precise and habitual that Damian was positive it wasn't his first rodeo. Cole didn't fight him—most likely too weak and hurt to make a move—terrible bleeding ulcers covering his skin, drops of blood sliding from his eyes, nose and ears.

"This one is old, Mr. Torres," said the guard, rising. "Has to be at least five hundred years old if not more and in good physical shape."

Mr. Torres... This is Ricardo Torres. A thought flashed through Damian's fogged mind as he turned back to the man with the box.

"Find out his name," Ricardo Torres commanded as the guard returned to the hall, wiping his hands on his pants.

"Should we package them both?" asked the guard, halting before him. "We have two sets of restraints ready, sir."

Ricardo Torres peered down at Damian with a calculating look in his dark eyes and rubbed his lower lip with his finger, a deep vertical wrinkle materializing between his straight eyebrows. He thrust the box into the guard's hand, making sure that the lid remained just slightly open.

"Hold it like this and don't open any wider. I need him conscious..." He switched his attention to Damian and squatted in front of him. "Normally, this would be the moment where my guards would restrain you with the kind of restraints no creature of magic can escape from." He ran his fingers over his mustache, narrowing his eyes. "I don't know what's so special about you, but my intuition tells me I shouldn't do it, and I learned to respect my intuition." He got up and looked at Cole through the bars. "What did they try to steal?"

The guard approached him, offering him the dagger with the eagle-head pommel. Ricardo took it and twirled it between his fingers, his eyebrows rising.

"Really?" he asked, lowering to Damian's level again, shock imprinted on his features. "Really?? Out of everything I have, all the magical artifacts in that room, you decided to steal the most useless one? You could have walked into my kitchen and steal my steak knives. They are worth about the same. What's so special about this dagger that you risked everything to have it? It has no magical properties and even though it's old, I couldn't discover anything interesting about its history."

Damian looked straight into Ricardo's eyes but said nothing.

"Okay," Ricardo said softly. "Let's try to have a little conversation first. My name is Ricardo Torres. You can call me Ricardo. I don't like all that official bullshit." He smiled as if he were talking to his best friend. "I own this house and everything around you. Would you like to tell me your name?"

Damian sighed, dropping his head. Even holding his head upright was taking too much of his energy. "Damian," he replied quietly.

"Aw, wonderful, you do have a human name. I'm sure there is a last name too, but we'll get to it later." Ricardo chuckled, flushing his paper-white teeth. "Well, Damian, I'm prepared to make you an offer, and if you have any brains in that head of yours, you will accept it, because—and my guards can attest to that—this is the first time in many years I'm offering something like this to a being of magic as yourself. Besides, the alternative is not going to be pleasant either for you or for your vampire pet."

Damian grunted, anger spiking through him at Ricardo's last words. "I'm all ears," he growled, raising his eyes.

"Oh?" Ricardo searched his face with new interest and then glanced at Cole. "Or maybe this vampire is not your pet, but someone a lot more important—"

"What's your offer?" Damian interrupted him, and an uneven smirk crossed Ricardo's face.

"Good, you do have brains after all," he murmured, twirling

the dagger between his fingers. "Well, Damian, if you promise to behave, I'm going to remove the gray stone from the room and allow you to gain your strength. After that, we'll talk in private, like any civilized individuals should. I'm a businessman, you know, so I have a business proposition for you."

Damian glanced at him in shock. "Not without my friend," he said coldly.

"But of course. I apologize I didn't say it right away." Ricardo snapped his fingers, jerking his chin at his guard. "The vamp is coming with the two of us." A few seconds later, the guard walked out of the collection room with Cole thrown over his shoulder. "Do I have your word now, Damian?"

Damian glanced at his brother, and his heart jolted painfully. While he knew Cole was as alive as a vampire could be, his arms hung limply, swaying with every step the guard took, and his blond hair was soaked with blood.

"You have my word, Ricardo," he said, his vocal cords too sore to produce any sound louder than a whisper.

"Aw, come on, Damian." Ricardo shook his head reproachfully. "We both know how it works in the World of Magic." He put the dagger into Damian's hand, wrapping his weak fingers around the grip. "You know what needs to be done."

Damian nodded, still feeling weak and lightheaded, and he wasn't sure if it was the gray stone that made him feel so sick or if it was the idea of getting into some kind of agreement with this slippery man.

With effort, he squeezed the hilt of the dagger, noticing that neither Az nor Ricardo had lied about it—the dagger had absolutely no magic in it. Placing its tip against the floor, he tried to bring one knee up to assume the proper position but was too weak to do it. He sighed and raised his eyes at Ricardo.

"I can't take one knee," he said, feeling more drained by the moment.

"That's okay. I'm an understanding kind of fellow." Ricardo

waved his hand dismissively and winked. "Your position is fine. Just say the right words."

Damian nodded. "I swear..." His voice cut off, and he groaned, forcing himself to pronounce the words clearly. "Ricardo Torres, I swear that for as long as I'm under your roof, you won't be harmed either by me or by my vampire friend."

"Perfect," Ricardo breathed out, straightening. He took the box from his guard's hands and closed the lid tightly. Holding the box in one hand, he seized Cole's hair with the other hand, yanking his head up, and quickly explored his face. Cole moaned, his tortured gaze meeting Ricardo's cold eyes. "Take this vamp into a shower and wash the silver off of him. Get him a clean set of clothes and a blood bag. Once he's ready, escort him to my office."

"No," groaned Damian, struggling to get up, but to no avail. Even though the gray stone was no longer affecting him, he knew it would take a while for him to restore his strength. "I'll take care of him myself."

"Damian, Damian, Damian." Ricardo threw his hands up. "A little trust, please? Now that we're friends, I promise... No, I swear, your precious vamp is not going to be abused in any way. While he's under my roof, he'll be treated as my guest with appropriate respect." He threw a pointed stare at the guard holding Cole.

"Yes, sir," the guard replied, moving Cole carefully off his shoulder and into his arms.

"You may go." He waved at the guard and turned to Damian. "Follow me."

"One second, sir." Damian raised his hand, looking around. "I need to use just a small amount of magic. Is it possible to do it here without triggering any kind of unwanted consequences?"

Ricardo glanced down at him with curiosity and smirked proudly. "Did you like my security tech? One of a kind." He pulled out his cellphone and quickly clicked something on the screen. "Go ahead. Do what you need to do."

Damian placed his palms flat against the floor and reached out to his element. It didn't come right away, but soon, warmth spread through him, gathering in his chest, energizing him and partially restoring his strength. He let out a harsh breath, his eyes igniting with a bright orange light, and Ricardo gasped, staring at him intently.

"*Magnifico*," he breathed out, shaking his head slightly.

Damian sat back on his heels and picked up the tiny magpie. Placing the bird in his palm, he moved his other hand over it and channeled the healing energy through it. The magpie twitched, jerked its black wings open and flipped to its feet, staring around wildly.

"*Heeellooo wooorld! I'm alive... ehhhhh... Hallelujah! Praise the Lord, the gods and the Kid of Earth, no Child... Thank you, gracias, spasibo...*"

Unable to contain a smile, Damian placed the bird on his shoulder and got up to his feet.

"I think I'm not going to ask about that one," mumbled Ricardo, staring at Damian in awe.

"It would be better if you didn't," Damian replied and followed Ricardo through the long hallways and up the stairs to the second floor.

Fu-u-ck... What could possibly go wrong with this little agreement...

CHAPTER 16

~ DAMIAN BLAKE ~

Just like everything else in this opulent estate, Ricardo's office was furnished with luxury and comfort in mind. A large room was dimly lit by an invisible chain of lights installed around its perimeter. A dark mahogany desk stood at the far end of the office with two large computer monitors positioned on the side of it. Heavy panels tightly covered the tall windows, and a few oil paintings that looked authentically antique decorated the walls. A faint scent of expensive cologne lingered in the cool air, entwined with the odor of papers and printing ink.

As soon as they walked in, Ricardo took his suit jacket off and threw it on the back of a large leather sofa. His tie followed, and he sighed with relief, opening a few top buttons of his white dress shirt. His face relaxed, and he looked like a completely different person, the layer of malevolent cruelty seemingly gone.

"Finally, I can breathe," he exhaled, pulling the top of his shirt apart, exposing his muscled chest covered with short black hair.

Damian closed the door but remained standing next to it, following Ricardo's every move with suspicion. Ricardo turned around and smiled weakly, and for the first time since Damian met this dangerous man, he noticed a touch of exhaustion showing on his hard features.

"Sit down, Damian," he said, waving in the direction of the sofa. "Relax. Trust me, the worst part is over."

Damian hesitated for a moment, but then walked toward the sofa and sat down, sinking between the soft pillows. The magpie hopped off his shoulder and flew up to the curtain rod. Damian leaned back and folded his arms across his chest, closing his eyes for a brief moment to get over the dizziness. The effects of the gray stone weren't gone completely, and he still felt slightly lightheaded and nauseous.

Ricardo glanced at him, shaking his head. "I've heard those gray stones are a bitch, and I've seen how they work quite a few times, but the way you reacted..."

Shaking his head almost as if he couldn't believe his own memory, he headed toward a small cabinet and opened it. Pulling a bottle of expensive cognac out, he partially filled two glasses.

"I need something stronger than water." His full lips twitched in the semblance of a smile, but deep, bitter wrinkles settled around his mouth, partially hidden by his facial hair. "I think you could do with a stiff drink, too."

He offered one glass to Damian, and once he took it from his hand, Ricardo pulled an armchair and sat down to face him, still tugging at the collar of his shirt as though it were strangling him.

"*Salud!*" Ricardo smirked over the rim of his glass, taking a sip of his drink. Then he closed his eyes, holding his breath for a brief moment.

Damian drank slowly, enjoying the feeling of the burning

liquid traveling down his throat. With all his senses on high alert, he observed Ricardo's every move, trying to understand why he brought him to this office and what this man's true agenda was. Perhaps Ricardo didn't have any magic of his own, but unlike Az thought, he was at least exposed to the World of Magic.

Ricardo leaned forward, reaching for his jacket. He grabbed it and pulled the dagger out of the pocket. Twirling it between his fingers, he glanced at Damian, a question in his cold, dark eyes. Then he exhaled and took the weapon by the blade, offering it to him.

"You went through a lot of trouble to get this dagger," he said softly. "Here. Take it." He took a sip of his drink and gave a short nod. "It's yours if you still want it, but I would like to know why."

"Why what?" asked Damian, taking the dagger.

"Why *this* dagger?" replied Ricardo, placing some weight on the word 'this'. "You don't strike me as a common supernatural thief. I've met too many of them not to recognize an honest man when I see one. So, why did you and your undead friend break into my house, trying to steal it?"

"You've met many supernatural thieves?" muttered Damian, recalling how easy it had been for Ace, Cole and Jamie to identify the methods of security in the house, and how simple it had been to break into the building and reach the collection room. It had been a trap—a well-positioned, elaborately designed and perfectly thought-through supernatural trap. Ricardo used his collection as bait.

Ricardo observed him, his attentive eyes crinkling at the corners as his lips curved into an uneven smirk. "I see you figured out that my collection is nothing more than bait. A magnet for supernatural assholes... no offense." Damian nodded, and Ricardo continued, "But before we jump into this conversation, I want you to tell me why you wanted this useless dagger. My usual visitors go for expensive pieces under the glass, those that have powerful magical properties."

Making a split-second decision, Damian chose to stick to the truth as much as it was possible in this situation. There was something strange about this man. Intuitive and perceptive, he looked like a smart individual, and despite his previous display of cold indifference bordering on cruelty, there was more to him than he originally thought. In so many words, he told him about the necromancer creating a dangerous situation, igniting a war between the werewolves and the vampires.

"So, you think this dagger used to belong to a powerful necromancer?" Ricardo's eyes halted on the weapon in Damian's hands. "Fascinating." He raked his hand through his black hair, and a chain of emotions crossed his face—starting with doubt, morphing into fear and then settling on the cold indifference Damian had seen before. "I'm glad I decided to spare you and your friend. The war between vamps and lycanthropes would be damaging for my business, too."

"I had no idea the construction and real estate business was directly related to the status of the Arizona Vampire Court or to the number of werewolves in the state," said Damian without hiding his sarcasm.

"My *other* business." Ricardo cringed visibly, and for a heartbeat, a shadow of self-loathing darkened his eyes. "As you can see, my collection attracts a lot of attention from the supernatural community. Just like you, they all arrogantly rely on their magic or their true nature, hoping it will help them to break in, tricking mundane security tech with ease, and steal unnoticed. What they don't realize is that their magic—or in the case of your undead friend, his vampiric essence—is their worst enemy."

He got up and headed to his desk. Opening one of the drawers, he shuffled around for a bit and pulled out a box the size of a small shoebox. Holding it in his hands, he came back to his seat and took the lid off. A few white plastic boxes lay inside. Visibly, there was absolutely nothing special about them.

"What is it?" asked Damian, reaching forward to touch one of the items.

Ricardo took one and placed it in Damian's hand. "Don't worry. There is no security in this room. I think you're one of those rare magical beings who have the *other* sight. Go ahead, check it."

Damian explored the box, probing it with his other sight as well as his senses, and shook his head. He couldn't sense any magic in them.

"It's not magical," explained Ricardo. "Pure human tech. It's made to respond to any magical energy, including elemental powers, vampiric and demonic essence, and even the slight magical waves the werewolves emit. These devices are installed everywhere in my house and around the gates." He waved his hand around and added, "With the exception of this room, of course." He sighed and leaned back, stretching his legs. "This is how I knew you were coming. As soon as your vampire stepped closer to the gatehouse, a silent alarm was activated. So, all I had to do was sit, relax, and wait for the mousetrap to snap shut."

Dammit, I knew something was off, but who could expect that... Damian ran his hand down his face, exhaling a ragged breath as he threw a quick glance at the door. *Where is Cole? What's taking him so long?*

Ricardo probably noticed because he reached for his phone and pressed a few numbers. "Leo, how is our guest doing? Did he recover?" He listened to the reply and added, "Yes, get him anything he asks for. I want him in good shape as soon as possible." He nodded to Damian, hanging up the phone. "Your friend is fine. Don't worry. He should be here in about fifteen minutes."

"Thank you," replied Damian, wondering about Ricardo's heightened perceptiveness.

"The devices in the collection room reacted to your friend's vampiric essence, dropping the bars and releasing the silver mist in the air. As far as the bars blocking the entrance," Ricardo continued with a light flick of his hand, "the alloy they are made of has powder of gray stones in it. This is why it absorbed your magic."

"Why didn't I detect your guards on the premises?" asked Damian. "The second sight allows me to see the glow of human souls. Unless they're not human?"

"Everyone in my household is human, but they all know what goes bump in the night. And just like myself, none of my staff members have magic. But did you notice the vests the guards were wearing?" asked Ricardo, pride lighting up his eyes. "Blocks any kind of vision—human or magical—including the other sight."

"Goddammit," mumbled Damian. "I didn't know tech like this even existed."

"No one does. The world's best-kept secret." Ricardo got up and put the box back into his desk. "I don't think even the Destiny Council knows about it."

"For a mundane, you know an awful a lot about the World of Magic," murmured Damian, shaking his head.

"I grew up with it. My sister and I had been exposed to the supernatural since I was a child," replied Ricardo. "My mother was human, but my father was a powerful *Brujo*. I guess I took after my dear mom. I have zero magic."

He got up and walked to the window, pulling one of the panels aside. Crossing his hands behind his back, he stared outside, his gaze traveling over the night desert. A vibe of unease rose around him, and Damian decided to give him a moment, patiently waiting for him to continue.

"That brings us to the reason we're talking right now,"

THE SHADOW DECEPTION

Ricardo said at length, his voice hoarse. "The reason I didn't restrain you and your vamp and didn't sell you both to the highest bidder."

Feeling the blood drain from his face, Damian swallowed hard, rising. "You are—"

"Yes, I am," Ricardo interrupted him, turning around. A haunted look changed his eyes, his tanned face so pale, it looked sickeningly yellow. "I capture supernatural beings and sell them to the underground circles, mostly the fighting pits. And as you figured out, I use the magical artifacts in my collection as bait. Works like a charm." He sighed, shaking his head. "That's my second business."

He walked back to the wine cabinet and brought the bottle of cognac back, refilling his and Damian's glass. Lifting his glass, he drank it in one gulp and refilled it again.

"Sit down, Damian. I gave you my word—you're safe here," he said softly, his voice almost pleading.

Damian lowered himself on the sofa, his fingers digging into its leather upholstery.

Like a plague, the underground supernatural fighting pits spread not only through the United States but all over the world. In the United States, every state had an individual owner who managed all the underground affairs and shady dealings, including the fighting events and activities associated with them, as well as betting procedures and the payoffs. Rich and insidious, the Heads of each state's Fighting House spared no expense to find the best supernatural fighters their money could buy, and acquiring the Captive Fighters had turned into nothing more than a modern-day slave trade.

The specialized divisions of the FBI, who were well aware of the situation with the underground supernatural fighting pits, put a lot of effort into destroying this malicious circle, but unfortunately, all their work was good for nothing. A few years ago, they had managed to destroy a few Fighting Houses, arresting their Heads, and bringing all their operations down. Unfortunately, fighting the supernatural mob was equivalent to fighting the Hydra. As the FBI removed one Head of a House, another one took their place, and the business ran as smooth and uninterrupted as ever.

"I was the older child of two poor Mexican immigrants," continued Ricardo, his fingers playing with the empty glass. Then he shrugged, and his lips twitched as if he were repeating something to himself. "Anyway, by the age of twenty, I had enough of counting every penny, wondering if I'd have food to feed my little sister or a roof over our heads tomorrow.

"Both my parents passed away, and the local gangs were beating at my doors. So, my sister and I decided to move from California to Arizona, where I wanted to start my own business. The real estate in Arizona, as well as the cost of living, was a lot cheaper, so I found a partner who was willing to back me up and started flipping houses." He rolled his eyes, pursing his lips at the memory. *"Stupido..."*

"Didn't work out, I gather?" asked Damian quietly, putting effort into hiding his disgust.

Ricardo shook his head and leaned forward, resting his forearms on his lap. Then he glanced up at Damian and smirked darkly.

"Disgusting, right? I'm a"—he slammed his fist on his knee and straightened—"disgusting, dirty, no code, no honor... I know." He laughed bitterly. "After a few deals, my business flopped, and both my partner and I lost everything we had." He fell silent, staring into space over Damian's head. "You probably don't know how it feels to work your ass off day in and day out with nothing to show for it. I was a good person, Damian, honest and kind, and every night when I went to bed thinking how I was going to pay my bills, I prayed, asking God what I was doing wrong. I didn't ask him to help me get rich overnight. I prayed to find a job where I could work hard and make enough to be able to pay for my sister's education..." He chuckled bitterly, staring down at his clenched hands. "Anyway, I'm sure you don't want to know all the details... At some point, I stopped praying, and when I hit rock bottom, I met this man..."

Ricardo lowered his face into his hands and stopped talking again. A few seconds later, he refilled his glass and drank it in one gulp.

"I sold my soul, Damian... for thirty pieces of silver," he whispered without meeting Damian's eyes.

"Is that a figure of speech?" asked Damian, stiffening. "Or did you really make some kind of Mephistophelean deal?"

"I don't know," replied Ricardo, biting his lip. "All I know is that I want out. I can't do it anymore. Every time I capture a person and sell them, it's harder and harder for me to play the heartless asshole everyone believes I am. But I made a deal, and I must hold up my end or suffer the consequences... And if it was only me suffering, I would say screw it. But my sister... what he would do to her..."

His voice trailed off, and he pressed his hands to his face. His shoulders shook, and for a few long seconds, he remained silent and motionless.

"The moment I saw you in my house," he continued, lifting his head, "I knew you were the man who could get me out of this mess, Damian. Don't ask me how I knew it. Sometimes, it's just the voice of my intuition, but I learned to trust it. It has saved my hide more than once." He rose with a heavy groan and swayed slightly. "So, I'm giving you your freedom, Damian, in exchange for mine and my sister's. Your freedom and the life of your precious vamp, in exchange for you breaking my"—he waved his hand—"Mephistophelean deal."

"Dammit, Ricardo," muttered Damian, feeling goosebumps covering his arms. "And what makes you think you could hold me restrained long enough to sell, anyway?"

Ricardo huffed, and for a moment, his former look of icy

superiority returned to his face. "Gray stone jewelry can hold down even gods. Something tells me that as powerful as you are, you're not a god."

"I'm not."

"So, what would happen if I decorated your neck, wrists and ankles with the gray-stone-infested silver, creating an inverted pentagram out of your giant body? Huh?"

Damian dropped back in his seat and rubbed his forehead, feeling the wetness of sweat under his fingers.

"I would be in pain for a few days," he replied, his throat as dry as an old parchment. "The pain would be so extreme that over the course of that time, I would die from the pain shock and get resurrected a few times since I'm an immortal being."

"Immortal...?"

"Yes, immortal. Not a god, though," said Damian calmly. "After my body adjusted to the effect of the inverted pentagram, it would take me a few hours to break through its magic and shed your restraints like they were nothing." A dark smile crossed his lips, and he tilted his head slightly, pinning Ricardo with a heavy gaze. "And after I set myself free..." He got up and channeled some of his elemental power, making the walls tremble. "I'd be extremely and profoundly angry with the person who put me through that kind of torture."

"You swore—," croaked Ricardo, taking a few unsteady steps back.

"Oh, yeah, I did. This was just a little demo." Damian smiled with a dismissive wave of his hand. "I gave you an oath—you're safe with me."

"*Oh, dude... ehhh... you're terrifying... Hold your horses though...right? Your fanged buddy is still not here...*" The magpie's voice sounded in Damian's mind, and he flinched, reminded of the bird's presence in the room.

"There are other ways to contain your powers, Damian," said Ricardo, slowly regaining his composure. "I brought you to your knees with large gray stones once, and I can do it again. I have holding cells made of this material and enchanted with the God's snare spell. As we both know, the God's snare circle can disable any being of magic, including you. Am I correct?"

"Yes, you are absolutely correct," agreed Damian, sitting back down, propping his elbow on one of the pillows. "You can hold me in the God's snare for a long time, but nothing lasts forever. Well... except me, of course." He laughed, his laughter sounding scary even to his own ears. "Immortal and all. Anyway, trust me, after I get free, your Mephistophelean deal will seem like a blessing to you."

"Damian, I'm asking you for help," Ricardo said, desperation in his voice.

"And what an awesome job you're doing at that," growled Damian. "You're asking for help by threatening me with slavery, torture and imprisonment? By hurting me and my friend?"

"Come on! Be fair. You broke into my house and tried to steal from me!" Ricardo threw his hands up.

Damian took a deep breath, getting his stretched nerves under control. "Anyway, Ricardo, you need to stop what you're doing. You turned yourself into a slave trader, you know that, right?"

"I know. I don't care about what happens to me, but I don't know how to stop all that without my sister suffering the consequences. Like I said, I made the deal years ago, and now, I have no idea how to break it."

Damian rubbed the back of his neck, moving his head from left to right, exhaustion buzzing through his muscles.

"I can't help you now, Ricardo. I have no idea who your Mephistopheles is and how to break the deal," he said quietly. "But even if I knew how to do it, I have my hands full with the necromancer now."

Ricardo nodded, dropping his head. "As soon as your vamp

is back, you're free to go," he said without looking at Damian. "The dagger is yours."

Dammit... Don't do something you will most certainly regret later... Don't do it... Don't do it... Just say no...

"Ricardo, give me your phone number," he said, silently cursing himself. "Once I'm done with the necromancer, I'll call you. We have to discuss your situation again and see if there is anything that can be done to set you free."

Ricardo raised his face, his eyes alight with hope. He opened his mouth to say something, but a loud knock on the door interrupted him, and he snapped around.

"Come in," he croaked and cleared his throat.

The door opened, and Cole, escorted by a guard, walked into the room. He wore a pair of jeans and a black shirt unbuttoned on his chest. His skin bore no signs of bleeding ulcers, and his eyes didn't glow with thirst.

"Damian," he said, his eyes quickly exploring his brother's body for any visible injuries.

The guard walked up to Ricardo and whispered something into his ear before leaving the room. Ricardo's eyes darted to Cole, and his mouth dropped open.

"Mr. Cole Adams," he whispered with an elegant bow. "Your Majesty."

"Oh, just cut the crap," Cole growled in Ricardo's direction and headed toward Damian. He took in Damian's appearance, and a muscle twitched in his jaw. "You okay?"

Damian gave him a short nod. "You?"

"I'm fine. Mostly," replied Cole, and Damian could see his brother was pissed, barely containing his aggravation. "What are we doing here?"

"We're almost done," replied Damian, turning to Ricardo. "Your phone number, Ricardo?"

Ricardo stilled, his eyes darting from Damian to Cole and then back to Damian. "You two..." he whispered, and a smile crossed his face. It wasn't dark or sarcastic. It was genuine and warm. He went to his desk and grabbed a piece of paper from a stand and a pen. Quickly scribbling a phone number on it, he offered it to Damian. "Now I know you're going to help me, Damian."

Damian took the business card, staring at Ricardo with curiosity. "I already told you that I would. As soon as I'm done with the necromancer, I will call you."

"Yes, you gave me your word." Ricardo smiled again. "But now I know you understand me."

Damian rubbed his forehead, exhaustion of this endless night making his moves slow and fatigued. "Sorry, I think I'm too tired, or maybe the gray stones magic is still affecting me, but I don't follow."

"Your vampire." Ricardo pointed at Cole. "Originally, I thought he was your pet or your sword for hire, but then I saw the way you reacted to his pain back in the collection hall. That made me change my mind, and I thought you were partners or lovers." He cocked his head slightly, and his eyebrows pulled down a little. "Then when I learned that your vampire was the King of the Arizona Court, for a split second, I thought you were his bodyguard."

"Well, I am." Damian chuckled. "I've been guarding his useless body for as long as I can remember."

"Who's guarding who, doofus?" Cole grumbled back.

Ricardo chuckled, shaking his head, his eyes warming up with humor. "Just what I thought." He waved his hand at Damian and then pointed at Cole. "You two are brothers." He sobered up and drew in a long breath. "You would die to protect him, Damian, despite him being a vampire, and I would do the same and more for my sister." He walked toward the door and opened it, gesturing for Damian and Cole to leave. "You can't teleport from my house without triggering the protection mechanisms installed here, but once you are outside, feel free to leave. No one will stop you."

Ricardo bowed to Cole and offered his hand to Damian. Damian swallowed, staring down at the hand of the man who had sold into terrible slavery hundreds of beings of magic, and for a brief moment, all he wanted was to be far away from this place and to never come back here. Ricardo was right—he would do almost anything for his brother, but there were certain lines he wouldn't cross even for Cole. At least, he hoped he wouldn't.

Until you're in the exact same situation as Ricardo, you don't know what you would or wouldn't do. So don't judge...

Making an effort, he took Ricardo's hand and squeezed it.

"Ricardo, be careful," he said quietly. "No one should know about our agreement. For your safety and for the safety of your sister. I'll call you as soon as I can."

He lifted his arm and whistled through his teeth. The magpie flew down from the curtain rod and landed on his shoulder.

"*Hallelujah,*" it muttered, moving its long tail up and down. "*Humans... Just... too... much... talking!*" The bird rolled its eyes and slapped Damian on the back of his head with its wing, making him flinch. "*Stop yapping and get us all the hell out of here while you still can.*"

"I can't agree more," Damian murmured, petting the bird's back, and ushered Cole out the door.

Dammit... Cole was right... I'm a friggin' magnet for trouble, he thought, walking toward the main entrance.

For years, the Destiny Enforcers had been circling the underground supernatural swamp, but no one wanted to kick this hornet's nest willingly. Even Moore and his crazy teams stayed away from it, finding all sorts of excuses. Unlike the FBI, the Destiny Council didn't care about taking apart individual houses. They wanted to find the person who stood above it all, pulling all the strings. Now, thanks to Ricardo, Damian had no choice but to start an investigation.

Who knows, maybe Ricardo's Mephistopheles is the one Magnus has been searching for—, Damian cut his thought short. *The paths of the Board of Destiny are truly unpredictable...*

CHAPTER 17

~ DAMIAN BLAKE ~

It was still dark when Damian and Cole manifested in front of the main entrance into Paradise Manor. Damian opened the door and halted on the threshold. Before letting his brother in, he scanned the building and the surrounding area for any supernatural presence and then nodded, allowing Cole through first.

They walked through the long hallway as quietly as they could, but as Damian expected, no one was sleeping. River, Ace and Jamie sat in the living room with Gypsy curled up on the couch next to River. The TV was playing, but he doubted anyone was watching. The tension between Ace and Jamie seemed to be palpable, but as soon as Damian walked inside, all three of them got up.

"Aw... Sasquatch... You brought me dinner?" purred Gypsy, stretching her paws, her green eyes fixed on Damian's shoulder. "How sweet. You didn't have to."

"Who are you calling dinner, furball!" the magpie screeched, reminding Damian of its presence, and flew up to the curtain rod. "We'll see who's going to eat who."

The stiffness left River's shoulders as her gaze lingered on

Damian's face and then slid down his body, searching for injuries. For a split second, her eyes darted to the little bird chirping under the ceiling, but she just pursed her lips, warmth suffusing her features.

"Damian..." River whispered his name barely audibly. She crossed the living room and wrapped her arms tightly around his neck, rising on tiptoes to kiss him on the cheek. Her fingers threaded through the short hair on the back of his head, and he couldn't help but close his eyes, enjoying her touch, but didn't embrace her, holding his arms down. She pulled away a moment later and gave Cole a quick hug, ruffling his unruly curls. "I'm so glad you are home and safe, boys."

Cole nodded. "Sorry, I need to take a shower and change," he muttered and walked out of the room, barely meeting anyone's eyes.

Damian followed him with his eyes, and dread spread through him, making small hairs on his arms rise.

"I'm sorry," he said apologetically. "I know you haven't slept all night, waiting for us, but give me a few minutes, please. I'll tell you everything as soon as I come back."

He almost ran along the hallway and didn't stop until he reached Cole's bedroom. Without knocking, he pushed the door open and walked inside. Cole wasn't in his room, but the sound of running water suggested his brother was in the shower.

"Cole, are you okay?" Damian knocked on the door, but since no one answered, he walked inside.

The lights were off, and the spacious bathroom was semi-dark, illuminated only by the nightlight installed above the sink. Completely dressed, Cole sat on the floor inside the shower stall, cold water running down on him, plastering his hair to his cheeks. His eyes were wide open, and he was absolutely still in that unnerving vampire's way.

Damian slid the shower door open and walked inside the stall, ignoring the cold rivulets engulfing him. He shut down the faucet and squatted in front of Cole, gently pushing the wet strands of hair from his face.

"What happened?" he asked, but Cole just shook his head and shrugged indifferently. "When the guard carried you away from the collection hall, you were poisoned by silver and absolutely helpless. What did they do to you, Nikolai?"

A deep shudder ran through Cole, his jaw clenched so tightly, his teeth squeaked, but he just shook his head again.

"If they abused you..." exhaled Damian, anger spiking his power. "Ricardo ordered them to treat you well. If they just looked at you the wrong way—"

"They treated me well, alright." Bitter laughter escaped Cole's tightly pressed lips. "They treated me like I was an exotic animal or an expensive toy... touch but don't break. And I was completely helpless against them. They made me feel so... dirty, you know? All this time I felt like my skin was on fire, and I couldn't wait to take a shower to wash their stench off of me. I'm fine, don't worry." He shuddered and looked away. "I went through a lot of shit in my life, Dima. Both of us did. We lived through the dark ages, and we saw things that weren't written in any history books. But I swear to God, never was I treated like an inanimate object." He raised his gaze, and Damian cringed inwardly at the icy hatred in his brother's eyes.

"Oh, Cole..." Damian bit his lip, shaking his head, guilt shredding his insides. "It's my fault you had to suffer through something like this. I should never have let them take you anywhere without me—"

Cole smirked tiredly, running his fingers through his wet hair. "No, Dima, not your fault," he said softly. "And it doesn't really bother me much. In a way, I'm glad it happened."

"You lost me. Is it something vampire-related? How can anyone be happy about being abused?"

"You'll understand in a minute," replied Cole with a faint smirk. "But first tell me, is Ricardo an underground trader?"

"The short answer is yes," Damian said. "He's a trader, but it's not all black and white. I'll tell you everything once you get out of the shower and change. Sorry, bro, but unlike you, I do feel cold, and right now I'm freezing my ass off, sitting with you here—wet, in a puddle of icy water."

Damian got up and offered his hand to Cole. Taking it, Cole rose to his feet and walked out of the stall, dripping cold water on the floor. Damian pulled his own shirt off and grabbed a towel, drying his body as much as he could, shivers running through him.

"I'll be right back," he muttered and walked out the door. He ran to his own bedroom, leaving wet footprints on River's carpet. Without slowing down, he stripped his wet clothes, throwing everything on the floor, quickly changed and returned to his brother.

By the time he came back, the vampire had changed into a fresh set of clothes and sat in a chair with his legs stretched, his face calm and relaxed. Damian sat down on the bed across from him, leaning forward with his arms resting on his lap.

"The guards talked. They just couldn't keep their fucking mouths shut for a goddamn second," growled Cole. "From their conversation, I got a pretty good idea of what Ricardo's *real* business was." An uneven smirk—a mix of undiluted fury and disdain—distorted his lips. "They couldn't stand the idea that Ricardo decided to let us go, saying that someone as powerful as you and a vampire as old as myself could've been sold for a big buck and that would mean a happy payday for them."

"Cole—," started Damian, but his brother shook his head, interrupting him.

"Don't get me wrong, all that was quite unpleasant, but not the end of the world," he continued. "However, there was something they said that made me..." He froze for a moment, his fingers clenched into tight fists. "How do I put it... It made me want to tear their throats with my own fangs!"

Cole growled the last words, anger igniting his eyes with a bright scarlet glow. He laughed again, a cold and dangerous sound rumbling in his chest, and for a brief moment, Damian saw his brother for what he truly was—a deadly, ancient vampire.

"What did they say?" asked Damian, watching Cole close his eyes to force his anger under control.

"They spoke of a vampire who was even older than me. They 'processed' him a few years ago, taking a big chunk of cash in return." Cole glanced out the window where the sky just started to lighten up with the grayish colors of the upcoming sunrise. "Anyway, I'm not going to repeat all the disgusting crap they said. The gist is, I'm positive they were talking about Ruslan, my maker. He disappeared without a trace a few years ago."

"Cole," Damian said softly, "you realize it could have been anyone. There are quite a few old vampires in Arizona."

"No," objected Cole. "Not as many as you think. With Roxana and Luciano gone and Ruslan missing, I'm the oldest vampire in the Greater Phoenix area now, as far as I know. I'm positive they spoke about him. Ruslan is a few thousand years old and an unmatched swordsman. It would make all the sense in the world to sell him to one of the Fighting Houses." He fell silent and punched the air with his fist, anger darkening his features. "But I searched for Ruslan everywhere, including the underground fighting pits. I receive invitations to their high-level events all the time, and as much as I hate being there, I went to every single event—Ruslan wasn't there. I checked every goddamn House in the United States personally, traveling from state to state. He wasn't one of the Captive or Unattached fighters."

"How can you be so sure the guards spoke about him?"

Cole chuckled. "I asked them a few questions, and they actually answered. They said that the Queen of the Vampire Court herself delivered this vampire to them. They said without her help they could never have captured someone like him. Roxana used to hate Ruslan, Dima. That goddamn vindictive bitch..." He bit his lip, a deep wrinkle crossing his forehead. "I'm positive. It was him. Now, the question is, would Ricardo be willing to help me save my maker?"

Damian let out a harsh breath, raking his fingers through his wet hair, feeling as if the noose Ricardo had placed around his neck just became tighter.

"Something tells me he might be quite agreeable," murmured Damian, rising. "If your maker is alive, we'll find him, Cole. One problem at the time, though. Let me take care of the necromancer issue first, and then we'll see what needs to be done."

* * *

IT DIDN'T TAKE LONG for Damian and Cole to tell everything that had happened since they left Paradise Manor. For the most part, it was Cole speaking. Now calm and relaxed, Cole delivered the story in such a lighthearted and humorous manner that even though everything he said was true, it didn't seem as terrifying as it really had been.

Too tired to go through the motions, Damian sat on the couch next to River, barely able to keep his eyes open, his fingers threading through Gypsy's long fur absentmindedly. When Cole was done, Damian filled in some blanks, only skipping the parts of his conversation with Ricardo that he considered confidential. He didn't want to get into the explanation of how the underground fighting pits worked and what part Ricardo played in delivering new fighters to the Heads of Houses, so he left all of it out.

"So, now that you have the dagger, what's your next step?" asked River when they finished their story.

Damian sighed and leaned back, closing his eyes. "What time

is it?" he asked, too tired to raise his hand and look at his wristwatch.

"Ten to five," replied Ace, stifling a yawn.

"I need to get some sleep," he said. "The gray stone magic drained me, and I need to get some rest to restore my power. As soon as I wake up, I'll visit Az. Let's see if he can scry for the necromancer." He got up with a low groan and rolled his sore shoulders. "Cole, if I'm not up by five P.M., wake me."

Damian walked out of the living room, barely understanding what his friends were saying. All this time, the stress of the mission had charged his system with adrenalin, and he didn't feel how truly tired physically and drained magically he was. He staggered along the hallway, supporting himself with his arm against the wall, and when he finally made it to his room, he dropped on top of his bed, dead to the world.

★ ★ ★

"Damian, wake up... wake up..."

At the first touch of his shoulder, Damian jolted upright. With his mind frazzled by the infinite loop of nightmares, he couldn't see clearly right away. Terrifying visions were flashing before his wide-open eyes nonstop. Cries of pain, screams of terror and pleas for help invaded his hearing, turning into a continuous cacophony. Acting on pure instinct, he rolled over his shoulder, sliding to the floor on the other side of the bed, and crouched in a defensive position with his back pressed against the wall, his daggers blazing in his hands.

"Damian! Wake up!"

The voice sounded familiar, but through the overwhelming noise in his ears, he couldn't recognize it.

"Dima!"

A strong arm yanked him away from the wall and wrapped around his neck, cutting his air. Someone's hand applied brutal pressure to the back of his head, forcing it down. He struggled against the hold, but as his oxygen-deprived brain fogged, he lowered his arms powerlessly, and his daggers dropped to the floor with a loud clatter.

"Dima, wake up, brother... You must wake up!"

The voice was familiar. He knew it... he recognized it.

"Cole..." he whispered, his fingers clutching at his brother's arm wrapped around his throat. The blood-curdling pandemonium in his hearing dwindled to nothing, and the visions slowed down, gradually disappearing. "Cole, I'm awake... let go... you're suffocating me."

Cole released the pressure on his head and throat just a little. "Easy now," he whispered into his ear. "Can you stand on your own?"

"I'm fine," he replied, tapping Cole's arm.

The vampire let go slowly, supporting him with his shoulder. Damian straightened and blinked a few times. What he saw made him stagger a step backward, running into Cole, and he froze in place, unable to believe his eyes. His mattress and blanket were destroyed, cut to shreds. Pillows were ripped apart, feathers covering everything around him. River stood a few feet away, clutching her upper arm with her hand, blood trickling between her fingers. She stared at him, her wide eyes overflowing with sympathy.

"Did I do it?" he whispered, feeling cold sweat dripping down his back. He glanced down to see his daggers lying on the floor, the tip of one coated in a bright red liquid. He approached River and gently moved her hand away to expose a shallow cut on her upper arm. "I'm sorry, River. Please, let me heal it."

"It's okay," she said calmly with a dismissive wave of her hand. "Just a scratch."

Cole walked around the destroyed bed and frowned as he stared at Damian, crossing his arms. "Do you wanna talk?"

"No," Damian snapped, glancing at his wristwatch showing a quarter to five. "I need to clean up this mess and leave."

"Not before I have a word with you," River objected dryly and turned to Cole. "Cole, please give us the room."

Cole threw a glance at Damian, a smile of a trickster stretching his lips. "My pleasure." He bowed, hiding the humorous twinkles in his eyes, and headed toward the exit. "Dima, don't do anything I wouldn't do."

"I doubt it's possible," Damian murmured, following his brother with his eyes.

The door closed with a soft thud, and Damian flinched, meeting River's icy-blue eyes. Taking a deep breath, he threw the shredded sheets, blanket and pillows to the floor, shaking his head. He didn't remember doing any of it.

"What was it? PTSD?"

Damian heard River's voice and snapped his head up. "Yeah, I guess you could say that."

"It was almost five, and you were screaming in your sleep, making the entire house shake," River said, pulling a chair closer to the bed and lowering herself on it. "So, I thought I'd wake you up from whatever nightmare you were having..." Her voice trailed, and she looked away, readjusting the strap of her tank top.

"Magnus is right," he whispered. "I need to protect my mind."

"Who's Magnus?" asked River, gazing at him with curiosity.

"Hard to explain. He's the Head of the Destiny Council and my superior. As a Shadow Enforcer, I report directly to him." Damian stopped talking, running his fingers over his chin, the new stubble prickling the tip of his fingers. "But he's also..." He sighed, chewing on his lip. "When Cole and I were killed in the year nine hundred ninety-six, he was the one who brought me back, taught me everything I know, supported me when I was grieving, thinking my only brother was dead. In a way, he was like..."

He cut himself off, his mind skipping through centuries of the love-hate relationship he'd had with Magnus. Then he lifted his face, and a guilty smile touched his lips.

"River, if you hear me screaming like this again, don't try to wake me up," he said with a sigh. "Could be dangerous, and I would never forgive myself if I hurt you."

"When I walked into your room," she continued, ignoring his statement, "the entire room was flooded with a blinding light." She pointed at him, her eyes alight with awe. "Your light or your daggers', or both. You were screaming as if someone was tearing your beating heart out of your chest."

"River—"

"I've seen men suffering from PTSD before, but I swear to God, I've never seen so much pain in one human being." She looked away, her hands clenched on her lap. "What was it, Dima? You can tell me. You can trust me to do whatever it takes to help you."

"I know I can trust you." He got up and approached her, taking one knee by her side. "But I don't want to talk about it, River. And as cliché as it sounds, it's truly not you. It's me."

He channeled the power of Earth, collecting some of the healing energy in his right hand. She looked at him, her large blue eyes surrounded by long copper lashes just inches away from his. Without breaking their eye contact, he moved his right hand over the laceration on her upper arm, channeling the healing energy of Earth through it. As a soft, orange glow surrounded his hand, she gasped, her gaze turning slightly drunk, and a tender smile touched her full lips.

"Your eyes are glowing orange," she whispered in one breath.

He ignored her, watching her wound close up slowly. Once it was completely healed, he removed his hand, ready to get up, but she turned slightly in her chair to face him and seized his chin with her fingers, lifting his face.

"Look at me, soldier," she whispered, gently moving the long strands of his hair drenched with sweat to expose his face. "You're beautiful."

"That's new... no one has ever told me something like that yet..."

She lowered her face a little, just enough for him to feel the warm touch of her breath to his skin, and he froze in place, unable to move. The Destiny Enforcer in him screamed, fighting, demanding to get up and leave, but he couldn't, his heart thumping in his chest. She leaned forward, and her lips touched his. It wasn't even a kiss. The connection was so light and so fast that he barely felt it, but everything inside him buzzed with desire, with the need the likes of which he hadn't felt in centuries. It wasn't just sexual desire. For the first time in many years, he needed and wanted more than just physical connection, and that scared him.

Destiny Enforcers can't have attachments... The words he had said to Ace a while ago rang in his fogged mind. This rule was placed there for a good reason.

"River, please," he moaned, somewhere in the depth of his mind realizing he was on one knee, begging for mercy. "Please, I can't—"

She cupped his scarred cheek with her hand, and he seized her wrist but had neither strength nor desire to pull it away. A warmth expanded in his chest, his body responding to her tender touch despite the commands of his mind. She pulled away just a little, taking in his appearance, and a dreamy smile ghosted her lips.

"Maybe you can't, but I can..." She lowered her face to his and kissed him, her tongue forcing his lips apart, her hand seizing his hair on the back of his head, pulling him closer.

A low growl rumbled somewhere in his throat, and in one motion, he got up and scooped her off the chair, pressing her to his chest. He made his way to the bed, lowered her on top of the shredded mattress and leaned over her, bracing his arms on either side of her body. She looked up at him, and her lips parted with a soft gasp. Her eyelashes fluttered, her gaze drunk with desire, and he couldn't take his eyes off of her.

Heat coursed in his veins, fogging his mind, and passion took hold of him. He kissed her, his kiss demanding and hard, a lot harder than he intended, but he had a hard time controlling himself. In response, she moaned and encircled his neck, pulling him down.

"Dima..." she breathed, and hearing his real name on her lips sent electricity down his spine.

He moaned, every inch of his body craving her touch. "River, please stop..." Gathering whatever willpower he still had in his body and mind consumed by desire, he pulled away slightly, his chest rising and falling with rapid breaths. "I shouldn't... I can't..." He couldn't speak, he could barely think.

Her arms unlocked, releasing his neck, but her hand slipped down, grazing his side before settling on his groin. A low growl rumbled in his chest, turning into a hiss as she stroked him gently.

"Ahh... I think you can..." She chuckled, sounding a little intoxicated. "You so-so-so can..."

She let go of him and slipped down from the bed, moving to the side to escape the prison of his arms. His elbows wobbled and gave in, and he fell flat on the bed, turning on his back. She glanced at him, and a tender smile touched her lips.

"Well, as you wish then." She tapped her wristwatch and flicked her eyebrow at him. "I think you may need to take a nice, cold shower before you go to see Az." She waved her hand and headed toward the door. Halting in the doorway, she turned around and added, "Don't worry about cleaning your room. I'll take care of it for you while you're away."

As soon as she left, Damian scrabbled into a sitting position and shook his head, rubbing his cheeks with his hands.

"Dammit. How did I let it happen?" he asked himself out

loud and got up, heading toward the shower, his mind still scrambled, thousands of thoughts rushing through it at the same time.

I can't get attached... I can't let her get... Sam is going to kill me if he finds out... and he'll be right... It's too dangerous... For her and for me... What if... what if...

What if...

CHAPTER 18

~ DAMIAN BLAKE ~

The sun disappeared behind the horizon, and bluish shades of early dusk colored the surroundings, giving everything a mysterious look. A gust of cold wind made Damian shiver in his light leather jacket as he halted in front of Az's door. The neon 'Open' sign in his window was off, and Damian could only hope that the old man was home. He quickly scanned the house and the neighborhood with his other sight. As before, he didn't find anything alarming and knocked on the door.

A soft shuffling noise announced that Az was home, and a moment later, the lock clicked, and the door opened no more than an inch. A giant eye behind a thick lens of eyeglasses peered through the crack, and the door closed again. The chain jingled, Az opened the door and peeked outside, observing the street in front of his house before ushering Damian in.

As soon as he walked inside, Az slammed the door shut and turned to face him. "Do you have it?" he asked, shoving his skinny arms into the pockets of his robe. Unlike last time, he was fully dressed beneath his robe, but the addition of jeans and a shirt didn't do him any favors, instead making him look even frailer.

"I have it." Damian reached in his pocket and produced the dagger, holding it at his shoulder level where Az couldn't reach it.

Az's gaze darted to the dagger and for the briefest of moments, a gluttonous light ignited in the bottom of his enlarged eyes. However, it was so fast that Damian wasn't sure he hadn't imagined it.

"This is it. Perfect," Az murmured calmly and separated the bamboo curtain, gesturing for him to come in.

Damian walked inside and headed toward the table. Pulling a chair out, he sat down, twirling the dagger in his hand. Somewhere far away, a dog howled—the sound filled with so much despair that his skin crawled. He closed his eyes and connected with the power of Earth, hoping to understand the animal, but the dog remained silent.

Feeling a tap on his shoulder, he let go and opened his eyes. Az stood across from him with a folded paper and a small crystal in his hands. He unfolded the paper on the table, carefully ironing all the creases with his hands, and placed the crystal on top of it. Damian glanced at a large map of three states divided by county lines and showing the major cities and then raised his eyes at the old wizard.

"This map shows only three states—California, Arizona and Nevada. What if JB is not in one of these states?" he asked.

Az smirked, his thin lips stretching enough to show off his overly bleached teeth.

"Very much possible." He shrugged indifferently. "There is a chance he's not in the realm of humans at all. However"—he raised a finger—"there is only one necromancer that I know of who's capable of conjuring wurdulaks, and it's JB. So, something tells me he is somewhere here. If everything you told me is true, he can't be far. Let's start with these three states, and we'll take it from there." He ran his finger over the crystal and smiled, taking a deep breath. "Let's see if I have what it takes to find this old bugger."

He extended his hand palm up, giving Damian a pointed stare. Damian glanced at his hand and something twitched in him, his heart sinking to his knees with dread. The dog howled again, and a few more answered its call, echoing through the neighborhood.

Az raised his head, staring around, concern reflecting on his face. "Damn animals," he muttered, shaking his head. "It's been like this all day long. Howling and barking. I wonder if someone has died." He glanced at Damian as if searching for his support. "You know how animals are. They can see a lot more than we can." He sighed, pursing his lips, and moved his hand closer to Damian. "This is that moment where I need the dagger for a few minutes to cast the scrying spell. I promise I'll give it back to you as soon as I'm done."

Stifling a sigh, Damian placed the dagger in the wizard's hand, his heart speeding up. Az took it and put it on the table in front of the crystal. Barely paying attention to the weapon, he focused strictly on the map. For a moment, he studied it with his eyes, then he touched the crystal, muttering something under his breath. A soft light ignited in the depths of the rock, and a shimmering cloak of magical energy wrapped around it.

"Ready?" muttered Az, but Damian wasn't sure he was asking him. "Here goes..."

He placed his hands on either side of the dagger without actually touching it and started to chant. In the beginning, his words sounded like a soft murmur and Damian couldn't make out anything he was saying. As he progressed with his enchantment, his voice became louder, his words carrying through the house loud and clear. A glowing orb materialized between his opened palms, and the weapon lifted a few inches in the air, surrounded by the glow of Az's magic.

The orb of light encapsulating the dagger became brighter, and all of a sudden, a single ray extended from it, creating a bridge between the blade and the crystal. It shone brighter and brighter, and soon the entire room was flooded with its light, making it impossible to see anything. Damian grunted and opened his second sight, but except for the brightness of Az's magical energy, he could see nothing.

"Az!" yelled Damian, raising his arm to protect his vision.

"Here... Almost..."

Damian heard the strained voice of the old wizard right in front of him, and a moment later, the light subsided. He pressed his hands to his eyes, blinking the dancing red and white spots from his vision. When he could finally see again, he saw Az sitting in his chair, breathing hard as if he had just ran a few miles. The dagger still lay on the table next to the crystal, seemingly untouched.

"Take it," whispered Az, barely moving his lips. His face was gray with exhaustion, and he looked like he was ready to cross the veil. "I'm done. I'm too old and not powerful enough for this kind of spell, but it worked nonetheless." With an effort, he pushed himself up and leaned over the map, pointing down at the state of California, a winning smile stretching his lips. "I was right. JB is still in the same place. He didn't move. I know exactly where you can find him."

Az grabbed his notepad and a pen and quickly scribbled something on it. Ripping the page off, he offered it to Damian. Damian took the paper and grabbed the dagger from the table, putting it back in his pocket.

"Are you kidding me?" he mumbled as he read the address on the paper. "The world's most dangerous Master of the Dark Arts lives in Encino?"

Az chuckled faintly, wiping sweat off his forehead. "What can I tell you, slayer. He was always an eccentric fellow." He got up and swayed slightly. "When you find him, tell him Az said hello—"

A loud howl interrupted the old wizard, and he stilled, frowning. Another howl followed, and at least ten more joined in a gut-wrenching chorus. Somewhere nearby, a cat's terrified meow joined the cacophony of the dogs' voices, and Damian froze in place, small hairs rising on the back of his neck.

"Something is not right..." mumbled Az, but Damian raised his hand, silencing him.

Connecting with the energy of Earth, he sharpened his hearing, trying to distinguish separate words in the cacophony of voices. The words came muffled and unclear, but it was enough for him to capture the meaning, and for a split second, sticky fingers of fear wrapped around his heart.

"Hide... run... it's coming... death is coming... hide..."

The voices of the animals repeated the same phrase over and over, making the blood run cold in Damian's veins. Suddenly, a heavy silence enveloped the neighborhood. It came so unexpectedly that for a moment, he thought a silencing spell was cast in the area. The dogs stopped barking and howling. The shrilling meows of the cats died down. Even the birds and cicadas fell silent.

"What's happening—," started Az, but Damian frowned, holding his hand up.

He opened his second sight and held his breath, sweat trickling down his back. The entire area, for as far as he could reach with his sight, was under a heavy cloak of dark magical energy. He recognized the energy signature, and his stomach twisted painfully, alarm ringing in his mind.

"Procedia Amnia," he whispered with a light wave of his hand, placing a protection spell over the room.

"A basic protection spell? Are you kidding me?" Az raised his hands, backing away from Damian. "On, no. No, no, no... What's coming?"

"Death is coming," Damian muttered over his shoulder, pushing the table to the side of the room. "It could be coming for you or for me—take your pick. It makes no difference. I can't let monsters run amok in a residential neighborhood." His daggers materialized in his hands, and he channeled his magic through them, igniting them with a brilliant, white light.

"You're no slayer... What are you?" mumbled Az, raising his arms, fear contorting his features.

"Does it matter?" asked Damian, switching his attention to the entrance just in time to see the door explode inward. A shower of wooden splinters and dust impacted his shield, obscuring his vision for a moment.

"Oh, God... My home... My business..." Az moaned, burying his hands into his fluffy hair, devastation in his words.

"Or your life," growled Damian without taking his eyes off the doorway as a few shadowy figures burst inside the house.

They halted for a second, their glowing, red eyes darting from Damian to Az, and their lips drew back in a snarl, exposing four terrifying fangs. There were at least five of them inside the house, and as far as Damian could see, a few more stood in the front yard, waiting for the opportunity to jump into action.

One of the men stepped forward and pulled out a small orb glowing with a sinister purple light. Meeting Damian's eyes, a horrendous smile distorted his face, stretching his lips wider than it was humanly possible. He touched the orb and growled something incomprehensible. A dark ray of purple light burst from under his fingers, impacting the shield of Damian's protective magic. Damian channeled more of his power through it, but to his shock, the ray of dark magic cut through it as if it were nothing. As the protective magic collapsed, the man snickered and opened his mouth wider, saliva dripping from his fangs.

"*Moderius*," Damian shouted. Expecting for the wurdulaks to run forward at their full speed, he wanted to slow them down, but he had no idea how wrong he was.

Moving too fast despite Damian's spell, the front wurdulak touched the glowing orb again, muttering something under his breath, and it morphed into a short spear shimmering with a dark, purple mist. He pulled his massive arm back and propelled it at Damian's chest.

With no time left to think, Damian raised his daggers, hoping to deflect the magical energy of the spear at least partially and protect the old wizard, but Az seized his arm and pushed him with more strength than he expected, making him stagger aside. The spear impacted the old man in the shoulder, piercing it through, and then dissipated. Az cried out in pain and collapsed, blood gushing from the deep hole, soaking his robe through.

"*Ventius*," shouted Damian, reinforcing his spell with his elemental power. A powerful blast of wind rushed forward, throwing the wurdulaks back and out of the house. Damian gathered the energy of Earth in his hands and spread his arms wide. The ground shook and shifted, and thick, thorny bushes broke through. Entwining, they grew higher and higher until the doorway was completely blocked.

Damian knew this wasn't going to hold the wurdulaks forever. It would take them just a few minutes to break through, but this gave him an opportunity to take care of Az. Making his daggers vanish, he lowered to his knees, quickly examining the wound on the old man's shoulder. While it was bleeding profusely, it wasn't fatal. Healing him wasn't an option, however, as the healing magic would take a lot of his strength, and he still had to deal with the wurdulaks.

"Az," he whispered, shaking him gently.

The old wizard cracked his eyes open and hissed in pain, clasping his injured shoulder. Quickly visualizing the entrance into the emergency room of the Blue Creek Memorial, Damian cringed inwardly, hoping that no one would notice the old man appear from thin air.

"Az, I'm going to teleport you to the hospital," he whispered quickly. "I can't have you materialize in front of all the people there. So, I'll send you to the small alley on the left side of the main building. Can you make it from there to the ER?"

"I think so," mumbled the old man, struggling to sit up. As Damian placed his hand to his shoulder and raised his other hand, ready to snap his finger, Az stopped him. "How about you, Damian? Come with me. You can't fight all these monsters alone."

Damian chuckled, shaking his head. "I can't leave. Someone needs to deal with these fanged assholes. Besides, 'alone' is what I do best." He snapped his fingers, and Az vanished from the house, leaving a small puddle of blood on the floor.

The walls of the building shook, and the windows exploded with a violent bang, a cloud of sparkling glass splinters bursting inside. An avalanche of monsters forced themselves through the openings, struggling to push their massive frames into the small entrance hall. With his mind working on overdrive, Damian looked for the best way to handle the situation, and as a crazy thought flashed through his mind, a dark smirk crossed his face.

Without waiting for all of them to make it inside, Damian waved his hand, removing the shield of the thorny bushes. Moving as fast as he could muster, he bolted toward the exit. A few wurdulaks stepped in his way, but he didn't slow down. His blazing daggers materialized in his hands, and he spun around, decapitating the wurdulak closest to him, cutting through the chests of the other two. They hissed furiously, staggering back. Damian rushed past them out the door, avoiding their hands with sharp claws. Before the rest of the monsters could realize what he was up to, he ran to the fence and stopped there, spinning around to face them. Placing two fingers in his mouth, he whistled.

"Hey, assholes!" he yelled, waving his arms. "Looking for someone?"

For a heartbeat, the wurdulaks stilled, but as they realized they had lost their prey, they spun around and rushed toward him, creating a stampede.

"Moderius," yelled Damian, casting the same spell again to slow them down to a more or less reasonable speed.

The monsters roared angrily, fighting the resistance of his magic. He laughed, the excitement of the fight charging him with adrenaline. He jumped over the fence and quickly surveyed the area. While the street seemed to be empty, he wasn't oblivious to the fact that anyone could have been watching him from behind closed blinds, filming everything with their smartphones.

"Moderius Amplio," he hissed, increasing the potency of his spell to slow the monsters down some more. Turning toward them, he roared, "You want me? Catch me if you can!"

The wurdulaks responded with furious screams. Damian laughed again, a wild excitement breaking to the surface. He turned around and took off running toward the abandoned building he used as his teleportation spot. Glancing over his shoulder, he ensured that the wurdulaks followed him, counting fifteen of them. Without slowing down, he burst through the door of the half-demolished building.

As he zoomed through the large living area and then through the kitchen, he waved his hand and shouted, *"Exitius!"*

The wall blew up with a thunderous bang, pieces of concrete, wood and debris flying around. Choking on the dust lingering in the air, he slipped through the opening into the spacious backyard. Once outside, he twirled around and channeled the power of Earth, completely surrendering to it.

As soon as he saw all fifteen wurdulaks enter the house, he moved his hand in a wide arch and muttered a spell, encapsulating the building in a powerful shield to block the wurdulaks from leaving. Then he spread his arms wide, and the ground shook violently, responding to his mental command. Deep fractures slithered through the walls and the roof caved in completely, but Damian didn't stop, localizing the earthquake to the area under the base of the house. The walls gave in, collapsing on top of the monsters, and a cloud of dust and debris rose in the air, a mighty boom shattering the stillness of the night.

Damian didn't stop. Burying the wurdulaks under a few tons of bricks and concrete wasn't enough to kill them. Powered by magic, these monsters weren't easy to destroy. Dropping to one knee, he rooted his fists into the ground. Channeling more and more power, he screamed, the muscles on his back and arms bulging from unimaginable strain. A thick pulsing vein appeared on his neck as he pushed himself to the extreme. The ground separated beneath the house, and the entire building—or what was left of it—fell into the deep, giant pit he had created. Breathing hard, he jumped to his feet and ran to the edge of the hole. Channeling all the magic he could gather from nature and from within, he extended his arms toward the bottom of the pit.

"*Ignius Amplio!*" he shouted, barely able to breathe. Two powerful jets of fire escaped his hands, flooding the pit, turning it into a flaming inferno. The screams of the burning monsters reached his ears, and a cold smirk crossed his face.

A few seconds later, it was over. Damian let go of his magic and stood, swaying, observing his handiwork. The house was gone, replaced by a giant hole in the ground. The fire still crackled at the bottom, dark swirls of smoke rising high above it, probably visible from miles away. He felt so drained by the extreme use of his magic and elemental power, he could barely keep an upright position, but his work wasn't done yet. With an effort of will, he connected with his element again, and the pit closed slowly, concealing the leftovers of the house and the piles of ash left by the wurdulaks.

Magnus is going to kill me... A faint thought flashed through his mind. *If this didn't expose the World of Magic, I don't know what would have...*

He snapped his fingers and vanished from the now empty lot.

CHAPTER 19

~ DAMIAN BLAKE ~

Damian materialized next to the backdoor of a tiny bookshop owned by the representative of the Wardens Order in the back alley of a small plaza. Breathing hard, with sweat plastering his shirt to his body, he leaned forward, bracing his arms against the door, trying to compose himself enough to speak coherently. Taking a few deep breaths, he pushed away and knocked, feeling the world starting to spin around him.

The door opened almost immediately, and an older man appeared in the doorway. As his eyes halted on Damian, taking in his appearance, his mouth dropped open, his gray, bushy eyebrows rising. Even though they had met only once previously when Cole introduced him to Master Warden Luc de la Crosse, Damian recognized the human Warden right away.

"Mr. Cooper," said Damian faintly. "Please... can I... I... need..."

"Commander Blake, are you okay?" mumbled Aaron, ushering him inside. "What can I do to help you, my lord?"

"Water... and an empty room," Damian managed to say, sounding apologetic. "I need just a few minutes of solitude, please... Also... sorry to... bother... need the Master Warden here."

Aaron escorted Damian into an empty room at the back of the shop and brought a bottle of water, placing it on the table in front of him. As soon as the Warden left, closing the door, Damian channeled some of his power and drew a rune in the air. Touching the Shadow Enforcer's rune on his shoulder, he connected them and whispered, "Magnus, I summon thee..."

An oval communication window replaced the rune, but a few seconds later, it still remained dark and silent.

"Come on, Magnus," whispered Damian, dropping back on the chair powerlessly, the room around him swimming and flowing in a continuous nauseating motion. "I know you're ready to make a few new belts out of my hide, but—"

"Right you are, Dmitri!" Magnus' voice sounded above him. Damian got up, swaying on his feet, and met the blazing gaze of his superior without blinking. Magnus frowned and continued, "What the hell is wrong with you, Commander! You exposed the World of Magic to anyone who cared to see!"

The Head of the Destiny Council waved his hand and stepped aside, showing him the screen of a large TV. A cheerful lady from the local News Channel happily delivered breaking news about the unusual seismic activity with the epicenter in Blue Creek, Arizona. Magnus snapped his fingers, switching the TV to a YouTube video of Damian standing next to a giant hole in the ground where a house used to be, his entire body glowing with bright, orange light.

"Ah..." Damian moaned, running his hand over his face, just now realizing that his skin was covered in dirt, blood and sweat. "I hate modern tech... How do they have all that just a few minutes later?" Meeting Magnus' infuriated gaze, he shrugged, spreading his arms, a guilty smile tugging at his lips. "I had to. This was the only way I could kill fifteen wurdulaks. Or did you want me to leave them running around Blue Creek, sir?"

"The proper salutation is *'my lord'*, Dmitri!" barked Magnus, throwing his hands up. "What the hell were you thinking, Commander? Why did you have to drop the entire building six fit under? Couldn't you just lock the wurdulaks in that house with your spell and set it on fire? No one would have questioned it twice!"

"I'm not a friggin' Phoenix or a Fire Salamander," shouted Damian, slamming his hand on the table. "I can't control fire! The wind would spread it around before I could snap my fingers. Burning them inside a pit was the safest way to kill them all!"

"You damn right, you're not a Fire Salamander," Magnus shouted back. "That boy is only thirty, and he's a hundred times better than you with his power! I would never have had this kind of problem on my hands if he was in your place. Why can't—"

"Why can't I be more like him?" asked Damian snidely, folding his arms as his frustration started to dwindle. "Aw, Magnus, *my lord*." He cocked his head a little, all but pouting. "And here I thought Daddy loved all his Children of Elements equally. But you do have favorites. I'm wounded."

"You... what... what the..." Magnus stuttered but then threw his hands up, shaking his head. "I already forgot what kind of shenanigans I could expect from you, Dmitri." He waved his head, his anger visibly dissipating.

"Admit it, you miss my shenanigans." Damian chuckled, lowering on the chair.

"Not in the slightest," huffed Magnus, his silvery eyes laughing. "Well, maybe just a little. Between you and your Cossack, you used to drive me crazy." He waved his hand dismissively. "Anyway, why did you summon me besides covering your PR disaster?"

Damian sighed, sobering up. "Mostly, I needed you to cover the exposure," he said quietly. "But also, I wanted to give you the report on the situation with the necromancer." As briefly as he could, he told the Head of the Destiny Council everything he found out so far and his plan.

Magnus stilled, and his eyes lit up a bright white. A few seconds later, he let out a soft breath, and the light in his eyes dwindled. "I don't know any Dark Wizards residing in Encino. That's strange, but I'll check my books again after we're done," he said quietly. "If you find the necromancer, summon Cossack. I'll have him on standby in case you need him. I think you'll need all the help you can get, and your brother can't help you in this case."

"Yes, my lord," replied Damian, slightly inclining his head.

"And I do hope"—he stressed the word *'do'*—"that after you're done in California, Arizona is not going to become a coastal state, Dmitri," grumbled the Head of the Destiny Council, placing his hands on his hips.

Damian snorted. "I'll do my best," he said. "But you know, it could improve the value of Real Estate in Arizona."

"I'm going to flog you next time you show your face in the Destiny Council realm," murmured Magnus, resigned. "On a serious note, Commander, be careful and report to me as soon as you're back." The Head of the Destiny Council waved his hand and closed the communication window.

Damian sighed in relief and took the water bottle, taking a few gulps. Then he folded his arms on the table and lowered his head on top of his arms. Closing his eyes, he took a deep breath, feeling as if he were on a boat, the floor wobbly and shaky under his feet. He didn't fall asleep, but his mind kept drifting on and off, lingering on the border with unconsciousness.

A soft knock on the door was too loud to his overly stretched senses, and he jolted to his feet, staring in the direction of the sound with wide-open eyes. Luc de la Crosse walked inside, holding his hands up. Dressed in black attire with a clerical collar, he looked just like a regular young priest, but

Damian knew better—he was looking at an ancient warrior, forged in the many battles he had survived through the centuries.

"Commander Blake," Luc greeted him, giving him a quick once-over. "Aaron informed me that you needed my assistance."

Damian released a ragged breath and inclined his head. "Brother de la Crosse, thank you for coming."

Luc's lips twitched in a tiny smile as he pulled a chair out and sat down across from Damian. "Since I've become a Master Warden, no one calls me 'Brother' anymore."

"I'm sorry, I didn't mean to—," started Damian, lowering on his chair, but Luc waved his hand dismissively.

"Actually, it's nice. Brings back some good memories." His gaze fogged, his mind traveling down memory lane. He sighed and focused his bright, hazel eyes on Damian. "What can I do for you, Commander?"

"I need a potion that can open a portal to a location of my choice," replied Damian.

"Oh?" Luc's eyebrows shot up. "That is an unusual request for a Destiny Enforcer. I believe you all can teleport, so if you know the exact location, you don't need a portal. If I'm not mistaken, you can also open portals by using runes. Besides, as a Commander, you have wings." He leaned back in his chair and tilted his head a little, humorous sparkles dancing in his attentive eyes. "Please, Commander Blake, indulge my curiosity. With all the powers you harbor in this massive body of yours, why would you need a potion to open a portal?"

Damian stifled a sigh. As nice and friendly as Luc was, he was a typical representative of his Order—there was absolutely nothing that Wardens would do until they had all the information and understood everything to the tiniest detail.

"It's not for me, Master Warden," he said softly. "It's for my brother and River Evans. I'm going to leave Blue Creek as soon as I get some rest, and I have no idea how long I'll be away. With the werewolves on the war path, I need them to have a way to leave Paradise Manor without attracting any unwanted attention."

"As ancient and unique as your brother is, he's still just a vampire. He has no magic. He can't cast a spell to sustain a portal, even if he has a potion. And River is human," objected Luc de la Crosse, his youthful features becoming harder. "If you don't believe they are safe in Paradise Manor, would you like me to take Cole to one of the Destiny Council's holding facilities? If he's out of Paradise Manor, River will be safe in her home. Besides, you can't take a chance of the wards in the left wing failing, and you know it."

Feeling the blood draining from his face, Damian swallowed. "Perun almighty. No, Luc, please don't do it," he replied. "I would never do something like that to my brother."

Luc smirked with a half-shrug. "He's not going to enjoy the stay, but he'll be absolutely safe there, and the safety of the dangerous magical artifact will be guaranteed."

"I just need the potion, Master Warden. It's a precaution," replied Damian, rubbing his sore shoulder, feeling the exhaustion settling in his very bones. "I have a Junior Enforcer guarding Cole twenty-four-seven and a young wizard. I'm sure one of them can sustain a portal open for a short time."

Luc de la Crosse got up and waved his hand, opening a portal. "Give me a moment, *mon ami*. Don't go anywhere."

He walked through the rotating and shimmering cerulean mass and disappeared on the other side. He came back just a few minutes later, holding a small vial with a semi-transparent liquid inside.

"Here is the potion you need, Commander," he said, placing the vial on the table in front of Damian. "I trust you know how to complete it to make sure it'll open in the right destination."

"Yes, sir," replied Damian, placing the vial in the pocket of his jacket. Then he pressed his fist to his chest over his heart and slightly inclined his head. "Thank you. I owe you one."

Luc smiled, offering him his hand. "I've met quite a few of your kind in my line of business," he said as Damian shook his hand. "Rigid bunch of self-centered arseholes, forgive my French... Especially Moore." Luc visibly shuddered, his French accent heavier than ever. "But you don't seem to be like the rest. Peculiar." He scratched the back of his head and then readjusted his low ponytail, but since Damian remained silent, he smiled and added, "Godspeed, Commander." He made a sign of the cross, blessing him. "May the Lord be with you."

An uneven smirk curved Damian's lips before he could stop it, but he managed to refrain from saying anything that could potentially insult the Master Warden and inclined his head in a light bow.

"Thank you for your help, Master Warden." He snapped his fingers and vanished from the bookshop.

* * *

HE MATERIALIZED next to the entrance into Paradise Manor. His phone buzzed in his pocket, vibrating vigorously, and he lowered himself on the cold steps, pulling out the device to answer the call.

"Damian?" a deep, raspy voice said on the other side of the line. "This is Hawk. Can you talk?"

"Hey, Hawk... Yeah, perfect timing." He frowned, an expectation of trouble coiling in the pit of his stomach. "As a matter of fact, I was going to call you myself. What's going on?"

"You were?" A vibe of unease was almost palpable in the old Alpha's voice. "You go first then."

"Hawk, does your offer still stand?" asked Damian, pressing the phone closer to his ear. "In case of emergency, can Cole seek your protection?"

"Of course." The answer came immediately, without a shadow of hesitation. "You and your brother have my word and the protection of my pack. What's going on?"

"I have no idea," replied Damian with a sigh. "Just a few hours ago, I was attacked by fifteen wurdulaks in the middle of a residential neighborhood." He fell silent, raking his hand through his hair. "It's getting worse, Hawk, and the only thing I know is that I must stop this necromancer now, before the situation escalates into a major disaster. I have only one lead, so I have no choice but to follow it. So, tomorrow, I'm leaving for California early in the morning, and I want to make sure that if push comes to shove, Cole can count on you."

"Yes, he can. You and your brother are always welcome here," replied Hawk. "Actually, this is the reason I called you, Lord Enforcer. In case you didn't know, I wanted to tell you that an entire family of werewolves has been slaughtered by something with fangs just a few hours ago." He stopped talking and a heavy silence invaded the phone line. "Five people, Damian... three of them were just kids..." He let out a shuddering breath. "They were Simon's wolves. I'm afraid there is nothing I can do to stop them from retaliating with full force. They're coming for your brother and his vamps."

"Perun almighty," exhaled Damian, pinching the bridge of his nose. "Why now?" He closed his eyes for a moment and took a deep breath. "I have a potion that can open a portal straight to your gates. If Simon's pack attacks Paradise Manor, Cole will use it. He may have River Evans and a young woman with him. She is a Destiny Enforcer in training charged to shadow him. Is that okay with you?"

"In training?" Hawk chuckled mirthlessly. "Are you playing a schoolteacher now, Commander?"

"You have no idea," muttered Damian, rising. "Thank you for your help, Hawk."

"Don't mention it," grumbled the old Alpha. "I mean it—

don't mention it to anyone. If anyone finds out that I gave the protection of my pack to a vamp..." A soft growl sounded in the phone, followed by a deep sigh. "Good luck, Commander. The sooner you sort this mess out, the better it is for us all."

"Thanks... I was going to get some rest and leave in the morning, but after talking to you, I think I'll leave tonight. I'll call you as soon as I'm back in Blue Creek."

Damian hung up the phone and moved toward the entrance, his feet seeming too heavy to take another step. He knew no one was going to be asleep, waiting for his return, so he headed straight to the living room. He halted in the doorway, leaning heavily against the doorframe. Cole got up but didn't come closer, taking in Damian's appearance.

"When?" he asked quietly, understanding darkening his features.

"Right away," replied Damian, pushing off the doorframe. "Mercedes?"

"It's yours," replied Cole with a half-shrug.

Damian approached his brother, and for a heartbeat, they stood silently, their eyes locked. Then Damian reached in his pocket and produced the small vial. Channeling his magic, he touched it, drawing a shining rune on its side. Once the rune dissipated, he took Cole's hand and placed the vial in his palm.

"Cole, I had a call from Hawk," he said softly. "He can no longer hold the werewolves back. They will be coming for you, and it's not going to take them long to find you here." He observed River, Ace and Jamie who were staring at him in shock.

"The house is warded," said Ace, her face ashen. "The wards were placed by the Guardians. They will hold."

"Only the left wing of the house is warded, and any wards can be broken, given enough hard work and perseverance," replied Damian, speaking through gritted teeth. "I can't count on that, and I can't jeopardize the integrity of the Guardians' magic."

"I don't understand." River threw her hands up. "These wards were enough to hold gods. Why are you worried about a few angry lycanthropes?"

Damian sighed, rubbing his forehead.

"Mara is still in the wind, River. I can't find her, and I don't know if she's somehow involved in all this." He waved his hand around. "If Simon's attacks weaken the protective magic just a little, Mara may step in, and who knows if the combined force of werewolves and an ancient dark deity will do the job. I can't take this chance, sorry. The magical lake under Paradise Manor must be protected at all costs. So, if Simon and his pack attacks, we must take the fight away from Paradise Manor."

"I understand." River dropped her head, unease lingering over her.

Damian jerked his thumb at the potion Cole held in his hands. "This potion will take you to the gates into Hawk's property. His wards have been placed by a Celtic god and the Fire Elemental and reinforced by elven magic. Besides, Hawk offered the protection of his pack. If the werewolves attack Paradise Manor, don't wait here to see if the wards will hold—"

"But Damian, I don't—," Ace started with unconcealed defiance in her words, but fell silent as Damian sent a frosty gaze her way.

"Ace, you will use your magic to open the portal," he said quietly, iron tones in his voice. "I trust you know how to keep the portal open long enough for everyone to go through?"

"Yes, Commander Blake," she replied, throwing a quick glance at Cole.

Damian switched his attention to River, icy dread coiling in the pit of his stomach like a poisonous serpent. He stepped closer to her and took her hand into his.

"River, I know you have your duty and work obligations. I

can't order you to do what I say, but I'm begging you to listen," he said, gazing down at her. "Stay home. Don't go to work, and no matter what you do, do not leave Paradise Manor. If the werewolves attack, I want you to leave with Cole and Ace." He stopped talking, searching her face. "Please... Do it for me."

She met his eyes, and her lips tightened into a straight line, the bitter wrinkles he hadn't seen for a while materializing around her mouth.

"Dima, you can't leave like this." Her fingers clenched his, her thumb caressing his knuckles. "You look like you're at the end of your rope. You can't drive that far in this condition and in the middle of the night. If you fall asleep behind the wheel—"

"This is why I'm not going to drive," he cut her off. Pulling his hand out of hers gently, he switched his attention to Jamie and gave him a short nod. "Jamie, you're coming with me. I need you to drive, so I can get a few minutes shuteye."

"Yes, Lord Commander," replied Jamie, his former training taking over.

"Get ready." Damian glanced at his watch. "We're leaving right away."

He headed toward the door but halted in front of his brother. His hand moved up, but he changed his mind and dropped it.

"Cole..."

"I know. I'll watch my back," Cole replied. "You too."

Damian nodded and pulled his brother into a quick embrace, giving him a light tap on his back. "Take care of River and Ace, little brother," he whispered so softly that only Cole could hear him. "And for once, do as I say."

As Cole's lips quirked up at the corners, Damian threw a reproachful glance at him and walked out the living room.

CHAPTER 20

~ DAMIAN BLAKE ~

It was late evening when Jamie drove the Mercedes G-Class SUV out of Blue Creek, taking the ramp onto the I-10 West, heading toward Los Angeles. The freeway was mostly empty, so Damian lowered the back of his seat and relaxed, folding his hands on his stomach. Despite his dislike of confined places, and cars in particular, the exhaustion took its toll, and he fell asleep almost immediately.

Oblivion swallowed him whole, and for once, he slept without any nightmares or dreams. He woke up a few hours later because the car jerked violently and came to a sharp stop, Jamie's colorful curses sounding somewhere on his left. He jolted upright but fell back, held by the seatbelt.

"Damian, relax." Jamie tapped his knee. "We just hit the LA traffic." He chuckled, shaking his head. "Now we're going to be crawling stop-and-go all the way until we reach Studio City."

"What time is it?" mumbled Damian, raising his seat back up, blinking sleepily at the ocean of red brake lights in front of him.

"Four fifteen. There has to be an accident somewhere," replied Jamie, dancing on the pedals as traffic congestion became thicker. "Do you feel better? You looked like the walking dead when we left."

Damian took a deep breath, stretching his shoulders as much as he could inside the vehicle. The soreness was gone, and he felt stronger now—not a hundred percent restored but refreshed enough to function effectively in a combat situation.

The use of magic and elemental power didn't come without a price, and the more he used it, the weaker and more worn out he felt. Even though he was channeling magical energy from nature, it was impossible not to tap into the internal resources of his own body, and after prolonged use of magic, his body was getting drained of magical energy, which weakened him physically.

Masters of Power, who were considered being at the top of the food chain in respect to power and magic, could get drained even faster if they used their magic excessively, and it could take them quite a bit of time to regain their strength. Like everything in life, the bigger they were, the harder they fell. One of the perks of being a Destiny Enforcer, however, was that Damian could restore his strength much faster than any other being of Magic of equal power. Nevertheless, he always had to keep in the back of his mind that his body was human, and its resources weren't endless.

"I'm fine," he replied, readjusting his position.

"How do you know when to stop?" asked Jamie, throwing a quick glance at him.

"Stop what?"

"Not to overuse your magic, I mean," said Jamie. "During the fight, when adrenalin is pumping, how can you measure your resources."

"Comes with experience, I guess," he replied unwillingly. He liked Jamie, but he was too young as a person and too inexperienced as a wizard. He needed a lot of training, and Damian wasn't sure he was the right person to teach him. "Jamie, are you sure you don't want to come back to the Guardians Academy as an apprentice? They know how to teach young wizards like yourself. I am..." His voice trailed off, and he stifled a sigh. "I lived on my own for most of my life. I'm not mentor material."

"Yeah, I'm sure." Jamie pressed his lips into a stubborn line. "You're the only mentor I want. It's either you teaching me, or I'm on my own."

Dammit, kid... Why me? he thought, staring out the window wistfully.

"When all this is over, hopefully, I'll have more time to devote to your training," Damian said out loud. "To know your limits, you have to be placed in a real high-pressure combat situation. This is the only way you can learn how far you can push yourself. Trust me, you'll feel when you're getting drained. The truth is, sometimes you have no choice but to push through the exhaustion and stretch your abilities to the maximum." He thought for a moment and added, "Especially when your life or the lives of others depend on it."

He smirked, throwing a veiled gaze at the young wizard from under the long strands of his hair. "Let's survive this trip first, though."

Thinking about what was coming and all the uncertainties, Damian ran his fingers over his dark stubble and whispered more to himself than to Jamie, "I wish I didn't have to drag you with me to California, putting you into this situation—"

"Ehhh... But you always do, don't you? You're a magnet for trouble, Kid of Earth, and everyone around you is always in danger, whether you like it or not," a screechy little voice sounded in Damian's mind, and he flinched, turning around. The magpie sat on the headrest of the back seat, its white chest prominent in the darkness of the vehicle.

"How did you get here?" Damian grumbled, making Jamie flinch and look back. As he spotted the bird, his jaw dropped.

"Ohhh... I'm glad you finally asked," chirped the bird, flying

forward and landing on the dashboard to Jamie's utter displeasure. *"You know I'm Canadian. Toronto—a beautiful city. You should visit when you get a chance. Anyway, one day, I was talking to my friend Jack, and he was like, hey, dude, I heard there is no winter in California, and it's warm all year round. Why don't we go? And I was like, yeah, dude, awesome idea—"*

"Perun almighty," exhaled Damian, rolling his eyes. "Can you answer one question without turning it into a full-length novel?"

"I wish I could understand what he's saying," murmured Jamie, his eyes darting from the bird to Damian.

"Trust me, you don't. He'll talk your ears off," Damian muttered, switching his attention to the bird. "I didn't ask you about your life story. I asked you what you are doing in this car and how you got here."

"Ekhhhhkh," chirped the magpie, spreading its wings. *"Well, I heard you two were going to take a road trip to the City of Angels, and I was like, a road trip? Alright, babe, count me in. Hollywood is where I wanna be, anyway. And Gypsy was like, yeah, a good idea, dude. You go to Hollywood, pick up some nice chick and live your life on the hills. And I was like—"*

Damian grunted, and the magpie flew up, landing on Jamie's left shoulder away from Damian.

"Anyway, Kid of Earth, just drop me off as soon as you get off the freeway," said the bird. *"I'll find my way to Hollywood on my own. It's not safe around you by any stretch of the imagination."*

"Thank God for small mercies," murmured Damian, watching Jamie trying to wave the bird off his shoulder. "I'm just curious... Why Hollywood?"

For a moment, the bird stared at him, cocking his head. *"Movie stars! Shiny!"* the magpie sang, and Damian could swear it winked at him.

* * *

JAMIE WAS RIGHT. Once they passed Studio City, traffic became handleable, and soon, he took the car off the freeway and onto the street. At the first stoplight, Damian opened the window and let the magpie out. The bird chirped its goodbyes and disappeared into the dark sky. For a moment, he stared into the darkness, trying to calm his mind and focus on the mission ahead.

"Damian!"

Jamie's voice broke his train of thought, and he raised his face, gazing at the young man, doubt tearing at his soul.

"Damian," said Jamie, staring at him with concern. "We're here. I parked the car at the Ralphs supermarket parking lot. The address you gave me is just a block away." He pulled the key out of the ignition and gave it to Damian. "Are you sure you're okay? Do you need more rest before we go?"

"Thanks, Jamie, I don't need rest," Damian replied calmly. "But I need you to stay in the car and wait for me. I don't know what we're going to run into and—"

"I know I made a stupid mistake a few days ago when Cole was in trouble, but I learned my lesson. Something like that will never happen again." Jamie glanced up at Damian, his eyes pleading. "This is the only way I can learn. All the practice you give me at home is not enough. You said it yourself—only in a real combat situation can I learn how to use my magic and what to expect on the field."

"Hey, don't use what I've said against me." Damian chuckled mirthlessly. "And it's not true," he objected quietly. "I went through rigorous training when I started as a Destiny Enforcer. My Commander would never put me on the field before I passed their tests." He fell silent, shivering at the memory of his initial training. "Come on, Jamie. Use common sense. We have no idea what we're going to find there." He waved at the dark street, worry gnawing at him. "Possibly, I will have to face one of the most powerful Masters of the Dark Arts I've ever met—a man who can conjure wurdulaks in groups of fifteen. I'll be honest with you, I'm afraid. I've never heard of a Dark Wizard wielding so much power."

"You're afraid... You?" Jamie's eyes widened in disbelief. "You're never afraid of anything. I saw you fight. You enjoy it... your power, your strength. You toy with your opponents, and the more dangerous and skilled they are, the more fun you have. You have no idea what the word 'fear' means."

Damian smirked, shaking his head. "Of course, I do," he objected, a warm smile touching his lips. "Only complete idiots are scared of nothing. Every time when I have to face a dangerous adversary, fear is twisting my gut into a tight knot." His hand went up to his chest of its own accord, his fingers clenching over his heart. "Being brave doesn't mean being fearless, Jamie. It means controlling your fears and doing what's right, no matter how scared you are. Actually, fear—if you know how to control it—makes you more careful, more alert, and that's exactly what you need in a combat situation where being reckless means certain death."

"Wow, if you hadn't told me, I never would've guessed," mumbled Jamie, gazing at him in awe.

"I *am* afraid. I'm terrified, Jamie, but not for myself. I'm afraid of what could happen if I fail. I have failed too many times over the course of my life..." Damian's voice melted into the silence of the night, and he dropped back in his seat, pressing his hand over his eyes. "Right now, I'm a ball of nerves, but I know when the time comes to face the enemy, I'll be all right."

"Damian—," started Jamie, but Damian held his hand up, interrupting him.

"Every time I fail," he said, numbness spreading through his chest, "people get hurt. I can't fail now, and I can't put you in the line of fire either. You're going to stay here and wait for me, and I'm going to face JB on my own, whoever or whatever he is."

"Yeah... no." Jamie opened the car door and stepped outside. Turning around, he bent a little, looking at Damian, and said, "Dream on. Get your terrified ass out of the car. We're going together. Someone has to watch your doublewide back."

"Dammit, kid," muttered Damian, stepping out of the SUV. *I've made possibly the longest speech in my entire life, and it successfully fell on deaf ears...*

* * *

THE SKY gradually began to change, pale shades of yellow and pink advancing to the deep ultramarine color of the night along the horizon. Slowly and unwillingly, the city started to wake, getting ready for the upcoming day. Following a two-lane street toward the designated address, Jamie kept checking the numbers on the houses, and after a short while, he halted in front of a gate into an apartment complex, observing it with curiosity.

Three two-story buildings positioned at ninety degrees to each other encircled a large court with a swimming pool and fitness center in the middle. Decorative palms and other leafy trees, strategically planted inside the complex, created a tropical atmosphere of relaxation and comfort. A few windows were lit up with the yellow light of electric lamps, suggesting that some of the residents were getting ready to start their day. Everything looked so quiet and peaceful that no one could even suspect that possibly one of the most dangerous Dark Wizards resided within the walls of this complex.

"Are you sure you have the right address?" asked Jamie, checking the number on the gate again.

Damian nodded and opened his second sight, carefully probing the area. He couldn't sense anything alarming, but he didn't expect that he would. If JB truly was the necromancer behind all the attacks in Blue Creek and Phoenix, he wouldn't let anyone detect his presence. Moving his hands over the surface of the gate, he probed it for wards but found none.

"Jamie," whispered Damian, switching his attention to his young friend, "remember what I taught you about shadowing your magical energy signature?" Jamie nodded, and he continued, sounding as calm as he could muster, "Do it now."

Carefully, he pushed the gate, and it opened with a light squeak. Holding his friend back, Damian walked inside first, following the narrow asphalt road toward the building on the right. As he reached the swimming pool, he halted in the shadow of the fitness center, checking the address.

"Building A, apartment Two-Twelve," he said, cringing inwardly. The apartment was on the second floor, which meant he would be a little weaker than he would be standing on the ground.

"Right there." Jamie pointed at the building on the left. The door with large numbers two-twelve was located in the middle of the second-floor balcony.

Damian nodded and headed toward the staircase leading to the second floor, silently cursing his bad luck. Taking a deep breath, he walked up the stairs, feeling his connection with his element weakening with every step he took. As he reached the top, he halted, leaning heavily on the railing to check his surroundings. The balcony ran in both directions for quite some distance, but the entrance into the apartment they needed was just three doors away. Opening his other sight, he surveyed the door and the wall around it but couldn't find any sign of either protective or concealment magic. For a heartbeat, he started to wonder if Az had sent him on a wild goose chase when something changed, immediately setting his mind on high alert.

A barely noticeable wave of magical energy touched his senses, and the floor swayed under his feet. Damian wasn't sure what it was, but he knew it was just the beginning. Turning to

Jamie, he hissed, "Hold on to the railing and don't move. Something is coming—"

He didn't finish the statement when their surroundings shimmered with a dark mist, slowly morphing into something entirely different. He was still in the same apartment building, but its looks had changed, turning into something blood-chilling and sinister. The walls wobbled as if they were made of some disgusting, gray jelly, and dark, thick drops fell from the edge of the roof. The temperature dropped considerably, and the suffocating stench of sulfur invaded his senses, making his stomach spasm painfully.

In the place of the tropical paradise, twisted, thorny bushes stretched their dry branches toward the sky, purple goo seeping from them like a putrid, revolting sap. The light was gone from the windows, and they stood dark and hollow, staring at him like the empty eye sockets of a skull. Glancing down, Damian grunted and swallowed hard, hiding his nose and mouth into the crook of his elbow. The pool was filled with a thick, dark liquid, its nauseating copper odor permeating the air. Semi-translucent swirls of steam rose above its surface, hanging over the pool like a disgusting curtain.

A constrained gasp reminded him that Jamie was nearby, even though he couldn't see him.

"Jamie, hold on. Don't be afraid," Damian whispered, channeling his magic. "I think it's just an illusion."

"Oh, yeah?" Damian heard Jamie's terrified voice and turned in his direction but could see only his dark silhouette. "I hope you're right," continued Jamie, "because I would hate for this to be real." He pointed at something behind Damian.

Damian spun around, and the hair rose on the back of his neck. The entire space of the balcony was filled to the brim with assorted monsters—pureblood demons, by the looks of them. They stood shoulder to shoulder in the narrow space between the wall and the railing, their eyes glowing with malice and hostility. A low growl rumbled through their rows, and Damian took a step back, running into Jamie.

"All this is not real," he whispered, not quite sure if he was trying to reassure the young wizard or himself. "It can't be real." He moved his arm in a wide arch and whispered, "*Veritatius Revelare.*"

The dark mist dissipated, the wall stopped wobbling, and now he could see the shimmering outlines of the demonic army coming in and out of focus. He was right. All this was an illusion —powerful and skillfully crafted, but still nothing more than an illusion. The goo dripping from the roof and the pool filled with blood were still there, however, and that sent chills down Damian's back, making him wonder how powerful this Dark Wizard truly was if a Destiny Enforcer of his caliber couldn't see through this illusion and dislodge it. He heard a loud bang and spun around a moment too late.

"Damian, watch out!" Jamie yelled, desperate tones ringing in his voice.

An enormous monster appeared seemingly out of nowhere and pushed off the floor, leaping in the air. In a way, it looked like an oversized Rottweiler, but its chest was a lot wider with thick ropes of muscles working under its black fur, and two webbed wings protruded from its back. Before Damian could do anything to stop him, Jamie pushed him away, unbalancing him, and threw himself in the beast's way, shielding Damian with his body. The monster roared, its eyes igniting with a deep blue light as it impacted Jamie on his chest with enormous force.

Jamie fell, propelled a few feet back by the impact, and a howl of anguish erupted from his lips as the monster pinned him to the floor with its heavy paws and sunk its enormous fangs into his shoulder. Bright red spurts of blood rushed down his chest, neck and arm, his face contorted by the debilitating pain. His arms fell to the floor, his body arching against the monster standing over him.

In less than a heartbeat, Damian was back on his feet, daggers blazing in his hands. He crossed the distance in two long strides and plunged his dagger into the monster's back between its wings. The blade bounced up, doing it absolutely no harm. Damian staggered a step back, staring at the creature in shock, the force of the impact still reverberating through his arm. The beast lifted his head and looked back at Damian, blood dripping from its fangs, the semblance of a smile stretching its ferocious muzzle.

As anger spiraled through him, Damian connected with his magic, and his daggers vanished, replaced by a high-voltage energy orb in the palm of his right hand.

"Hey, mutt," he roared, stepping closer to the beast, and as the monster turned its ugly head again, he shoved the energy orb into its maw.

The beast shut its jaws and swallowed the orb as if it were nothing more than a dog treat. His glowing stare pinned Damian in place as the beast turned around, a sound similar to laughter rumbling in its wide chest.

"My turn, puny wizard..." a growling voice sounded in Damian's mind.

"Oh, fu-uuu-ck!" Damian jumped aside as the monster charged him like an infuriated bull, the balcony shaking with its every step.

Even though the beast missed him, it turned around with a speed Damian didn't expect from such a sizable creature. Its webby wings spread wide as it glowered at him, ready to charge again. Damian glanced back at Jamie, realizing that if he would step out of the line of attack, the beast would rampage over the young man. Without thinking twice, Damian jumped on top of the balcony railing and whistled.

"Hey, monster, catch me if you can." He dove down, his

wings opening to their full width. To his relief, the monster followed him, reacting to his every move with a swiftness and agility unbelievable for such a heavy creature.

Cursing inwardly, Damian rose higher in the air, now truly feeling the distance from Earth, weakness slowly taking hold of him. The monster followed him, forcing him to rise higher and higher. Making a loop-de-loop, Damian attempted to outmaneuver it, searching for a way to lower himself to the ground, but to no avail. Faster and stronger, the creature whirled in the air and met him face to face. It wrapped its mighty paws around his waist, squeezing him in a deadly embrace.

He pushed against the beast's chest, struggling to get free, but it squeezed him tighter, its muscled paws as hard as rock. Something cracked, and Damian cried out in pain. The monster roared in response and flapped its wings, moving higher and higher. As weakness assailed him with full force, Damian stopped fighting and hung limply in the monster's paws, his black wings gone. Somewhere high above him, stark-black against the pinkish backdrop of the morning sky, a white-tailed eagle was flying like a soundless shadow. Even from this distance, the bird looked a bit too big to his eye.

"A little higher, Bulat... About a hundred yards more and hold him there..."

Damian wasn't sure if it was his frazzled mind overpowered by weakness playing tricks on him, or if it was really the eagle who said that, but the beast obeyed. It flapped its wings, rising even higher, holding him firmly in its paws.

"Now, bring him down," commanded the eagle and vanished.

The monster obeyed again and spiraled down from the sky. Coming to a halt above the balcony, he lowered Damian carefully to the floor next to Jamie. Damian stirred weakly and reached for the energy of Earth, trying to recharge as much as he could without the direct connection with his element. The beast sat back, looking like a regular dog now. Tilting his head from left to right, he observed Damian's every move, a doggish grin splitting its muzzle.

What the hell?

Ignoring the monster and its odd behavior, Damian scrambled to all fours and turned to Jamie, quickly checking his vitals. The young wizard was alive, but he was losing a lot of blood and if Damian couldn't heal him right away, he would most certainly die. He channeled as much of his element as he could gather in his condition, moving the energy to the palms of his hands. But as soon as a bright, orange glow enveloped his hands, the dog got up, and its wings opened up again.

"Don't move, Child of Earth, or I will take you to the stratosphere," he growled, his eyes shining brighter with a deep blue light.

"If I don't heal him, my friend will die," snapped Damian, with shock recognizing how weak his voice sounded. "I have to heal him now."

"You're no match for me, Child of Earth," growled the dog, taking a step closer, baring its giant fangs. *"I have my orders. Disobey me, and I'll make sure to take you as high as my wings can carry me."*

"I know that in my current condition, I'm weakened, and you can most likely deliver on your promise," hissed Damian, his fingers clenching into fists, "but Jamie is my friend, and he's innocent in all this. So, you do what you must—kill me for all I care—but I swear I'll find a way to destroy you if you try to stop me from saving his life."

Turning away from the beast, Damian focused on Jamie. He placed his hands over the young man's chest and forehead and started the healing process. The monster growled behind him warningly, but Damian ignored him.

"Bulat, stand down. Good boy," the voice of the eagle sounded in Damian's mind again. *"Let him do his thing."*

As Damian circulated more and more healing energy through his friend, his hands shook with the strain, sweat trickling down his forehead. Gradually, the bleeding stopped, and the wound closed. Jamie cracked his eyelids open, his gaze still unfocused.

"Jamie," Damian exhaled, sitting back on his heels. The world swayed and spun around him, and he closed his eyes for a moment to deal with the nauseating weakness. "Jeez, man, you scared me shitless. Why did you do that?"

"Do what?" The shock sounded in the young man's voice as he raised his hand to touch his shoulder, and a faint smile ghosted his pale lips.

"Took the proverbial bullet for me." Damian chuckled, gazing down at his friend with reproach, warmth and sadness spreading through him. "I'm immortal, you dumbass. They can't kill me."

"But they can still hurt you..." Jamie shrugged with a sheepish grin. "Seemed like the right thing to do at the time. What happened? Did you heal me?"

"I hope I did. Although foolhardiness is an incurable disease, I believe." Damian glanced down at him, wiping sweat off his face with his hand. "Anyway..." He bit his lip and looked away, warmth rising in his chest. "Thank you."

"What a wonderful reunion. So touching." The eagle's voice, filled with sarcasm, sounded in Damian's head, causing him to flinch and turn around just in time to see the enormous bird land on the balcony.

A dark mist surrounded the eagle, and once it dissipated, a tall man in his late forties, dressed in blue cargo jeans and a long-sleeved, black shirt, stood in front of him, observing him with interest in his attentive dark-brown eyes. His black hair fell to his shoulders, ruffled by the breeze, and he raked his hand through it, throwing it off his face impatiently. His arched eyebrows lowered, and two deep wrinkles materialized between them, making him look older. Damian froze in place, carefully channeling his magic, knowing ahead of time that after the air-battle and performing healing magic, he was too weak to fight.

An uneven smirk lifted the corner of the man's mouth, and he tapped his thigh with his hand, calling to the monstrous dog. The beast approached him and sat at his feet, wagging its short tail.

"Disengage from your magic, Child of Earth," the man said frostily. "I believe you're experienced enough to know that after performing the healing and your little trip to the"—he chuckled, pointing up—"high heaven, you are too weak magically and physically." He moved closer, the beast following his every step. "That was my goal—to weaken you enough so we could talk like civilized people without guns blazing or swords swinging."

Damian smirked, stifling the boiling fury within him. "So, you almost kill this innocent young man, who did nothing wrong except for being loyal to his friend, just to drain me? You call that civilized?"

The man shrugged. "No, killing him was never my goal," he said, shoving his hands into the pockets of his wide pants, "but I did want him injured. It was a test. I wanted to see if this boy was loyal enough to you to sacrifice himself, and then I wanted to check how far you would go to save him." He tilted his head a little, and his lower lip puffed out, before he waved his hand as if dismissing the matter. "I guess you do deserve his blind loyalty after all."

A growl rumbled in Damian's throat, his chest rising and falling with strenuous breaths as he struggled to contain his rising anger. "Are you satisfied?"

"Very much so." A wide smirk split the man's face, leaving his eyes alert and cold.

"What do you want?" growled Damian. As Jamie stirred on the floor, attempting to get up, he helped him to his feet, supporting him with his shoulder.

"What do I want?" The man shook his head, staring at

Damian with unconcealed sarcasm. "The real question is what you want, Child of Earth. You came here with hostile intent, so I want to know why." Since Damian remained silent, he waved his hand dismissively and continued. "I couldn't sense your magic, but I could detect your hostility from a mile away. So I created this little illusion to make you use your magic and reveal your supernatural identity."

"There is nothing to reveal. I'm a Child of Earth," replied Damian dryly.

"Oh, you're a lot more than that," objected the man, shaking his head. "But we'll get back to that subject later. In the meantime, allow me to introduce myself." He held out his hand. "My name is Yakov Vilimovich Bruce, but the locals call me Jacob Bruce or—"

"JB," whispered Damian, goosebumps rising on his arms.

CHAPTER 21

~ DAMIAN BLAKE ~

"I'm Damian Blake," said Damian, taking JB's hand, "and this is Jamie Coldwell."

JB squeezed Damian's hand, sending a wave of his magic through him to explore his abilities. Damian hissed and jerked his hand back, realizing that in his weakened state, most likely, he wasn't a hundred percent successful at concealing his energy. JB's lips stretched wider, and he waved in the direction of his apartment.

"Well, come in, boys," he said not without a hefty load of sarcasm in his voice, heading toward the door with the large numbers two-one-two on it. "You came unannounced, but since you're already here, be my guests."

He halted by the doorway, allowing his pet-monster to pass through first, and then ushered Damian and Jamie inside.

Damian halted by the door, observing the apartment in shock. Whatever he expected to find there, this wasn't it. The place looked more like a modern science lab than the home of a dangerous necromancer. Most of the living area was taken by strange machines and computers, wires dangling from them like some oversized spider web. A light scent of chemicals lingered in the air, and the dim light of multiple monitors illuminated the semi-dark room.

Noticing Damian's hesitation, JB shrugged and pursed his lips. "Not what you expected?" he asked. Gesturing for them to sit down on a small sofa by the wall, he flipped the light switch on.

"Not at all," replied Damian, taking a seat. The sofa moaned under his weight, and he shifted to the edge, leaning forward slightly. "When I think of a powerful and dangerous Master of the Dark Arts, a school science lab is not what I envision."

"Powerful and dangerous, eh?" JB's eyebrows rose, confusion written all over his face. "Powerful—yes. Dangerous—no, unless you force me to be, like you did earlier." He leaned against the counter, folding his arms. "Why are you here, Child of Earth? You didn't come in peace, and I would like to know how you found me, and why you were searching for me in the first place."

"Why would you assume I didn't come in peace?" asked Damian coldly, his eyes darting to the monster-dog sitting next to JB's feet. "We barely made our way into your apartment complex when you attacked us with your illusions and set your dog on us."

"Dog, eh? Bulat is the one who can sense the hostile intent, but he's so much more than a dog." JB chuckled, gazing heavenward. "I can't believe someone as old as you didn't recognize him for what he is. And don't try to lie." He twirled his hand impatiently, frowning. "I have no patience for lies. You have to be one of the immortals since you're a Child of Earth and God knows what else. I can sense your magic, and you're as powerful and as dangerous as I am, if not more so."

Opening his other sight, Damian carefully scanned the large animal sitting next to JB's feet, and the hairs rose on the back of his neck and his arms. The dog gave him a wide grin, his powerful magical energy swirling around him.

"Dammit, I can't believe I missed it," he whispered, shaking his head. "All the signs were right in front of me. He's as heavy as a ton of bricks and incredibly strong. My dagger couldn't penetrate his hide, and he can detect potential danger. He's—"

"A gargoyle," said Jamie, his voice a terrified whisper. The young man raised his eyes at JB, staring at him in awe. "But a gargoyle would never serve anyone evil... And Bulat seems to be loyal to you through and through."

"Tuh-duh." JB spread his arms. "The proof is in the pudding. Like I said, I'm powerful, but not evil. So, let's start from the beginning. My name is Yakov Bruce. I consider myself to be more scientist than a magician." He waved his hand around the apartment. "Since the early seventeen hundreds, I've lived and breathed science. Astronomy, astrology, chemistry, mathematics, physics, medicine, history, art—you name it, I studied it."

Damian exchanged a quick look with Jamie, noticing a dumbstruck expression on his face. "I think I know who you are," said Damian, meeting JB's calm gaze. "You're Count Yakov Bruce, Tsar Peter the Great's righthand man. After your death, all sorts of wild gossips and legends spread across the land. You were named a dark sorcerer and warlock. Peasants were talking about some Water of Life you had created, that could heal any wound, even resurrect the dead."

"Sorcerer-shmorcer," muttered JB, rolling his eyes. "You can't stop people from wagging their tongues no matter what century it is." He thought for a moment, but then sighed and added, "There is such a thing as Water of Life, of course, but I didn't invent it. The real Water of Life comes from a well in the sacred garden of the magical nexus, the Land of Dreams. There is another liquid substance that can heal any wound. It's called vampire's blood. I didn't invent it either."

"But you did practice necromancy, alchemy, summoning, and other forbidden Dark Arts." Damian rubbed his forehead, thousands of thoughts rushing through his mind. "Not everything you studied was pure science."

"Oh, that?" Yakov shrugged, a crooked smirk lifting one corner of his mouth. "Of course, I did! It's called the normal curiosity of an inquisitive mind. Still, it doesn't make me evil, just like it doesn't explain your intentions."

"Something doesn't add up, Count." Damian got up, towering at least a few inches over JB. "If you've practiced forbidden arts, how are you still living in the human realm and not in one of the Destiny Council's holding cells?"

"I said I practiced the Dark Arts, but not for long. I haven't done that for centuries," growled JB, stepping closer to Damian. But as his eyes slipped from Damian's chest up, he chuckled. "Intimidating SOB, aren't yah, Damian Blake?"

Damian didn't reply, staring at JB without blinking. The old wizard threw his hands up and then started unbuttoning the cuff of his shirt on his right wrist. He folded his sleeve all the way, exposing his arm. The entire surface of his skin was covered in an intricate tattoo, letters of the Dragon tongue intertwining with the design. Under the ink, the barely visible scar of an old burn marred the inner side of his forearm. JB pressed his hand over his upper arm, murmuring something under his breath. As he removed his hand, a rune glowing with a brilliant white light materialized on his skin.

He pointed at the rune and said with a deep sigh, "The reason I'm not in the Destiny Council prison is that I work for them—for the secret division of the Wardens Order sponsored by the Destiny Council, to be precise. After I died, they brought me back and made me an offer I just couldn't refuse. They placed all the resources of the Wardens Archives and Libraries at my disposal. Well, almost all of them. How could anyone in their right mind refuse such a generous offer?"

Damian recognized the signature rune of the Destiny Council, and desperation spread through him, twisting his stomach into a tight knot.

"God damn it all," he whispered, moving his hand over the

rune to confirm its authenticity. "What a giant waste of time." He inclined his head, pressing his fist to his chest. "I apologize for the intrusion, Count Bruce. Jamie and I will be on our way." He gestured for Jamie to get up.

"Whoa, not so fast." JB held his hands in a timeout sign. "Obviously, there was some kind of misunderstanding here, and if I'm not mistaken, we do work on the same side. Maybe I can help you if you tell me who you are and what brought you here in the first place."

"Yes, we do work on the same side," confirmed Damian. "I'm a Commander of the Destiny Enforcers."

He slipped his jacket off his shoulder and touched his upper arm to reveal his own rune. Then he reached in his pocket, producing the dagger with the eagle-head pommel. He extended his hand, offering the dagger to JB, the electric light igniting bright sparkles in the small stones embedded into the eagle's eyes. The wizard took it, his hands trembling as he brushed his fingertips over the blade.

"Oh, my God... Oh, God..." he exhaled, a mix of emotions reflected in his eyes. "Damian, how did you find it? Where? I lost it a long time ago. It's..." His voice shook, and he pressed his fingers to his eyes. "Tsar Peter the Great gifted this dagger to me in the year seventeen twenty-one, and I never parted with it since. Until I lost it, or it was stolen from me, that is." He raised his eyes at Damian, liquid gathering in the corners. "How did you come in possession of it, Commander, and can I—" He cut himself off and exhaled a ragged breath, unable to voice his plea.

"You can keep it," said Damian, lowering back on the sofa with a heavy sigh.

In so many words, he told JB the problem he was facing in his state, about his meeting with Az and how he acquired the dagger. As the wizard listened to him, his features hardened, a shadow of concern settling on his face, but at the place where

Damian told him about the unsuccessful heist, he chuckled, for a brief moment pride twinkling in his dark eyes.

Once Damian finished, a winning smile graced his face. "My inventions truly work."

"Which inventions?" asked Jamie, staring at him with curiosity.

"The magic detectors," replied JB with pride, pointing at the pile of small plastic boxes lying on top of the kitchen counter Damian hadn't noticed before. "I invented and produced the first magic detector ever and improved them as time went on. Now, they detect not only the magical and elemental energies but also the vampiric and demonic essence as well as the energy waves of werewolves and shifters."

"Nice," muttered Damian, shaking his head. "Your invention almost sent my brother and me into supernatural slavery." He shuddered. "Does your boss at the Destiny Council know about your invention?"

"Who do you think finances this venture? Yeah, I'm an alchemist, but I don't turn kitchen utensils into gold, you know," said JB with a slight shrug. "The Destiny Council wanted chosen human authorities to have something to identify the presence of magic. I'm talking about special divisions of the FBI and some people in the Secret Service who are exposed to the World of Magic. Don't ask me why they wanted me to create something like this. You know how the Destiny Council works—the paths of the Board of Destiny and so forth and so on." He waved his hand, pursing his lips. "Anyway, I invented it with the blessing and support of the Destiny Council. The question is how my invention fell into the hands of a private collector?"

"I'm not going to worry about that," murmured Damian. "To be honest, right now, my head is spinning. All this time, I believed you were the necromancer in question. But now, I have no idea where to go from here."

"Who was this man who scried for me? Az was his name?" JB

asked, his fingers caressing the pommel of the dagger. "I don't recall knowing anyone with this name. Does he have a last name?"

"He said he met you in California years ago," muttered Damian. "His full name is Azul Moreno. He is a low-grade wizard with psychic abilities."

JB averted his gaze, shaking his head. "I don't know him." His eyes fell on the dagger, and the color drained from his face. "Please, no," he whispered.

His fingers trembled as he took the blade in his left hand and applied some pressure on the eyes of the eagle with the thumb and middle finger of his right hand.

"What?" asked Damian through clenched teeth, his heart beating in his throat.

With a soft click, a hidden door in the grip of the dagger opened. JB peered inside, and his face fell.

"Oh, Commander," he mumbled, showing a tiny, empty compartment to Damian, "I hate to do this to you, but I think you have a lot bigger problem than the war between the vampires and werewolves or the unrest in the Arizona Vampire Court."

CHAPTER 22

~ COLE ADAMS ~

"It's sunrise already." River glanced at the lock screen of her cellphone, checking the time, and then put it back into the pocket of her business suit. "Your brother is a selfish ass, you know that? He could have at least called to tell us that he arrived, and everything is fine. He's just so... infuriating." She tilted her empty cup, rolling it in her hands, almost knocking it over. "Ugh... I don't think there is even a remote family resemblance between the two of you—either in your looks or personality."

Cole glanced out the kitchen window, watching the shy morning light reflecting in the purple rock formation in the distance, his throat tightening with worry. Then he turned toward River, an easy smile playing on his lips. He grabbed the coffee cup out of her hands and put it on the counter next to the coffeemaker. With a habitual move, he refilled the cup, added some milk and sugar, and turned around, placing it in front of River.

"Did you deduce it all on your own, detective River Holms?" Cole laughed, lowering on the chair next to her. "My brother and I are nothing alike. Damian is a good man—a lot better than

I am—but he's not what you may call a modern man, if you haven't noticed yet. The best technology in his hands is a pile of useless metal." He chuckled, shaking his head, asking himself how she managed to suck him into a conversation about his brother again. "Despite his youthful appearance, he's over a thousand years old with a huge luggage of good, bad and ugly."

"So are you," replied River with a half-shrug, taking a sip of her coffee. "It's amazing how different you both are, even though you're biological brothers. How much is he older than you?"

"About six years," replied Cole. "Not the point. What are six years in comparison to a thousand?"

"Exactly the point." River put the cup down, spilling some coffee on the table. "You live and behave like a modern man, easygoing and gregarious. And he is—"

"Introverted? Socially awkward? Guarded? The dark and brooding type?"

"Yes, and I can add a few more descriptions to your list," she replied, getting up to grab a piece of paper towel. "I'm sorry. I shouldn't be asking you all that, but I just want to understand him. Be there for him, you know? It's a lot easier with you. I can speak with you pretty much about anything I want. With Damian around, I feel like I need to tread on eggshells all the time. I never know when he will just get his ass up and leave."

"First of all, even as young people—human—we were very different. After our death..." Cole cleared his throat, gauging her reaction, but she just nodded, seemingly accepting it for what it was. "We were separated for many centuries. While my life wasn't easy, I had my maker watching over me, helping me through the transition and protecting me. I was heartbroken, thinking that Damian was dead, and if not for Ruslan, I don't think I would have survived. He had become my father, my friend, my family. I was never alone..."

His voice trailed off, and he averted his gaze, reminded of

the two people who meant so much to him, but who were gone from his life now. He still hoped to find Ruslan—now more than ever—but Luciano was dead. By his hand... And there was no way to undo it.

"Both Ruslan and Luciano supported me in anything I wanted to try, no matter how crazy my ideas were. So, when I decided to try to live a 'human' life, they helped me to get where I wanted to be, including attending a college to earn a Master's in computer science, opening my own business and anything else that came with owning a tech company. I'm sure on the sidelines they were laughing and shaking their heads—an old vampire trying to be human—but they never stopped me. Instead, they taught me how to control my thirst around humans and block the sound of beating hearts and rushing blood. Damian, on the other hand..."

He stopped talking, his fingers raking through the mass of his hair nervously. River was a smart and strong woman, but she was human, a young person to boot, and he wasn't sure her mind could easily comprehend and accept everything he was trying to explain to her.

"I don't know much about his life back then," he continued at length. "He doesn't talk to me either. Here is what I know. After he died a human death, the Destiny Council made him an offer, and he accepted the mantle of a Destiny Enforcer. But about five hundred years ago, he lost the only woman he had ever loved, and that turned his life upside down. He resigned, accepting the *no one* status, which was a terrible price to pay, by the way. For five hundred years, he lived alone, constantly on the move, in hiding, unable to create any kind of connections—"

"Cole, I'm sorry. I didn't mean to pry. I don't know what I was thinking..." A pink shade crept up River's cheeks as she touched his hand gently. "Sometimes I forget that you both are not the same age as me, even though you look young."

Cole got up and turned away, bracing his arms against the

kitchen counter, his fingers nearly crushing the granite countertop.

"You're probably right. I shouldn't be telling you all of this, but maybe you're right—it's a good idea for you to understand him a little better." He turned around, leaning against the counter with his arms folded over his chest. "For five hundred years, my brother blamed himself for the death of the only woman he had ever loved. I'm not a detective or a psychologist, but I can safely assume that Damian's greatest fear is the fear of loss. This is one of the reasons he has doomed himself to a solitary existence. And now that he's back on the Destiny Council payroll, there are rules in place. You've heard him speaking about it with Ace—a Destiny Enforcer cannot have personal attachments," said Cole, perfectly imitating his brother's voice, eliciting a burst of chuckles out of River.

He smiled, watching the twinkles of humor dancing in her blue eyes.

"Well, when it comes to you, I don't think Ace cares much about these rules," River pointed out, taking another sip of her coffee.

"That's because she's young, inexperienced and stubborn." Cole glanced at the door as if expecting Ace to barge in. "Give her a few hundred years on the job, and she'll be a lot more like my brother. The truth is, the Destiny Enforcers have more enemies than friends in all layers of the supernatural community. They are feared and hated by many, and sometimes they have to carry out orders they don't understand or agree with. They have no personal life, they don't own anything, and they don't know where they will wake up tomorrow. This is the kind of life my brother has lived for most of his life." He opened his arms with a slight shrug. "So, you can see where Damian's fabulous personality traits come from."

"It's amazing when you think about it," mused River, circling the rim of her cup with her finger. "You two have lived through the dark ages and beyond... Sometimes, I look at you and your brother and I can't even wrap my mind around it... There are probably things you've seen with your own eyes that are not written in any history books. I would love to ask you a few questions and pick your brains one day."

Cole smirked, his blue eyes crinkling at the corners. "Sure," he replied, his voice a soft purr. "You do that with Damian and watch him get up and walk out on you while muttering something like 'this discussion is over'. Trust me, even my vampire strength won't be enough to stop him. I wouldn't—"

Suddenly, a loud bang rolled through the area, causing Cole to flinch and still, listening intently. A noise of hundreds of voices assailed his sensitive hearing, and a moment later, a low buzzing and vibration filled the room. River jumped to her feet, knocking her cup off the table. It broke with a loud crunch, pieces of ceramic scattering over the tiles.

"What's going on?" River's voice shook, her hand reaching down to her gun holster of their own accord.

"Someone triggered the magical alarm system the Guardians placed over the property." Cole closed his eyes, sharpening his sense of smell, and then pressed his hand over his nose. "Frigging werewolves... the reek..." He glanced at River, thinking of the best course of action. "Get Ace and go to the left wing of the house. You'll be safe there. Just stay inside and wait for me. I'll check what's going on and find you there."

Without waiting for her reply, he grabbed his trench coat and put it on as he jetted out the door. At his full speed, he crossed the hall and zoomed into an empty room at the opposite end. Carefully moving blinds aside, he peeked outside, and the small hairs on the back of his neck rose. The gates were broken by a powerful impact, warped into a metal ball. He didn't think something like this could have been done by a human or even a purebred lycanthrope. It meant the werewolves had at least one wizard with them.

As far as he could see, the perimeter of the property, following the line of the fence, was surrounded by men and their vehicles—mostly trucks. A large group of men was walking toward the doors of the house, armed with firearms, swords and knives, silver-infested clubs, and silver chains and nets. Even from the inside of the house, Cole could detect the powerful energy signature they projected, and he had no doubt quite a few of them were purebred lycanthropes. It meant they were strong, fast, and could transform into their wolf form at any time of the month.

Cole crossed the room and ran to the left wing of the house. To his relief, River and Ace were there already.

"The property is surrounded. There are just too many of them," he said quietly. Reaching into his pocket, he produced the small vial with the potion and gave it to Ace. "Open the portal—"

A loud banging on the entrance door interrupted him, and he spun in the direction of the sound, his eyes igniting with a murderous scarlet glow.

"Detective Evans!" a deep male voice shouted from outside. "We know you're harboring Cole Adams. Give him to us, and I promise no one will get hurt. Except him, of course." An outburst of wild laughter accompanied the man's words.

River winced as if the words physically hurt her and took a step toward the entrance into the foyer, anger twisting her face. The buzzing and vibration of the wards became louder. Cole seized her arm, staring down at her heavily.

"What are you doing, River? Don't you dare open that door," he hissed, his fingers digging into her forearm. Turning to Ace, he growled, "Open the goddamn portal, Ace. Now!"

"Wait, Cole," River whispered, prying his fingers off her arm. "Maybe I can talk to them. After all, I am a police officer."

"River, there is no reasoning with werewolves, especially

when they are hell-bent on revenge. They're not going to care about your badge. We have to leave," he said quietly.

"I hate running just because a bunch of rabid dogs are banging on the door. The wards will hold! The Guardians Mages placed them. Do you always do what your brother says?" grumbled Ace, searching for something in her pocket. She found a piece of chalk and started to draw a large pentagram on the wall.

"No," growled Cole, throwing his hands up. "Only when he's right! Do what I say, Ace!"

"Detective Evens!" shouted the werewolf. "Open the door. Last warning!"

The sound of police sirens broke through the shouting of the attackers and the loud buzzing of the wards.

"Christ almighty! Who called the police?" yelled Cole, slamming his fist against the wall, leaving a gaping hole in the drywall. "All I need is for the local human authorities to get involved." He dropped his arms, shaking his head. "Dammit! Angry werewolves will eat them for breakfast."

Metallic clicks of armed weapons reached Cole's ears, and he pressed his hands to his face, thousands of thoughts rushing through his mind. Like a chess player, he tried to see all possible moves and combinations ahead, but nothing he could think of looked good.

If he left now, the werewolves would break into the house. The police would try to stop them, and it'd be a massacre. If he didn't leave, trying to stand his ground, they would break in anyway, possibly damaging the wards and exposing the entrance to the sacred lake hidden under Paradise Manor. The police would get involved with the same deadly outcome. If he gave himself up, the police would still step in to deal with the possible hostage situation, anyway.

No matter how he twisted and turned the situation, both the

death of humans and the possible exposure of the World of Magic were unavoidable.

River's phone rang, breaking through the disarray of thoughts in his mind. She pulled it out and answered the call, putting it on speaker.

"River," Jesse's troubled voice sounded across the line. "Are you okay? Is Cole Adams with you?"

"Jesse, I'm fine," replied River, sounding absolutely calm and even. "Cole is with me, but I need you to take your people and leave as soon as possible. I promise I'll be fine."

"What are you talking about?" yelled Jesse, tones of desperation clear in his voice. "Paradise Manor is under siege! I've never seen anything like this. They're all armed, and I bet you anything, unless you're going to give them Cole, they're not going to stop. Their leader, Simon Cox, is open for negotiations, but only if I come in person and unarmed. I can't leave you in this situation, River. I'm coming up to see if I can reason with him."

"Jesse, no!" yelled River. "I'm begging you! Stay back and take your people as far away from here as possible. They're all werewolves, Jesse. You're dealing with the World of Magic. They will kill you!"

"I know," replied Jesse, his voice calm and resolute, "but as far as I can see, there is no winning here, and I will never leave you unprotected. River, I'm an experienced negotiator, and it's not the first tough situation for me. Just let me do my job."

Short beeps announced that Jesse hung up the phone. Cole turned to Ace, his pale face ashen.

"Goddamn idiot," Cole moaned, realizing with painful clarity that the situation had just become worse. "Ace, open the portal. You and River are leaving now."

"No, Cole, please. For once, don't listen to your brother," Ace whispered, tears gathering in her eyes. "Don't you understand? I can't leave you behind. Besides, Moore would skin me alive for leaving my charge unprotected... What am I saying? Cole, I—"

"Do it," Cole interrupted her. "I'll see if I can save Jesse and get the police out of harm's way. After that, Jesse and I will stay in the left wing and pray that the wards will hold."

"Wait..." Ace rushed into the foyer and halted in front of the entrance door. Cole and River exchanged a quick look and followed her. She moved her arm in a wide arch, whispering something, and the soft yellow glow of her spell surrounded the doorway. "It's just a basic protection spell. Sorry, I've never learned anything more potent." She threw a guilty look at Cole. "Not a studious type... But if you stay on this side of the threshold, you should be safe... At least from bullets."

"Thank you." Cole nodded. He didn't believe Ace's protection magic could withhold a major attack, but he hoped it would be enough to protect him from mundane weapons. Pointing back at the hallway on the left, he added, "Now you and River must go."

Switching his focus to the events unfolding outside and with all his senses stretched to the maximum, he approached the door and opened it, making sure to remain behind the threshold. The entire area in front of the house was crowded with the attackers. Jesse stood on the steps with his back toward the entrance. One of the werewolves—purebred, judging by the powerful energy he was projecting—held a gun trained at Jesse's chest. An older man with untidy gray hair stood next to the werewolf. He was dressed in leather pants and a jacket, and despite the absence of any kind of weapons in his hands, he looked like a poster child for a motorcycle gang.

"Release Detective Williams, and I will come with you willingly," said Cole, raising his voice over the noise of the crowd.

Simon lowered his gun and exchanged a quick look with the man next to him. Jesse let out a ragged breath, throwing a glance at Cole over his shoulder.

"Who said we want you to go with us, anyway? We just want you dead. I mean the true death, where you're a pile of ashes under my boots. You and the rest of your vamps," said Simon with a nonchalant shrug. He looked at his companion again, giving him a curt nod, and they barked laughing.

"*Moderius*," the biker-looking man in leather yelled, and his eyes ignited with a sinister purple glow as he directed the flow of his magic at Cole. The feeble shield Ace had conjured wasn't potent enough to stop it, and the stream of magical energy wrapped tightly around Cole. A high-voltage orb crackling with electrical discharges materialized in the man's other hand, and he pulled his arm back, propelling it at Cole's chest.

Cole growled, struggling against the hold of the man's magic, but his moves were lethargically slow. Jesse gasped and darted to the side, taking the energy orb in his chest as he shielded Cole with his body. The orb burned through his bullet-proof vest and dissipated, leaving a bleeding hole the size of a golf ball behind. For a brief moment, Jesse stood still, his fingers grasping at his chest. Then he swayed and collapsed to the side, blood seeping from the corner of his mouth. His slowly fading eyes found Cole's, and his lips twitched, forming a faint smile.

"Protect River... I can't..." he whispered with his last breath.

CHAPTER 23

~ COLE ADAMS ~

Cole roared as an overwhelming fury seared through him, his fingers elongating into sharp claws. His eyes ignited brighter with a deadly scarlet light, and his fangs expanded to their full length. But as he glanced back, he saw River and Ace still standing at the entrance into the foyer, staring at Jesse's lifeless body in shock. River didn't scream, but her face reflected a mix of horror and undiluted anger.

The group of werewolves that stood a few feet away from the house advanced forward, running toward the door, shouting threats and brandishing their weapons. The wizard regrouped and conjured another energy orb, ready to send it flying. Even though the spell's effect started to wear off, Cole moved a lot slower than he normally would, but he was still faster than the lycanthropes. In one move, he slammed the door shut and locked it, spinning in place.

"What the hell, Ace!" he shouted, making his way toward them. "Why are you still here?"

He yanked the potion out of her hand and smashed the vial against the pentagram Ace had drawn earlier. The fragile bottle exploded in a shower of sparkling splinters, cutting his hand.

The sharp pain just fueled the anger he felt, and a feral growl rumbled in his chest. As the thick blue liquid mixed in with his blood dripped down the wall, he turned to face Ace.

"Start chanting, goddammit!" he yelled, placing his hands on River's shoulders.

The banging on the door became louder, and the house rattled, impacted by a powerful spell. The wards buzzed louder, responding to the assault of magical energy. Ace started to chant, her voice trembling with effort. The air in front of the pentagram shimmered, and finally, a large vortex rotating with sparkling blue lights opened up before them. River gasped, her shoulders stiffening under Cole's grip.

"River, go!" Cole didn't wait for her response and pushed her through the portal.

The house shook again, and the door blew up, pieces of wood scattering all over the foyer. Cole grabbed Ace's hand, pulling her closer to the portal.

"Together," he growled and jumped through it, yanking Ace with him.

"*Incanto Comlium,*" she yelled, closing the portal behind them.

COLE WALKED out of the portal and halted, staring around. He stood in front of a long white fence surrounding a large piece of land with a small ranch house visible in the distance. There was nothing except for the endless plains of the Sonoran Desert for miles around.

"Where are we?" asked River, staring around in shock.

"Arizona," muttered Cole absentmindedly, reaching in his pocket.

He pulled out his phone and quickly scrolled through his contact list. Then he pressed the dial button and listened to the dialing tone, tapping his foot impatiently.

"Hawk, hello," he said with relief. "This is Cole Adams. Damian's—"

"I know who you are, King," replied the old Alpha, his voice coming muffled through the phone. "I'm going to send my son to walk you through the wards."

"Please, do it fast." Cole looked around, searching for any sign of trouble. "Simon had a wizard with him. I'm sure it won't take him long to trace my portal to your location."

He heard a loud thud as Hawk slammed his fist against something, followed by a slew of profanities. "I'm coming, Cole. Hang in there."

As soon as Hawk hung up, Cole found another phone number in the contact list and dialed it, his fingers nearly crushing the device.

"*Monsieur* Adams, I think I know why you're calling," Luc's voice sounded on the other end of the line. "The situation at Paradise Manor, I presume?"

"Yes, my lord," replied Cole. As fast as he could, he told the latest events to Luc de la Crosse.

"Yes, I expected that. After Commander Blake showed up at my doorsteps, asking for a portal potion, I expected something like this to happen. The unrest in Arizona has been growing for a while, and now, it's finally spilled into the realm of humans." The Master Warden sighed and fell silent for a brief moment. "Where are you, Cole? Is Detective Evans safe?"

"We're in the middle of nowhere, at Hawk's ranch," replied Cole, throwing a quick glance at the house. "He offered Damian and me the protection of his pack. River Evans and Ace are with me."

"Perfect," murmured Luc. "Stay there, *mon ami*. My Wardens are already at Paradise Manor, and from what they can see, the wards are still intact. We'll speak soon."

As Luc hung up, Cole put the phone back into his pocket and turned to Ace and River. "Hawk is coming to walk us through the wards. We should be safe here. At least for a while."

A few seconds later, an older man came running across the property. He halted in front of the white fence, breathing heavily with his hand pressed to his chest. Giving a quick nod to Cole, he unlocked the gate, pulling it open, and walked outside.

"Mr. Adams," he said. "Please, come in." He gestured at the entrance and turned to River and Ace. "Detective Evans? Ace?" River and Ace exchanged a surprised look and nodded. "Please, come inside. All of you are welcome in my home."

Cole walked through the property, following Hawk. Despite the hour, the ranch was empty, and the machine shop at the far end of the land remained dark and silent. Everything looked quiet and peaceful, but Cole couldn't get rid of the feeling of being watched. Even though until now Arizona's vampires and werewolves had lived in peace, there had never been any warm feelings between these two powerful supernatural clans, and Cole wasn't sure what to expect. With his sharp vampiric senses, he couldn't help but detect the presence of werewolves all around him, and his skin crawled with anticipation of trouble. Nevertheless, he clenched his teeth and kept walking, his eyes registering the smallest details and the tiniest movements.

Hawk stepped up the short staircase leading to the porch and opened the door, allowing Ace and River to pass through first. But as Cole approached him, he put his hand on his arm, halting him.

"Cole, my house is not much, but I want you to know that you are a welcome guest," he said quietly. "I'm sure you don't feel comfortable in the presence of my pack, so before you meet them, I wanted to reassure you that you are absolutely safe here. I promised your brother that my pack and I will protect you, and I stand by my words."

Cole met the old Alpha's eyes, which were glowing with a soft golden light characteristic to purebred werewolves on high alert and they reminded him of the eyes of his brother. A soft smile touched his lips, and he offered his hand to Hawk.

"Thank you," he said, squeezing Hawk's callused hand. "I will never forget your kindness."

Hawk winked, gesturing for him to come in. "It's nice to have a king owing you a favor."

Cole chuckled and walked inside. As soon as he crossed the threshold, the magical energy of lycanthropes enveloped him, invading all his senses with renewed strength, and he had to make an effort not to clasp his hand over his mouth and nose. The small lobby was empty, but the soft sound of chatter came from an open door leading into the kitchen. Hawk motioned for him to follow and walked inside.

The kitchen wasn't large, but like everything Cole had seen so far, it was clean and well taken care of. White curtains with a floral design adorned the only window, and a pot with a small decorative cactus sat on the windowsill. A scent of freshly made coffee permeated the air, and a young man with shoulder-length black hair served the hot beverage to Ace and River, who sat by the table located in the middle of the room. A second man stood by the window, leaning his back against the wall with his arms crossed over his chest. Dressed in plain blue jeans and plaid shirts, the men looked like they could have been brothers. Both were long-legged and muscular, and judging by their energy signature and the slightly glowing golden eyes, they were purebred werewolves.

As soon as they noticed Cole, they froze in place and their eyes lit up brighter. Hawk raised his hand warningly and turned to Cole.

"Mr. Adams," he said, pulling a chair out and gesturing for him to sit down. "These are my sons, Griffin"—he pointed at the man next to the window—"and Atticus. I summoned them after I talked to Commander Blake."

The older man pushed away from the wall and slightly

inclined his head, a crooked smirk on his lips. "Your Majesty," he said in an attempt to sound respectful, but a layer of sarcasm underlay his every word. "Pleased to make your acquaintance."

"My liege." A wide grin split Atticus' face as he gave Cole a ceremonious bow infused with good-natured humor.

Cole glanced at Hawk, slightly confused by such a welcome, but the old Alpha just shrugged, wagging his finger at his sons.

"My name is Cole," he said as calmly as he could muster in the situation. "There is no need for titles and bows. I appreciate your help."

"Well, that's something I haven't done yet." Atticus lowered on the chair next to Ace, his golden eyes darting to her for a brief moment.

"What would that be?" asked Cole, leaning his shoulder against the doorframe as he observed the young man with curiosity.

"Being a bodyguard to a king, of course," he replied, arching his eyebrow.

"A Vampire King," muttered Griffin dryly, looking away, disdain curving his lips.

"We discussed it, Griffin." Hawk frowned, taking a step toward his older son, but Cole raised his hand, stopping him.

He crossed the kitchen and halted in front of Griffin. The werewolf straightened, staring down at him coldly, and just now Cole realized that the man had to be at least six-foot-seven as he towered a few inches over him. He looked at River and Ace and then turned back to Griffin.

"Yes, I'm a vampire," he said, his voice soft but firm. "I was turned over a thousand years ago—" He heard a high-pitched whistle and glanced over his shoulder to see Atticus' widened eyes. Giving him a lopsided smirk, he switched his attention to Griffin. "It wasn't my choice to become one, just like it wasn't your choice to be born a werewolf. But I am what I am, and I accept it. However, if it's hard for you to tolerate my presence,

I'll gladly leave your home as long as you promise to protect my friends." He pointed at River and Ace.

Ace got up, her face turning ashen, her hand lowering to her hip, but River gave her a slight shake of her head and turned in her chair to face Griffin.

"Listen, Griffin," she said with a sigh. "I'm new to the World of Magic, and I have a hard time understanding this silent hostility between werewolves and vampires, but there is one thing I must tell you." She got up, her moves weary as if she were too tired to move. "I am human, and I'm not Cole's blood donor or lover. But a few months ago, Cole and his brother saved my life, risking everything for me, even though they barely knew me. I'll never forget it."

She walked up to Cole, wrapped her arm around his waist and looked into his eyes, a gentle smile lighting up her features.

"Damian and Cole are my brothers in everything but blood," she continued, switching her gaze to Griffin. "Besides my father, they are the only family I have, and I would do anything to keep them both safe." She pulled up to her tiptoes and gently kissed Cole on his cheek. Giving him a tiny smile, she returned to the table and sat down, staring at Griffin pointedly.

"Griffin—," started Cole but fell silent as the amount of werewolves' energy in the area suddenly increased tenfold, pressing on his senses. He spun around, meeting Hawk's troubled eyes, and then turned back to his son. "Griffin, Simon and his pack are here. You can throw me outside your property line, and there is a chance they will leave your pack alone." He glanced back at Hawk and Atticus, and a wild smirk crossed his face. "Or we can fight. Together. So, what is it going to be? Make your choice, and I swear to honor your decision."

Before Griffin could reply, a young man, no older than twenty, rushed into the room and stopped, gasping for air with his mouth open.

"Hawk," he managed to say between breaths. "Simon is here.

His pack is"—he made a wide gesture with both arms—"enormous. I've never seen anything like this. You got to see it, Pack Master. The rest of our men are already by the gates."

"So, what is it going to be, Griffin?" Cole pulled the side of his trench coat open, showing his sword sheathed beneath it.

The werewolf looked down at Cole, his mouth pressed into a stubborn line. He grunted and shook his head, but then held out his hand, and Cole took it, squeezing it in a firm handshake.

"This goes against everything I grew up believing in," Griffin growled, and the air around him shimmered as he partially transformed, seemingly getting taller and more muscled than he had already been. "But, what the hell? I hate Simon Cox, anyway, and it's about time someone taught him a lesson. We stand together, King. I don't betray people... um... vampires to whom my father offered the pack's protection."

"Good choice," River murmured, rising, her gun in her hand. Ace stood by her side, holding her sword.

"Whoa, timeout, Detective," said Atticus, shaking his head. "You're human. And you are"—he threw a quizzical glance at Ace—"just a little girl. You're staying here."

"A little girl?" Ace gasped indignantly.

"Try stopping me," River snapped, raking the young werewolf with an icy stare. "It's about time I meet this Simon face to face. He killed my ex-partner, and I believe I owe him a nice silver bullet with my undying gratitude." She jerked her chin toward the door. "Cole, Ace, are you coming?"

With her gun in her hand, she walked out the door.

"Damn, girl." Atticus laughed, throwing his head back, the excitement of the upcoming fight igniting his eyes with a bright golden light.

Cole just shook his head and rushed out to catch up with River.

CHAPTER 24

~ COLE ADAMS ~

Cole walked out on the porch and stopped dead in his tracks. When the young messenger said Simon's pack was enormous, he didn't give it justice. Back in Paradise Manor, Cole neither had the time nor opportunity to truly estimate the size of the opposing forces, but now, as he took in the sheer number of men in Simon's pack, cold shivers ran down his back.

The army of werewolves stretched as far as he could see, following the shape of the fence that was surrounding the ranch. The men spoke and laughed loudly, their chatter turning into a continuous growling noise. The thick cloud of werewolves' magical energy mixed in with the odor of their bodies polluted the air, making him groan and press his hand over his nose and mouth. But as he forced himself to lower his hand and sharpen his senses, he realized that Simon's army consisted of not only werewolves but also demons and possibly other beings of magic he couldn't identify from this distance. Compared to them, Hawk's entire pack looked like a drop in the bucket.

A light tap on his shoulder ripped him out of his thoughts,

and he snapped his head to find Atticus standing next to him. The young werewolf smiled his friendly, open-hearted smile, pointing at the dark line of the enemy forces.

"Wow, I didn't realize Simon wanted you that bad," he muttered, shaking his head. "He's really outdone himself."

"I don't think he wants only Cole." Hawk stepped on Cole's other side. The old Alpha looked calm on the outside, but his tightly clenched fists showed his real state of mind. "He wants our land, and he wants my pack. I think he's using the situation to his advantage. Getting vengeance for the fallen is just an excuse."

"There are too many of them," said Griffin quietly. "Even with an ancient vampire on our side, we stand no chance."

"This is why we're not going to fight," Hawk replied and headed toward the fence, motioning for them to follow him. "As long as we stand behind the fence, there is nothing they can do."

Once they approached the line of Hawk's werewolves, the men stepped aside, allowing them to pass through. Hawk halted in front of the fence and tilted his head, folding his arms. Cole stopped next to him, observing the opposing army with interest. Now closer, Simon's pack looked even more impressive. Most of the werewolves, however, weren't purebred, and since it wasn't the time of the full moon, they couldn't transform. Despite that, they still presented a dangerous power—all of them stronger and faster than average humans. Besides werewolves, quite a few demons and shifters stood mixed in with the pack, and it was clear Simon spent a pretty penny to hire all these supernatural mercenaries.

Feeling a soft touch to his shoulder, he turned around to see River and Ace standing behind him. He smiled at them calmly, hoping that his acting ability didn't fail him and that his smile was reassuring enough.

"It's going to be okay," he said, taking River's hand into his.

"They can't cross the property line, and these wards will hold for quite some time."

River gave him a reproachful gaze, all but rolling her eyes. "For an old vampire, you're a pretty bad liar, Cole Adams, but I appreciate the effort."

A tall werewolf approached the fence and put his hand on it, eliciting a furious reaction out of the wards. Cole recognized him right away. It was the same man with whom he had spoken at the door in Paradise Manor, the same man who put the order to kill him but murdered Jesse instead. It was Simon Cox.

"Hawk," Simon said, disdain distorting his wolfish features, deep creases crossing his narrow forehead with a protruding brow bone. "And here I thought you couldn't fall any lower. Your preaching the Vampire Court's innocence in murders of our kind was one thing, but you offering your pack's protection to a bloodsucker is—"

He cut himself off and shook his head, turning toward his wolves as if asking for their support. The loud shouts, the angry downpour of profanities and raised weapons were the answer to his words.

"Simon, you know Hawk is right." A man moved forward from behind Hawk's back, stepping next to him. "I have proof of that. I witnessed the attack of the wurdulaks myself—"

"Kaleb!" Simon growled, and his lips drew back in a snarl. "You're a fuckin' turncoat. You left your pack to support this traitor and his vamp?"

"Why are you talking to them, Simon?" Simon's wizard approached the fence and moved his hand, probing the wards.

The wards buzzed, and for a brief moment, a dome built of glowing red lines materialized over Hawk's property, completely encapsulating it. The wizard pulled his hand away, raking his short, knobby fingers through his long, greasy hair, discomfort reflected on his wrinkled face.

"Enjoying the view, old meat-bag?" asked Hawk snidely, cocking his head.

"These wards are quite potent," the wizard replied, placing his hands on his hips. "But I'm sure you know there is no such thing as unbreakable protection magic, no matter who cast it. If one being of magic conjured wards, the other can break them. And I'm here to prove that theory." He raised his hand above his head and twirled his wrist. Four people separated from the crowd—three men and a woman. "Let me know when you're in position."

The four nodded and took off running—two men went to the left, and a woman and man to the right.

"Dammit," muttered Cole, biting his lips. "I think I know what they're planning to do."

"It doesn't matter," replied Hawk with an indifferent shrug of his shoulders. "I've seen a hundred of Guardian Witches trying to break these wards and they had a hard time. I'm not going to worry about four self-taught, immature spell-slingers."

"I understand, but just in case, we should be ready," Cole said quietly.

Just as if to prove his words, the wizard pulled the sleeves of his jacket up and placed his palms on the fence, chanting softly under his breath. His hands lit up with a sinister purple glow, and a thick ray of dark magical energy escaped his hands, traveling up the protective dome. Cole twirled around, noticing four more similar rays of purple light running up and connecting into a single point high above their heads.

Dammit... They're building a pentagram. Anything could happen after they are done with that. Cole reached into his pocket and pulled his phone out, quickly checking the lock screen. There were no messages or notifications. He dialed Damian's phone number, but after a few short beeps, the call went to his brother's voice mail. *Dima, come on... Don't you know that when the little black box in your pocket rings, you need to press the green button?* He exhaled a ragged breath and hung up the phone, putting it back into his pocket. *Dima, I need you to be all right...*

"Cole, what is that?" He heard River's troubled voice and glanced at her. She was pointing up, her eyes wide with wonderment.

A few more lines crossed the dome, and the wards howled, vibrating angrily.

"They completed the pentagram," answered Cole, keeping his eyes on the opposing army as the werewolves and demons took a step closer to the fence, a carnivorous hunger and bloodlust reflected on their faces void of any humanity.

"What do we do?" River whispered, taking his elbow.

"We do the hardest thing in the world—we wait." Cole glanced down at her but didn't find fear in her calm face, just cold determination.

As the dark wizards kept chanting, the purple light grew brighter, and the buzz of the wards became so loud, it was nearly unbearable. The web of blazing, red lines crisscrossed over the property. However, their light started to dim down a little, overpowered by the purple glow. Cole knew it would only be a matter of time before the wards fell. It might take them quite a few hours—days, even—to break them, but if they had more wizards to replace the exhausted ones, sooner or later, they would have it done.

"Hey, King," Atticus' voice sounded on Cole's left, and he turned his head. "I've never seen a vampire fight." The young werewolf smiled, showing his elongated fangs.

Cole gave him a quick once-over, wondering how young Hawk's son was. "If we survive this, I promise to spar with you. If you want, of course."

"If I want?" Atticus laughed, tapping Cole on his shoulder. "Hell, yeah. Bring it on, Majesty."

A terrible ruckus rose in the air. It was so sudden that Cole yelped, pressing his hands to his ears to protect his overly sensitive hearing. The wards lit up with a blinding red light, and fire ignited at the top of the glowing dome, smoldering flames slowly gliding up and down the red lines.

"Heaven and Earth," growled Hawk, his entire body locked with rage. "This asshole is going to do it... They'll break the goddamn wards."

As if hearing his words, the dark mass of the opposing army shifted forward and raised their assorted weapons, positioning themselves closer to the fence, ready to spring into action at the first command of their pack master.

Suddenly, a bright flare of light ignited somewhere in the desert behind the enemy line, and the ground shook violently. A bright zigzag of a lightning bolt split the sky, and thunder rolled across it, rising over the noise of the wards. Most of the men spun around, but the wizards kept at what they were doing, ignoring everything around them.

"Put down your weapons and stop what you're doing at once!" A magically magnified voice rose above the pandemonium.

"Damian," whispered Cole. As he recognized his brother's voice, happiness bubbled up in him. "But how...?"

"Let me through!" Simon shouted, yanking his men out of his way.

The crowd parted, allowing Simon to pass, and now Cole could see his brother standing with his fists clenched, his entire body locked with fury. A tall man Cole had never seen before stood next to Damian, a derisive smirk playing on his lips as he glowered at the wizards working on the wards.

Simon shoved his hands into his pockets and spat, giving Damian a demonstrative once-over. Then he glanced back at his massive army, and a burst of laughter erupted from his mouth, accompanied by wild snorts as he bent forward, slapping his hands on his thighs.

"Make us stop, giant," he said, cutting his laughter abruptly. "I wanna see you do that."

"No problem," Damian replied through gritted teeth, and the glowing daggers materialized in his hands. His eyes swept along the length of the massive army, and a dark smirk curved his lips. "Looks like a nice workout. I needed one."

"Uhhh, scary." Simon shivered, rubbing his arms with his hands. Then he looked back and waved his hand.

Five men separated from the crowd and approached him, exuding a vibe of superiority with their every move. Without slowing down, they muttered something, and energy orbs materialized in their palms. They propelled them forward, aiming at Damian, but Damian moved his hand, and a thin, glowing layer of his protection spell wrapped around him and his companion.

Unfortunately, the wizards didn't get discouraged, and neither did they become any smarter. They kept conjuring one energy orb after another, bombarding Damian's shield with a mighty force but with nothing to show for it. Damian folded his arms, the smirk on his face growing wider and wider with every next failed attempt. Finally, his companion groaned and stepped forward with an impatient wave of his hand.

"Allow me to teach you how it's done," he grumbled, raising his arms.

He muttered something under his breath, and a powerful wave of magical energy spread around him. It impacted Simon and his wizards with a mighty force, sending them flying backward into the other members of his army and creating momentary confusion and disorder.

"They call themselves wizards. A bunch of amateurs." The man tongued his cheek, staring at Simon's wizards struggling to get to their feet. "These young ones truly have no idea what they're doing. They used to make them better in my days."

Finally, Simon was able to restore order, and with furious roars, his men rushed toward Damian and his companion. But as another flare of light ignited behind Damian, they came to a screeching halt. Unable to stop right away, the back lines smashed into the front ones, making them stagger forward and causing some people to fall, cursing angrily.

Five horsemen, dressed in ancient armor with white coats over it, rode from the desert and halted next to Damian, sunlight throwing playful flares on their breastplates. The front horseman leaned down slightly to tap Damian's shoulder and then raised his leather-gloved hand. Cole froze in place as he recognized Luc de la Crosse. He had seen the Master Warden before, but never had he seen him in his full regalia and his true form.

"In the name of the Destiny Council, Simon Cox, I command you to stop what you're doing or suffer the consequences." Luc wasn't shouting, but his strong voice carried through the desert, rising above the ruckus of the wards.

"I second that," Damian added, and his entire body lit up with a blinding white light as he assumed his Destiny Enforcer form, his mighty black wings expanding behind his back. Then he looked up at the Master Warden and a lopsided smirk touched his lips. "What took you so long, man? I know you ordered us to hold back and avoid the fight for as long as possible, but if you waited a few more minutes..." He chuckled darkly.

Doofus... Cole snorted at his brother's familiar behavior and the lack of manners appropriate to the World of Magic, and he shook his head slightly, just happy to see Damian here and in one piece.

"Whoa..." Atticus breathed, his eyes alight with awe. "Who are these people?"

"On the horse—the Master Warden of Arizona," Cole answered quietly. "With the wings"—he looked at the young man and smiled, pride constricting his throat—"my brother... The Commander of the Destiny Enforcers."

A collective gasp rushed through the lines of Simon's army,

and a shuffling noise rose above the men as they dropped their weapons and kneeled.

"Simon Cox," Luc de la Crosse continued, pointing at the Alpha. "You're under arrest for exposing the World of Magic and killing a human in cold blood. I offer safety to all the members of your pack if you comply with my orders willingly." He looked at Damian and gave him a curt nod. "Do your duty, Commander Blake."

Simon looked back at his people, and then his eyes darted to Cole and Hawk. For a brief moment, deep loathing distorted his features, but he didn't say anything and turned away, facing the Master Warden.

Moving slowly, he kneeled and bowed his head. Damian extended his hand and his daggers vanished, replaced by a pair of handcuffs glowing with bright white light. He approached Simon and touched his head. The Destiny Cuffs shone brighter and disappeared just to materialize on Simon's wrists, binding them together. The werewolf moaned, his eyes rolled back, and he fell to the side, unconscious.

"This war between the werewolves and the Arizona Vampire Court is over! On behalf of the Destiny Council, I attest that Cole Adams and his subjects are not responsible for the deaths of the werewolves." Luc de la Crosse looked down at Simon's army and sighed. "You are free to go," he said with a dismissive wave of his hand. "Next time, choose your alliances wiser."

As the crowd dispersed, all but running into the desert, Luc dismounted and approached Damian.

"Commander Blake," he said softly, pointing at the other Wardens. "My Brothers will take the werewolf to the Destiny Council holding facility." His hazel eyes flashed to Damian's companion, and he gave him a slight nod. "I see you found Yakov Bruce. I'm not going to ask why or how because we need a powerful ally. In light of the latest events, we need to have a serious discussion."

Cole approached the fence, his eyes meeting Damian's glowing gaze. "I was trying to call you to let you know we were here," he said, his voice hoarse, "but I couldn't get through. How did you know? Dima—"

"I'll explain everything in a moment, Cole." Damian stepped closer, switching his attention to Hawk. "Hawk, would you kindly invite the three of us in? Like the Master Warden said—we have a serious issue on our hands."

CHAPTER 25

~ DAMIAN BLAKE ~

Hawk's kitchen seemed to be too small to accommodate all the people gathered there. While everyone settled down, Atticus brewed a fresh pot of coffee, and the warm, bitter aroma spread through the air. Moving fluidly and weightlessly for a man of his size, he filled a few cups with the hot drink, taking care of everyone in the room.

With so many people crammed into the small kitchen, Damian's claustrophobia reared its ugly head, and he had to make an effort to suppress the debilitating need to be out of there and remain calm. He took a large gulp of hot coffee, nearly burning his tongue, and started talking.

It didn't take long for him to brief everyone in, going over everything that had happened since Jamie and he arrived in Encino and found JB. When he was done, he dropped his arms on the table. His eyes swept over the faces of the people gathered in the small kitchen, and bitter disappointment in himself twisted his gut, his scalp prickling with shame.

"I can't believe I made such a stupid mistake," he said, lowering his head. "Since the moment I started searching for a necromancer, I had a feeling that he was toying with me, playing some kind of twisted cat-and-mouse game. It felt as if he wanted me to find him, leading me toward him." He slammed his fist on the table, making the cups jump and spill some of their contents. "God damn it all! How could I be so blind?"

"Damian, you couldn't have known all that. We all make mistakes," started River but pulled back under his pained stare.

"I'm a Destiny Enforcer. When I make mistakes, people get hurt," he said, his voice strained. "Jesse is dead because I made this mistake."

"Take a notch down on the self-loathing, Commander." Luc de la Crosse touched his shoulder, his chainmail rustling softly with his every move. "First, Jesse is dead because he didn't listen to Cole and River when they told him to stay back. Second, you're not the only one who was blindsided. You reported to me on every move you made, and it never even crossed my mind that JB was Yakov Bruce. If I had realized it sooner, I would've told you that Yakov works for the Destiny Council, and you would've known that Az is not who he claims to be."

The old wizard chuckled, taking a sip of his coffee. "Yeah, JB is not the name I use commonly, but some people do call me that. Imagine my shock when these two showed up at my doorstep, claiming I was an evil necromancer." He smirked, shaking his head.

"Where is Jamie?" asked Ace, shifting her way closer to Cole. "Is he okay?"

"He's fine," replied Damian. "He should be here in a few hours. When Luc called me, telling me about the situation at Paradise Manor and a possible confrontation at Hawk's ranch, Yakov and I teleported here right away, but Jamie stayed behind to drive the SUV back to Cole's house."

Luc leaned against the counter, the metallic sound of his armor too loud in the silence of the room.

"By the way," he said, "I checked Az's name against the Wardens Archives. Guess what? Azul Moreno is a registered small-time wizard with some clairvoyance. So, who in their right mind could think he mustered such a complex branch of forbidden magic as necromancy?"

"Well, Luc, I think there is a lot more to this Azul Moreno than your archives have registered." Yakov shook his head, reaching in the pocket of his pants. "Unless Az is not Azul Moreno as he claims to be." He placed the dagger on the table and pressed on the eyes of the eagle's head, opening the empty secret compartment. "But unfortunately, no matter who he is, we have a huge problem."

Luc took the dagger from the table. His fingers lit up with a barely noticeable glow of his magic as he probed the weapon with it.

"The blade has no magical properties," he said, giving it back to Yakov. "If I understand you right, something is missing from this small compartment?"

"Yes." Yakov took the dagger, placing it back on the table. "In the year of one thousand eight hundred and twelve of our Lord, I hid a small crystal inside the hilt of this dagger." His fingers traced the shape of the eagle head on the pommel as he sighed and shook his head. "The crystal was a key that locked a dangerous and powerful magical device."

"How powerful?" asked Cole.

"Powerful enough to bring gods to their knees." Yakov rubbed his forehead. "I searched for this device for many years, and finally, in eighteen-twelve, I discovered it among all the treasures Napoleon stole during his Russian invasion. The device is protected by its ancient magic, so it can't be destroyed. I had no choice but to seal it in a box and hide it on the bottom of a lake to make sure that no one ever would find it. Obviously, this Az, whoever he might be, found out about the device and its location." He threw a glance at Damian. "Sorry, Commander, but he manipulated you into stealing the dagger from that private collector for himself and took the key while he was 'scrying' for me."

"The unrest in the Vampire Court, the war between the werewolves and vampires." Damian groaned, hiding his face in his hands. "He did all that just to manipulate me. He made sure that I would find the wurdulak's bite on Ace's neck and start looking for a necromancer. The escalating war between the vampires and werewolves pushed me into a tight spot, and just to make sure I would have no other options but to find the necromancer, he broke the sanctuary law. So, after I knocked on his door, asking questions, all he had to do was give me the answer I desperately wanted to hear."

Damian laughed bitterly, shaking his head. "He even went as far as ordering the wurdulaks he conjured to attack his own house, pretending to save me during the fight." He ran his hands over his face and dropped them on the table with a dull thud. "Dammit! I gave him the key with my own hands and then teleported him out of his house, setting him free." He pressed his hands to his face again and moaned.

"Forget it, Damian," Luc cut him off. "At this point, it's no longer important how he did it and who he manipulated. The important questions are what this device is and why he went through so much trouble to get it?"

"I can answer the first question," said Yakov, throwing the long strands of his hair off his face. "It's a Hollow Band."

Luc pushed away from the counter, his face turning ghostly pale. "What?"

"You heard me, Luc." Yakov met the Warden's widened eyes and then looked away with a deep sigh. "A Hollow Band. There are only two sets in all the worlds—human and magical."

"I know that..." Luc swayed and braced his hands against the table, dropping his head, his long black hair obscuring his face. "Of course, I know that. An unknown Master of the Dark Arts is going through a world of trouble to retrieve a magical device that can bend a god to his will, turning any being of magic, no matter how powerful, into his mindless puppet." He raised his hand, setting his lips into a firm line. "Nope. There is absolutely nothing to worry about." He laughed, his laughter sounding almost hysterical.

"There is only one thing we can do now," said Yakov, rising. "Damian, when was the last time you saw Az?"

Damian glanced at his wristwatch. "About twelve hours ago."

"That's good!" A tentative smile crossed Yakov's face. "Not all is lost then. The lake is not easy to find, and to find the box at the bottom of it is even harder. If Az hasn't been there, it'll take him a long time to find the place. He won't be able to teleport or open a portal, so if we're lucky, he'll have to use mundane methods of transportation, at least for a part of the journey. I can open a portal directly to the lake." He observed everyone in the room, excitement in his eyes. "If Damian and I leave immediately, we can retrieve the device from the lake before Az gets there."

Damian frowned, nibbling on his lip. While Yakov's suggestion sounded like the only option they had, something was bothering him, his intuition throwing red flags in his mind like a football referee.

"JB... um... Yakov," he corrected himself. "There is one question that has been bothering me since I've learned that you're not the necromancer."

"What's that?" Yakov turned to him, his smile slowly morphing into an expression of concern.

"Why did Az send me to find you? He could have told me that the dagger belonged to someone in China, and I would be none the wiser," said Damian. "You're the only person in the entire world who knows about the crystal and the Hollow Band, and he sent me after you."

Yakov frowned, and his shoulders tensed. "You think I didn't ask this very same question myself?" He stifled a sigh, his eyes sliding from Damian to Luc. "The only answer I could come up with was that he wanted me dead, and he hoped that the immortal Commander of the Destiny Enforcers had enough power and magic to end me."

"We don't know Az's supernatural identity or his motives, but if we keep wasting time, we may miss the only window of opportunity we have to retrieve the Hollow Band." Luc straightened and pulled at his chainmail coif as if it were suffocating him. "How much time do you need to prepare the potion, Yakov?"

"Thirty minutes." The wizard replied and turned to Hawk. "Hawk, this potion is pretty simple to brew, and I'm sure I can find all the ingredients I need here, if you allow me to check your kitchen cabinets." He waved his hand around the room.

"Everything I have is at your disposal," replied the Alpha, slightly inclining his head, and then turned to his older son. "Griffin, please make sure the Lord Wizard has everything he needs."

As Yakov started to go through all the herbs and spices Hawk had in his kitchen, Cole approached Damian and touched his shoulder. "Damian, I'm coming with you. Don't argue with me, brother."

"Cole, we're going after a man who can possibly control a vampire with a simple spell." Damian got up, his every cell responding with soreness. "While I would love to have you by my side, I don't think it's a smart idea."

"Actually..." Yakov glanced over his shoulder at Damian. "I think it's the smartest idea I've heard since this morning. I can protect a vampire from the influence of a necromancer, but if for some reason I can't summon mavka Kostroma, Cole is the only one among us all who doesn't need oxygen to survive." He gave Damian another arched stare and returned to his work.

Damian ran both hands through his uneven hair, exhaling a

ragged breath. "Fine. As soon as the potion is ready, Yakov, Cole and I are leaving."

"Perfect. I believe I'm no longer needed here." Luc touched Damian's shoulder, calling for his attention. "Commander, I expect you to contact me as soon as you're back."

"Yes, sir," replied Damian, slightly inclining his head.

Luc said his goodbyes, wishing them good luck, and then snapped his fingers, vanishing from Hawk's house.

Once Luc was gone, Damian turned to River, worry gnawing at his heart. She caught his troubled gaze and warmth suffused her features.

"I have to go back home somehow," she said, making her way closer to him. "I guess I'll call Uber. I'll be all right, though. Don't worry."

"Detective," said Hawk. "You're welcome to stay here until Damian and Cole return. My home is open to all of you at any time."

"Thank you, Hawk." River smiled at the old Alpha. "I appreciate the offer and everything you've done for all of us today, but I have to go to work and call my father to fix my door. Again. I live with a handyman in my house, but my door keeps breaking on a weekly basis." She chuckled softly, giving a slight wink to Damian. "I wonder if I should just leave it off. It'll be cheaper."

"Ace, you're going to return to Paradise Manor with River and wait there for Jamie to brief him in," Damian said and raised his hand as he noticed that Ace jolted up, ready to argue with him. "It's an order, recruit. Don't argue with me. Cole's not only my charge, but he's also my brother. I can protect him."

"Fine," she grumbled, throwing a murderous stare at Damian, eliciting a snort out of Cole.

Damian gave his brother a loaded look and turned to Ace. "Is that the appropriate reply to your Commander?" he asked frostily. "Where are your manners, recruit?"

"The same place where yours are," she muttered, but pressed her fist to her chest and bowed to him. "My lord, I'm yours to command."

Damian groaned, throwing his head back and pressing the heels of his hands to his eyes. Cole chuckled, shaking his head.

"Ace, stop driving my brother crazy," he said pleadingly. "It will come back on me later."

Atticus laughed, but then sobered up and approached Damian. "If you think it's a good idea, I could drive Ace and River back to Blue Creek and stick around to help River's father install the door."

River was about to object, but Damian turned to her, mouthing 'please', and she sighed, gazing at him with reproach.

Turning to the young werewolf, she gave him a warm smile. "Thank you, Atticus. That would be wonderful."

Damian glanced at his wristwatch and took River's elbow. "We have about twenty minutes before the potion is ready," he said, ushering her out of the kitchen. "Can I have a word with you?"

He crossed the small lobby and opened the door, allowing River to walk outside first. The sun was blasting from the clear sky, but the air was still crisp with the morning coolness and filled with the fresh, earthy scent of the desert. He lowered himself on the steps and patted the cold wood next to him, inviting her to sit down.

He rested his shoulder against the railing at the edge of the steps and dropped his arms, closing his eyes. She pushed her arm through the crook of his elbow and lowered her head on his shoulder.

"What did you want to talk about?" she asked, caressing his hand with her thumb.

"Nothing," he replied without opening his eyes. "I just wanted a few minutes of peace with no one asking me any questions."

She chuckled softly. "I wish I could believe you." She rubbed her cheek against his shoulder. "But for such old men, both you and your brother are terrible liars."

He cracked his eyelids open and glanced at her. "We're exceptional liars," he objected, laughter rumbling in his chest. "It's not us. It's you. You're too good at what you do, my lady Detective."

"Nice avoidance maneuver, my lord Commander," she replied in kind, slapping his hand slightly. "You are here with me because there is something you're worried about, but as usual, you can't articulate your feelings even if your life depended on it."

"Feelings? What kind of mythological beasties are those?" He plastered a fake frown on his face. "We manly Destiny Enforcers don't have feelings. We're always cold-minded, and we respond in the same manner whether we're happy or sad."

"Smartass," she murmured, closing her eyes.

For a few seconds, they sat in silence, and Damian couldn't help but enjoy her closeness. Then River shifted and raised her head.

"Dima, is it true?" she asked, gazing up at him. "There is more than one world? Something Yakov had said earlier…" Her voice faded into silence as she expected his answer.

"It's true," he replied at length, considering how much he could tell her without giving too much information to a human who was new to the World of Magic. "You live in what we call the Realm of Humans. Besides that, there is the World of Magic, as in the actual physical place. It's called Kendral, and it is located outside the human realm. Also, there are three magical nexuses here on Earth—the Land of Dreams, the Isle of Legends and the Hidden Kingdom. I don't know much about the Hidden Kingdom, but I've been to Kendral and the other two nexuses."

"Oh, wow," she whispered, her blue eyes lighting up with wonderment. "I wish I could see all that."

He chuckled, and before he could stop himself, his hand went up to her face, caressing her cheek. "Maybe one day?" he said. "Anything to do with magic is never safe, and you must always expect the unexpected. But while all these places are prone to danger, they are also beautiful and mystifying. Every fairytale you've heard as a child, every myth and legend you've ever read, comes to life there. I hope one day I'll be able to show you at least some of these magical places."

She shifted closer to him and encircled his waist, slipping under his arm. He didn't resist, too troubled with the latest revelations. Instead, he planted a soft kiss on the top of her head and pulled her closer to his side.

They didn't speak and didn't move until Cole came out to the porch and tapped his shoulder. "Hey, big bro," he said gently. "I'm sorry, but Yakov is ready. It's time to go."

Damian got up and offered his hand to River. She took it, rising easily to her feet, but before he moved toward the house, she held him back.

"Dima," she whispered, her voice deeper than usual and raspy. "I need you to come back home to me." He didn't reply, a thick lump stuck in his throat, so she placed her hand against his cheek and added, "You hear me, manly, emotionless, antiquated doofus? I need you to return to me. It's an order, soldier."

"Yes, ma'am," he replied, forcing himself to sound even, and pressed his fist to his chest, inclining his head. "I'm yours to command, my lady."

CHAPTER 26

~ DAMIAN BLAKE ~

Damian walked out of the portal and halted, carefully observing his surroundings. The sun was gone, and the velvety dark sky was covered with stars. He was in the middle of a forest. The trees, prepared for the winter, had lost their hefty foliage and stood naked. Through the heavy smell of the damp dirt and musky-sweet odor of decaying leaves, a barely noticeable scent of water touched his nostrils, suggesting they weren't far away from a lake or some kind of body of water. As a light gust of wind rushed through the woods, a rush of cold air grazed Damian's skin, and he shivered, zipping up his jacket.

"Don't move." He heard Yakov's voice and turned in the direction of the sound.

Both Cole and the wizard stood right behind him. Yakov squatted and placed his hands flat against the ground, whispering something under his breath. A wave of magical energy spread around him, moving in all directions. Yakov got up and brushed his palms against his pants.

"That's better," he muttered, but catching Damian's puzzled gaze, he added, "Swamps are all around us. It's not deep, but if you don't know where you're going, you're not going to enjoy the experience." He passed Damian and moved forward, gesturing for them to follow.

A few minutes later, Yakov halted at the edge of the forest and raised his hand, stopping them. Past a narrow clearing, a dark lake spread before them, its motionless waters reflecting the dim light of the moon and stars. The silence seemed to be unnaturally heavy, sending chills down Damian's back. He opened his other sight and quickly scanned the lake and the area around it as far as he could reach.

"I don't sense anything supernatural here," he whispered, tapping Yakov's shoulder. "But the silence…" He shivered like from a gust of cold wind. "It can't be normal."

"It's normal, alright. It's always been like this. This is why the locals call this place the Dead Lake." The old wizard sighed, shaking his head. "You Destiny Enforcers are so limited. When it comes to magic, all you know is the combat aspect of it. Magic is a lot more than just that."

Damian shrugged. "In my line of work, combat magic is what I need."

"Like I said—limited." Yakov waved his hand as if dismissing the issue and walked out into the clearing.

The old wizard approached the lake and took one knee, placing one hand on the ground. He closed his eyes and sucked in a deep breath, the air around him shimmering with a soft white light. Cole and Damian exchanged a look, but neither of them said anything. A few seconds later, Yakov opened his eyes and got up.

"Well, boys, I have good news for you," he said, his eyes darting from Cole to Damian. "If I'm not mistaken, our friendly neighborhood necromancer hasn't been here yet. No one cast any spells or wielded any magic over the lake for quite some time."

"How can you be so sure?" asked Cole, his blue eyes searching the still pool of the lake.

"Magic is a lot more science than you can imagine," replied Yakov. "After all—magical or elemental—it's energy, and just like any energy in nature, it doesn't come out from nowhere and doesn't disappear without a trace. Even the lightest casting leaves a magical energy residue behind." He glanced at Damian, and humorous twinkles appeared in his eyes as he jerked his chin in his direction. "Even your magically illiterate brother can sense it. Am I right, Commander?"

"Yes, sir," replied Damian, inclining his head.

"Well, this area is absolutely clear." Yakov waved his arm in a wide arch and muttered a few words. A large oval window, similar to a communication window, materialized before him, hanging in midair. "Come here, see for yourselves."

Damian stepped behind Yakov and held his breath. Through the window, he could see the flow of magical and elemental energy a lot brighter and clearer than through his other sight. Everything around him shimmered with the four colors of elemental energy and sparkling brilliance of the magical energy. The flow of the energy looked undisturbed and natural, not a touch of man-made magic.

"I've never seen anything like this," whispered Cole, gazing through the window in awe. "I had no idea…"

"You're a vamp, boy." Yakov chuckled, closing the window. "Sorry, but you can't wield or see magic." He gave Cole a quick once-over and shrugged. "It's a shame. You're a clever one."

"You're right, I can't see it," Cole agreed. "I never could, but lately I noticed I can detect its presence."

"Oh?" Yakov glanced at him with renewed interest. "Peculiar. I've never heard of a vampire with such a gift. When all this is over, I would like to run a few tests—"

"My brother is not a lab rat, Yakov," Damian interrupted him dryly, putting his hand on his brother's shoulder.

The old wizard smirked, rolling his eyes. "Relax, Commander. I wouldn't dare hurt the Vampire King of Arizona. Especially now that I know who his brother is." He wagged his eyebrows at Damian.

"So, what do we need to do next?" asked Damian, switching the subject.

"Now, we're going to check if the magical device in question is still here." Yakov moved closer to the lake and took one knee at the edge of the water.

Whispering a spell, he stretched his arms forward, and a heartbeat later, the entire surface of the lake lit up with a shimmering blue light. A weightless, sparkling mist rose above the water and lingered in the air for a few seconds before dissipating.

Yakov expelled a ragged breath and got up, relief lighting up his features. "Yes," he whispered without taking his eyes off the lake. "The portal is still available to me. It's a good sign."

He reached into his pocket and produced an old piece of paper. It was wrinkled, and time had stained it with yellow and brown spots. As he unfolded the paper, Damian peered at it with disbelief—it was absolutely blank. But as the wizard moved his hand over the page, a bright rune lit up on its surface.

"What is it?" asked Damian. "I've never seen a rune like this."

"Unfortunately, what you don't know about magic can fill the Grand Canyon," mumbled Yakov, watching the rune slowly melt in the background. He glanced up at Damian. "If you wish, I could teach you and that pupil of yours... Jamie. You both have quite a natural gift for magic. I know Jamie is marked by the Guardians, but between us, he's not Guardians material. He should be studying with the Wardens. Knowledge and science are his true calling, not combat magic."

"Agreed," murmured Damian. "I wish I had time for learning." He sighed, moving his gaze away from the wizard, staring into the dark forest on the other side of the lake. "I had more than enough training in combat magic, but barely learned the other types of magic when I was sent in the field. After that, it was mission after mission, and then…" His voice broke, and he smirked. "Anyway, I would love to learn more, but time never works in my favor."

"It's understandable. Besides, you're immortal. Immortality presents certain opportunities mortals don't have." He shrugged with a kind smile. "Allow me to explain." Yakov pointed at the paper. "This rune is a marker. The twin-brother of this rune—a so-called base rune—is inscribed on the box with the Hollow Band. If I throw the marker into the water, it will react to the base rune. Assuming the box is still at the bottom of the lake, that is. Fingers crossed…"

He stepped into the water and threw the paper into the lake. For a moment, the paper lingered on the surface of the water and then sank, disappearing into the darkness. A heartbeat later, a large glowing rune materialized, hanging slightly above the surface.

"Yes!" Yakov slapped Damian on his back. "We're not late. The box is still here."

"Perun almighty," exhaled Damian, wiping sweat off his forehead. "At least something went right today…"

"Thank God," murmured Cole, stepping next to him. "I guess now it's my turn?" He turned to Yakov. "How am I going to know where to look for this box? And how does it look?"

"Hold on, Cole. If mavkas still inhabit this lake, you may not need to go for a swim." Yakov bent down and touched the lake, sending a small amount of his magic into the water. Shimmering circles spread over the surface, running away from his hand.

"Mavka Kostroma," he called, gently threading his fingers through the water, "I summon thee, my old friend…"

They waited a few extremely long minutes, but no one answered the summons. Yakov straightened and stepped back on the shore, shaking water off his boots.

"I guess this is where our luck ran out," he muttered and

turned toward Cole, a troubled expression on his face. "Cole, the portal is open." He waved at the lake. "This lake has what locals call a double-bottom. But they are wrong. The lake doesn't have a double-bottom. It has no bottom at all, just a barrier of sorts. Below the lake, there is a different..." His voice trailed off, and he scratched the back of his head. "Once you reach the barrier, you will see the portal. It's a large, rotating vortex. You can't miss it. Go through it, and you'll end up in a different underwater realm, guarded by rusalkas."

"Rusalkas?" asked Damian, chills running down his back. "They're not friendly creatures. Especially not to a man."

"Then it's a good thing your brother is not a man," Yakov murmured. "He's a vampire, and he has no heartbeat. I don't think rusalkas' charms would work on him. At least their influence on him is not going to be as potent as it would be on you or me."

Damian swallowed hard, realizing that as much as he hated to put Cole in any kind of danger, Yakov was right. His vampiric nature would protect his brother from rusalkas' magic. At least he hoped it would. Rusalkas, Slavic spirits inhabiting lakes, swamps, and rivers, were powerful and dangerous. They weren't friendly to humans, and when it came to men, they were extremely hostile. No man could fight their charm and live to tell the tale. Contrary to popular belief, most types of rusalka had legs and looked absolutely normal, so their victims had no idea who they were dealing with until it was too late.

"What other types of rusalkas possess this lake?" asked Damian, watching Cole take his clothes and shoes off, leaving just his pants on.

"Just mavkas," replied Yakov. "They are probably the least dangerous type."

"Uh-huh," murmured Damian, thinking that at least with mavkas Cole could negotiate, and knowing his brother, he could talk his way out of any sticky situation. "Are you sure there are no lobastas here? Fighting with them will present a problem. Even iron and silver can't kill them."

"Good. You do have some knowledge outside combat magic after all." Yakov chuckled, but there was no humor in his laughter. He pulled a gold chain with a small round pendant from under his shirt, taking it off. "No, I've never seen lobastas in this lake. They are too aggressive and territorial to share their domains with other types of water spirits."

Yakov approached Cole and halted, waiting until the vampire put his back-scabbard with his sword on and readjusted the leather straps to make sure they wrapped tightly around his body. Then the wizard put the chain around Cole's neck and pulled at the straps one more time, checking them.

"Cole, when you get there, ask for a mavka named Kostroma," he said, throwing a quick glance at the lake, concern shadowing his features. "Give her this chain, and she'll give you the box in exchange."

Cole inclined his head. "Is there anything else I need to know?"

The wizard ran his fingers over his unshaven chin and sighed. "Just in case… be careful, Cole. Avoid direct eye contact and their touch. Like your brother said, the rusalkas, even mavkas, have power over men. Even though your heart is not beating, I'm sure your other body parts are still functioning." His eyes slipped to Cole's groin pointedly, and he smirked. "I hope you're not sexually deprived, or vampire or not, you stand no chance against their charms."

A wide grin split Cole's face. "I'll be fine." He approached the edge of the lake and turned toward Damian, giving him a quick nod. Then he took a few steps forward and dove in, quickly disappearing under the layer of dark water.

"Be careful, brother mine," whispered Damian, lowering himself to the cold ground.

"You know your brother is an ancient vamp." Yakov sat

down next to him, a low groan escaping his lips. "Between the three of us, he is the best choice for this mission. Besides, he's not an easy-to-kill prey. He is a predator himself."

"You're wrong. I killed more vampires than I can count. It's easy to kill them if you know what you're doing," replied Damian, staring at the lake, unease twisting his gut into a tight knot. "Cole is my little brother, my family, my flesh and blood. I can't help but worry about him."

"It truly is amazing, Damian." Yakov picked up a small twig from the ground, twirling it between his fingers. "I don't know if you're religious, but you may want to ask the god you worship why they punished you by letting your brother, whom you love so deeply, be turned into the very thing you're supposed to hate and kill—"

Suddenly, he cut himself off, and the energy of his magic spiked around him. He slapped his left hand over the tattoo on his right arm, and his face turned into a stone mask.

"What's going, Yakov?" Damian rose to his feet, opening his second sight, but couldn't detect anything alarming.

"My gargoyle tells me we're in danger," whispered Yakov, getting up, "but I can't sense anything and…"

Yakov's voice melted into a soft buzz in Damian's mind, and he turned to him, ready to ask if the wizard could hear this strange noise when the forest and the lake started to spin around him. He swayed on his feet, struggling to keep his balance.

"Yakov—," he groaned. His stomach heaved, and he dropped to all fours, fighting nausea. With his blurry vision, he watched Yakov collapse to the ground, his long, dark hair fanning around his pale face, an expression of shock in his wide-open eyes.

Damian reached for him, but his limbs were too heavy to move. The world tilted, and he started to fall, everything around him soft and disgustingly mushy. With his fading vision, he glanced at the lake but could see nothing except endless darkness.

"Cole," he whispered his brother's name, and his eyelids closed.

He felt a soft touch to his chest and forehead but had no strength to open his eyes. An icy wave spread through his body, freezing him to the core, and he jerked helplessly, holding on to the last rays of consciousness for as long as he could.

"Daaa-mi-aaaa-n..."

CHAPTER 27

~ COLE ADAMS ~

As soon as Cole dove into the lake, darkness surrounded him, wrapping its icy arms around his body. He made a few strokes, submerging deeper, and then stopped, treading his hands through the water to keep in place. Something cold and slippery brushed his bare back, and he spun around but could see nothing except for the unsteady, blurry shadows gliding soundlessly in the depth of the lake.

He swallowed hard as the glacial eyes of fear stared back at him from the infinite blackness, chilling him from the inside. Below him, the glowing blue light of the portal shimmered dimly, giving him the direction he needed, and he turned toward it, swimming as fast as he could. With every stroke he made, the pressure on his chest intensified, but he ignored it and kept moving ahead at a steady pace.

The closer he moved to the portal, the brighter it became. The shadows jerked and shied away from the light, as if scorched by its brightness, and Cole doubled his efforts, his arms breaking the stillness of the water. Soon, he reached what seemed to be an enormous luminous vortex that spun slowly in a clockwise motion. Stretching his already heightened senses to the maximum, he detected the slight presence of magical energy, but since he couldn't see it, he had to assume it was the magic of the portal.

Here goes nothing...

With a powerful kick of his legs, he dove into the portal headfirst. The dancing blue lights surrounded him in a never-ending merry-go-round. As the rotating vortex picked him up, the lights spun faster and faster, making him dizzy and light-headed. He twisted, struggling to regain control of his body, but to no avail. Powerful jets of water propelled him forward, and he stopped fighting, realizing that the only way out of this situation was through it. He made an effort to relax and let go completely, surrendering himself to the power of the magical portal.

Suddenly, all the lights vanished, and for a heartbeat he felt disoriented by the absolute darkness. The water pressure eased up and soon disappeared, and he felt weightless and powerless, at the mercy of whatever was coming. The stop was abrupt and painful. He hit his head on something hard and cried out in pain, but no sound came out from his constricted throat. Somehow, the darkness became heavier, physically pressing on his chest, and a moment later, he blacked out.

* * *

AN UNFAMILIAR YET DELICATE scent invaded his nostrils, and through the fog in his mind, Cole heard a couple of musical voices speaking somewhere next to him. A soft touch to his arm confirmed that he wasn't alone. Someone brushed the hair off his face, and it took all the power of will he had not to react, pretending to be unconscious.

"He should have been up by now," said a woman on his left, tones of concern in her voice.

"He banged his head pretty hard though," replied the second woman.

"I checked his head," objected the first one. "He healed almost instantly, which is strange. The room is filled with air, but his chest doesn't move, so I believe he doesn't breathe. He looks like a man, but he can't be human."

"A wizard maybe, or a Child of the Elements? Or he could be one of the undead..." A cold hand pressed on his chest as if checking for a sign of breathing. "The Queen will figure out what he is and what he's doing here. But we have to get him ready for the audience and to do that, he must be awake."

A slight slap on his cheek followed her words, and he decided that he had no choice but to pretend to wake up and meet with the Queen, hoping she was the one Yakov called mavka Kostroma. He cracked his eyelids open and moaned, reaching for the back of his head with his hand. To his satisfaction, he noticed that he wasn't restrained, and his sword was still in his scabbard.

Cole blinked a few times to adjust his vision to the semi-dark surroundings. He was in a small, windowless room, lying on a soft bed. A black silk sheet covered him from the waist down, and his back was propped up against a couple of large pillows. A few strange green orbs levitated under the low ceiling, illuminating the room with dim, shimmering light. They didn't look like the light orbs Damian used to summon, but he had no doubt they had a magical origin.

Two young women sat on the bed on either side of him. Both had long blonde hair that seemed to flow through the air even though there was no wind. Their tender faces were pale and looked almost translucent as their flawless complexion reflected the green light of the orbs. They stared at him without blinking, their overly large eyes filled with curiosity. Their long, sheer dresses flowed weightlessly around their willowy bodies, effectively underlying every curve of their figures.

"Greetings, traveler," said the woman on his right with a gentle smile that exposed a perfect set of small, white teeth. She leaned closer to him and cupped his face with her hands. "What is your name?"

"Cole," he replied, avoiding direct eye contact.

She laughed softly, the sound of her voice as musical as the sound of a bubbling creek. "Your name is as unusual as you are."

She caressed his cheek, and the light wave of her magical energy touched his senses. For a heartbeat, the room spun around him, and his vision became blurry again. A moan broke from his lips, warmth traveling down his body. She smiled wider and upturned his face more, now her eyes right in front of his. Their gazes locked, and a fog obscured his mind, blocking everything out except for the desire to touch, caress and kiss the spellbinding creature next to him.

Rusalkas... The thought flashed through his dimming mind, and he braced himself against their overpowering magic. With a low groan, he forced himself to close his eyes and break their eye contact, focusing on blocking their magical energy.

"Open your eyes, Cole," the rusalka whispered. She was so close now that her lips grazed his ear, but he didn't detect either warmth or the touch of her breath to his skin. Before he could say anything, her icy lips pressed against his, and the amount of magical energy she sent through him seemed to double.

He struggled against her hold, realizing with satisfaction that the more he fought, the weaker her influence on his mind and body became. However, he decided to play their game and cracked his eyelids open, gazing at the rusalka from under his eyelashes. His lips parted, and he arched his body slightly with a deep moan.

"Well, hello there," the rusalka purred and caressed his cheek with her long fingers, satisfied by his reaction. "Whatever you are, you are not immune to our magic after all, are you? I wonder…"

She brushed her hand over his lips and then forced her index finger into his mouth, probing his teeth with her fingertip. He touched it with his tongue, closing his lips around it for a brief moment. She laughed and leaned down to his kiss his cheek, sending another wave of magical energy through him.

Turning to her friend, the rusalka shrugged. "He looks just like a human man, but he has no heartbeat. So strange. I thought he might be a vamp, but he can't be. When vampires are sexually aroused, their fangs expand. He has no fangs."

"My lady," Cole whispered, reaching for her hand.

She pressed her finger to his lips but then hopped off the bed, tittering. "I think he's ready, Iriada," she said to the second woman. "Just keep him under your charm while I fetch the Queen."

As soon as she was gone, Iriada turned to Cole. She lifted the gold pendant off his chest and peered at it, her blonde eyebrows lowering over her bright, green eyes.

"Where did you get this pendant, Cole?" she asked softly, her voice almost pleading. He met her eyes, realizing with interest that she wasn't trying to use her magic on him. "Please, tell me the truth. It used to belong to someone dear to me."

Making a split-second decision, Cole dropped his act. "I'm looking for mavka Kostroma," he replied, taking the pendant out of her hand. "My friend gave this necklace to me. I believe it belongs to her."

"Oh, Cole." She took his hand and gave it a gentle squeeze, glancing over her shoulder at the door. "Don't say anything about Kostroma to the Queen. She is—" She cut herself off, her eyes becoming even wider if that were even possible. Then she lowered closer to him and whispered into his ear. "Evil... pure evil. It's been quite a few years since she took over the Black Lake. Kostroma and all those who refused to obey her are in her dungeons, outside the—"

The squeak of the door interrupted her, and she jumped off

the bed, lowering into a graceful curtsy. Cole half-closed his eyes and relaxed, staring at the entrance through his eyelashes.

A tall woman dressed in a shimmering, silvery dress walked into the room and halted at the foot of the bed, observing Cole with frosty contempt in her oversized green eyes. She was slightly taller than the other two rusalkas, and her face was just as tender and enchanting. She moved with fluid grace, stepping soundlessly on the floor with her bare feet. Her flowing, slightly green hair moved about her in soft waves as if the room was filled with water.

She smiled and glided around the bed to lower herself on its edge. Seizing his chin, she lifted his head just a little and peered into his eyes. As her powerful magic washed over him, Cole moaned, horrified by the realization that his body reacted to her charm more eagerly than he anticipated. Her magical energy felt different from that of the other two rusalkas, its dark touch raising goosebumps on his arms.

"Hello, traveler," she purred, caressing his cheek, her every move sending more and more magic through him. "Let's see what kind of beastie you are."

As debilitating weakness spread through him, he tried to fight, but his body was refusing to obey the command of his mind. She reached forward and forced his lips apart, running her fingers over his teeth. Then she let go and wiped her hand on the sheet.

"Just as I thought," she said, turning to the other two women. "He is a vampire." She laughed, slapping his cheek gently. "He might have been able to fight your charm, but his true nature is not going to help him escape *my* magic."

She leaned forward, looming over him with malice. He closed his eyes and turned his head to the side. She didn't object, but her hand landed on his chest, steadily moving south—touching, probing, exploring. Her malignant magic spread through him, making his entire body pulse and throb with desire, but he resisted with everything he possessed in his frazzled mind.

"He resists," she whispered, anger making her musical voice deeper. "How can he still fight me?" She seized his chin, crushing it with her fingers, and jerked his head up. "Look into my eyes, vamp!"

A sharp, pulsating pain took hold of him, becoming stronger with every passing moment. His body shuddered and convulsed of its own accord, and his mouth opened, a howl of pain escaping his dry throat.

"Open your eyes, vampire," she commanded, her long fingernails cutting into his cheeks. "Obey, and the pain will stop."

He opened his eyes and met the Queen's malignant stare. A deep shudder rushed through him as for a heartbeat, he saw her true form. The image of a beautiful young woman was just an illusion. Beneath the shimmering layer of magic, there was an old crone with a wrinkled face and yellowish-brown, sharp teeth. Her skin, the color of a swamp, was stretched over her bones, and a large hump decorated her back, bending her forward.

Cole wasn't sure how he was able to see through her illusion, but at this moment, he couldn't care less. Seeing her true form broke her charm, setting him free. He rolled over his shoulder and dropped to the floor on the other side of the bed, his sword in his hand.

"Lobasta," he growled and laughed, feeling the leftovers of the rusalka's charm being expelled from his body, clearing his mind completely.

"How did you..." she seethed, baring her pointed teeth. She charged at him, vaulting her deformed body over the bed.

Cole sidestepped her, grazing her side with his sword. She hissed in pain and spun in place, bluish-green liquid staining her gray, dirty dress. She lifted her bony arm with deformed fingers and long claws and stared at her own blood dripping off her shaking hand. Cole backed away, searching for a position inside the small room that would give him a better fighting chance.

Iriada cowered in a corner, but her eyes gazed at him with hope and encouragement, her pale lips moving like in silent prayer, her hands pressed to her chest. He searched the room with his eyes for the second rusalka but couldn't find her anywhere. As he switched his attention back to the Queen, a high-pitched shriek cut his hearing, and something heavy dropped onto his shoulders, a slender but strong arm wrapping around his throat.

Cole reached back with his left hand and seized a handful of hair, eliciting a furious hiss from the rusalka. Using the opportunity, the Queen charged him again, reaching forward with her skinny arms covered in something resembling fish scales. Her gray claws started to elongate, turning into dangerously sharp blades before his eyes. Wrapping the rusalka's hair around his wrist, he spun in place just in time for the Queen's claws to pierce her servant's back.

The rusalka screamed in pain and dropped to the floor, releasing Cole's neck. Without slowing down, he swung his sword, decapitating her. Her head rolled off her shoulders, falling to the stone tiles with a dull thump. A burst of thick, green blood erupted from her neck before her body finally fell to the side. The Queen backed away, her nostrils flaring as she inhaled the reek of stale water radiated by the paddle of thick, green liquid spreading under the quickly decomposing corpse.

Cole turned toward her, raising his sword to his shoulder. But instead of attacking him, she spread her arms wide and threw her head back. A terrible high-pitched screech erupted from her wide-open mouth. Cole groaned and staggered back, momentarily overwhelmed by the ferocity of the sound.

A few seconds later, the door burst open and at least ten women barged into the room. All of them were armed with swords and daggers and had strange armor on that looked like metallic scales. Quickly assessing the situation, they turned to Cole, their large eyes burning with animosity and unconcealed hostility.

Before they could surround and attack him, cutting all his ways out, Cole jumped on the bed, bending his knees slightly to keep his balance on the soft mattress. His fangs elongated, his fingers turning into claws almost as terrifying as that of the lobasta. A strange burst of energy rushed through him, and his lips drew back into a snarl, a low growl rumbling deep in his chest.

For a brief moment, the rusalkas stilled with their mouths open, visibly shocked by his reaction. The illusion surrounding them shimmered, and the image of beautiful women disappeared. Deformed, old hags stood before him, training their swords at his chest. Their gaping mouths were filled with sharp teeth, disgusting green goo dripping from their thin, black lips.

Lobastas... all of them... how can I fight so many of them alone... Cole wrapped his fingers tighter around the grip of his sword, preparing for what could be his last fight. *O Lord, if I don't survive this ordeal, protect my brother...*

The calm before the storm was over, and earsplitting shrieks rose in the air as the lobastas assailed him, seemingly coming from every direction at once. Even though they moved almost as fast as him, Cole was still a little faster. He screamed and drove his sword forward. As his blade pierced the nearest lobasta's armor, he pushed it through her chest in one powerful thrust. The rusalka screamed and grabbed the blade with her hands, struggling to get away. Fueled by anger, a wave of energy rushed through his sword arm. The blade lit up with a bright scarlet light, and the lobasta shrieked, pain turning her already ugly face into a terrifying mask.

There was no fire, but the nauseating reek of scorched flesh polluted the air. The lobasta's body arched back, her arms flailing, and a moment later, she went down in flames. Cole moved back, away from the hungry fire devouring the monster's body with an admirable speed. The other lobastas, including the Queen, froze in place, staring at Cole without blinking, and a collective gasp of horror, anger and shock rustled through the room.

"You're just a disgusting vamp!" screeched the Queen, her green eyes turning the poisonous color of a swamp. "How are you doing this? How did you manage to kill a lobasta? How can you wield the Fire? It's impossible—"

"I have no idea, but I'm about to find out if I can do it again." Cole roared and spun around as the lobastas sprang into action, their claws slicing through his flesh. He didn't care where his blade landed as long as it found a target. Liquid like the water itself, the lobastas kept shifting, moving and exchanging places to avoid his strikes. However, even in the limited space of the room, with his speed and strength, he still had the upper hand, making every strike of his sword count.

A sharp pain in his back made Cole growl more from annoyance than from pain, and he staggered backward until his back with a shrieking lobasta attached to it hit the wall. She yelped, and for a short moment, her grip weakened. While blocking an attack of another monster, Cole slammed his back against the wall again, causing the lobasta to black out and let go of him. As his sword found his next victim, turning her into a stinking pile of ashes and goo, he spun in place, decapitating the unconscious lobasta by the wall with one swing of his blade.

Turning around, he observed the room and rolled his shoulders, feeling the warm wetness of blood as it dripped down his back and chest. Charged with the excitement of the fight and with the strange energy still rushing through him, he couldn't feel the pain. He didn't care how severe his injuries were either, knowing that they would heal sooner rather than later.

He stood on top of the bed with the sheets and the mattress

soaked with sticky, green goo. All the lobastas were dead, turned into ashes. He stared at the sword in his hand in disbelief. It was a gift from his maker, and Cole had had this sword for centuries. He had been in countless sword fights through his long life, yet never had he experienced anything like this. It was almost as though he were wielding magic.

Impossible. Vampires can't wield magic.

Shoving the troubling thought to the back of his mind, he switched his attention to the Queen. She stood by the wall, her ugly, grotesque figure cowering in the corner between the wall and the bed, her hand clasping the wound on her side. Her malicious cockiness was gone as she stared at Cole with widened eyes. He jumped off the bed, landing on the floor soundlessly. Not in a rush, he made his way to her and brought his sword up, placing the tip of his blade against her chest.

"What are you?" whispered the Queen. "That was…" Her voice turned into a hoarse whisper as she pointed at his sword. "I have no idea how it is possible, but I know magic when I see it. You're not a vampire. Vamps can't cast."

"Agreed," Cole snarled, exposing his long fangs. "But my fangs beg to differ. I *am* a vampire. I've been a vampire for over a thousand years. So, trust me, water-bitch, I know what I am. Whatever this was—magic, powers, God or the devil himself—I don't give a damn. I enjoyed every second of it!"

He thrust his sword forward, forcing it through the Queen's heart. She didn't scream. Her mouth opened wider, green goo dripping down her hairy chin, and her eyes bulged as she gripped the blade with both hands. Her skin seared and blistered at the touch of the steel, and a heartbeat later, she collapsed to the floor, her body slowly turning into ashes.

Cole wiped the blade on his pants and turned to Iriada, a faint smirk lifting the corners of his mouth.

"So, now that we're done with that… where can I find mavka Kostroma?"

CHAPTER 28

~ COLE ADAMS ~

Cole followed Iriada through the long hallways and passages of the underwater palace. She moved quickly and soundlessly, constantly glancing over her shoulder to make sure he was still behind her.

"Are there other lobastas in the lake?" he asked, falling into step with her.

"Not here," she replied without slowing down, "but there are more. Now that their Queen is dead, it'll be a while before they attempt to come back to our realm, and when they return, we'll be ready for them." Her eyes lit up with a furious glimmer, her hair flowing around her in soft waves.

They walked out of the palace through a hidden backdoor and crossed an empty courtyard toward a tall stone wall. Iriada halted in front of it and drew an invisible rectangle in the shape of a door, whispering something under her breath. With a grinding noise, the stone blocks moved and pulled apart, creating a low, narrow doorway. Iriada turned sideways and slipped through the opening, motioning for him to follow.

Cole pressed his hand to his mouth, his eyebrows rising as he assessed the size of the opening. "There is not a chance in hell I can go through this," he muttered to himself but turned sideways just like Iriada had done and pushed his shoulder through the doorway. To his shock, he slipped through easily, but when he glanced back, the opening in the wall was gone, and the wall remained as untouched and solid as it had been before.

"Don't worry," whispered Iriada, grabbing his hand and pulling him forward. "I can open this doorway again."

He moved through a dark corridor, following Iriada, the sound of her steps echoing loudly in the heavy silence of this place. The putrid stench of stale water and drainage assailed his senses, and he pressed his hand over his nose. Dirty water was dripping from the low ceiling, sliding down the slimy walls covered in green goo. Something slipped and moved under his feet, but he didn't care to find out what it was. The floor was covered in a slushy mix of mud and water, and he had to slow down to keep his balance on the slippery surface.

Soon, the corridor ran into a wooden door with a dirty old lock on it. Iriada touched it and whispered a few words in a language he didn't recognize. The lock clicked and fell to the floor with a loud bang. She grabbed the handle and pushed, but the door wouldn't budge. Cole smiled and gently moved her aside. Applying pressure with his shoulder, he pushed with all his strength, and the door moved with a mournful squeak. A musty, unclean smell rushed from the room behind the door, and he stalled for a moment, sharpening his senses.

"We're here," said Iriada.

They crossed the threshold into a large hall with a low ceiling. The room was dark, but with his sharp vision, Cole could see a chain of small cells with rusty iron bars lined up against the walls. Iriada moved forward and stopped in front of one of the cells. A black shadow moved in the darkness of the space, rushing toward the entrance.

"Iriada? But how did you get here?" A female voice, hushed and raspy, sounded from behind the bars.

"Kostroma!" Iriada grabbed the bars and hissed in pain, jerking her hand away. "Iron. Dammit! There are no locks on these doors, and I won't be able to open them with my magic." She threw an anxious glance back at Cole, her shoulders dropping.

Cole nodded and smirk. "Well, I don't have magic," he said calmly. "But I hope we won't need it."

He seized two bars and tried to force them apart, the muscles rippling under his skin. The bars screeched, slowly moving under his force. He screamed, applying more strength, and the bars gave in, creating an opening big enough for a person to slip through.

A young woman stepped through the opening he created and halted in front of him. Except for lobastas in their natural form, all types of rusalkas were beautiful, but mavkas had that special, tender beauty that left any man who was unfortunate enough to lay his eyes upon them breathless, making him forget about everything else.

Just like all mavkas, Kostroma was breathtakingly gorgeous, her long blonde hair flowing around her as if carried by a light current. Her large, green eyes slipped up and down his unobstructed torso covered in dried blood and splatters of green slime. But as her gaze halted on the gold pendant on his chest, her lips parted, shaping the letter 'O'. Her slender arm reached for the chain but halted halfway, her fingers trembling slightly.

"Where did you get it?" she asked, staring straight into his eyes as if she were trying to read his soul.

Detecting a fluctuation of the magical energy field around her, Cole clenched his teeth and averted his gaze. Then he took the chain off and put it in her hand. "Yakov Bruce says hello." He massaged his shoulder with his hand, feeling an unusual weariness in all his muscles. "He needs the box he gave you in eighteen twelve. Do you still have it, my lady?"

"I do," she replied airily.

She lifted her hand, her fingers brushing over his lips, but he seized her wrist and stepped back, letting go of her arm.

"I'm sorry, my lady," he said dryly, a crooked smirk curving his lips, "but if one more rusalka forces her fingers into my mouth to check my fangs, I'll have to bite." He gave her a light bow filled with mockery. "I am a vampire, if that's what you wanted to know. And yes, Yakov Bruce sent me here."

She gasped and pressed her hand to her chest, a vibe of discomfort lingering over her. "My apologies..." she exhaled, dropping her head. "The Queen must have put you through hell."

"The Queen is dead," Cole replied calmly. "I'm sorry, but Yakov is waiting for me on the shore, and time is working against us. I really need that box, my lady."

"Thank you for helping me and my people." She inclined her head in a light bow and moved around Cole toward the exit, gesturing for him and Iriada to follow.

Kostroma crossed the hall and halted by the door, staring at Cole with doubt in her green eyes. "It'll be a lot easier if I use a portal," she said with an apologetic shrug. "It'll be a little unpleasant for you, but if you don't mind some discomfort, we could get the box a lot faster."

"Go for it." Cole nodded.

She turned her back to him and started to chant, accompanying her words with a circular motion of her hand. The air in front of her shimmered like a mirage, and a large vortex filled with rotating water opened before her.

"Iriada," she said, a warm smile playing on her lips, "please help our friend through the portal. I don't want him to suffer..." Her voice trailed as she turned to Cole. "Brace yourself."

She jumped into the portal headfirst as if she were diving into a lake. Iriada stepped next to Cole and took his hand.

"We'll go together." She smiled, stepping closer to the whirlpool. "It'll be quick. Just don't let go."

She stepped closer, wrapping her arm around Cole's waist, and they dove into the swirling mass at the same time. Streams of water enveloped him in their icy embrace, completely immobilizing him. Even though he didn't need air, for a brief second, he felt as if he were drowning. His lungs burned, and his muscles spasmed painfully. He opened his eyes but could see nothing but the blur of twirling water. Fear—overwhelming and debilitating—squeezed his heart, and he jerked, struggling against the hold of the portal.

Iriada's arm held him tighter, and her other arm seized the hair on the back of his head. Her cold lips found his, and as she kissed him, unusual calmness spread through him. His body went limp in her embrace, and his arms dropped. A heartbeat later, everything was over. The feeling of weightlessness was gone, and with relief, he felt firm ground beneath his back.

"Cole?" Iriada's voice sounded above him, and he opened his eyes. She offered him her hand. He took it and got up, looking around in awe.

"Where are we?"

He stood in a large clearing surrounded by a strange forest. Brilliant, bluish light flooded the area, seemingly coming from nowhere. The trees weren't tall, but their leaves sparkled like sapphires, and their trunks were a deep ultramarine. The ground was covered with lush, cerulean grass, and it moved like the ocean waves with every gust of the light wind.

This place was as beautiful as it was remarkable, but that wasn't what shocked Cole. Everywhere, as far as he could see, gold and silver coins, precious and semiprecious gems, jewelry, priceless pieces of art, weapons, icons, crosses and other religious artifacts were scattered all over the clearing.

"You're still beneath the lake." Kostroma's voice sounded behind him, and he spun around. She stood in front of him with a plain wooden box in her hands. "This is the place where Yakov Bruce had Napoleon dump all his treasures." She smirked, a look of superiority reflected on her face. "No human will ever be able to put their greedy hands on any of it." She stepped closer and offered the box to Cole. "Here is what you need. I hope Yakov knows what he's doing." She shook her head with a deep sigh. "This device is extremely dangerous, vampire. Make sure it doesn't fall into the wrong hands."

"I will, my lady," replied Cole, taking the box from her hands.

"I have a bad feeling about this." She bit her lips, her green eyes turning a shade darker. "First, lobastas invading my realm. Now, Yakov wants to retrieve this box... There are no coincidences in the World of Magic. There has to be a connection."

"I don't know what to say." Cole glanced at the mavka, readjusting the straps of his scabbard. "Someone extremely dangerous has learned about the location of the device, and Yakov is trying to protect it. This is the reason he sent me here."

"Like I said..." Kostroma frowned. "I hope he knows what he's doing." She turned to Iriada. "I'm going to open a portal to the surface. Please take our guest back to shore. Even though he's a vampire, I noticed the portal affected him more than I expected."

Cole cringed inwardly, thinking about going through a rusalka's portal again. Swallowing his doubts and fears, he thanked her for her assistance and bowed to her, his natural elegance taking over. As Kostroma opened the swirling and splashing vortex, Iriada took the box from him and encircled his waist with her arm, pulling him inside of the portal.

* * *

THE MOON SHONE above the lake, its silvery light reflecting on its still surface. Iriada pushed Cole slightly on his back, directing him toward the shore, the soft splashes of water sounding like thunder in the surrounding silence. She halted a few yards away from the land and took his hand, stopping him. She gave him the box with the device and gently moved the wet strands of his hair off his face, sadness suffusing her features.

"Farewell, my friend. I hope we meet again one day." She waved her hand and dove into the darkness of the lake.

"Hopefully, under better circumstances," murmured Cole and turned around, heading to shore as fast as he could.

He stepped on the slippery, cold ground, moving heavily to the place where he left Damian and Yakov. As he crossed through the thickets of reeds, he almost tripped over Yakov's body. The wizard lay sprawled on the shore, his dark hair soaked with water, and he appeared to be asleep. Cole dropped to his knees, quickly checking his vitals. He found a pulse right away, but no matter how hard he tried, he couldn't wake him up.

Cole moved the box to his left hand and unsheathed his sword, wincing from the soft metallic sound the blade produced. Light like a shadow, he rose to his feet and moved along the shore, hiding behind the tall reeds. He found his brother almost right away, and what he saw caused him to freeze in place with his skin crawling.

A tiny, scrawny man was kneeling next to Damian. He wasn't armed, but a tight noose of magical energy, glowing with a sinister, purple light, was wrapped around his brother's neck. Damian lay motionless, either asleep or unconscious. His chest was rising and falling with even breaths and his face was relaxed, so Cole assumed he was still alive.

The man readjusted his thick glasses, pushing them higher on the bridge of his nose, and waved in the direction where Cole was hiding, rolling his eyes.

"Come closer, vampire," the man said, disdain pulling his lips back in a snarl. "I can detect your essence with my eyes closed." Without waiting for Cole to answer, he seized Damian's hair and yanked his head back. "And don't get smart with me, vamp, or I'll show you how to kill an immortal Child of Earth." He snickered, the sound so malevolent and carnivorous that Cole shuddered inwardly. "Trust me, there is a way to kill him, and I'm sure he knows that, too."

Cole didn't move, remaining in the thickets, his mind going through thousands of possible options, seeing nothing useful.

"Dammit," cursed the old man, adding a few more choice words. "Do I have to do everything myself?"

He snapped his fingers, and his magical energy spiked around him. Pointing in Cole's direction, he muttered something, his smirk becoming wider and more sinister by the moment.

Cole wasn't sure what happened, but suddenly his mind went completely blank. He could see and hear. He could also understand everything clearly enough, but he was no longer in command of his own body. He stood absolutely still, unable to move a muscle.

"Now, come here, boy," said the man, gesturing for him to approach.

No, I'm not going to—

But before he knew it, he separated the reeds and moved toward the man, everything inside him screaming to fight the influence of his magic. He halted in front the man, staring at him in horror.

"Much better." The man got up and detached Cole's unbending fingers from the box and took it, lowering back next to Damian. "Now kneel, boy."

Cole fell to his knees, unable to fight, think, or resist.

"My name is Az," said the man softly, but then glanced at Cole and smirked. "Well, not really. But that's the name your brother will recognize. When he wakes up—if he ever wakes up, that is—give him my deepest gratitude. Without him and the old wizard there"—he waved in Yakov's direction—"I would have never been able to get this box... Not true. I would still find a way to get it even without them, but it would take me a lot longer, and time is of the essence."

Cole opened his mouth to speak, but no sound came out from his throat. He wanted to lift his hand, but he couldn't. Az noticed his attempts, and his smile grew wider.

"You can't fight my influence, vampire," he said, his voice soft and indifferent. "I wield one of the oldest and most powerful branches of magic—necromancy. Anything dead or undead, like yourself, is powerless against me. I can tell you to take this extraordinary sword of yours and thrust it through your beloved brother's heart, and you'll do it without a moment of hesitation."

He placed the box on the ground, his fingers trembling slightly as he moved his hands over it. Then he glanced at Cole and twirled his wrist.

"You may speak, by the way," he said, reaching into his pocket.

He produced a tiny crystal and moved it around the lid of the box, chanting quietly. After a moment, the box lit up with a soft, white light, and the lid opened, revealing two silver bands resting on a bed of black silk. Az moved his fingers over the bands, a wistful expression on his face. Carefully, he picked up the smaller one and put it on the middle finger of his right hand.

"This is all I need." He closed the box and rose to his feet, showing his hand with the ring to Cole.

"Why?" asked Cole. "Why did you need to trick Damian and Yakov? You obviously knew the location of the device, and I'm sure a swim in the lake wouldn't stop you. Why did you need them? Why all these shadow games and deception?"

Az looked down, running his fingers through Cole's hair. "You're quite clever for a vamp. I would love to have you as my pet, but right now, I have no time to play with you." He glanced back at Damian. "It wasn't easy to find the lake. The old wizard was too smart for his own good. He never gave Napoleon the true rune. But sooner or later, I found it, anyway." He chuckled, shaking his head. "I also knew the location of the crystal that unlocks the box, and I needed to find a way to put my hands on that eagle-head dagger."

"So why didn't you break into Ricardo's house yourself? Obviously, you're powerful enough to do something as trivial as a robbery?"

"Haven't you seen all the magic detectors Ricardo has in his house?" Az rolled his eyes, fixing up his sliding glasses. "Besides, I could feel the presence of gray stones all around the house, and I didn't want to bother with this man's defense mechanisms. As you know, the more powerful you are, the heavier and more painful the effect of the gray stones magic."

He stopped talking, his eyes shifting from Damian to Cole and then back to Damian.

"Knowing how much your brother cared for you," he continued at length, "I made sure to create a hostile situation in the state, placing your rule and your life in enough peril for him to get desperate. And just to drive that proverbial nail, I made sure that my wurdulaks broke the sanctuary law. So now, your brother wasn't only protecting you, he was under a direct obligation to find the person responsible." He laughed, pointing at his chest. "Me."

"But why did you send him after Yakov Bruce?" asked Cole. "He was the only person who knew about the Hollow Band. He could have ruined all your plans."

"Exactly, he was the only person who knew about the device," Az agreed airily. "He was also the only person in the world who could open the portal and communicate with mavka

Kostroma who held the box hidden. A while ago, I sent my loyal lobastas to deal with her, but no matter how much they tried, she wouldn't tell them where the box was hidden."

"Damn..." Cole dropped his head, biting his lip. They had fallen into every trap this insidious man had set for them.

Az snickered, patting Cole's cheek, and Cole growled, struggling to turn away from his touch.

"Don't beat yourself up, vampire. I'm the master of deception and shadow games, as you put it. No one can beat me at that." He glanced around, his eyes lingering on Damian's motionless form for a moment. "Well, boy, I have what I need, thanks to all of you, and it's time for me to go. Good luck waking up your beloved brother and the wizard." A sinister smirk curved his lips. "It'll take a divine intervention to break my enchantment."

Az snapped his fingers and vanished from the cold lakeside.

As soon as he was gone, the influence of the necromancer's magic dissipated and Cole fell to all fours, finally in control of his body. Scrambling to his feet, he rushed to his brother's side, lowering himself next to him. He seized his shoulders and shook him a few times, but Damian didn't react. For the next few minutes, he tried everything he could think of to wake him up, but nothing worked. Feeling numb on the inside, he sat back on his heels and ran his trembling fingers over Damian's scarred cheek, his shoulders slumped.

"Damian, please wake up... Dima... I need you to wake up, brother mine," he whispered, the last ray of hope gone from his soul.

CHAPTER 29

~ DAMIAN BLAKE ~

"Daaa-mi-aaaa-n... Open your eyes..."

He was warm and comfortable. Nothing was tormenting his soul, and his body wasn't sore. No one was trying to force him to do anything he didn't want to do, and no one was trying to kill him or his brother. For once in his life, he felt safe and happy. If it was just a dream, he didn't want to wake up... Ever.

"Damian, come on. I need you to open your eyes..."

The voice pleaded and nagged. It sounded familiar, but he couldn't place his finger on who it was.

"Damian, please..." the voice whispered, and someone slapped his cheek gently. "If you don't open your eyes now, you will die. Your brother will die. The old eagle will die. The world as you know it will perish forever. Can you live knowing that all you had to do to save everyone was open... your... eyes..."

Damian moaned, everything inside him screaming and begging to stay asleep. He cracked his eyelids open, staring straight up at a blue sky with a single fluffy cloud. It wasn't the Arizona sky with its merciless sun. It wasn't the midnight sky above the Black Lake in Russia either. With a groan, he pushed himself up into a sitting position and observed his surroundings.

He sat at the edge of a cliff next to a large pine tree. Below, surrounded by a forest, a wide river rolled its waves, disappearing behind a curve. A narrow bridge led across the river toward a city encircled by a tall, stone wall.

He knew this place. He used to love it. A long time ago. In another life.

"Hello, Damian," a soft female voice sounded on his left.

He turned his head and smirked. A young woman—short and slender—sat by his side. Her long black hair fell to her back and chest, blending with her black dress. She glanced at him sideways and answered his smirk with a sad smile.

"Hello, Mara," he said calmly, turning away from her. "I should have known it was you all along." He rubbed his eyes and sighed. "Would you like to tell me what I'm doing here and why?"

"No, it wasn't me. I didn't put you to sleep, but I used the situation to contact you." The corners of her lips quirked up. "I didn't have much time, but I did what I could in the time I had," she said, touching his elbow. "Once you fell asleep, I searched through your memories, trying to find your happiest moments. There wasn't much happiness in your life, was there?"

Damian shrugged indifferently and shook his head no. "Whatever you say…"

"From what I understand, in your human life, you used to love this place. You felt happy here." Mara waved her hand. "This is why I brought you here."

"Good choice," replied Damian after a short pause. He pulled a small daisy out, plucking off one petal at a time absentmindedly. "As a twelve-year-old boy, I used to love this place. I'm not sure I was happy here, but for some reason, it used to make me feel safe." He glanced at the Slavic goddess of Nightmares, and an expectation of trouble squeezed his heart. "I know you want something, Mara, and unless you get what you want, I won't be able to wake up. So, why don't we get to business because I don't have time for your games."

"That's the problem, Damian," she replied, caressing his arm. "Today, I'm not here to torment you. I'm here to help you. But before we get to business, can I ask you something personal?"

Damian chuckled, shaking his head. "You just admitted that you went through all my memories. How much more personal can it be?" He waved his hand dismissively. "Go ahead. What would you like to know?"

She didn't reply but pushed her arm through the crook of his elbow and snapped her fingers. The surroundings shimmered and became blurry. Damian groaned as the world spun around him, feeling Mara's arm supporting him. When his vision cleared, he was in a small, half-demolished hut. Heavy rain bombarded the roof, cold water flowing down through the holes in the ceiling.

Two small boys—about twelve and six—lay on the cold, hard floor, shaking in their thin, torn clothes. Damian stared at the boys, and his every muscle tensed as he remembered this night.

The younger boy sat up, pulled his knees to his chest and wrapped his arms around his legs. Glancing at his older brother, his pale lips quivered, tears gathering in his blue eyes.

"Dima," he whispered, wiping the tears mixed in with the icy rainwater off his face. "I'm so cold. I can't sleep."

The older boy took the only shirt he had off and put it on his brother, wrapping it tighter around him. Then he lay down on his side and pulled his brother closer to his bare chest, encircling him with his arms to share his body heat with him.

"Nikolai..." Damian whispered his brother's name, watching the little blond boy fall asleep in his arms. He swallowed and dropped his head, biting his lip.

"How many nights did you spend like this when you were kids?" she asked.

"Too many…"

"You still sleep in this position—on your side, hugging your pillow. You know?"

"I know. How do *you* know my sleeping habits?" He waved his hand, dismissing the matter. "Never mind that. Was that your question?" He exhaled, unable to take his eyes off his little brother's innocent face. "You've gone through so much trouble just to find out why I sleep on my side?"

"Of course not." She rolled her eyes and pointed at the two boys. "At this moment, both you and your brother are frozen to the bone and hungry. I wanted to know why you consider it a happy memory," she replied, gazing up at him with interest.

Damian smirked, averting his gaze so the goddess wouldn't see the haunted expression in his eyes. "My brother was alive, and we were together," he replied, his voice raspy.

"Your brother is still alive, and you're together once more." Mara frowned and snapped her fingers.

The surroundings spun and blurred, and once Damian could see again, they were back on the cliff over the river.

"My brother is *undead*," said Damian, taking her hand off his arm, "and we spent over a thousand years apart." He shifted, resting his back against the trunk of the pine tree. "I answered your question, Mara. Now it's your turn to tell me why I am here."

For a moment, she remained silent, studying his face with her icy eyes. Then she sighed and turned slightly to face him.

"You're here because a powerful and dangerous being of magic put a spell on you," she said, taking his hand. "But like I mentioned before, I'm here to help you."

He flinched at her touch but didn't pull away. "Help me? How so? And more importantly, what do you want in return?"

"You're in danger, Damian. You, and your brother, and even the old eagle Yakov Bruce," she replied. "You're all mistaken, and your mistake has some costly consequences."

"What are you talking about?" Damian growled, squeezing her hand in his. "If you're truly here to help, stop speaking riddles."

"Fine." Mara pulled her hand out of his grip and got up. "I'll be as plain as I can. The person you are dealing with is not a necromancer or a Master of the Dark Arts. He's a lot more deadly and powerful than you think. He placed you and Yakov in a magical coma, and with all your power, you could do nothing to stop him. I have no idea what he's planning, but to be honest, your chances of stopping him are anywhere between zero and nil, anyway. Having said that, if I wake you up in the next few minutes, maybe you can save your brother and the old eagle."

He stared at her with widened eyes, his limbs filled with lead. "Who is he? If Az is not a necromancer or a Master of the Dark Arts, what kind of monster is he?"

"Az?" Mara laughed, the sound of her frosty laughter echoing through the forest. "How cute. I'm sure you meant to say Azazel."

"Azazel?" Damian repeated, barely able to breathe. He rose slowly and staggered back a couple of steps, his heart beating desperately somewhere in his throat.

"That's right, Lord Enforcer." She approached him and halted a step away, barely reaching to his chest. "Don't blame yourself, Damian. Who would recognize a dangerous Fallen in a tiny, old, magically challenged wizard?"

"Perun almighty," whispered Damian, cold sweat running down his back. "Can you break his spell and wake me up?"

She shrugged, a playful smirk on her puffy lips. "Even though I'm not in my full power, I'm still a goddess, am I not? Sleep is my domain. Here, I'm the Queen." She tilted her head slightly, raising her eyebrows.

He squeezed his head with his hands, his fingers digging into his hair. "What do you want from me, Mara? What's your price?" he asked, his chest tightened with anxiety.

"Almost the same thing I wanted the last time we met," she replied quietly, and there was neither derision nor mockery in her voice. "Last time, I wanted my powers back so I could go home..." She stepped closer, now her body flat against his, and placed her arms on his chest, looking up into his eyes. "I can't live like this anymore. The realm of humans is not for me, Damian. I'm alone and miserable. If I can't return to the Prav, I would even accept the Dark Nav. Help me, Damian. You are a Destiny Enforcer. You have the power and the connections to get me home. I'm not even asking for my full power, just safe passage to the World Tree through the Land of Dreams."

"Oh, Mara, I'm sorry," he whispered with sincere regret. "I don't think I have the power to do that. Prav is a locked realm of the Slavic gods. Even as a Destiny Enforcer, I'm not welcome there. Not even all the Slavic gods have access to the Prav. Only the god of the Three Realms, Veles, or the great Svarog himself can open the door for you. As far as the Dark Nav, it's ruled by Chernobog, one of the most dangerous and twisted dark gods of the Slavic pantheon. I wouldn't even know where to start." He opened his arms in a half-shrug, but then dropped them at his sides.

She nodded, tears sliding down her pale face, and for a brief moment, Damian forgot that she wasn't a regular person but a dangerous, ancient goddess. All he could see was a woman in distress, begging for his help.

"I believe you," she whispered, breaking their eye contact. "I also believe that if an opportunity presents itself, you will try to help me." He didn't say anything, but a tiny smile ghosted her lips. "You're too tall, Damian. Kneel so I can try to wake you up."

He lowered down to one knee, Mara's eyes right in front of his now. She cupped his face and upturned it slightly.

"Now, close your golden eyes, Child of Earth," she whispered, her lips nearly touching his. "It's time to wake up."

He squeezed his eyes shut, feeling her thumbs caressing his cheeks. Her lips brushed his, just a gentle touch, and the ground vanished from under his feet.

"Damian, please wake up... Dima... I need you to wake up, brother mine."

CHAPTER 30

~ DAMIAN BLAKE ~

Damian opened his eyes but could see nothing except for the dark sky with two glowing red stars above him. He blinked a few times, dispelling the blurriness from his vision. Two red stars turned into a pair of glowing scarlet eyes, gazing at him without blinking.

"Cole..." Damian reached up, his arm heavy and stiff. His fingers brushed over his brother's cheek.

"You're awake. Thank God." Cole sat back on his heels, a tortured smile tugging at his lips, the tips of his fangs showing.

Damian pushed himself up into a sitting position, realizing how weak he was. "Actually, you should thank the Slavic goddess of Nightmares that I'm awake."

"Divine intervention..." Cole whispered, staring at his brother incredulously.

"Something like that," replied Damian.

He searched the lakeside but couldn't see Yakov anywhere. Cole got up and headed toward the lake. He returned a few seconds later, carrying the old wizard in his arms. Yakov was awake, but his arms hung limply, bouncing with every step his brother took. Cole lowered him to the ground next to Damian and then brought the box, placing it on the ground between them.

"Az was here when I surfaced," he said quietly, a haunted expression settling in his dimming eyes. "I'm sorry. He controlled me, and I could do nothing to stop him." He punched the air with his fist and looked up in the dark sky, biting his lip.

"He only took the controlling ring," Yakov pointed out, his fingers tracing the shape of the large silver band. "Why is that?"

"He didn't say," replied Cole.

"There are only two Hollow Band sets," said Damian. He closed the box and picked it up, rising to his feet with a strenuous groan. "Are they interchangeable? Can the controlling ring from this set control the band from the other?"

Yakov looked up at him, his face turning a sickening yellow. "Yes," he whispered. "I believe so. Do you know who owns the second set?"

"I think so. The last I heard, it was in Kendral," replied Damian. "But that was more than five hundred years ago." He switched his attention to his brother. "Cole, help Yakov get up. We're going home. We need to find out where the second set is and that will tell us where Azazel is going next."

Leaning heavily on Cole's shoulder, Yakov froze in place, and his jaw dropped. "Did you just say Azazel?" he asked, his voice barely above a whisper. Damian nodded. "Azazel? Are you out of your fucking mind, Commander? We can't fight the Fallen! It's suicide! Even for you!"

"I know." Damian smiled a humorless smile, his eyes meeting Cole's shocked gaze. "Yakov, neither you nor Cole have to go with me, but I have no choice. It's my obligation to face Azazel and stop him." He placed his hand on his brother's shoulder, giving him a reassuring squeeze. "Are you ready?"

Cole nodded, and Damian snapped his fingers, teleporting them from the Dead Lake.

* * *

It was past noon when Damian, Cole and Yakov materialized on the steps of Paradise Manor. A Mercedes SUV was parked on the driveway in front of the entrance, and that told Damian that Jamie was back home. The entrance door still wasn't fixed, and Atticus was busy working with a broom, cleaning the splinters of wood from the foyer. As soon as the young werewolf noticed them, he pressed his fist to his chest, inclining his head. Then he stepped aside, gesturing for them to come in.

Damian headed straight to the kitchen. As he suspected, River, Ace and Jamie were there, discussing something animatedly. As soon as he walked in, they fell silent, and Ace moved her infuriated gaze from Jamie to Damian and then to Cole. Damian frowned, wondering what that was all about, but at the moment, he had no time to deal with drama. He pulled one of the chairs out and sat down heavily, placing the box on the table.

"Cole," he said, turning to his brother. "Can you please make a cup of strong coffee for Yakov? Maybe get him something to eat. He still feels weak after the number Azazel did on both of us. The weakness should be gone in a short while, but some food and caffeine in his system might help him recover sooner."

Cole just nodded, helped Yakov to sit down and headed to the coffee machine. River got up, taking a tentative step toward Damian, but he raised his hand, stopping her.

"River, I'm really sorry," he said, his every move sharp and jerky. "We have a situation on our hands, and I need to deal with it as soon as possible. You'll understand everything later."

River threw a reproachful glance at him and turned to Cole. "Why don't you sit down, Cole," she said, moving a chair for him. "For a vampire, you look like you're ready to drop yourself. I'll take care of our guest." She smiled at Yakov and headed toward the refrigerator.

Feeling heat creeping up his cheeks, Damian turned away and stifled a sigh, cursing himself inwardly for his usual awkwardness and unusual nervousness. Then he channeled his magic and drew a rune glowing with the orange light of his elemental energy in the air. He touched it with his fingers and whispered a summoning spell.

"Luc de la Crosse, I summon thee." He completed the summons and stilled as the empty oval of a communication window replaced the rune. After a few seconds, a flare of light lit up the window, and the Master Warden approached it, still in his full medieval regalia.

"Commander," he said, his face tense, "were you able to recover the Hollow Band?"

"Yes and no," replied Damian, showing the Master Warden the open box. He told him everything that had happened at the Dead Lake, omitting some personal parts of his conversation with Mara.

"Azazel," muttered Luc, his French accent thickening as it always did when he was troubled. "O Lord, save us all." He crossed himself, all color draining from his face. "How could I not realize—"

"It's okay, Luc. Do you know where the second set of the Hollow Band is?" asked Damian, drumming his fingers on the table impatiently. "I'm sure that whoever owns the second set is in danger. Since Azazel took only the controlling ring, it means he is after the second band, otherwise, the ring is useless."

"Yes, I'm sorry, *mon ami*." Luc ran his hand through his hair. "The second set is in Kendral. Originally, it was passed from one Master of Kendral to the next. At some point, the Ancient Master of Power, Mrak Delar, owned it. When he was at his darkest, he used it to control Alliandr." Luc frowned and rubbed his forehead, his gaze going out of focus. "From what I recall, in the end, Mrak Delar passed the ownership of the Hollow Band together with the power and the throne to Master Alliandr, the young King of Kendral."

"Then I believe Azazel is on his way to Kendral," said Damian. "I have to contact Master Alliandr and warn him. After that, I'm going to ask his permission to enter his realm. I have to find Azazel and deal with him."

"Oh, Damian." The Master Warden stepped closer to the communication window, his eyes widened. "You can't…" He slammed his fist against the surface of the window and looked away for a brief moment. "I'm afraid you don't have the kind of power you need to stop a Fallen, Commander."

Damian smirked, meeting his brother's tense gaze. "Do I have a choice?" he asked quietly, switching his attention back to Luc. "Do Destiny Enforcers ever have a choice? I'm going to go to Kendral and do whatever it takes to stop Azazel and at least attempt to capture him. Besides, the young King of Kendral is a skilled Master of Power. I'm not going to be alone."

"God be with you, Commander," said Luc de la Crosse. "Please, keep me updated." He waved his hand and closed the communication window.

Damian leaned forward, bracing his fists against the table, and dropped his head. A stampede of thoughts rushed through his mind, and he couldn't focus on anything. Feeling a gentle touch to his shoulder, he snapped his head up to see River standing next to him.

"A Fallen," she said, lowering her hand. "As in a fallen angel? Is that what Azazel is?"

"Yes, something like that, but a lot worse," replied Damian, straightening. "In his true form, he's a powerful demon, evil to the core. He is more powerful than any angel." A bitter smirk crossed his face. "Just like any evil being of magic, he doesn't bother with the rules and laws of the World of Magic. He doesn't care how many people die or if the World of Magic gets exposed. For him, purpose justifies the means. All that in combination with his great and dangerous power, makes him…" His voice trailed off, and he looked out the window at the familiar desert view.

"Unstoppable?" River whispered.

"Not unstoppable, Detective," chimed in Cole, taking the cup of steaming coffee out of her hands and placing it in front of Yakov next to a plate with a sandwich. "No one is unstoppable. But it makes him hard to beat."

Damian channeled his magic and assumed his true form. Folding his wings behind his back, he held his finger to his lips, asking everyone for silence. Then he drew another rune in midair and pressed his palm against it, channeling his magic through it.

"Master Alliandr, I summon thee," he whispered and stepped back, staring at the blank communication window.

A moment later, the window lit up, and a young man stepped in front of it. He was at least as tall as Damian, if not a little taller, and his jet-black hair fell to his shoulders in soft strands. While he looked muscular in his tight black pants and white shirt laced on his wide chest, there was an unmistakable vibe of elegance and a certain charm about him. His obsidian eyes observed everyone in the room with interest, and a soft smile touched his full lips.

"Master of Kendral." Damian pressed his fist to his chest and lowered to one knee. Except for River, everyone kneeled before the King of the World of Magic.

"Oh, my," mumbled River, staring at the young Master of Power in awe. Damian glanced at her, and a jolt of pain surged through him, tightening his chest. Not sure what that was all about, he dropped his head lower, clenching his jaw.

"Please rise." Alliandr waved his hand, gesturing for them to get up. His black eyes stopped on Damian, taking in his appearance, and his chiseled features hardened. "You are a Commander of the Destiny Enforcers, aren't you?"

"Yes, my lord," replied Damian, approaching the window. "My name is Damian Blake."

"Damian Blake." The young Master frowned, clasping his hands behind his back. "I've never heard of you. The only Commander I know of is Moore, and I hope I'll never have to meet with that man again." His frown deepened, his lips forming a firm line. "What can I do for you, Commander?"

Damian cringed inwardly at the icy tone of the young Master of Power, wondering what happened between him and Commander Moore.

"It's about the Hollow Band you have in your possession, Master," said Damian.

Master Alliandr paled, and his hand went up to his neck involuntarily. "What about it?"

Once more, Damian repeated the entire story. As he finished, the Master of Power stepped closer to the window, bracing his arms on either side of it, and dropped his head, his long hair obscuring his face.

"Master Alliandr," Damian called after a short pause, chills running down his spine. "If you give me permission to enter your realm—"

"That's the problem," the Master of Power interrupted him, raising his head. "You don't need to cross over into my realm, Commander. The Hollow Band that belongs to me is in yours." He raised his right hand and pointed at the silver ring on his finger. "At least the main band is in your realm, and I believe that's what the Fallen is searching for."

Damian exchanged a bewildered look with Yakov. "Why?" he asked.

"A while ago, I used my Hollow Band to control an extremely dangerous dark being of magic," said Alliandr. "He was one of the immortals, so killing him wasn't an option. At the time, I was too young and inexperienced as the Master of Power, so the only way I could subdue him was by using the

Hollow Band. I did that, and then I wrapped him in iron chains and locked him in a tiny cell I made out of solid rock. He's been there all this time…" His voice trailed off, and he raised his eyes flooded with the blackness of his power, staring at Damian without blinking. "Commander, you must stop Azazel. This monster…" He swallowed hard and squared his shoulders. "You can't allow for this monster to walk the world of humans ever again."

"Who are you talking about, Master?" asked Damian calmly.

"Koschei the Deathless," replied Master Alliandr. The darkness vanished from his eyes, replaced by endless exhaustion. He rubbed his forehead, throwing his hair off his face. "I'm talking about the ancient sorcerer, Koschei the Deathless. But from what I've been told, his immortality is conditional. He can be killed. I just don't know how."

"*Gospodi Iisuse Hriste, pomiluj mya greshnogo,*" Yakov exhaled, crossing himself.

"I haven't heard anyone praying in old Russian for a while." Damian smirked, looking at the wizard from under his hair. "Don't tell me you're scared, old eagle?"

Yakov got up and leaned forward, propping his fists against the table. "Yes, I am," he said, his eyes darting from Damian to Alliandr. "And you should be too. With all due respect, Master of Kendral, you're wrong. Koschei the Deathless is not a sorcerer. I mean, yes, he can wield magic. As a matter of fact, he is one of the most powerful Masters of the Dark Arts, but that is the least of our worries."

Alliandr inclined his head respectfully. "Please tell us everything you know, my lord," he said, gesturing for Yakov to proceed.

"Koschei is not just a Master of the Dark Arts," Yakov continued, lowering on his chair. "Born by Mother Earth herself at the time of Creation, he's as old as Svarog and the first gods of the Slavic pantheon. Russian fairytales downplayed his power and importance. Even his name was explained wrong. Many think his name 'Koschei' comes from the word 'kosti', which means bones. Don't get me wrong—the man is as skinny as a skeleton, so it does seem to be appropriate." Yakov chuckled mirthlessly. "But that is not what his name means. His name comes from the old Slovenian word 'koschun', which means evil sorcerer. He is not of this world. He draws his power from the realm of the dead, from the darkest corners of the Dark Nav, and in his power, he's equal to Chernobog himself."

"Can you take it all back?" murmured Cole, shaking his head. "I don't think I wanted to know all that." He glanced at Damian, his hands nearly crushing the counter he leaned against. "Are you saying the Fallen is trying to free some crazy, evil, ancient god?"

Yakov shrugged, falling back in his chair. "Well, maybe not quite a god anymore, but an equal in power for sure," he said. "Just like Master Alliandr said, Koschei's immortality is conditional. He has death, but he hides it well. His death is a physical object. Slavic fairytales say that his death is hidden in a needle. The needle is hidden in an egg. But I think there is some kind of misinterpretation here, just like with his name. Perhaps, we're talking about the World Egg, which is a symbol of the Sun. Anyway, this is nothing more than speculation. I would have to talk to the Master Warden and return to the Wardens Library and Archives. But one thing is for sure—he can be killed."

"Thank you," said Alliandr, slightly inclining his head. "If at some point you feel you need more information, the Riders Library in Kendral is available to you." He turned to Damian, his expression hardening again. "In the meantime, Commander, you'd do well to stop the Fallen before he can free Koschei."

"Yes, Master." Damian pressed his fist to his chest, wondering what Moore had done to anger the young Master to the point where he couldn't look at another Destiny Enforcer without getting hot under the collar. "It would help me a great deal if you could tell me the location of the cell where you have Koschei imprisoned. I'm sure this is where Azazel will go."

Alliandr exhaled and pinched the bridge of his nose, nibbling on his lip. "That's another problem, Commander. I can't give you the direction. This place is a cave without any ways in or out of it. It is located underground on the border between the world of the living and the realm of spirits and demons. Between the Yav and the Nav. The only way to get there is by teleporting. And the only way you can teleport there is if you know where it is located."

"Catch twenty-two," breathed Ace, and everyone turned to her.

Alliandr smiled. "Yes, my lady," he said softly. "It would be, considering the fact that as the Master of Kendral I'm bound to my realm and can't leave it for long, but I think I do have a solution." He turned to Damian and for the first time, his face didn't harden. "If I'm not mistaken, you're a Child of Earth, Commander?"

"Yes, Master," replied Damian, cringing inwardly, reminded that any Master of Power could control his element and him.

"It's so strange to see such a rare and powerful being of magic taking on the mantle of a Destiny Enforcer," he muttered, shaking his head.

"I accepted this position before I knew what I was," Damian replied with a shrug.

Alliandr looked at Damian as if sizing him up. Damian met his heavy gaze without blinking, and for a heartbeat, they both fell silent.

"Anyway, Damian," said the young Master at length, and Damian's eyebrows rose as he realized that for the first time, Alliandr used his name. "Give me about thirty minutes, and I will send someone who can help you. He's my friend, so do me a favor and take good care of him." A sad smile crossed his face. "He was with me when I imprisoned Koschei, so he can take you to the cave and assist you in your fight against the Fallen. He's a powerful wizard and... well... you'll see." Alliandr raised his hand, ready to close the communication window. "I'll summon you as soon as I'm ready. I'll need a location rune, so I can open a portal to your house. Can you do it?"

"Yes, sir," replied Damian.

"Sir?" A lopsided smirk curved Alliandr's lips. "Yes, I believe you and my friend will find quite a few things in common. Thirty minutes, Commander. That's all I need."

He snapped his fingers and closed the communication window.

CHAPTER 31

~ DAMIAN BLAKE ~

As soon as the communication window closed, Yakov got up. Reaching for Damian's shoulder, he nudged him slightly, ripping him out of his thoughts. Damian closed his eyes and took a deep breath, returning to his human form.

"Damian, are you sure you want to do this?" Yakov shook his head, looking more than troubled.

"Do what?" asked Damian flatly.

"Go after the Fallen and Koschei the Deathless," replied Yakov, placing the empty coffee cup and the plate into the sink.

"Someone has to, and I'm already neck-deep in this mayhem. Besides, being a Destiny Enforcer, I don't have a choice in the matter." Damian shrugged, switching his attention to his brother. "Cole, please—"

"No." Cole pushed away from the counter and folded his arms.

"Cole, be reasonable." Damian sighed, feeling too exhausted to argue with anyone. "Az already controlled you once. You know you're powerless against his magic."

Ignoring Damian, Cole turned to Yakov. "You told me once that there is a way to protect me from the influence of necromancy. Can you do it, Yakov?" He smirked, throwing Damian an arched stare. "Even though my brother is a Mister I-Work-Alone, I would rather die than leave him without any support in this situation."

As an answer to Cole's question, a wide grin crossed Yakov's face, and Damian threw his hands up—there was no way he could talk his brother out of this mission now.

"Come here, my friend," said Yakov, gesturing for Cole to sit down. "Not many wizards know how to protect a vampire from necromancy, but I do." A glimmer of pride ignited in his eyes for a brief moment, but then he tapped Cole on his shoulder, an expression of pride morphing into a semblance of guilt. "There is one serious drawback that you may want to consider, though. This spell is extremely unpleasant. Just a fair warning, you know?"

"Do it." Cole sat down on the chair, looking up at the wizard, and Damian threw his hands up again, making Cole chuckle.

Yakov glanced at Cole's unclothed chest, rubbing his chin, and then placed his hand over his heart. A soft glow of his magical energy surrounded his hand, and he started to chant. Cole clenched his teeth, bearing down on his chair. His eyes widened and muscles bulged on his tense shoulders as he fought to suppress a scream of pain. Thin red veins sprouted from under Yakov's palm, slithering under Cole's skin, moving in all directions.

Cole groaned, red liquid gathering in the corners of his eyes, his face strained. Then he threw his head back and screamed, his cry of pain turning into a low growl. In a heartbeat, Damian was next to him, taking his brother's hand into his. Cole's fingers crushed his, but he didn't move and didn't make a sound.

Both River and Ace moved closer to Cole, and Ace, with her hand on the pommel of her sword, looked like she was ready to split the wizard in two. Atticus ran into the room, but

Jamie halted him in the doorway, whispering something into his ear.

Yakov stopped chanting and lifted his hand. For a few seconds, a bright red rune shone on Cole's chest before gradually disappearing. Slithering red veins slowly withdrew and dissipated. Cole's head dropped backward, his eyes closed, a few drops of blood escaping from under his tightly shut eyelids.

"He's okay." Yakov glanced at Damian, giving him a reassuring nod. He slapped Cole's cheek slightly, and the vampire opened his eyes, straightening.

"Jesus, man," muttered Cole, wiping bloody tears off his face. "Extremely unpleasant? You couldn't have said it was going to hurt like a bitch?"

"The benefits outweigh the cost?" Yakov winked at him slyly, but then quickly sobered up. "Never again a necromancer, no matter how powerful, will be able to control you, Cole. I embedded the protection rune into your very bones."

"It sure felt like that." Cole got up, swaying slightly, his eyes moving from one face to the next. "If the great assembly doesn't mind"—he bowed, humorous twinkles dancing in his blue eyes—"I'm going to steal my brother for a few minutes. I need to have a quick *tête-à-tête* with him before we leave." He glanced down and scratched the back of his head. "Getting dressed also sounds like a good idea. I promise we'll be right back."

Without waiting for anyone's response, he grabbed Damian's elbow and ushered him out the door. They walked through the dark hallway in silence until they reached Cole's bedroom. Damian opened the door, allowing Cole in first. The vampire crossed the room and sat down on the floor, leaning his back against the wall. Damian looked down at him, guessing what Cole wanted to tell him.

"You're right." Damian lowered himself to the floor in front of Cole and crossed his legs. "We should have done it a long time ago, but now that we're about to face..." His voice trailed, and he exhaled a short breath. "I wish you let me go alone, Cole..."

"No."

Damian nodded, nibbling on his lips. "Let's do it then. We should have a way to communicate with each other when we're apart. What happened at the lake could have been prevented if we had a blood bond established. With Mara's help, I could have contacted you even in the enchanted sleep." He dropped his head, looking at his clenched hands.

"Come here, brother." Cole grabbed Damian's hand, pulling him closer. "Sit next to me, I'm not gonna bite." A lopsided smirk crossed his face, sadness remaining in his glowing eyes. "Oh, wait. That is exactly what I'm going to do."

Damian changed his position, sitting down next to his brother, and offered him his arm. Cole took it, his fingers brushing over a thick blue vein running from Damian's elbow to his wrist.

"Ready?" he asked softly.

"I'm never ready to drink vampire's blood, but let's do it."

Cole lowered his face over Damian's arm, and his fangs penetrated his skin. Damian sucked in a sharp breath, but the momentary pain was replaced by a feeling of warmth and contentment. He moaned and leaned back, closing his eyes. His mind fogged, his muscles turning into mush.

"When you're done, I'll kill you," he exhaled, his weak fingers seizing Cole's hair on the back of his head. He could feel Cole's lips stretching into a smile over his arm but had no strength to push him away. "You little bloodsucking monster..."

A heartbeat later, Cole pulled away. Damian looked at him with his eyes half-closed but had neither the desire nor strength to move. Cole pulled him over, propping him against his shoulder, and then bit his own wrist. As dark, thick blood spilled from two puncture wounds, he moved his arm over Damian's mouth.

"Drink," he said, supporting his head gently. "I'll let you know when to stop."

As the first drop of thick, sweet liquid fell into Damian's mouth, he closed his eyes, his mind blissfully blank. He wasn't sure how much blood he took, but when Cole moved him away, resting his back against the wall, he felt something close to regret, fighting the need for more.

"Do you still want to kill me, big bro?" Cole's voice sounded in Damian's mind, his scarlet eyes laughing.

"No," muttered Damian, and as the fog in his mind started to clear out, he tried to communicate through their psychic link created by the blood bond. *"What I wanted to do to you was a lot worse than death."*

The corners of Cole's mouth lifted, and Damian knew his brother heard him.

"Listen, Dima," said Cole, suddenly serious. "Now that you've agreed on me going with you, Ace would want to follow." He fell silent, rubbing his hand with his thumb. "You can't let her go with us. Use your authority as a Commander or do whatever you need to do but don't let her follow us into that..." He took a pause as if searching for a better word, and finally added, "Battle. You know it's going to be hell there, right?"

Damian glanced at his brother sideways and leaned forward, resting his arms atop his bent knees. "I agree, but I want to know what brought this up."

"She's not ready, Dima," Cole said, his shoulders tense. "Neither as a Destiny Enforcer nor as a person. I like Ace, but after what happened when Simon's pack attacked Paradise Manor, I feel that her physical attraction to me will be the death of her in a real combat situation. We're about to face a monster of our childhood nightmares, and when the shit hits the fan, I don't think I'll be able to protect her. I can't have it on my conscience."

"This is why there is a rule in place—Destiny Enforcers can't have personal connections with their charges. In our line of work, any personal attachment becomes a dangerous liability." Damian massaged the back of his neck. "If Moore ever finds out..." He whistled, shaking his head. "He'll skin her alive, and he'll try to put his hands on you as well, blaming you for seducing her. He would do it just to hurt me. I don't know why, but this man hates me with a passion. He would do anything to bring me down, and your situation with Ace gives him all—" Damian didn't finish the statement, nibbling on his lip. "Anyway, if he tries to hurt you, I'll do what I have to do to stop him."

Cole shuddered visibly. "I hope it's not going to come to that." He got up and headed toward the closet. "Just make sure Ace stays in Paradise Manor."

Damian rose to his feet and swayed slightly, his head still a little heavy after the influence of the vampire bite. He stretched his arms and shoulders and sat down on the bed, waiting for Cole to come out. His thoughts circled back to Ace's infatuation with his brother, and a painful heaviness settled in his chest.

I hope you don't feel the same about her, brother mine, Damian thought, forgetting about the psychic link they just created, his fingers rubbing the edge of his bracelet absentmindedly. *That would be a true disaster.*

Cole walked out of the closet, a wide grin on his face. "You need to learn how to block our connection, so I don't hear your thoughts directed at me unless you want me to hear them. It's easy. Try."

Dammit...

"I heard that." Cole laughed, bending down to lace his combat boots. "No, Dima, I'm not in love. She's a beautiful young woman, and I like her. I care about her, but it's not love." He straightened, readjusting his scabbard. "I don't think it's possible." He sat down next to Damian, gazing at him sideways. "I'm a thousand years old. The things I've seen... and done..." He hid his face in his hands for a short moment. "She's what?

Twenty-five? She's a child, Dima. I didn't think about the consequences of having sex with her. It was wrong on many different levels, and I should have stopped her."

"Damn right, you didn't think. Or you thought with the wrong head," replied Damian. "Anyway, what's done is done, but if you care about her future, you have to stop it now."

Cole dropped his head. "I'm so curious to find out how she became a Destiny Enforcer in the first place, and why the Destiny Council sent someone so inexperienced, young and unprepared to shadow me. Apparently, they knew my situation before your arrival, and after you arrived in Blue Creek, it became even more dangerous. It doesn't make any sense."

"I've been thinking the same thing for a while," replied Damian, "and I have no answer to that. But I will find out." He glanced at his wristwatch and tapped his brother's knee. "Alliandr should summon me in five minutes. It's time to go."

They got up, but as they moved toward the door, a light knock stopped them in their tracks.

"River. I can smell her perfume," projected Cole, using their link, a mischievous grin crossing his face. *"Speaking of—"*

"She's not a child, despite her age," objected Damian.

"No, she's not, but when she's around, you behave like you are a child." Cole chuckled, shaking his head, and placed his hand on the door handle. *"Man up, big bro."*

He opened the door and gestured for River to come in, making a move to leave, but she seized his arm, halting him in the doorway. Her eyes moved from Damian to Cole and then settled on Damian.

"I know you're about to summon that young man... um... Master of Kendral," she said, pulling Cole back inside. "I know you both want me to stay behind." Damian tilted his head a little, taking a step closer, but she raised her hand, stopping him. "You don't have to say anything, Dima. You're doing the right thing. I'm just a human with no magical powers. As much as I wish I could, it would be stupid and reckless for me to go with you. But there is one question I wanted to ask both of you."

"What is it?" asked Damian unwillingly, raising his eyes at her.

"He is a vampire," she said, pointing at Cole. "I've seen enough fantasy movies and read enough books to know his immortality is conditional. He can be killed. But I don't understand anything about Destiny Enforcers. Can a Destiny Enforcer be killed, Dima?"

"Don't believe everything you read in fantasy books," murmured Cole, a lopsided grin on his lips. "Some of them are written by vampires to deceive humans."

"Destiny Enforcers are not immortal, River," replied Damian. "Their lives are a lot longer than an average human life, though. When you accept the mantle of a Destiny Enforcer, you receive new powers and your own powers are amplified to a degree, but it doesn't make you immortal. It's my connection with the elemental Earth that gives me the immortality."

"Can you die?" she asked calmly, looking directly into his eyes. "Answer my question straight."

"Yes, I can, River," replied Damian softly. "Even gods can be killed, and I'm not a god." He approached her, placing his hands on her shoulders. "I'll be all right. We both will be fine." Glancing at his wristwatch again, he frowned, throwing a quick glance at his brother. Then he gestured at the door. "Master Alliandr should be summoning me any moment now. It's time."

River didn't add anything else but squared her shoulders and silently walked out the door without looking back.

* * *

DAMIAN STEPPED into the kitchen and halted, observing everyone in the room. Ace and Jamie weren't getting along, and Atticus had taken a place between them, keeping them at arm's length. Yakov sat in the same place, a set of glowing runes scrolling in the air in front of him. He kept touching one rune at a time, shaking his head, and then scrolling farther down. Once he noticed Damian, he moved his hand across the set of runes, and they vanished.

With a low groan, he got up. "I can't find anything about Koschei the Deathless and the location of his death," he said, staring down at the table. "I need to get back to the Wardens Library as soon as possible and start the research. In case, you won't be able to stop Azazel, we have to be ready, Commander." He lifted his face, angst reflected in his eyes. "When it comes to combat magic, I'm not—"

Damian raised his hand, stopping him. "It's okay, Yakov. You made the right choice. You should go to the Wardens Library and take Jamie with you. I'm sure between the two of you, you'll find everything we need."

Jamie's eyes lit up with excitement, but he swallowed and shook his head. "Wait, Damian. I should go with you and Cole."

Damian stifled a sigh, noticing a torn expression on the young man's face. It was obvious that on one hand, Jamie wanted to visit the Wardens Library and Archives. After all, it was a legendary place filled with ancient books, scrolls and wisdom collected over thousands of years, and Jamie with his natural hunger for knowledge yearned to spend time in a place like this. On the other hand, he felt that he was betraying his friend, and his honor wouldn't let him do it.

"It's okay, Jamie," Damian said softly. "What Yakov's doing is just as important, and he needs your help. Cole and I will be fine. Besides, Master Alliandr is sending someone to help us." He switched his attention to Ace, mentally preparing for a storm. "Ace, I need you to sit this one out."

"But Damian—," she started but fell silent under his heavy gaze.

"Please, Ace," he said softly. "I can order you as a Commander, but I'm asking you as a friend. Please, stay here. If you care about my brother, you'll do as I say."

As defiance vanished from her eyes, she glanced at Cole, her gaze pleading with him. The vampire frowned but made his way around the table and halted next to her. Placing his hand on her shoulder, he leaned down.

"Today, we all are going to do as Damian says," he whispered into her ear. "Not because he's a Commander and it's his mission, and not because he's my older brother, but because he's right. Do it for me, Ace." He gave her shoulder a reassuring squeeze and stepped back.

Feeling a slight headache of a summoning call originating behind his eyes, Damian channeled his power and drew a rune in the air, opening a communication window. Master Alliandr and an unfamiliar tall man stood in front of the window.

"Commander," said the Master of Power, slightly inclining his head. He waved his hand at the man and introduced him. "This is Oleg Svetlov—my friend I've told you about earlier. I've explained your situation to Oleg, and he is willing to take you to the cave and stay with you to support you in case you need help." Alliandr glanced at the man, warmth transforming his face. "Oleg, this is Damian Blake, a Commander of the Destiny Enforcers."

Oleg's attentive hazel eyes met Damian's, and a wide, open smile split his face, dimpling his cheeks.

"Nice to meet you, sir," he said, generously rolling his R's, and Damian had to wonder why this man spoke with such a heavy Russian accent when he could use his magic to speak fluently and without an accent in any language.

Damian smiled back at him, inclining his head. "Thank you, Oleg. I appreciate your help."

He stepped away from the window and channeled his magic. As his hands lit up with a soft orange glow, he heard Oleg's soft gasp and glanced back at him, noticing surprise bordering on shock written on his face. Turning away, he drew a bright rune in the air and returned to the communication window.

"Master Alliandr," he said, "the location rune is ready. You can open your portal."

The young King of Kendral turned to his friend, his eyes filled with concern. They locked their hands in a forearm handshake, and Oleg tapped Alliandr's upper arm slightly.

"I'll be fine, Alliandr," he said with a half-shrug. "We've been through worse, yes?"

"Yes." Alliandr released his arm. "You know my girlfriend will kill me if something happens to you." He turned to Damian, and a slight smile ghosted his lips. "Damian, you better take care of my friend or my girlfriend will come after you, too."

"God save us all in that case." Oleg laughed, his light eyes shining with humor. "Open the portal, my friend. I will see you soon."

A heartbeat later, a portal rotating with bright blue lights opened next to Damian, and Oleg walked through it. He turned to Damian and offered his hand.

"It is great to meet you in person, sir," he said.

Damian glanced at Oleg's hand, noticing a thin silver ring on his middle finger, which looked like the one Master Alliandr had. For a brief moment, he wondered if the Master of Power had given the controlling ring of the Hollow Band to his friend or if it was just a plain piece of jewelry. Then he smiled and took Oleg's hand. A wave of elemental energy of Earth rushed through him, and the ground responded to their connection with a light tremor. Yakov got up, his eyes wide with awe.

"You don't say," he mumbled, tilting his head. "Well, you don't see something like this every day."

"You're a Child of Earth." Damian released Oleg's hand, taking a step back. "I've heard that there was a Child of Earth in Kendral, but I never thought I would meet..." His voice trailed off as he observed the man with new interest.

"I had no idea there was another Child of Earth," admitted Oleg, his eyes narrowing slightly. "I wonder if Sandhya knows." Catching Damian's puzzled look, he added, "Sandhya... You know? She is the Elemental of Earth."

"The Queen of Kendral's Underworld?" Damian stared at him in awe.

He knew that the Elemental of Earth resided in Kendral, and from what he'd been told, the Queen didn't like to leave her kingdom of dwarfs. Wise and kind to her subjects, she regarded strangers with open wariness. While she lived in peace with the people on the surface, trading gems, minerals and iron for food and some supplies she couldn't produce in her realm, she never allowed anyone from the outside to enter her underground domain. However, this man spoke about her with such ease and familiarity as if she were his best friend.

"Yes, the Queen of the Underworld." Oleg thought for a moment and added, "If we survive all this, there is a big chance you will see her soon, and I will be happy to introduce you to her."

His eyes slipped across the room as he studied everyone present, and a slightly apologetic smile touched his lips.

"My apologies. There is no time for introductions, but I hope to see you all later on today." Switching his attention to Damian, his face grew harder, a muscle working in his tightly pressed jaw. "Damian, once I teleport us into the cave, we will be right in the middle of whatever is going on there. I have no idea what we will find there, but it cannot be any good. Unfortunately, there are no other ways to get into the cave as it exists between our world and the Dark Nav. There is no place to hide there either. It is a large open space with a small lake on the right side of it. So, brace yourself, Commander, and expect the unexpected."

Damian motioned for Cole to come closer and put his hand

on his shoulder. "This is my brother Cole. He is coming with us."

Oleg gave Cole a quick once-over followed by a curt nod and took Damian's elbow, raising his hand. "Here goes…"

As Oleg snapped his fingers to teleport them out of Paradise Manor, Ace crossed the distance between her and Cole in one step and grabbed his arm. Damian noticed her move, but it was too late to do anything as the world swirled around him, darkness taking over.

CHAPTER 32

~ DAMIAN BLAKE ~

The reek of sulfur mixed in with a musty, unclean smell assaulted his senses, and Damian held his breath, hiding his face in the crook of his elbow. The flickering orange light of torches illuminated a spacious cave, unsteady shadows moving away from the circles of light. A small lake was right behind him. With nothing disturbing its smooth, mirror-like surface, it spread, black and motionless, unknown dangers hiding in the depths of its waters. In front of him, a wide circle of dark, hooded figures obscured everything that was going on at the other end of the cave. The soft sound of their monotonous, emotionless chant filled the space with a continuous hum that sent chills down Damian's back.

"*We're too late,*" Cole's voice sounded in Damian's mind as he stared at the people in long, black cloaks, trying to figure out what they were.

"*Maybe not... Can you detect what they are? I don't want to use any magic if I can help it,*" projected Damian. He threw a warning glance at Oleg and Ace, raising his finger to his lips.

"*Not humans,*" replied Cole. "*At least most of them are neither humans nor vampires. My guess some kind of demonic entities.*"

Oleg placed his hand on the pommel of his sword and gave Damian an arched stare, jerking his chin toward the monsters. Damian nodded but didn't move, his jaw clenched so tight he didn't think he could speak. He wasn't sure what he was waiting for, but he stared at the enemy army like in a trance. He knew that even the tiniest sound or a fluctuation in the magical energy field around them could alert the chanting monsters as well as the Fallen.

Even though he couldn't see Azazel anywhere, he was positive the demon was here. The biggest surprise, however, was that the Fallen hadn't noticed the spike of magical energy they had created when they teleported into the cave, as well as that he still hadn't detected Cole's presence since vampires couldn't shield their energy signature. At least, he didn't acknowledge their presence, and that fact alone made Damian's stomach twist with dread.

A thin metallic sound was so faint that Damian barely noticed it. He glanced in the direction of the sound to see Ace standing with her sword in her hand and cursed inwardly at her inexperience.

He wasn't sure if it happened because of the sound Ace produced or because Azazel finally decided to acknowledge their presence, but the change came immediately. The chant ceased abruptly, and a heavy silence enveloped the cave, pressing on Damian's stretched nerves. Somewhere at the far end of the cave, a few rocks fell, rolling across the hard ground, their sound prominent in the surrounding quietness.

All cloaked figures turned around at once, a heavy shuffling noise following their movement. Their black hoods were pulled low over their faces, and he couldn't distinguish their features. But as their black lips drew back in a snarl, a set of terrifying fangs reflected the light of the torches, and it seemed as though their mouths were filled with blood. The reek of demonic essence intensified, leaving no doubt—most of these monsters were demons in their pure form, which made the situation a lot more dangerous.

Most of the demons who walked the realm of humans weren't in their natural state, but rather human bodies possessed by demonic essence. More often than not, the owners of the possessed bodies were long dead. However, in some cases, for reasons known to them only, the demon kept the soul of the human they were possessing intact. While these kinds of demons were dangerous and magically well-endowed, they were relatively easy to kill, and in their power, they were nothing compared to the demons in their natural state.

It wasn't easy to summon pure demons from the realms of demons and spirit. It was even harder to control them and make them do your bidding. So, seeing so many of them gathered inside the cave just confirmed the seriousness of Azazel's intentions and his enormous power.

Both Oleg and Cole unsheathed their swords, and Damian summoned his daggers but didn't channel his magic through them, waiting to see what would happen next. A soft wave of whispers rushed through the crowd, and the demons parted, creating a narrow passage between them.

"What the hell?" Cole projected, and his vampiric essence spiked around him, his eyes igniting with a scarlet glow.

"Azazel is coming," replied Damian.

A short, scrawny man walked among giant demons and halted one step ahead of them. His eyes, enlarged by the giant lenses of his eyeglasses, swept from left to right, halting for a brief moment on each of them. His lips stretched into a wide smile, exposing overly bleached teeth, and he took one more step forward, now standing right in front of his army. He glanced back at the demons and waved his hand.

"What are you staring at?" he asked impatiently, displeasure clear in his voice. "Keep going. The location is not going to reveal itself."

Right away, the demons turned around and started to chant again, their whispers flowing through the cave once more.

"Commander Blake," Azazel said, switching his attention to Damian. "I see you found me." His eyes darted from Cole to Oleg, and his smirk became wider. "And I see you brought your biological brother and your brother in element with you. How sweet." His eyes explored Oleg's body, moving up and down his brawny figure, and he pointed at him with his slightly deformed finger. "I've heard of you. If I'm not mistaken, you're the Child of Earth from Kendral—the infamous Captain Oleg Svetlov, personal friend and bodyguard of the Master of Kendral. Am I right?" An almost a child-like excitement lit up his eyes.

Oleg shrugged nonchalantly, a cold smile tugging at his lips. "What if I am? Does it make any difference?"

Azazel lifted his skinny shoulders, pursing his lips. "Alas, you're right, Captain. No matter who you are, you stand no chance against me. I'll kill you all." His eyes halted on Ace, and his eyebrows rose dangerously close to his hairline. "And who might this enchanting, tiny creature among you giants be?" He reached for Ace, but she stepped back, raising her sword.

"I'll kill you, demonic scumbag," she growled, squeezing the grip of her sword tighter.

"Aw... I'm sure you'll try, dear." Azazel chuckled, shaking his head, the fluffy cloud of his hair flowing with his every move. He stepped away from Ace and returned to Damian. "How did you find out where I was, Commander? Just curious. I thought I covered my tracks well."

"Not as well as you thought," replied Damian, calmly. "You made a mistake, Azazel. You took only the controlling ring of the Hollow Band."

"Oh?" The Fallen cocked his head, staring at him intently. "You also know who I am. Kudos to you, Commander. I didn't figure you were smart enough to figure it out."

"Underestimating your opponents is another mistake you've

made and are still making." Damian smirked, placing his hand of Ace's shoulder.

"You're probably right. In this case, the masquerade is over." The Fallen roared, spreading his arms, and his magical energy mixed in with his demonic essence spiked to the next level.

The air around him shimmered, and a dark-purple mist rose from the ground, wrapping around him like a shimmering veil. The walls trembled, causing a few more rocks to slide at the other end. A gust of wind swept across the cave, raising dust in the air, and then spun around Azazel into a purple funnel, its howls earsplitting within the limited space of the cave.

A moment later, the wind died down, and the mist vanished, revealing a figure of a giant man towering at least a foot over Damian. His narrow, black lips stretched into a malignant smirk as he stared down from his height, the look of his long, sharp fangs making the small hairs rise on the back of Damian's neck. The Fallen rolled his massive shoulders covered with grotesquely bulging muscles, and a pair of giant, webbed wings sprouted behind his back.

Ace gasped, taking a step back involuntarily. A wild grin split Cole's face as he brought his sword to his shoulder, and for some reason, his blade emitted a soft scarlet glow, characteristic of the energy of magic. Damian threw a troubled glance at his brother but had no time to think about it.

"That is all you have?" Oleg asked calmly, staring at the monster. A dark smirk appeared on his face, leaving his eyes cold and hard.

The demon glowered down at him and cocked his head a little, throwing the long strands of his black hair to his back. He didn't grace Oleg with an answer. Instead, he pivoted on his heels, the metal soles of his heavy boots scraping the ground.

"I'll take it from here," he said to his army, his deep voice bouncing off the tall ceiling of the cave. He waved his giant arm in Damian's direction. "Kill the girl and the vampire. Children of Elements are immortal. Subdue and restrain them until I have time to deal with them."

For a brief second, Azazel looked back at Damian, his eyes glowing with the malignant glimmer of his magic, and the corner of his mouth went up as if teasing him to try to stop him. He folded his massive wings and moved toward the opposite end of the cave, his every step producing soft tremors.

The demonic army shifted forward, taking their hoods off. Their ugly faces had nothing human about them, and the carnivorous light in their eyes was unmistakable. They ripped their cloaks off, bringing forth an assortment of terrifyingly large weapons—swords, daggers, battle axes and hammers, as well as spike-infested clubs and chains.

Oleg whistled between his teeth. "Bring it on, *ublyudki*..."

Damian smirked, thinking that he hadn't heard someone cursing in Russian for a while.

"What he said," murmured Cole, throwing a gaze sparkling with laughter at Oleg.

The demons howled and roared as they charged forward, brandishing their weapons.

"Procedia Amnia," roared Damian and Oleg at the same time.

The glowing shield of their magical energy unfolded before them, and the front line of the demonic army ran into it, pounding it with their weapons but unable to break through. The impact vibrated through Damian's arms, and he strained to maintain his magic. Oleg's face tensed, and a thick pulsing vein crossed his forehead, the muscles of his arms and shoulders rippling under his shirt. The demons hadn't expected it and bounced back, running into the monsters behind them.

"Stay behind us," yelled Oleg, addressing Cole and Ace.

He exchanged a look with Damian and gave him a sharp nod. Understanding him without words, Damian dropped the shield at the same time as Oleg. The daggers in Damian's hands lit up with the pure energy of Creation as he assumed his true form, folding his wings behind his back.

Oleg charged forward, moving lightly on his feet despite his size. He swung his sword. There was nothing magical about his weapon, but the man was so strong, he was able to decapitate a demon in its natural state with one swing of his blade. The monster froze in place, its head rolling off its deformed shoulders. Oleg applied a powerful push kick, propelling the massive body back into the group of demons behind it.

The presence of the elemental energy of Earth doubled as Oleg channeled his power. Endeavoring to make his way to the other end of the cave where Azazel was weaving his deadly magic, Damian moved forward. The purifying energy of Creation projected by his blades cut into the mass of the demonic army, burning through them as if they were nothing but butter under a hot kitchen knife.

The demons roared and parted, moving in two directions as they attempted to surround them. Watching every move of the opposing army, Damian knew that despite his effort, he and his friends were in trouble. There were just too many monsters here, and only four of them. They were severely outmanned. They couldn't stop them. Sooner or later, they would be squeezed into a tight circle with no way to escape and no space to maneuver.

"Cole," he projected, *"keep an eye on Ace and be careful. We're about to get outflanked."*

A momentary distraction caused him to lose track of his opponents. As a giant monster with four hairy arms spun toward him, waving his spiked club, Damian steered to the side to avoid the club just to run into another demon. Multiple tentacles wrapped around his torso, pinning his arms to his body. The suction cups of the tentacles attached to his skin, and Damian cried out as the poison produced by the monster scorched his skin. The massive fist of another demon connected with his jaw. His head jerked to the side, the copper taste of blood filling his mouth, his vision turning blurry for a few seconds.

Channeling more of his power, Damian threw his head back and screamed, opening his wings to full extent, placing all his strength into this move. The tentacles burst apart, releasing him, but as their suction cups broke off, they took parts of his skin with them, leaving bleeding ulcers in their wake. The demon howled and dropped to its knees. Cole stepped forward and swung his sword at the monster's head, splitting it in two.

Three more demons replaced the fallen one, and it seemed like there was no end to them. Damian thrust his dagger forward, penetrating the monster's chest.

"Illucious!" he yelled, amplifying the purifying power of Creation, and the demon melted into a pile of disgusting mush.

Spinning in place, Damian almost lost his footing on the sticky goo. Oleg was fighting across from him, deflecting the attacks of two demons at once, but all he could do was keep a defensive position, overwhelmed by the sheer number of attackers coming at him from every direction.

"Cole," Damian called to his brother. *"Oleg and I need just a few seconds to regroup. Can you and Ace give us a short breather?"*

"Ask and you shall receive," Cole's voice roared in his head, and the vampire vanished.

Damian opened his other sight, watching his brother as he moved around the perimeter of surrounding attackers. While the vampire couldn't kill the demons in their natural form easily, he produced enough chaos and confusion in their lines to distract them. Shouts of anger and howls of pain accompanied Cole's speedy progress, and the demons pulled back slightly, focusing on stopping him.

"Oleg," Damian shouted, magnifying his voice with his magic to raise it over the clamor of the battle. Oleg snapped his head, glancing at him over his shoulder with his eyebrows raised, and

Damian added in a deep growl, "Let's bury them once and for all."

Oleg nodded, an orange light igniting in his eyes. "Be careful, Damian," he shouted back. "We're in a cave." Sheathing his sword, he dropped to one knee, placing both palms flat against the ground.

"Ace," yelled Damian, pulling her closer. "Watch Oleg's back." Making his daggers vanish, he dropped to one knee, mirroring Oleg's position, and reached out to his brother. *"Cole, come back now and keep an eye on the demons while we're working."*

Detecting his brother's presence behind him, Damian allowed the elemental energy of Earth to flow freely through him. He had never worked with another Child of Earth before, and now that Oleg was with him, he could detect the fluctuation in the elemental energy field as it split between them. With delight, he noticed that Oleg was skilled and precise, directing his energy through the ground between them and the demonic army.

The Earth responded to them, and the ground quaked. A thin fracture ran through the rocky floor, growing thicker with every passing moment. Careful not to rattle the floor of the cave too much, Damian focused on the crack, enlarging it. A few monsters fell into the trench, their screams of horror echoing through the cave. The others growled and hissed, cowering away from the danger. The front lines crushed the back lines, and the air filled with howls of pain, fury almost palpable around them.

Without giving them time to regroup and attack again, Damian rose to his feet and touched his bracelet. As it turned into the whip, he swung it, directing it forward. The thong wrapped around a demon's neck, silver burning its gray skin. He channeled his power through it, and dirty tendrils of smoke rose in the air, permeating it with the reek of scorched flesh. Damian yanked the whip back, sending the monster into the trench. Fast and deadly, he kept working with his weapon, sending one monster after the other crashing down. The demons roared, their ugly faces distorted by overwhelming anger, but none of them dared to even try to cross the trench.

Conjuring one energy orb after another, Oleg kept propelling them at the opposing army, each orb finding a target. As the army of demons started dwindling, Damian saw Azazel through a small opening in their lines. With his back turned toward the center of the cave, the Fallen was casting a spell, the malignant energy of his magic wrapping around his enormous body. The wall of the cave in front of him was shimmering with purple sparkles that were outlining an area about three feet wide and seven feet high.

Dammit, he found the cell... The bone-chilling thought flashed through Damian's mind, and he turned toward Oleg, waving to attract his attention. Oleg's face lost all color as his eyes fell on Azazel, and he swore colorfully in Russian.

As if feeling their eyes on his back, the Fallen turned his head, and a sinister smirk crossed his face. He pointed in their direction, muttered something under his breath and returned to the task at hand.

"What the hell is this now!" Ace's furious voice sounded behind Damian.

He spun around, and his heart thundered in his chest, his arms numb. Like in a stupor, he saw Ace raising her sword and taking a step forward.

"Ace, no!" he shouted, reaching for her. "This is not what you think!"

CHAPTER 33

~ DAMIAN BLAKE ~

Under the ceiling of the cave, a giant dragon-like monster levitated, supported by enormous wings. Its large body was covered in blood-red scales that seamlessly morphed into a rich burgundy on its stomach and chest. Its four massive paws ended in sharp, hooked claws, and its flaming eyes stared at them with carnivorous hunger. Puffs of gray smoke exited its nostrils and mouth with every breath, tiny flames and sparks breaking through between its sharp fangs. The wings of the monster, however, contrasted with its general appearance. While they were large enough to sustain its heavy body in the air, they seemed to be thin and slightly blue, resembling plain paper.

"What do you mean, it's not what I think!" yelled Ace, holding her sword at the ready. "If it looks like a duck, swims like a duck, and quacks like a duck, it probably is a friggin' duck." She threw a furious glance back at Damian and extended her sword up. "It's a goddamn dragon. Open your eyes!"

"It's not a dragon!" shouted Damian and Cole at the same time.

"Procedia Amnia!" Oleg yelled, encapsulating all four of them

into a protective shield just in time as the dragon-like creature sucked in a huge gulp of air, the scales on its chest lifting and spreading out a little. A heartbeat later, the monster exhaled with an ear-splitting hiss, showering them with a powerful downpour of fire. Oleg grunted, but his shield withheld the attack.

"Definitely not a dragon," muttered Damian, watching the creature getting ready for the next fire blast. He turned to Cole. "Fire is deadly for you, brother. Stay within Oleg's shield and don't try anything crazy."

"Damian, I believe you know with whom we are dealing," Oleg said calmly, and it wasn't a question. He simply confirmed the fact.

"Whom? Did you mean what?" asked Ace, narrowing her eyes at him.

"Nuh, it is he—a man. Never thought he was real, though." Oleg raked his fingers through his shortly cropped hair and turned to Damian. "Can you wield water, Commander?" he asked, following the monster's progress with his eyes as it made another circle above their heads, either looking for a better place to attack or deciding who to munch on first.

"No, I can't wield the elemental energy of Water, but I can conjure enough of physical water to do the job—," started Damian, but a low growl rolled through the cave, interrupting him, and he winced, spinning in place.

Even though they had destroyed more than half of the demonic army, a small group of them still remained. The few short minutes Damian and his team switched their attention to the new threat had given the demons the opportunity they needed to pull back and regroup.

Now, a few of them stood behind the Fallen, channeling their demonic essence through him to reinforce his magic. But the rest of them restored order and pulled closer to the trench, chanting in low, growling voices. With every word they uttered, the edges of the trench pulled closer together, and Damian had no doubt that if they didn't find a way to stop the monsters, soon he and his team would be attacked by the demonic army from the back and the flying monster from the front.

He felt Oleg's back pressed against his as he changed his position, and Cole took a place next to him, leaving Ace at Damian's side.

"Oleg, I'll deal with the flying monster," Damian whispered, pointing at the dragon-like creature. "I need you to take care of the rest of the demons, and I need you to do it fast. Cole and Ace are coming with you. You must break through to the Fallen before he completes his incantation and before his demons cross the trench. I'll be fine on my own."

"Let's do it." Oleg gave him a curt nod, gesturing for Cole and Ace to follow him. "Watch your back, Commander."

As soon as Damian stepped outside the protective shield, the monster sucked in air again with a loud hissing noise and immediately exhaled the next blast of fire, aiming at Damian. He spun out of the way, but not fast enough. The fire set his jacket on the left side ablaze, and a few scorching flames licked the exposed skin of his neck and face, eliciting a groan of pain from him. He ripped the jacket off and threw it to the ground, cursing the Slavic fairy tales and their deadly creatures of magic.

Channeling his magic, he pointed at the monster and shouted, *"Aquamius!"*

Two powerful streams of water erupted from his palms, and he directed them at the monster's wings. The creature howled and hissed, twirling in the air, the terrible sound it emitted making the walls vibrate. In an instant, its paper-like wings were soaked through with water and hung at its sides, limp and useless. The creature spiraled down, its deafening howls overwhelming the cacophony of the fight unfolding at the other end of the cave. It hit the ground with a thunderous bang, and a fountain of dust and debris rose in the air like a thick, dirty veil, completely obscuring the point of impact.

Using the momentary reprieve, Damian channeled his magic again and drew a rune in the air, charging it with his magical energy. As the rune lit up brighter, he whispered a summoning spell, pressing his hand to the Shadow Enforcer rune on his upper arm. Immediately, a portal twirling with shimmering blue lights opened up next to him, and a man dressed in a black tactical uniform walked through it, halting next to him. His eyes widened as he observed the mayhem in the cave.

"What the hell, Dima?" the man roared, two cossack's sabers materializing in his hands. "Thank God I was dressed for the occasion. A little warning would go a long way, you know." Then he laughed, humor and the excitement of the upcoming fight sparkling in his blue eyes. "I already forgot how much fun it is to work with you. I never know in which shithole I will end up the next time you summon me." He pushed Damian with his shoulder slightly. "What do we have here?"

"We have a little zmey-problem on our hands. Tugarin Zmeyevich, to be precise," replied Damian, his eyes trained on the curtain of dust as it slowly started to dispel.

"You don't say," murmured Cossack, all mirth gone from his eyes. "I thought he was long dead."

"Apparently not." In one quick motion, Damian wrapped his whip around his wrist, turning it into a bracelet, and summoned his daggers, directing the flow of his magical energy through them. "Remember the Carpathian Mountains? The same plan should work."

Cossack grinned, flicking his eyebrow at Damian. "This time, you're the front."

"Fine," agreed Damian in a quick whisper. "We need him unconscious just long enough to destroy his physical body."

A low growl rattled through the cave, stretching Damian's already heightened senses to the next level. The dust settled down, and now an enormous man stood in the place where the creature's body had hit the ground. He was at least seven feet tall, his unclothed torso wrapped in grotesquely oversized muscles. His tanned skin reflected the reddish-orange flares of the torches, making him look as if he was engulfed in flames. Perhaps he was, since gray swirls of smoke rose above him, wrapping around his massive biceps. Black leather pants tucked into tall leather boots hugged his legs, and a long sword in a black sheath was attached to the wide belt fastened around his waist.

"Holy zmey," murmured Cossack, his sabers igniting as brightly as Damian's daggers.

A predatory smile stretched Tugarin's lips beneath his long black mustache, turning his narrow, sharply angled eyes into black slits. Touching his chest with his hand, he bowed a ceremonious old-Russian style bow, but it was filled with enough mockery and derision to give Damian a good idea of how little the ancient monster truly thought about him and his friend.

Straightening, Tugarin ran his hand over his head, which was shaved cleanly on the front and the sides with a long black braid left on the back.

"*Goi esi, dobri molodtsi*," he greeted them with an ancient Russian greeting. "How would you like me to kill you? I can burn you with fire. I can cut you with a sword. Or I can penetrate you with my long spear."

"Hmm..." murmured Cossack, ruffling his curly hair. "A tough choice. Dima, do you want to see his long spear? Or be penetrated by it?"

Damian snorted. "I think I can live for the rest of my life without ever seeing his... spear."

Tugarin Zmeyevich roared, fury igniting the flames on his arms and shoulders. In one swift move, he unsheathed his enormous sword and charged Damian. Without skipping a beat, Damian met his sword with his daggers. Bright red sparks flared in the air, the sound of metal striking metal ringing through the cave.

The fire ignited in Tugarin's eyes as he pushed down on his sword, his colossal biceps doubling in size. Damian groaned, fighting to hold his position. With his peripheral vision, he watched Cossack stealthily move around the monster. He wasn't sure if Tugarin could see his friend, but he had to make sure he was too busy to pay attention.

He channeled the energy of Earth, making the ground wobble slightly under their feet. The pressure Tugarin had been applying on his sword eased up just a little as the monster had to check his balance, and Damian used the opportunity to thrust forward, forcing the zmey to stumble backward. With his daggers free, Damian spun, closing the distance between himself and his opponent. His blade whistled through the air, biting into Tugarin's flesh between his ribs.

The monster roared in pain, fire engulfing his torso. Smoldering heat surrounded his entire body, expanding around him like a blast wave. Damian staggered a step back, struggling to fill his lungs with oxygen.

"Frail humans!" Tugarin Zmeyevich roared, laughing. "Killing you is too easy."

He twirled around, the flames around him creating a fire-filled funnel. Swinging his fist, he punched Cossack, sending him flying across the floor. He hit the opposite wall and slid to the floor, his hands unlocking. The sabers dropped with a loud clatter, their brilliant light extinguishing. A sinister smirk distorted Tugarin's features as he raised his sword, stepping closer to Cossack.

"Hey, you, origami dragon!" yelled Damian, trying to divert

the monster's attention away from his friend. "Why don't you pick on someone your own size? Or maybe you're afraid to lose a fight to a frail human?" He snickered, assuming a fighting stance.

With a furious growl, Tugarin spun in place, his double-wide chest rising and falling with furious breaths. Like an infuriated bull seeing red, Tugarin moved toward Damian with a speed no one would expect from such a large, heavy monster. He raised his giant sword, ready to crush it on Damian's head, and his blade went up in flames, spreading the waves of heat around.

In the last second, Damian sidestepped him, barely missing the sharp edge of the flaming weapon. However, this move came at a cost. Confined between the lake and the furious monster, he had no space to maneuver. As tall and strong as Damian was, Tugarin towered over him a few inches, and his unparalleled strength of an ancient monster gave him a serious advantage in their current position.

Raising his daggers, Damian braced himself for the next assault of the zmey when a harsh boom of a gunshot exploded in the cave. Like in a slow-motion movie, Damian watched a bullet exit Tugarin's forehead, pieces of bone and splatters of blood following its movement. For a split second, the monster stood still, shock and disbelief reflected on his features. Then his fingers unlocked, and his sword dropped to the ground with a loud clamor. His eyes rolled back, and he fell on his back, the floor of the cave trembling from the impact like from an earthquake.

Cossack stood behind him, a .500 S&W Magnum in his hand. He lowered the gun, and a rueful smile appeared on his face.

"Whatever works… Right, Dima?" He shrugged his shoulders almost apologetically and put the gun back into the holster attached to his belt. "Just because medieval assholes fight with medieval weapons doesn't mean we have to follow suit."

Damian nodded, swallowing hard. "We're not done, Cossack," he said, his vocal cords painfully hoarse from the heat and smoke. "You know what we have to do." He shuddered at the thought, his friend's expression mirroring his feelings.

"Let's do it." Swallowing hard, Cossack approached the monster sprawled on the floor and swung his sword, decapitating him. Blood burst from the severed neck, drenching him from head to toe. He grunted, pressing the back of his hand to his mouth for a brief moment but didn't stop. Damian joined his effort, and a few seconds later, they stood covered in blood over the monster's dismembered body.

"That should be sufficient," said Damian, channeling his magic toward his hands. "Ready?"

Cossack nodded, his lips pressed tight, his face slightly green.

"*Ignius Amplio,*" Damian said, and Cossack echoed his words.

Powerful jets of fire enveloped the body of the monster, hungrily devouring it. A swirl of dirty smoke went up in the air, and the reek of burned flesh mixed in with the nauseating odor of blood made it nearly unbreathable. Ignoring the heat and the stench, both Damian and Cossack kept the fire flowing until nothing was left of Tugarin Zmeyevich except for hot, steaming ashes and a few blackened bones.

Wiping the sweat and blood off his face with his hand, Damian turned toward the other end of the cave and froze, his limbs filled with lead. Feeling Cossack's fingers squeezing his elbow, he winced and glanced at his friend.

"What the fuck?" he moaned, throwing his hands up. "And here I thought it couldn't get any worse…"

CHAPTER 34

~ DAMIAN BLAKE ~

Damian took off running, jumping over piles of disintegrating bodies of demons, steaming puddles of sticky goo, and severed limbs and heads. The pounding of fast steps and a slew of profanities sounded behind him, and he knew Cossack was following him. The terrible stench overpowered his sense of smell, making him cough, but he didn't slow down until he reached Oleg and Cole. Both stood with their swords at the ready, but neither made a move, staring straight ahead.

The demonic army was gone, destroyed by his friends, but the Fallen was still alive and free. He stood in front of the wall with a sinister smirk on his face. A large area behind him glowed with the malignant presence of his magical energy. He was no longer chanting, but the light was steadily becoming brighter and brighter, small purple runes and sigils moving slowly around the perimeter of the affected area.

He held Ace in front of his stomach, his long, clawed fingers squeezing her throat. She didn't move, her arms hanging limply at her sides, her sword lying next to her feet. Her eyes halted on Damian, and an expression of hope flew across her face but quickly disappeared, replaced by that of despair.

"That's close enough, Commander Blake," the Fallen said, raising his free hand, his webbed wings expanding behind his back. The entire cave shook, and a web of thin, black fractures sprouted from the glowing area.

Damian ignored him and stepped forward, running into an invisible wall. Pushed backward by the resistance of the magical field, he growled and punched it with his fist. The power field lit up brighter, indicating a small dome encapsulating Azazel, Ace and the entire area behind them.

"I warned you that you were close enough," murmured Azazel, a crooked smirk stretching his thin, black lips. "Admit it, Commander"—he waved back, his smirk growing darker—"I won. You lost. End of story. There's nothing you can do now."

"We'll see about that." Damian threw a quick glance at Cossack, and he nodded, muttering something that sounded like 'sure, why not'. They both approached the power field and place their hands against it.

Oleg glanced at them, and understanding dawned on his face. He stepped closer, positioning himself on the other side of Damian, and pressed his hands against the invisible barrier of magic.

"Between the three of us," Oleg said quietly, "we can do it."

Damian glanced back at Cole. His brother stood behind them with his sword in his hand. Drenched in blood and slime from head to toe, it was impossible to see his expression, but his scarlet eyes blazed furiously from under the strands of matted hair, betraying his true state of mind. Damian nodded to him, and Cole smiled, his long fangs showing. His smile was so vicious and deadly that Damian couldn't help but shudder inwardly.

"Just break this barrier, brother," the vampire hissed, taking a step closer. "I'll tear him limb from limb with my bare hands."

Damian nodded and switched his attention to the task at hand. "Together," he said. He didn't look at his friends, but the magical and elemental field around them spiked, and he knew they were ready. As his hands lit up with the bright orange glow of his elemental energy, he pressed them tighter to the shield and started to chant.

"Stop that at once, Enforcer!" yelled Azazel, baring his terrifying fangs. He squeezed Ace's throat tighter, forcing a scream of pain out of her. "If you continue what you're doing, I swear on my power I will kill her."

Damian lifted his face, and his glowing eyes met the menacing stare of the Fallen. "Go ahead," he said calmly. For a second, his eyes moved to Ace, and he saw shock imprinted in her widened eyes. "You're trying to blackmail the wrong person, scumbag, and you chose the wrong person as your shield."

Everything inside him twisted with remorse, and his heart responded with a dull ache as with agonizing clarity, he realized that the Fallen would kill Ace as soon as they broke his protective shield, and there was nothing he could do about it. Besides, he couldn't let Azazel release another monster capable of destroying the world.

Averting his gaze, he continued his chant, Oleg's and Cossack's voices echoing every word he said. A soft light spread through the power field, devouring the purple glimmer of Azazel's magic.

"Her death will be on your hands!" shouted the Fallen, applying more pressure on Ace's throat.

"She's a Destiny Enforcer," growled Damian, directing more of his energy through the power field. "When she accepted the mantel, she swore to put her duty above all, including her own life. She's not afraid to die, because for a Destiny Enforcer death is never the end... So, do what you must."

"Cole..." Ace didn't really say his brother's name. Her lips barely moved, forming the word, but Damian had no doubt that Cole had heard her.

Damian winced, feeling the coolness of his brother's hand on his shoulder as the vampire halted next to him, but he couldn't stop what he was doing. He glanced from side to side, exchanging a quick look with Cossack and Oleg to confirm that they were ready and increased the potency of his magic. The power field began to vibrate under their joint assault, emitting a low buzzing noise.

"Ace, look at me," said Cole, coming as close to the barrier separating them as he could.

She met his eyes, her face contorted with fear. Cole clenched his teeth, his hands tightening into fists for a brief moment. Then he squared his shoulders, and his vampiric energy doubled around him. He sheathed his sword and moved his hand over the surface of the barrier without touching it.

"Look into my eyes, my sweet girl... It's going to be all right... relax... relax..." His whisper—a deep, insinuating purr—flowed through the cave in soft waves, intoxicating and compelling, and for the first time, Damian felt the true power of an ancient vampire up close and personal, even though it wasn't directed at him.

Ace's lips parted, and her eyelids closed slowly, tears escaping from under her fluttering eyelashes. Cole let go and stepped back, his arms dangling powerlessly at his sides, unadulterated torment and despair reflected in his dimming eyes.

Abruptly, a powerful tremor ran through the floor. The walls shook, and a grinding noise filled the cave. Azazel's eyes lit up with a poisonous purple shine, and he laughed, the sound of his laughter making Damian's blood run cold. A deep fracture ran up across the wall behind the Fallen, originating from the floor. It moved fast, outlining a semblance of a door.

The tremors increased, but Damian could sense it wasn't a

true earthquake since it wasn't powered by the energy of Earth. Its origin was so dark and evil, that his breath caught in his throat, and for a moment, everything around him spun, making his stomach clench. He glanced at Oleg, noticing that he looked just as sick as he felt. Cossack kept chanting, channeling more and more of his magic through the shield, seemingly unaffected by the influx of dark magical energy.

The crack ran its path, outlining a large rectangular area. Still holding a half-dazed Ace in his clutches, Azazel turned slightly and extended his right hand toward the wall, the silver of the Hollow Band's ring on his middle finger reflecting the light of the torches. With an ear-splitting noise, a giant piece of rock outlined by the fracture started to move forward.

"Keep going," Damian yelled to his friends, taking a step away from the power field.

He closed his eyes and surrendered himself to the elemental power of Earth. Then he pressed his hand over the rune on his shoulder, assuming his true form. Directing all the magic and power he had at the moving rock, he commanded it to stop. In response to his action, the Fallen increased the flow of his malignant magic, and the dark energy within the boundaries of the dome seemed to strengthen tenfold.

Damian screamed, his entire body straining, sweat running down his face and back. Leaning forward, he outstretched his arms toward the wall, but no matter how much power he applied, the rock still kept moving. With his free hand, Azazel squeezed Ace's throat, and she cried out in pain, ripped out of the peaceful oblivion Cole had put her in. Giving up on his efforts, Damian manifested his daggers and struck the barrier with all he had, applying all the power and physical strength he could gather.

The power field howled and screeched—the sound characteristic of failing wards, and at this moment, he knew he was close to demolishing it. The grinding of the moving rock increased, painfully reverberating in his head, and then with a thunderous bang, the stone blew up, shards of rock and debris propelled in all directions within the dome.

From the confinements of a small, dark cell, a tall man emerged, moving soundlessly as if he was incorporeal. His skeletal body was wrapped in massive iron chains. His thin, gray hair fell over his face that looked like a skull, his closed eyes surrounded by black shadows. A thin, silvery line of the Hollow Band encircled his neck. Azazel shouted four words in Dragon tongue, and the Hollow Band shimmered and vanished, appearing in the Fallen's hand.

The man opened his eyes, and they ignited with the malignant, yellow glow of his magic. He roared, rising a few inches off the ground, and spread his arms wide, the entire cave shaking and rattling, rocks falling from the ceiling. The chains fell off of him, turning into dust, and he lowered himself, stepping soundlessly on the floor with his bare feet.

Azazel let go of Ace, and she fell to the ground unconscious, a puddle of red liquid spreading under her body, soaking her long, black hair. He touched the man's skinny arm, and a fanatical glimmer ignited in his eyes. The Fallen held out the Hollow Band he was holding to the man and bowed to him. The man touched the silvery band with his dirty, hooked nail and it vanished, disappearing in a cloud of light, wispy smoke.

"You're free, my lord," the Fallen said. "Leave now to fight another day. I'll deal with them swiftly and join you later."

"No!" Damian shouted. "NO!" His desperate scream boomed through the cave as he attacked the vibrating power barrier with all he had in his exhausted body.

The man snickered, exposing his rotten, brown teeth, derision gleaming in his yellow eyes. Then he nodded to Azazel and snapped his fingers, vanishing from the cave.

For a heartbeat, Damian froze in place, unable to take a breath, his hands rising to his head. But adrenalin charged by despair surged through him, ripping him out of his stupor, and he screamed, striking the power field again and again with his bleeding fists and his daggers until it finally failed with an ear-splitting ruckus.

Azazel spun around and moved toward him, chanting something under his breath. His frame started to enlarge, and a split-second later, his head touched the ceiling of the cave, his webbed wings overshadowing the light of the torches. He threw his terrifying head back and roared, anger and excitement in his deafening voice.

Unable to bear the sound, Damian dropped his daggers and pressed his hands to his ears, blood streaming between his fingers. He leaned forward, the floor slipping from under his feet. From the corner of his eyes, he saw his brother. Blood was dripping from Cole's ears and eyes, but he was still on his feet.

"Oleg! Use your controlling ring!" Cole shouted, his voice barely audible in the surrounding cacophony.

He reached under his trench coat and threw something up in the air. With his blurred vision, Damian followed the trajectory of the shining object, recognizing the main band of the Hollow Band—the one they had retrieved from the lake.

For a heartbeat, Oleg's eyes widened, but he reacted almost immediately. Pointing at the Fallen, he shouted the same four words of the Dragon tongue the Fallen had used just a few seconds ago. Azazel's eyes flew wide open as he realized what had just happened, but it was too late to do anything. The Hollow Band vanished from the air and manifested around Azazel's neck.

The Fallen howled, his face contorted by an unbearable pain, his fingers clutching the silver band as if it were suffocating him. The gleam in his eyes vanished, and he returned to his normal size, lowering to the floor. He stopped before Oleg and dropped his head, his shoulders hunched. A low growl rumbled in Oleg's throat as he ripped the silver ring off Azazel's finger and put it in his pocket.

Damian straightened, wiping his bloodied hands on his half-torn tank top. He approached Oleg and extended his hand, a pair of glowing handcuffs materializing in his palm. Oleg froze in place, his face turning into a stone mask void of any emotions.

"Even though he is under the influence of the Hollow Band, this is the best way to control Azazel's power," Damian explained quietly. "The Destiny Cuffs will strip it."

"I know how the Destiny Cuffs work," snapped Oleg, taking a step back. "I tried them on my own skin." Then he cleared his throat and shuffled from foot to foot. "Sorry, Damian. That was uncalled for." He rubbed his forehead, a guilty smile touching his lips. "Just some bad memories I have. It has nothing to do with you. I hope you don't mind, but I have my orders from Master Alliandr. I have to bring the Fallen to his dungeons in Kendral. The Gray Tower can hold him imprisoned and his powers under control just as well as any Destiny Council's holding facilities. The Destiny Council has agreed with his decision, so if you have to, you can contact your... um... commanding officer, they will confirm it."

Master Alliandr was known for his loyalty to the World of Magic, and despite his young age, he was one of the most powerful and knowledgeable Masters of Power who had ever ruled Kendral. Besides, the young Master always fought on the side of light, and if Oleg said the Destiny Council had agreed with his choice, he had no reason to doubt his words. Making a quick decision, Damian nodded and stepped back, the Destiny Cuffs vanishing from his hands.

Opening his other sight, he glanced at Ace who was sprawled on the floor in a puddle of her own blood. Her face was drained of color, and her chest was barely moving, but the soft glow of her human soul was still intact even though polluted by strange purple inclusions, and that told him she was alive. As long as her heart was beating, he could heal her.

"Cole, see if you can heal Ace while Oleg and I will take care of the Fallen," he said, giving his brother a quick tap on his shoulder.

Cole nodded and headed toward Ace, lowering to his knees next to her. Lifting her limp body, he placed her on his lap and bit his wrist.

"Let's do it, Oleg," said Damian, approaching him.

Oleg took a knee and placed his hand against the rocky surface of the floor, closing his eyes. The elemental energy of Earth doubled, and his entire body lit up with the soft, orange glow of his power.

"Sandhya, my Queen" he whispered, calling to the Elemental of Earth, "I summon thee…"

A soft tremor rushed through the cave, and the air shimmered with bright orange sparks. A young woman, short and willowy, materialized in the cave and stilled, her glowing golden eyes slipping from one person to the next. As her gaze halted on Oleg, for a brief moment, her face lit up with happiness, and her coral lips parted. But then she turned to the rest of them and bowed, pressing her hands together in namaste. Her long copper hair cascaded down, touching the floor, and she threw it back, straightening up.

Damian lowered to one knee and pressed his fist to his chest, recognizing the power of his element surging through this woman with unprecedented strength. Cossack mirrored his position, and Cole tried to follow, but she raised her hand, stopping him, gesturing for him to continue what he was doing. Then she approached Oleg, her hand rising to thread through his hair. Even with him kneeling, he was slightly taller than her.

"Please rise," she said, addressing everyone in the cave, her voice beautifully melodic. "I'm Sandhya, the Queen of Kendral's Underworld, and the Elemental of Earth."

She approached Azazel and gave him a quick once-over, her lips curving in disgust, and then turned to Damian. "I'll take this monster off your hands, Lord Enforcer, and deliver him to Kendral."

"Thank you, my lady," replied Damian, slightly inclining his head

The Queen walked to Oleg and gazed up at him, craning her neck as if she were looking at the Empire State Building. "When are you coming home, my love?" she asked him, rising on her tiptoes to caress his cheek, and Damian's jaw dropped.

"I would like to spend a little time with Damian," he replied, taking the Queen's small hand and raising it to his lips. "He is my brother in element, but I never knew he existed. I would like to ask him a few—" He cut himself off, looking at Damian, a question in his eyes. "If you have time for that, Commander, maybe we could talk."

"I would love that," replied Damian, stifling a sigh, "but Cossack and I have to return to the Destiny Council realm. I must report to my superior first. If you don't mind waiting for me at Paradise Manor, I also have a few questions I'd like to ask you."

"I'll wait," replied Oleg, letting go of the Queen's hand.

She smiled at him and turned toward Damian, looking up at him with interest. Then she took his hand and a powerful wave of elemental Energy swept through his body. His eyes closed of their own accord, and a soft moan escaped his lips.

"You *are* a Child of Earth," she whispered, her golden gaze drilling through him. "How did it happen that I—the Elemental of Earth—did not know about your existence?"

"I don't know, my lady," replied Damian, wondering if it was Magnus' handiwork.

She reached up, rising on her tiptoes, and placed her hand on his cheek, sending more of the elemental energy through him. Damian let out a harsh breath, the cave starting to spin slowly around him, but she removed her hand, and everything went back to normal.

"You weren't claimed," she whispered more to herself than to Damian, her golden eyes igniting brighter.

"I'm not sure I know what it means, my lady," replied Damian, feeling lost.

"Oleg will explain it to you." Sandhya smiled and made her way to Azazel, stopping by his side. She placed her hand on his elbow, grimacing as if she were forced to touch a poisonous snake. "Farewell." She bowed and snapped her fingers, vanishing from the cave together with the Fallen.

* * *

FOR A MOMENT, Damian remained in place, his mind racing. He thought he knew all there was to know about being a Child of Earth, yet he had no idea what it meant to be claimed by the Elemental. As his memory went back to the fight with Azazel and the way Oleg wielded the power of Earth, he had to admit that the element obeyed this young man's every command, and he manipulated it with the ease of a person who had been doing it for centuries.

"Dima..." Cole's drained voice broke through Damian's train of thought, and he turned to his brother.

Cole sat on his heels, his lips and hands covered in fresh blood. Ace lay on his lap, unconscious, her long, black hair cascading down his legs and to the floor. Her face was smeared with blood, but her skin was colorless, and with the dark circles surrounding her eyes, her features looked sharper.

"Dima," Cole whispered again, a haunted look in his eyes, "I don't understand..."

Damian approached his brother and kneeled by his side. "What's going on, Cole?"

Cole shifted Ace's limp body slightly, exposing an incision

on her chest, an inch below the collarbone. It didn't seem to be deep, yet blood kept seeping from it without stop, streaming to the floor.

"This is the only visible injury," he said, his fingers threading through her hair absentmindedly. "But my blood doesn't heal it, and I can't wake her up. Nothing works…"

Feeling a quick tap on his shoulder, Damian raised his eyes to find Cossack standing next to him. He squatted and brushed his fingers over Ace's face, the soft light of his magic enveloping his hand.

"Open your other sight, Dima," he said, raking his fingers through his unruly curls. "Do you see what I see?"

Damian channeled his magic and opened his other sight. Ace's aura was still present, enveloping her with its soft white glow of a human soul, but the malignant purple patches he had noticed before were spreading through it, slowly devouring it.

"Dammit. This has to be a spell. The Fallen's magic," he muttered.

Placing his hands over Ace's chest and forehead, he started to circulate the healing energy of Earth through her. With his second sight, he could see his elemental energy working its way through her, and he increased the flow of his power. Oleg kneeled across from him and placed his hands over his, increasing the potency of the healing magic.

Ace's long lashes fluttered, eyeballs rolling from side to side under her tightly shut eyelids. A second later, she opened her eyes and winced, unable to stop a cry of pain.

"Stop, please stop…" she croaked, her voice shaky and weak. "You're hurting me…" She fell silent for a few seconds, her chest barely moving with uneven breaths. "You can't save me… the Fallen made sure of it… made sure I knew it."

Damian and Oleg pulled back, exchanging a troubled look.

She moved her eyes, searching around, her eyeballs rolling back for a brief moment. Then her fading gaze stopped on Cole, and her face fell, the shadows under her eyes and cheekbones growing deeper.

"Cole," she whispered, tugging feebly on his coat. He leaned forward slightly to be closer to her, and she continued, "I'm sorry... I never... loved you. I had to pretend... seduce and... I was ordered to—" Her voice cut off, and she closed her eyes.

"Ace?" Cole squeezed her hand gently. "What were you ordered to do? Who gave you the orders?"

She opened her eyes again, and her lips twitched in a faint smile. "You're a good man... the best I've ever met... You didn't deserve..."

"Ace." Damian leaned closer to her. "You told me your orders were to shadow and protect my brother."

"In the beginning... that was true," she replied. Blood spilled from the corner of her mouth, and she coughed, her chest spasming painfully. "My orders... changed... I was supposed to create a rift between you and your... stop all of you from..." She moved her eyes up to look at Damian and even this tiny move came with an effort to her. "Damian, be careful... you must help... Magnus is—"

Her lips kept moving, but she could speak no more. Her eyes widened. Her gaze flashed to Cole for a brief moment and then stilled, the last breath escaping her lips. For a few seconds, Cole sat still, his face a mask of despair. Then he moved his hand over her eyes, closing them forever, and looked up at his brother.

A pregnant silence enveloped the cave, and for a few endless seconds, no one said a word.

"Dima, it's impossible," Cossack said at length. "It sounded as if she was ordered to sabotage you and your brother. But I've heard with my own ears from the Destiny Council—they wanted to support the direction Cole took with the Arizona Vampire Court." He shook his head, spreading his arms. "That can't be true."

"She was dying," snapped Cole, gently moving Ace's lifeless body to the floor. "She had no reason to lie." He got up, his moves torturously slow, and bit his lip, the scarlet glow in his eyes fading. "And I must admit, I believe she was working against us. Her behavior in the last few weeks was strange—stupid and childish even. When Simon's pack attacked Paradise Manor, her action almost killed us all. I couldn't understand why…"

Damian lifted Ace's body with a strenuous grunt, his every muscle responding with soreness and aches.

"I intend to find out the truth about this," he said. "I want to know who sent her and why she was ordered to sabotage us." He turned to Oleg, different thoughts racing through his mind at the same time, tripping over each other. "Oleg, can you please take my brother to Paradise Manor? I have to return to the Destiny Council realm." He glanced at Ace and a heavy dread settled in his chest. "I have to take her home. Even though she was still in training, she *was* a Destiny Enforcer. Maybe it's not over for her… But if it is, she deserves a proper burial." He stifled a sigh, frowning. "Besides, I have to report to my superior and find out what's going on."

"No problem," Oleg replied, a weary smile ghosting his lips, and just now Damian noticed how truly drained this large man looked. "If you don't mind, I'll wait for you there." He ran his hand over his chin, smearing blood and dirt all over his skin. "I hope River won't mind me in her house."

"I don't think she will. But just so you know, Cole owns a house next to Paradise Manor, so you won't have to sleep outside." He chuckled mirthlessly.

"I love sleeping outside," murmured Oleg, giving him an arched stare. "I'm sure you do too." He approached Cole and placed his hand on his shoulder. "Ready?"

Cole nodded, and Oleg snapped his fingers, teleporting them out of the cave.

For a moment, Damian stood still. Drained physically and magically, he wasn't sure he could make even the smallest move. Then he took a deep breath and glanced at his friend. "Something tells me I'm going to be in a world of trouble." He sighed, expelling a ragged breath. "Why don't you take the wheel this time, Cossack."

"You didn't do anything wrong, Dima," objected Cossack, taking his elbow.

"Oh, yeah?" Damian laughed, but there was no humor in his laugher. "What's good about being right and dead?"

Cossack shook his head and snapped his fingers. The world around Damian spun, and the cursed cave melted into the darkness.

CHAPTER 35

~ DAMIAN BLAKE ~

They materialized in a small room illuminated by a soft blue light that seemingly was coming from nowhere. Over the centuries, nothing had changed here, and Damian knew where he was right away. Still holding Ace's body in his arms, he turned to his friend.

"Cossack," he said, worry coiling in the pit of his stomach, "why are we in your room? I'm so drained, I can barely stand on my feet, and while I'm still in the upright position, I must see Moore. He's the only one who has a chance to bring Ace back."

"Dima." Cossack took a tentative step toward him but then halted, a deep frown shadowing his features. "I brought you here so we could discuss the situation first." He rubbed the back of his neck and brought his hand forward, staring at the mix of blood and demonic goo on his palm. "You can't go to Moore. That man hated you from the moment he laid eyes on you. He'll use Ace's death to blame you. You were a Commander, and she was an inexperienced recruit. He'll find a way to turn it against you."

"I know, and I don't care," replied Damian, feeling too tired to continue this discussion. "What do you propose?"

"Let me take Ace to Moore and deal with the repercussions," said Cossack, putting his hand on Damian's shoulder. "You should go to Magnus and give him a full report. It'd be better if he heard the story from you. We captured the Fallen, but Koschei the Deathless is in the wind. He needs to know that."

"And I will tell him everything after I speak with Moore." Damian headed toward the door, but halted there, turning to his friend. "You really think I would allow you to take a beating for me?" He chuckled bitterly. "Five hundred years is a long time. You forgot me, my friend." He shrugged, carefully readjusting Ace's body in his arms. "Stay here, Adrian. As a Commander, I am equal to that asshole. Except for showering me with insults and threats, there is nothing he can do to me."

"Fine." Cossack threw his hands in the air. "I'm coming with you then."

"Stubborn ass," murmured Damian as his friend opened the door for him, gesturing for him to go first.

"It takes one to know one, Lord Commander." Cossack chuckled, following him into the perfectly white hallway.

They found Commander Moore in the training facility. Dressed in a white martial arts uniform, he was sparring with a large man —a purebred werewolf, judging by his powerful energy signature. Even though Moore wasn't short, the werewolf was at least a couple of inches taller, and his muscled body, glistening with perspiration, was worthy of any Mister Universe Contest.

Damian wasn't surprised to see that. Moore had quite a few teams of Enforcers working under his command. All his Enforcers were picked from the strongest and most powerful representatives of their supernatural types. All of them were well trained in different styles of martial arts and knew how to use their powers and magic in a combat situation. However, his personal team was the cream of the crop. It was small—no more than fifteen members—and to become a member of Moore's personal team wasn't an easy task.

As soon as Damian walked into the training facility, Moore stopped the sparring session and gestured for the werewolf to leave. Then he turned to Damian, wiping the sweat off his flushed face with the back of his hand. His brown eyes darted to Cossack, then to Ace, and his bulldog-like face hardened, a muscle twitching in his tightly pressed jaw.

Without any rush, he sauntered toward Damian, his bare feet stepping softly on the hardwood floor. He stopped a few feet away from him and put his hands on his hips, cocking his head slightly. His eyes lit up with the brilliant glow of his magic as he opened his other sight and scanned Ace. A heartbeat later, his eyes returned to their normal color, and a corner of his mouth lifted, forming an uneven smirk, as if a young woman whose dead body Damian held in his arms meant nothing to him.

"Look who the cat dragged in," he rasped. "Commander Dmitri Chernov—once again." He bowed mockingly, spreading his arms. "Oh, wait... It's Commander Damian Blake nowadays, isn't it?"

Damian lowered to one knee and placed Ace's body on the floor between them, his heart giving a painful jolt as he watched her head loll to the side lifelessly. Then he straightened and spread his shoulders, an overwhelming wave of weakness rushing through him, making him sway. After the battle with the Fallen, he was drained magically and exhausted physically, and getting in a confrontation with one of the most powerful Destiny Enforcers didn't seem like a good idea.

"Commander Moore," he said evenly, suppressing the burning desire to wipe that ugly smirk off Moore's face. "It's not about you or me. So, just cut the crap and bring your recruit back. She was one of yours. You can do it."

Without sparing a single glance to Ace, Moore took a step forward, nearly stepping on her arm. His eyes darkened with hatred, and his magical energy spiked around him.

"You're right, Chernov. It isn't about you or me. It's about you, only!" He stepped over Ace's body, invading Damian's personal space, his face contorted with icy contempt. "It was always about you. You're nothing. The biggest failure I've ever seen in the Destiny Council realm! Yet, you seem to do no wrong. Magnus always pulls your sorry ass out of any shithole you manage to dig yourself in. Why is that?"

"Moore, the young woman is dead, and you're the only one who can bring her back." Damian took a step back, trying to keep calm and civil for as long as he could.

"Damn right she is dead!" Moore shouted, pushing Damian on his chest. "She was an inexperienced recruit, and you were a Commander with at least five hundred years of experience, and you let her get killed. She died on your watch, and you're the only one who's responsible for her death! And if for one second you think I won't hold you accountable for that, think again!"

A low growl rumbled in Damian's chest as his forced patience start to lose the battle with anger. "If you cared for her so much, then why did you send such an unprepared recruit into the field? To shadow an ancient vampire to boot?"

"I had my orders!" Moore boomed. "But you don't know how to obey orders and comply with the chain of command, do you?"

"Stop! Stop arguing!" Cossack raised his arms up, stepping between Damian and the infuriated Moore. "The longer Ace stays dead, the harder it is to bring her back." He turned to face Moore, still holding his hands up. "My lord, please, bring her back, and then you and Commander Blake are free to beat each other into a bloody pulp."

Moore's glowing eyes shifted to Cossack, and for a brief moment, he stilled, a terrifying shade of magenta rising from his neck to his square face. "How dare you speak to your commander in this manner!"

He swung his arm, the glow of his magic surrounding his massive fist. But before his punch landed, Damian pushed his friend out of harm's way and blocked the powerful strike. The impact was so strong, however, it sent him staggering a few steps backward. In a heartbeat, Moore was in front of him, and Damian barely had any time to block his next punch. Moore didn't stop. With a ferocious growl, he increased the speed and the ferocity of his attacks, pushing Damian into a corner.

Damian raised his arms and lowered his head slightly to protect his face, feeling like a cornered animal. Every punch that landed on his sides and stomach made him cringe, pain reverberating through his insides. Severely weakened by the earlier events, he could do nothing to stop his opponent, and even the smallest use of his magic would only drain him more at this point. His vision blurred, and his knees trembled. He groaned, putting all his effort into keeping upright.

"Pathetic," Moore growled and stepped back, wiping his hands on his uniform pants. He tongued his cheek and spat on the perfectly clean floor. "Weak and pathetic. I could never understand why the Destiny Council granted you wings in the first place, holding you in higher esteem than everyone else." He stepped back and hooked his thumbs on his belt, his square face darkened by disdain.

"Is that what's been bothering you for centuries? That the Destiny Council trusted me more than you?" Damian chuckled and winced at the aches in his battered body. Taking a strained breath, he lowered his arms, his every move resulting in a jolt of pain. "I'm tired of your games, Moore. You want to see me bleed? Fine. Do what you must. I'm not going to fight you. But save your recruit first."

Moore glowered at him with scorn in his dark eyes and pivoted on his heels, turning toward Ace. But then he spun around and landed a bone-crushing hook into Damian's jaw. Damian cried out and collapsed to the floor, a blinding white light flooding his vision. Moore seized his hair and yanked his head back.

"Even if I wanted to bring her back," he hissed through gritted teeth, "I can't. I never bound her spirit to the Destiny Council realm. Once she crossed the veil, there was nothing I could do, and you know it."

With an effort, Damian opened his eyes, blinking the white spots from his vision. "But why?" he whispered. "She was a Destiny Enforcer. *Your* Destiny Enforcer. And she was human, just a young and inexperienced witch, a child compared to either of us. She wasn't one of the immortals. How could you send someone so unprepared to work with an ancient vampire and not bind her?"

Moore smirked and lowered himself to the floor next to Damian, releasing his hair.

"You see, Dmitri," he said, staring at him with mockery, "that's the difference between us. I get things done and make things happen, and if I need to make sacrifices, I'm not afraid to do so. Whereas you..." He chuckled, shaking his head. "Anyway, I never bound her because she was expendable. The binding procedure is complicated, and it takes a shitload of magical energy. I do it only for the elite members of my teams. When the Destiny Council ordered me to send someone to shadow a vampire, at first, I thought it was a joke. But as you know, the Destiny Council has no sense of humor."

"Neither do you," growled Damian. "You have no other senses except for the sense of self-importance, you egocentric douchebag. You care for no one except your precious self."

"Right you are," agreed Moore lightly. "I care only about myself and my mission." He waved his hand dismissively. "Anyway, when they asked me to send one of my people to shadow a vamp, I recruited Ace specifically for that mission. While she was completely incompetent as a witch, she was a perfect fit for the job in the vampire's company. So, I gave her basic training and sent her out. I never expected her to come back, anyway, and to be frank, I didn't care. She wasn't Destiny Enforcer material." He got up and straightened his uniform, tucking the lapels of his jacket into the belt. "So, no, Dmitri, I can't bring her back, and her death is on your hands. Live with it."

He laughed icily, throwing an indifferent glance at Ace's body sprawled on the floor.

As uncontrollable fury spiked through Damian, he pushed himself up into a sitting position, leaning on one hip. Before Moore realized what he was doing, he swung his leg back, supporting himself with his arms, and struck Moore's Achilles tendon, sweeping him to the floor. Unprepared, Moore hit the floor hard, and the air escaped his lungs in a loud gasp. With his last remaining strength, Damian launched himself at him and connected his fist with Moore's nose. It broke with a satisfying crunch, and blood flooded down his chin, dripping to his white jacket.

Moore yelped in pain, his hands rising to his face involuntarily, but he recovered a lot faster than Damian expected. With a roar of anger, Moore bridged, moving his hips up, forcing Damian to all fours. As he was falling forward, Moore seized Damian's right arm with his left, trapping it, and then punched him into his already damaged ribs. Damian cried out, falling on his chest, and Moore flipped him over, getting on top of him.

Shouting profanities, Moore kept punching him with admirable persistence. After a few punches, Damian stopped feeling the jolts of impacts, the pain becoming a continuous debilitating ache. His head jerked from left to right, and blood filled his mouth with its metallic taste, making him cough and choke, but Moore didn't stop. The world around him blurred, slipping into darkness.

In that obscurity, he noticed a flare of bright light and reached for it. He saw a familiar and kind face, surrounded by long, flowing hair. But it wasn't the black mane of his beloved Vita whose memory he carried in his heart throughout the centuries. It was shining with all the colors of sunrise in the desert, and all he wanted was to touch it.

"Stop it! Commander Moore, I command you to stand down at once!"

A loud voice broke into his oblivion, bringing him back to reality, and with that came pain. Harsh and debilitating, it rushed through him, and he moaned, unable to open his swollen eyelids. The pressure on his chest lifted, and then someone touched his forehead. A wave of magical energy rushed through him, easing the pain, and he moaned again.

"Dima, open your eyes," Cossack's voice sounded somewhere above him, and this time, he managed to crack his eyelids open to see his friend kneeling next to him. Magnus stood behind him, his eyes blazing with an angry light.

A smile of relief crossed Cossack's face, and he leaned closer to him. "I'm going to get you to your feet on the count of three. Ready?"

Damian nodded. Cossack pushed his arms under Damian's shoulder and counted to three before lifting him into a sitting position. Then he threw Damian's arm over his shoulder and helped him to his feet. With Cossack's help, he made it to the exit door but halted him there.

Looking over his shoulder at Moore, he smirked faintly.

"You're right, Moore," he said quietly, barely able to move his split lips. "I failed and made mistakes more times than I care to admit. I live surrounded by the shadows of my mistakes. But unlike you, I still have a beating heart in my chest and not the piece of cold rock that you have." Damian explored Moore's bloodied face, and his lips pulled up in a snarl. "And just a fair warning, Commander. The only reason you were able to get the best of me was that I was drained already. Next time you try to pull something like this, I swear on my power, I *will* kill you."

He pushed the door open and walked out, leaning heavily on his friend's shoulder.

CHAPTER 36

~ DAMIAN BLAKE ~

Damian glanced down at the white leather armchair in Magnus' office and stifled a sigh. Even though his wounds were no longer bleeding, he was covered in blood, dirt and some other substance from head to toe. Magnus noticed his hesitation and chuckled, gesturing for him to take a seat.

"Sit down, Commander," he said softly, perching himself on the edge of the desk in front of the armchair. "I healed you as much as I could in such a short time, but you still look like crap, and you probably feel even worse."

Damian pulled the chair back and lowered himself on it with Cossack's help. Magnus wasn't wrong. He felt broken. But it wasn't the pain of his wounds that bothered him. The image of Ace's motionless body lying on the floor at his feet was embedded in his mind, and the raw anguish of grief constricted his chest to the point where he could barely breathe. He hunched forward, resting his blood-splattered arms on his lap, and dropped his head.

"Adrian," said Magnus, "thank you for your help, but you look hurt and tired yourself. Why don't you go and see our healer? In the meantime, I'm going to have a word with

Commander Blake. Now that he's back with us, you can get together anytime you wish."

Damian didn't see Cossack leaving, but the soft thud of a closed door told him that now he was alone with the Head of the Destiny Council.

"Dmitri, I know you're tired, but we need to speak, my child." Magnus leaned forward and touched his shoulder gently. "In the few minutes Adrian and I had, he told me as much as he could about everything that transpired in the cave. Is there anything you'd like to tell me? Anything you think I should know?"

Damian raised his head, meeting Magnus' glowing eyes unwillingly. "In Arizona, the war between the werewolves and vampires was prevented. Since the unrest in the Arizona Vampire Court was mostly driven by Azazel, my brother's throne is secure, at least for now," he said, barely moving his lips. "We captured the Fallen, and he's in Master Alliandr's custody now, but we failed to stop him from raising Koschei the Deathless."

He frowned, staring at his skinned knuckles, a jumbled mess of thoughts rushing through his mind.

"I can see something bothers you," said Magnus. "Speak up, Dmitri. Outside of the obvious, what is it?"

Damian's frown deepened, his mind racing through the entangled disarray of thoughts. "Outside of the obvious..." he whispered. "Azazel and his plans, that's what's bothering me. Why would an ancient and powerful demon—the Fallen who was dormant, keeping to the shadows for centuries—decide to come out in the open? He knew who I was, and yet, he toyed with me from the beginning to the end despite the risks associated with that. After all, no matter how powerful he is, I'm a Destiny Enforcer with the power of the Destiny Council behind me. He couldn't have known that I am the Shadow Enforcer, working alone.

"Why would he risk everything just to free Koschei the Deathless? I doubt he did that out of the evilness of his black heart. Assholes like him won't lift a finger without getting something in return. What was his plan? Why did he need Koschei?" He exhaled, the dread of the unknown pressing on his heart. "*'Inside the obvious'*—yeah... It bothers me to no end that I failed to stop Koschei from rising."

"I didn't think you'd be able to stop that from happening," murmured Magnus.

Damian leaned back in his chair, a hiss of pain escaping his lips before he could suppress it.

"For years, I've been observing your work and the work of others in the Destiny Council." He traced the edge of his bracelet with his finger—a nervous habit he could never get rid of. "What's the point of having access to the Board of Destiny and the ability to read it if you can't use your knowledge for something good, or to prevent something evil from happening." He threw his hands up. "Please, indulge me, Magnus. Explain it to me once and for all."

"Oh, my boy..." whispered Magnus, shaking his head. "You know I'm an empath. I can feel your suffering..."

"I'll be all right. I just need time. There are no wounds time can't heal... at least partially." Damian closed his eyes, swallowing hard. "Don't avoid my question, Magnus. I need to understand."

"Some things I have no right to tell you, but I'll do my best to explain." Magnus rubbed the bridge of his nose and stopped talking, a heavy silence engulfing the room. Then he waved his hand, muttering a spell under his breath, and the heavy, yellow glow of a cloaking spell enveloped the office. "Trying to exploit the knowledge we gain by reading the Board of Destiny is a terrible crime prone to serious consequences. This is why my predecessor Aramir has been imprisoned for manipulating the Board of Destiny."

"I know all that," replied Damian. "Tell me something outside the basic knowledge. Did you know for sure that we wouldn't be able to stop Koschei from rising?"

"Yes, but it's not that simple," said Magnus. "When I read the Board of Destiny, I don't receive definitive answers. I see thousands of possible outcomes and scenarios. All there is and all there might be."

He moved his hand, his eyes going out of focus as if he were looking at the Board of Destiny now, and Damian couldn't help but wonder if he truly could see it, even from his office.

"Each possible outcome is different from the others, based on the decisions all the figures involved in the event make. The more people are involved, the more possible outcomes I receive while reading the Board of Destiny." Magnus fell silent, gazing down at Damian. "Unfortunately, there wasn't even a single chance of you stopping Koschei from rising. But there were other scenarios where you failed to capture Azazel, too, or where your brother was killed."

Damian nodded, nibbling on his lip. "Was there at least one scenario where—"

"No," Magnus interrupted him. "You couldn't save Ace, Commander, and it wasn't your fault she died."

Damian inhaled with an effort and smirked faintly. "I know it's not my fault she's dead, but it sure feels that way. I failed her in many other ways, Magnus."

He rubbed his unshaven chin, his fingers slipping on the wetness of sweat and blood covering his skin. His mind traveled back in time to the first moment he met Ace, quickly slipping through everything that happened after that to the moment the Fallen had taken her life.

"Moore should never have sent her to shadow my brother," he continued at length, every word coming with an effort. "She didn't have the level of knowledge or training she needed to handle an ancient vampire..." Damian's voice trailed off, and he sighed. "I failed her as a mentor. When I realized she was addicted to the vampire bite, it should have been a warning flag for me. I should have given her more attention. I should have taught her..." His voice cut off, words stuck in his throat, and he swallowed as if it could help him speak. "Never in my life did I think that someone would want me as a mentor... And I'm failing miserably at it. I need to change things before it's too late." He got up with a strained groan and swayed slightly. "There is something else you need to know, Magnus."

"What is it?"

"Before Ace died, she said a few things... Strange things that made no sense to me." Damian frowned, raking his fingers through his matted hair. "First, she said her original orders to protect Cole were changed a few weeks ago. She said she was supposed to seduce Cole, pretending to be in love with him. From what I understood, her orders were to drive me and my brother apart, and sabotage whatever we were doing. Who would order such a thing, and why? It has to be someone here."

"She was dying and in pain," Magnus said quietly. "Are you sure her words are reliable? It makes no sense. It wasn't my solo decision to support Cole's rule in Arizona. The entire Destiny Council voted unanimously on that. Who would want to sabotage that?"

"You tell me." Damian shrugged and pressed his hand to his side, pain striking through his fractured ribs. "One more thing, Magnus, and this one really bothers me."

"What is it?" Magnus asked again, his voice a hoarse whisper.

"I have no idea, but here are the words she said exactly the way she said them," replied Damian. "Damian, be careful... you must help... Magnus is..." He took a pause, drilling Magnus with his eyes. "Magnus is what? Who am I supposed to help and why should I be careful?"

Magnus slipped off the desk and straightened, spreading his long robe on the front to shove his hands into his pants' pockets. "Commander, I swear on my power, I don't know what it means. I also swear that I'll do my best to find out." He ran his hand over the stylish stubble on his cheeks, and for a moment, stilled in this position, deep in his thought. "What are you planning to do next?"

Damian massaged his sore shoulder and glanced down, just now realizing that his tank top was torn in so many places, it barely concealed his body covered in ugly blemishes of bruises, cuts and welts.

"My lord, if you don't mind," he said, "I would like to go home."

"Home," echoed Magnus, a warm smile changing his face. "It's been centuries since you had a place in any realm that you called *home*. I'm glad to hear that. You deserve some happiness in your life, my child."

The Destiny Council realm has never been my home, Damian thought, but then added aloud, "I'm not sure about happiness, but I need to heal myself, and I desperately need a good, hot shower and some rest. Besides, Oleg Svetlov is waiting for me at Paradise Manor, and I want to speak with him." Damian smirked, thinking that Magnus was right—Paradise Manor did feel like home.

"Captain Oleg Svetlov." Magnus nodded approvingly. "He's a good man. You can trust him." He waved his hand, and a portal, shimmering with the brilliance of his magic, opened next to Damian. "Go home, my boy. You need to heal in more ways than one, for terrible things lie ahead. The escape of Koschei is just the beginning. You need to be ready, my Shadow Enforcer."

Terrible things lie ahead... Magnus' words echoed through Damian's frazzled mind, and for the first time in over a thousand years, he looked at the Head of the Destiny Council with different eyes.

It was hard to be on the frontline of the fight between the Light and the Darkness. There was no chance anyone could survive this kind of confrontation unscarred, and the torment of pain and loss came with the territory. However, knowing what was coming and not being able to do anything to change the future was even harder. Magnus had carried this burden for centuries.

"Thank you, my lord," said Damian, inclining his head.

Magnus' glowing eyes widened for a fleeting moment, but then he smiled and gestured at the portal. "Farewell, Commander, and keep me updated on everything happening in your state."

Damian nodded and walked through the portal, leaving the Destiny Council realm behind.

✱ ✱ ✱

DAMIAN WALKED out of the portal in front of the entrance into Paradise Manor. The door was back in place, but the porch lights were broken, and the heavy cover of the night embraced the building. A dark shadow rose in front of the entrance, and a tall man stepped on the driveway, heading toward him.

"Oleg?" asked Damian, recognizing him. "Why are you outside?"

"Waiting for you." He smiled with a light shrug. "Do you have a place..." He moved his hand in the direction of the desert. "You know, a place where there is no one around, and you can just relax and let go?"

Damian chuckled softly, knowing well what Oleg had in mind and how he felt. As a true Child of Earth, he needed solitude and nature to relax and recharge. He approached Oleg, placed his hand on his shoulder, and snapped his fingers. They materialized on a small plateau surrounded by purple rock formations. The moonlight flooded the desert with its dim silvery light, shadows hiding behind every stone and cactus.

"It is a beautiful place... Peaceful..." Oleg looked around

with interest, lowering himself on a large boulder. "It reminds me of the Isle of Legends, the magical nexus here, in the realm of humans. Deserts in Kendral are nothing like this. More like the Sahara, I guess."

Damian sat down next to him and leaned forward, dropping his head. The effort of teleporting took a lot more out of him than he expected, and the desert around him kept shifting and flowing in nauseating waves. He glanced at Oleg sideways, realizing that he looked just as worn out as he felt.

"Do you need me to heal you?" asked Oleg, staring down at his feet. "I hate to say it, but you look like crap."

Damian chuckled. "I've been told that a few times today." He thought for a moment and then slipped off the boulder and lay down flat on the cold ground. The elemental energy of Earth embraced him like a tender lover, gently kissing his exposed skin. He inhaled deeply and then exhaled with a soft gasp that sounded almost like a moan. "No, thank you. Healing magic takes too much effort, and you're just as drained as I am. I'll be all right. Nothing that a good night's sleep can't fix."

Oleg nodded and leaned forward slightly to see his face. "Have you ever met another Child of Earth?"

"No," replied Damian. "You are the first." He lifted his head a little and threw a curious gaze at him. "When did you discover your power?"

Oleg shrugged, his eyes going out of focus for a brief moment. "About ten years ago or so?"

"You're so young," whispered Damian. "So new to all this…" His mind traveled back to the time when he was just as young and new to the World of Magic, and for a brief moment, something resembling pity took hold of him. He didn't know this man, but he didn't want him to suffer through the trenches of the World of Magic the way he had to do it. "Why do they call you Captain Svetlov?"

Oleg flashed him his wide, open-hearted smile. "It is my

military rank. I used to be a Captain of the Belorussian Special Forces. That was before I was driven out of my own country by gangsters who wanted to exploit my power."

"Belorussian?"

"Yeah. Where are you from?" asked Oleg.

"Originally?"

Oleg nodded.

"Kievan Rus," replied Damian, absentmindedly. "From the time of Prince Vladimir the Great." Even if Oleg was shocked by his statement, he didn't show it, and Damian continued, "A thousand years from now, you'll be talking to a young Child of Earth, probably sounding like me—tired and indifferent." He smirked. "Who helped you through the transition after you discovered your powers?"

"In the beginning, I had no idea what was happening to me. Back in Belarus, I had someone who taught me how to use my magic, but she gave me no insights into what I truly was. I did not learn my supernatural identity until I crossed over to Kendral and met Sandhya, the Elemental of Earth," replied Oleg. "But it was the Ancient Master of Power, Mrak Delar, who taught me how to use my power and magic. As much as I love Sandhya, I consider Mrak to be my mentor."

Damian lifted his head again, meeting Oleg's calm gaze. "Do you know how unusual it is? A Child of Earth in love with the Earth Elemental." He chuckled, dropping his head back down. "You won't find something like this in any fantasy novel or movie."

Oleg ran his hand over the ground and elemental energy responded to his move, flowing with his movement, wrapping around his body. "This brings us to what I wanted to tell you, Damian," he said softly and got up.

He spread his arms, his entire body emitting a soft, orange glow of his elemental power, and the desert responded to his call. The ground under his feet rolled and small rocks and pieces of dirt rose in the air. The night birds fell silent, and all the sounds disappeared. Damian pushed up on his elbow, watching the show with interest. Oleg brought his right arm up, pointing into a dark sky. A small bird, brown with gray and white spots, flew down and landed on his outstretched hand.

"Hello, my friend," he whispered, petting the bird's back gently with the tips of his fingers. The bird chirped its hellos and flapped its wings, disappearing back into the sky.

"You can speak to animals, of course," murmured Damian.

"Not only." Oleg sat down on the ground next to Damian, playing with a tiny pebble, throwing it up and catching it on the way down. "You are so much older than me, and you have the magic of a Destiny Enforcer, yet as a Child of Earth, I am more powerful than you. I can wield the energy of Earth and bend it to my will without channeling the power. Not only can I communicate with animals, but I can also transform myself into any living creature on Earth—shapeshifting is one of my powers. Do you know why I can do that?"

"Some beings of magic are more powerful than others?" murmured Damian, folding his arms under his head.

"No, my friend," replied Oleg. "This is not a reason for it. I allowed the Elemental of Earth to claim me, and that gave me extra power and sensitivity to the elemental energy."

"Wouldn't it also put you in servitude to the Elemental?" asked Damian.

Oleg shrugged. "You are a Child of Earth. Every cell in your body is infused with the energy of your element. It means the Earth Elemental can control you, suppressing your will, anyway. Any Master of Power who can control the elemental energy of Earth can control you. I am sure you know that."

"True," admitted Damian. "This is the part of being a Child of Earth I hate the most. After that comes the intolerance to high-rises and a minor case of claustrophobia."

"And then there is that." A faint smile crossed Oleg's face.

"My claustrophobia is not that bad. I do not let it affect my life. But the farther I am from Earth, the weaker I feel." He threw the little pebble up and made it freeze in midair. "I used to have the same concerns about subserviency and being controlled," he continued at length, slowly lowering the stone to the ground. "Kneeling and bowing is not my style, you know." He smirked, all but rolling his eyes. "In the end, I did it because my friends were about to face a formidable foe, and to help them, I needed more power." He tapped Damian on his shoulder and got up, offering him his hand. "Something tells me this is not the last time we fight side by side. So, if one day you change your mind and decide you need more power, visit me in Kendral."

Damian took his hand and got up, brushing the sand off his torn pants. "I hope you're wrong, Oleg," he said. "You have a life in Kendral—a woman you love who loves you back, friends, purpose. Diving back into the mayhem of the World of Magic brings nothing but pain and loss. I don't wish it for you."

"I guess we will see." Oleg waved his hand, whispering something, and a portal, shimmering with bright orange sparkles, opened next to him. "No matter what happens in the future, my offer stands, Damian. If you ever need me, all you have to do is call."

"In my line of work, it's not easy to make friends. Your offer means a lot to me," said Damian, holding out his hand. "Thank you."

Oleg shook his hand and stepped into the portal, disappearing into the clouds of swirling sparkles.

CHAPTER 37

~ DAMIAN BLAKE ~

Damian materialized next to the entrance door and braced his arms against it, dropping his head. He took a few deep breaths and grabbed the door handle, pulling the door open. The foyer stood dark and empty, and his steps echoed against the ceiling as he made his way to the kitchen. To his surprise, the kitchen was vacant, a few empty coffee cups sitting on the counter by the sink.

"Cole?" Damian reached out to his brother through their blood link and received the answer immediately.

"Living room."

He made his way to the living room and halted in the doorway. Jamie stood by the window, staring into the darkness of the desert, his hands clenched tightly behind his back. Cole sat in an armchair with his long legs outstretched before him, motionless in the way only vampires could be. His face bared no emotions, but as soon as Damian walked in, he got up and approached him.

"Dima, finally." His features softened, and relief reflected in his blue eyes.

But there were other scenarios where you failed to capture Azazel, too, or where your brother was killed. Magnus's words surfaced in Damian's mind, and he shuddered, realizing how close he had come to losing his brother again.

Without words, he took a step forward and pulled Cole into a tight hug.

"Hey, hey, I'm all right," Cole whispered, giving him a light tap on his back. "What happened, big bro?"

"Nothing. Thank the gods, nothing happened outside of what you know already." Damian pulled away. "I'm sorry, I couldn't save Ace. Moore never bound her spirit to the Destiny Council realm."

Cole nodded, averting his eyes. A deep vertical wrinkle materialized between his eyebrows, and his jaws clenched. He didn't say anything, but Damian had no doubt his brother blamed himself for the young woman's death.

Suppressing a sigh, he switched his attention to Jamie. The young man still stood by the window, just turned around to face him, his fingers fidgeting nervously with a cuff of his long-sleeved shirt. Catching Damian's gaze, he smiled, the smile never reaching his red-rimmed eyes.

"I'm glad to see you back," he said, his voice raspier than normal. "In one piece." He gave him a quick once-over and added, "More or less..." As a haunted expression shadowed his face, he averted his gaze. "I knew something wasn't right with her. I was trying to stop her, but she just—"

"What are you talking about?" asked Damian, taking a step closer.

"The last few days... No, actually, it'd been a couple of weeks already. Ace wasn't herself." Jamie raised his face, his eyes darting from Cole to Damian. "Stubborn and argumentative. More than usual, that is. And she was constantly unhappy about Cole hanging around you, Damian. According to her, when Cole was next to you, he behaved like a little boy in the presence of his parents, incapable of making his own decisions. I tried to figure out why she had suddenly developed such a severe allergic reaction to you, but I couldn't get anything out of her. I should have tried harder... I should have told you or Cole. Dammit!" He punched the air with his fist and turned away, biting his lip. "I should have pulled her back when she—"

"Jamie, stop." Damian approached him, placing his hand on his shoulder to give him a reassuring squeeze. "It's not your fault. You're right, something is going on, but so far, I have no idea what that is. Trust me, there was nothing you could do to stop her."

Jamie nodded, swallowing hard. "I always do. If there is anyone in this world whom I trust no questions asked, it's you, Damian."

At his words, something twitched in Damian's heart, and he pressed his hand to his mouth, gazing down at the young man, astonished. "Jamie, do you still want me to teach you?" he asked at length. "Or would you rather study with Luc and Yakov to become a part of the Wardens Order?"

Jamie and Cole exchanged a puzzled gaze, and a tentative smile graced Jamie's face. "Can't I have the best of both worlds?" he asked. "But if I have to make a hard choice—you're the only mentor I want."

Damian gave him an arched stare, considering a few options, but then nodded. "I'll see that you have your time with the Wardens," he said, sounding hoarse even to his own ears. "But if you want me to train you, get ready for pain."

Jamie's eyebrows climbed up, and he threw a quick look at Cole. "Cole, is your brother always this"—he twirled his wrist —"doom and gloom?"

"Nuh. Not at all." Cole waved his hand dismissively. "Only on special occasions." He took a brief pause and added, inching away from Damian, "But he does treat every day of his immortal life as a special occasion."

"Ugh, shut up, little bloodsucker," muttered Damian, catching the humorous look in his brother's eyes.

"Doofus," Cole didn't fail to reply in his usual manner.

"Where is Yakov?" asked Damian, switching back to serious mode. "I wanted to speak with him about Koschei. We can't let him roam the realm of humans freely, and I was counting on Yakov's help with the search."

"Oh, yeah." Cole lowered back in his chair, crossing his legs at the knee. "The old eagle asked me to give you a message. He said that he has something you need, but it'll take him about a month to find it and bring it here."

"Something I need?" parroted Damian, his eyebrows rising. "I have no idea what he's talking about. Did he say anything else?"

"Not much," replied Jamie. "Just this… And that he'll try to dig out anything he can on Koschei by the time he comes back here again. He asked you to be patient and not to enforce anything that doesn't need enforcing."

"Whatever that means," Damian grumbled, shaking his head. "This man can't speak plainly if his life depended on it." He glanced over his shoulder at the doorway, his eyes searching the darkness of the hallway. "Where is River? Is she home?"

"What do you think?" Cole leaned to the side, propping his elbow against the armrest. "She was so tired, she could barely keep her eyes open, but she was determined to wait for your return no matter what. So, I had to insist on her going to her room to lie down. I promised to wake her up as soon as you got home."

"Oh…" Damian raked his hand through his dirty hair, covering the left side of his face without realizing he was doing that. "I guess I'll see her in the morning then."

Cole and Jamie exchanged a flabbergasted look, and both said, "No."

Cole facepalmed, rolling his eyes. "Go to her room now. I

can bet you anything, she's not sleeping." Damian hesitated, and Cole's lips quirked up in a tiny smile. "Dumbass... When it comes to women, you're like—" He chuckled, not finishing his statement.

* * *

Damian stopped in front of River's bedroom and opened his second sight, quickly scanning her room and the area around it for any supernatural presence. He didn't need to do it, but he was so used to guarding her that it had become his second nature, his instinct.

The door was cracked open, and a narrow ray of the dim, yellow light fell on the carpet next to his feet. A small, dark shadow squeezed its way out of the room, making the door squeak. Damian smirked, recognizing Gypsy, mentally preparing himself for the verbal attack of the sarcastic furry monster. The cat sat and looked up at him, her jaw dropping in a very un-catlike manner.

"Well, now you do look like a real Sasquatch," she murmured, raising her paw and giving it a good lick. "I hope no one caught you on camera outside Paradise Manor. I can just see the newspaper and social media headlines tomorrow." She closed her eyes and moved her paw from left to right. "'Ten most convincing Sasquatch sightings in Arizona', or 'Bigfoot hunting season is opened in Blue Creek'. And all those videos going viral on YouTube...Yay! We're finally famous."

"Gypsy—," Damian started, but the cat got up, completely ignoring him. With her bushy tail up, she made a circle around him and finally halted in front of him again, narrowing her round, green eyes. He suppressed a sigh, not sure if he wanted to laugh or be angry at this unexpected delay.

"And the smell, the smell..." purred Gypsy, wrinkling her nose. "What is it? Let's see..." She sucked in a large gulp of air, pressing her ears with long furry brushes down. *"Black and puke-like green colors. A fine demonic essence bouquet, and a touch of dark magical energy with a hint of sulfur. Good balance."*

"Gypsy, I'm too tired to deal with your shenanigans," whispered Damian, throwing a gaze at the bedroom. "Is River awake?"

"Once a Sasquatch always a Sasquatch." The cat rolled her eyes furiously. *"What do yah think? She couldn't relax since y'all left. And when Cole returned with the news about Ace, she was heartbroken and terrified."* Gypsy stepped closer, rubbing her side against his legs. *"For you... She was terrified for you, silly Sasquatch. She was afraid that something could happen to you, too. I think until that moment, she didn't fully realize how perilous your job was..."* She took a short pause, giving him a pointed stare, then a wide feline grin appeared on her face. *"Anyway, she's not sleeping. Go already."*

As Gypsy strolled down the hallway toward the living room, Damian knocked softly, then pushed the door open and walked inside. The room was semi-dark, illuminated only by the weak light of a small nightlight. River lay on her bed with her knees pulled to her chest. Her copper hair cascaded down her chest and back, partially covering her face. But he could see her wide-open eyes gazing at him from under her long, golden eyelashes.

Silently, River sat up, her every move slow and measured. Throwing her hair to her back, she rose to her feet and walked toward him, her bare feet stepping soundlessly on the carpeted floor. He watched her approach, and for some reason, his limbs felt as if they were filled with lead. She halted in front of him and looked up, their eyes meeting just for a brief moment shorter than a heartbeat. Then she leaned forward and rested her forehead against his chest, her arms remaining at her sides.

He raised his arms to embrace her but froze halfway, unable to make a move. "River," he croaked, his vocal cords refusing to function. "I am—"

She lifted her head and took his hand, her slender fingers

squeezing his. Without saying a word, she pulled him toward the master bathroom. Flipping the light switch on, she moved a small vanity stool from under the counter and opened the faucet.

"Sit," she said, gesturing at the stool.

He sat down, and just now, he started to feel how truly drained he was. Partially healed injuries and bruises ached, and his muscles were so sore that he doubted he could hold his head upright. With a soft groan, he leaned his back against the counter and dropped his hands in his lap. She made sure the water was warm enough and put a small hand towel under the stream.

Then she took his chin and gently lifted his head. Pushing back the dirty strands of hair from his face, she proceeded with cleaning the partially healed wounds on his face, the strokes of her towel careful but precise and fast. After a while, she ripped his destroyed tank top off, throwing it on the floor, and proceeded with cleaning the wounds on his shoulders, chest and back. He closed his eyes, and the corners of his mouth lifted in a blissful smile as he enjoyed the treatment despite the occasional stings of pain.

Suddenly, she stopped what she was doing, and he opened his eyes, almost unwillingly, just to see River's blue eyes right in front of his.

"You're smiling," she whispered in disbelief, the warmth of her breath brushing his skin. "You have to be in pain, but you're smiling." Her fingers probed his bruised ribs, and he hissed, wincing. "Your ribs are probably broken, but you still look blissfully happy."

"Broken ribs? It's nothing. I know how to control physical pain, and I can self-heal," he replied. "I'm just too exhausted physically and drained magically to perform any kind of healing magic right now. I need a little rest before I can do it." He gazed at her and took a deep breath, feeling warm and content. "Just a little while ago, the Slavic goddess of Nightmares told me that I have no happy memories. I think I do now."

She straightened, her eyes sparkling with wonderment. "Dima, I drove Cole crazy with my questions about you and your past. I wasn't nosy. All I wanted was to understand you better, so I could be there for you." She threw the dirty towel into the sink and laughed softly. "I think you're still an enigma to me."

She pressed her hand to his scarred cheek, caressing his skin with her thumb. He placed his hand over hers and closed his eyes again, leaning against her palm. She bent forward slightly and planted a soft kiss on his forehead. Then her lips moved down his cheek, leaving a trail of tiny kisses that set his skin on fire.

"If we can't be anything more than friends, I accept that. I just want you to know that I'm ready to spend the rest of my short human life unraveling the mystery that you are, Damian Blake," she whispered, covering his lips with hers.

Damian wrapped his arms around River's waist, pulling her closer.

The Destiny Enforcers' rules be damned...

EPILOGUE

* * *

~ Damian Blake ~
Blue Creek, Paradise Manor.
One month later.

THE SOUND of metal clashing against metal rang through the desert. Cole laughed, easily deflecting Atticus' vigorous attack. The young werewolf was partially transformed, and Cole didn't use his vampiric strength and speed, yet the vampire had no problem holding Atticus at arm's length. He toyed with him like a cat with a mouse, dancing circles around him within a small amphitheater surrounded by boulders and rock formations. Damian sat on the ground with his back rested against a large rock, watching his brother having fun.

A few minutes later, Atticus stopped and dropped his sword, raising his hands.

"I give up," he panted, sweat running down his flushed face. He dropped next to Damian, laughing. "I need a few minutes of rest. I'm fast. I'm strong. But he is—"

"He's an ancient vampire who's practiced swordsmanship since he was six years old," Damian interrupted, tapping the werewolf on his knee. "And you're what? Fifteen?"

Atticus snorted. "I'm twenty-five, dude, come on!"

Damian got up, shaking the red-orange sand off his pants. "You're using your sword as if it is an oversized screwdriver in your father's machine shop. You have a lot to learn, and if you're serious about it, Cole is the best teacher you can wish for."

He held out his arms, and his daggers materialized in his hands, responding to his mental command.

"Whoa," exhaled Atticus, staring at the shining blades in Damian's hands in awe. "How do you do it? I've never seen anything like that."

"A Destiny Enforcer's weapons—daggers, in my case," he replied, offering one of his daggers to the werewolf. "After the training is complete, every Destiny Enforcer has to choose a weapon. Powerful wizards, who work only for the Destiny Council and never leave their realm, bind the Enforcer with the weapon of their choice. The daggers respond to my mental commands, and I can never lose them."

He snapped his fingers, and the dagger vanished from Atticus' hands, materializing back in his. Turning to his brother, Damian lifted his blades. "Care for a round?" he asked.

Cole assumed a guarding stance, flicking his eyebrow at him. "No Destiny Enforcer powers and earthquakes?"

"No vampire speed and strength?" retorted Damian, excitement spiking adrenalin in his system.

"Feeling lucky today?" Cole laughed.

Instead of answering, Damian glanced back at Atticus. "Watch and learn. Cole is an ancient vamp," he said, switching his attention back to his brother. "It means he is faster than you and stronger than you. You can't beat him at that. Even partially transformed, you're still slower and weaker. The only way you can beat him is by outsmarting him."

"Which is impossible." Cole laughed, starting with a powerful frontal attack.

Knowing Cole's fighting tactics, Damian was ready. He sidestepped him, forcing his brother to switch his position. Then he moved forward so quickly and forcefully that Cole had no choice but to take a few steps back, almost hitting a large boulder. The vampire pulled to the side, moving along the length of the rock, but Damian didn't stop. Cole increased his speed, his blade a silvery blur, but forced into the narrow space between two rocks, his maneuverability was severely limited.

Damian pressed forward, locking his brother in, and the only thing separating his daggers from his brother's throat was the shining blade of Cole's sword. Cole growled, and despite his effort to contain his nature, his eyes lit up with a bright, scarlet light and his fangs expanded. At the same time, his sword ignited with a slightly reddish glow of unusual magical energy. Damian gasped, staring at his brother in shock, and lowered his daggers, taking a step back.

"I told you," murmured Cole, sheathing his sword. He walked back to where Atticus sat and lowered next to him. Looking up at Damian, he added, "Dima, Yakov wanted to run some tests on me, remember?"

"Yes." Damian nodded, a heavy knot twisting in the pit of his stomach.

"I want him to do it." Cole bit his lip, staring into the evening desert, his fingers fidgeting with a small, dry branch. "I need to understand what's going on with me. Vampires are not supposed to have magic."

"You're probably right." Damian massaged his temples, feeling a nagging headache of a summoning spell originating somewhere behind his eyes. "Speaking of the devil..."

He got up and channeled his magic, drawing a rune in the air. Pressing his palm to it, he activated the rune, and a heartbeat later, it was replaced by the oval of a communication window. Yakov

Bruce looked at them through the window, a tiny smirk playing on his lips. His clothes looked like they'd seen better days and needed either a good laundry or a convenient garbage can. His long hair was in disarray, and his chin was covered in an overgrown stubble.

"Sorry for the interruption," he said, running his hands over the front of his button-down shirt in a futile effort to smooth out the wrinkles. "I came here straight from"—he twirled his wrist, a mischievous grin appearing on his face—"wherever I was. I didn't bother to take a shower and change because I wanted to see you first, Commander. I'm at Paradise Manor with the beautiful Ms. River. Can you come home now? I promise it's not going to take long."

"I'll see you in a minute," Damian replied and closed the communication window. Turning to Atticus, he asked, "Do you want to come with us or return to Hawk's ranch?"

Atticus got up, rubbing the back of his neck. "While it's been fun getting my ass kicked, it's getting late, and I had better go back home before my father has something to say about it." A guilty smile crossed his face, and he pointed to the west where the last rays of the setting sun colored the desert with their pink shades. He turned to Cole and offered his hand. "Thank you, Majesty. I hope we can do it again sometime. I really want to learn and improve my sword skills."

"Any time," replied Cole, squeezing his hand in a handshake. "Let's just keep our lessons away from my Court or my company." He winked, giving a quick tap on the young werewolf's shoulder.

Damian moved his hand and a portal shimmering with rotating blue and white sparkles opened in front of him.

"It'll take you to the gates of your father's property," he explained, shaking Atticus' hand. "Say hello to Hawk. I'll try to stop by sometime next week."

As Atticus walked through the portal, disappearing on the

other side, Damian closed it and placed his hand on his brother's shoulder.

"The fun is over," he said. "Let's see what the old eagle brought on his wings." He snapped his fingers, and they vanished from the desert.

* * *

DAMIAN AND COLE materialized in front of the entrance into Paradise Manor and headed straight for the kitchen. Since the time when Damian moved into this large mansion, the kitchen had become one of his favorite places. Early in the morning, while everyone was still asleep, he liked to sit down with a cup of hot coffee in his hand, watching the sun slowly rise over the desert. It was a beautiful view that never failed to give him a feeling of peace and a sense of belonging.

River sat at the table, her face flushed from laughing, and Yakov stood in front of her, telling her something animatedly. As soon as Damian and Cole walked in, he stopped talking and turned to them, inclining his head in a light bow.

"Commander Blake, Your Majesty," he greeted them, a lopsided smirk tugging at his lips.

"Yeah, right," murmured Cole, making his way to the table.

"I thought you weren't into the medieval formalities of the World of Magic," said Damian, shaking the wizard's hand.

"I'm not." Yakov sat down, crossing his legs, and shrugged. "Just seemed like the appropriate thing to do." He glanced at Cole and cocked his head, narrowing his eyes. "Changed your mind, eh?"

Cole's jaw dropped, and he exchanged a bewildered glance with Damian. Reaching behind his back, he unsheathed his sword and placed it on the table in front of Yakov.

"A while ago, I told you that I developed some extra sensitivity to magical energy," said Cole, his fingers running over the red stone embedded into the pommel of his sword.

"I remember," replied Yakov calmly. "At the time, I thought it wasn't something common to your kind. But it's not unheard of for an old vampire to develop some... eh... unusual talents. So, I thought it had something to do with your age. Also, since your brother is a Child of Earth, it's possible you may have magical gifts, too, but they had been suppressed when you were turned." He thought for a second, scratching the back of his head. "What happened, Cole? Something had to trigger this conversation."

"He wields magical energy, Yakov," replied Damian. "I saw it with my own eyes, and as a Destiny Enforcer I can attest, it was the real deal. The energy was emitted by his body and channeled through the sword. It was so powerful, I could see it without opening my second sight—a scarlet glow."

"The sword, eh?" Yakov took the weapon, holding it flat on the palms of his hands.

He closed his eyes, and the magical energy field spiked around him. The sword rose a few inches in the air, a sparkling blue mist surrounding it like a shimmering, see-through veil. A few seconds later, the mist dissipated, and the sword lowered into Yakov's hands. He pressed the red stone of the pommel to his forehead, whispering something, and a dim light ignited within the gem.

"Curious..." Yakov gave the sword back to Cole. "Inclusions of *Ardenium* steel and a gem in the pommel... This weapon is not a mundane sword. It has magical properties, and I believe this stone"—he pointed at the gem—"is special. I don't recognize its magical energy signature since it seems to be partially suppressed by the *Ardenium* steel, but I don't recommend removing it from its settings. I believe this stone allows Cole to channel magic. Possibly, I'm mistaken, but I can't be sure until I run a few tests on this weapon and Cole himself." He glanced at the vampire, two deep wrinkles crossing his forehead. "Where did you get this sword?"

"A gift from my maker," replied Cole, his face paler than usual. "I've had it for centuries, but I could never channel or detect any magical energy before. It can't be the sword."

"Yes, it can." Yakov got up and started pacing the small area in front of the table. "It can, I have no doubt. Something had to trigger the change, and unless we know the history of this weapon and the origin of this red stone, we can't be sure of anything. Is your maker still alive, Cole?"

"I hope so." Cole averted his gaze, a muscle working in his tightly pressed jaw. "He's been missing for a while, and I've been trying to find him all this time."

"Find him." Yakov drummed the table with his fingers, his eyes going out of focus for a heartbeat. "I will run some tests, but it would be a lot safer and easier if we could speak with your maker. What is his name, by the way?"

"Ruslan," replied Cole.

Yakov froze in place, and his jaw slacked as he stared at Cole with wide-open eyes. "Ruslan," he whispered, all color draining off his face. "Your maker is one of the oldest vampires who walks this realm."

"He's not *the* oldest." Cole shrugged.

"I know," replied Yakov dryly, switching his attention to Damian. "Commander, you need to find Ruslan. Cole would have known if his maker was dead, so I don't doubt for a second he's alive. As far as the Destiny Council's and Wardens' Archives recorded, over thousands of years of his life, Ruslan sired only one child"—he jerked his chin at Cole—"and he would never abandon his only child without saying a word. It means something or someone is holding him against his will." He shook his head, a dark shadow crossing his features. "It can't be good... It can't be good. Dammit!" He slammed his fist on the table, spilling the coffee. "Whoever holds him must be extremely powerful. You must find and free Ruslan as soon as possible."

Without saying another word, he headed toward the door, muttering something under his breath absentmindedly. But then he halted in the doorway and turned around, bowing to River slightly.

"I'm sorry, Detective," he said, pressing his hand to his heart. "Thank you for your hospitality, but I must leave. I need to process this new information and do some research as soon as possible."

"No problem, Yakov," replied River with a soft smile. "You're welcome here at any time. I hope to see you soon."

"Hold on, Yakov." Damian raised his hand to attract the wizard's attention. "Do you have anything on Koschei's whereabouts or anything on where he keeps his death?"

Yakov slapped his forehead with his hand, rolling his eyes. "Sorry, Commander, with this latest revelation, I almost forgot why I came here in the first place." He threw his hands up and made his way back to Damian. "I've spent a full month trying to trace this old monster, but it seems like he's in hiding and unless he makes a move, we won't be able to trace his location. However, I placed a few"—he twirled his hand, gazing heavenward—"magical traps for the lack of a better word in the realm of humans and all accessible magical nexuses. Should he make a move, we'll know right away."

"Thank you," said Damian. "I guess it's better than nothing. Keep me updated on your research."

Yakov nodded, but then a wide grin, which seemed completely inappropriate in the tense atmosphere of the room, split his face. He grabbed Damian's wrist, and a soft wave of magical energy surged from his palm, quickly spreading through Damian's body.

"I have a gift for you, Commander..." the old wizard

murmured, sending more and more of his magic through Damian. "I believe you need it."

Damian sucked in a sharp breath that sounded almost like a gasp, feeling as though his right arm was on fire. The pain grew sharper, spreading through his chest, moving steadily up toward his head. He gritted his teeth, and his hands clenched into tight fists, but he couldn't allow himself to scream in front of River in fear of scaring her.

"Wow, yours looks beautiful..."

Damian heard Yakov's voice through the fog of pain in his mind and opened his watering eyes, feeling slightly unsteady and lightheaded. The pain slowly vanished, and he exhaled, realizing that he had been holding his breath all this time.

"Take a look." Yakov released Damian's wrist and pointed at his arm.

Damian peered at his arm, and his eyebrows rose. An intricate tattoo covered the entire area of his arm, starting from his wrist to the middle of his bicep. Complicated symbols, runes and words in Dragon tongue he didn't recognize entwined with thorny vines crossed his skin in a beautiful design.

"What the hell did you do, Yakov? What is the meaning of this? And what in the world made you think I needed it?" he whispered. "I never wanted a tattoo. I like my body the way it is—clean and natural."

"There is nothing natural about your thousand-year-old body, Commander," Yakov huffed, heading toward the door. He stopped there and threw his hands up, shaking his head. "As I said earlier, Destiny Enforcers—ignorant in everything other than combat magic. When the time comes to face your next formidable foe—Koschei, for instance—you'll be happy I gave you this tattoo."

He waved his hand dismissively and walked out the door, tittering, but then came back a second later and stuck his head in the doorway.

"And Commander, don't forget to name him," he said, twinkles of humor dancing in his dark-brown eyes. "Give him a name of strength and power. It's important."

"Yakov!" yelled Damian, running after him as the wizard pivoted on his heels and walked away. "Name who? What are you talking about?" He rushed into the hallway, but Yakov was already gone.

Damian returned to the kitchen and dropped on a chair, turning his arm as he tried to read the words of the Dragon tongue but without any luck. He sighed and gave up, putting his hands on the table.

"I hate tattoos," he mumbled, throwing a tortured gaze at Cole, but his brother just shrugged, a lopsided grin on his face.

"For what it's worth," said River, approaching him, "this one is truly beautiful." She ran her finger over the lines, tracing the design wrapped around his bicep, and a tender pink shade colored her cheeks. "I love it."

Cole chuckled, and River stepped away, the blush on her cheeks becoming brighter. She sat down across from Damian and folded her hands on the table, leaning forward slightly.

"So, what are you going to do now?" she asked, her normal calmness returning to her. "This Koschei doesn't sound like someone to be taken lightly."

"He's not," replied Damian quietly. "We'll do what we always do."

"We'll find this prehistoric monster, and we'll fight," said Cole, his eyes igniting with the furious, scarlet light. He approached Damian and placed his cold hands on his shoulders. "Do your thing, brother. I'm with you all the way. No matter what—"

"—we stand together." Damian placed his hand over his brother's, squeezing it. "*Brat moi....*"

"Brother mine," Cole echoed his words, looking up at him.

EXCERPT

*Read on for an excerpt from
N.M. Thorn's new book
The Shadow Enforcer Series Book 3:*

*~ Damian Blake ~
Blue Creek, Arizona*

The large, orange disk of the moon hung low over the horizon, bathing the dark suburban neighborhood in its soft light. Despite the late hour, it was still too hot to be comfortable, and the asphalt road emitting additional waves of heat didn't improve the situation. The wind-deprived air felt stuffy, and the silence of this scorching evening seemed to be too heavy to be natural.

Damian halted in front of a dark intersection and raised his arm to stop Jamie. The young wizard halted by his side and pointed at a dark house on the south-east corner, across the road. Damian nodded and sharpened his senses, quickly scanning the area around. A barely noticeable spike in the magical energy field attracted his attention, and he channeled his magic, opening his other sight.

"Dammit," he cursed, frowning.

The magical energy flowed around the house in unsteady waves, spiking up and dropping to nearly nothing like some crazy EKG of a monstrous heart. Some of it was basic protective magic—a turn-away spell cast to keep humans as far away as possible. Besides that, he detected a strange dark energy he couldn't identify right away. It was pulsing in short, continuous bursts, dark-purple flares accentuating each spike, aligning with the overall uneven flow of magical energy around the building.

What bothered him the most, however, was that this unusual pulsating magic completely blocked his second sight, and he couldn't see what was going on inside of the building. The idea that someone was powerful enough to block his other sight made his skin crawl with the expectation of trouble, and he tensed, channeling more of his magical energy toward his eyes to enhance his vision.

"What do you see?" Jamie asked, shifting closer to him.

"River was right," Damian replied in a soft whisper, wishing with all his heart that she wasn't. "I have no idea how she does it, but whenever she tells me that her case is supernatural, she's always right."

"Do you know what we're dealing with?" Jamie shivered, rubbing his arms with his hands as if he were cold in this unusually steamy ninety-five degrees evening. "I can't get rid of the feeling that I need to leave this place and never come back." He huffed, catching Damian's reproachful stare. "Yeah, I know—a turn-away spell. I'm not gonna fall for it. You taught me well."

"Good, don't. I need you to keep it together..." Damian stared into the darkness behind the house and reached out to his brother through their blood bond. *"Cole, are you in position?"*

"Aye, aye, Captain. We're in position," Cole replied immediately, his voice sounding loud and clear in Damian's mind.

Damian stifled a sigh, thinking about his brother's inability to stay serious no matter how severe the situation was. *"You're a lot closer to the house. Can you detect any supernatural presence?"*

For a few seconds, Cole remained silent, then his voice sounded in Damian's mind again, humorous vibes replaced by tones of concern. *"A few vampires. Not mine. Either rogues or visitors from other states... Well, that's a big problem, and I need to handle it later."* Cole stopped talking, and the short pause he took felt like an hour-long silence to Damian's stretched nerves. *"Do me a favor, big bro. If you come across vampires, keep at least one of them alive if possible. I would like to ask them a few questions..."*

"You got it," replied Damian. *"Any other supernatural presence?"*

"Yes," replied Cole. *"Demons, at least two or three, judging by the amount of demonic essence they're emitting. Oh, and Atticus thinks there are a bunch of shifters among them. Most likely swords for hire."*

"Jeez," muttered Damian, wondering why this completely unremarkable suburban house was guarded like a medieval fortress. *"Okay. I believe there are wards around the place, so Jamie and I go first. If River is right, there could be humans inside. So, be careful. Don't go happy-go-lucky on me."*

"Oh, no, and here I was going to rush in, guns blazing." Cole snickered, and Damian could almost see his brother rolling his eyes.

"You and Atticus stay back and wait for my signal," he replied, ignoring Cole's sarcasm.

"What signal?"

"You'll know it when you see it." Damian severed their link and seized Jamie's elbow, directing him toward the house.

They crossed the road, and Damian halted by the decorative fence surrounding the property. The house was large—eight to nine thousand square feet, if not more by the looks of it. The only two-story building on the block, it stood out like a sore thumb, and he had to wonder why someone would pick this place if they wanted to stay under the radar of local human and

EXCERPT

supernatural authorities. The windows of the house were dark, shaded by thick curtains, and nothing seemed to be moving either inside the building or in its front yard.

Damian squatted, placed his palm flat against the ground, and sent a touch of his elemental energy through it. The small area of the fence in front of him lit up with a barely perceptible purple glow, and a chain of tiny, shimmering runes shone along the perimeter of the property for a heartbeat before vanishing.

Damian got up and turned to Jamie. "Did you see it?"

"Wards?" replied Jamie, shoving his hands into the pockets of his track pants.

Damian noticed his move but managed to stop himself from smiling. A few months ago, Jamie had touched the wards and activated them, giving away their presence to their enemies. He had obviously learned his lesson, and now he kept his hands firmly locked in his pockets to make sure he wouldn't touch anything he wasn't supposed to.

He got up, straightening his jeans, and nodded at Jamie. "Well, they are wards, but they are not built to keep anything supernatural out. They're built to alert whoever is inside as soon as someone with magic crosses the property line." He brushed his palms together, getting rid of the sand. "It's a supernatural alarm system."

"Can you disable it without activating the alarm?" asked Jamie, his troubled gaze traveling across the property, settling on the dark house.

"No. I need to use my magic to disable the wards, but these wards are designed to react to anything magical." Damian frowned, considering different options, but none of them looked good. "Unfortunately, this protective magic also blocks my other sight, so I have no idea how many monsters are waiting for us on the inside and where they are."

Jamie shrugged, and his eyes lit up with the soft reddish glow of his magic, determination reflecting on his face. "Then we do what we always do," he said quietly. "We make an entrance they will never forget."

"You are learning." Damian tapped Jamie's shoulder and reached out to his brother. *"Cole, there are alarm-type wards around the property. There is no way to get in quietly. Tell Atticus to be ready. We're going to go in first."*

"Ready." Cole's voice sounded in his mind like the low, dangerous growl of a predator.

"Jamie, now." Damian channeled his magic to his hands and shouted, pointing at the fence, *"Exitius!"*

The fence blew up with a thunderous bang, showering them with shards of wood, dust and debris. The wards crashed, and the ear-splitting sound of the supernatural alarms rang through the sleepy neighborhood. A few dogs replied with gut-wrenching howls that made the small hairs rise on the back of Damian's neck. A flock of birds went up in the air, their screeches adding to the cacophony of the alarm.

Damian held out his arms, and his daggers materialized in his hands, blazing in the surrounding darkness. He stepped through the opening he had created, registering from the corner of his eye that Jamie was following him. Opening his second sight, he ran soundlessly across the front yard toward the entrance into the house.

Halting on the circular driveway, he channeled more of his magic toward his hands, ready to break the door, when it opened with a soft squeak and remained ajar, exposing a light-less room behind it. Jamie came to a screeching halt, grabbing Damian's elbow.

"It's a trap," he exhaled, staring into the black rectangle of the doorway as if it were the maw of a monster.

"Of course, it is," murmured Damian, unable to hide his amusement. "Let's see who'll get trapped, though. I bet you a hundred dollars, it's not us."

"Make it two," replied Jamie, his hands clenching into fists.

EXCERPT

"Perfect. Now, give me some light, boy!" Damian laughed, adrenalin surging through him. He planted his feet firmly on the ground and spread his arms, connecting with his element. As the energy of Earth flowed freely through his body, he redirected it toward the house.

The entire building shook, tremors running through its walls. Damian took a step forward and twisted his arm, drawing a shining circle in the air with his blazing dagger. The tremors became stronger, the front wall wobbling as if it were made of jelly. Damian whispered a spell and drew another circle in the air.

A part of the front wall surrounding the doorway separated from the house, ripped by his magic. Deep fractures ran in every direction, but the building didn't collapse. For a brief moment, Damian held the chunk of wall suspended in mid-air, every muscle of his body tense with strain. Then he screamed and pushed his arms forward. The piece of wall flew through the opening into the house, exploding into a cloud of wood slivers and pieces of concrete. Loud screams of horror and cries of pain followed his move.

Jamie raised his arm, muttering a spell, and a swarm of tiny light orbs materialized over his hand. He flicked his wrist toward the building, and the orbs obeyed his command, zooming into the house.

"Ask and you shall receive." A winning smile crossed Jamie's face. "Light for you, my lord."

The light orbs illuminated a large hall covered in pieces of wood, slivers of glass, dust and other debris. There was no furniture in the room and the space was wide open with no place to hide. Two hallways ran in opposite directions, leading into the darkness. A group of dark figures cowered by the back wall, their eyes igniting with an angry glimmer as they started to recover from the initial shock. Jamie's magical orbs hovered above them, throwing flares of light against their blades and firearms.

Damian didn't need to use his other sight to know they were shifters for hire, their powerful energy signatures unmistakable from such close proximity.

"Shifters," hissed Jamie, unsheathing his sword.

"You're better off with your gun. Use the silver bullets," Damian whispered and crossed the threshold. At the same time, the clatter of broken glass and a furious slew of profanities sounded at the other end of the house. Damian's mouth twisted into a dark smirk as the sound of an unfolding fight confirmed that his brother was in, too.

The noise ripped the shifters out of their stupor, and the air around them shimmered as they started to transform. Soon, a pack of desert wolves stood before him, their light, sandy fur raised on their backs. With blood-curdling howls, they charged Damian and Jamie.

Damian spun in place, ducking the first monster as it leaped in the air. His arm went up, and the shining dagger cut through the wolf's side and stomach, ripping it open. The monster fell to the floor next to his feet, his body convulsing as it transformed back into human form. The man's hands clutched at his front and side, blood and entrails spilling out of the terrifying wound.

The sound of a gunshot rolled across the house, and another wolf fell, turning into a man on its way down. Damian didn't wait to see what would happen next. Deadly and precise, his daggers worked their way through the pack of shifters, leaving disfigured bodies in their wake. The screams of pain and howls of anger filled the house, and the nauseating stench of spilled blood permeated the air.

Damian wasn't sure how many shifters he killed. It was hard to count, especially since they kept shifting, taking on a different form every chance they had, but it seemed like they kept coming. Throwing a quick glance around, he noticed that the shifters outmaneuvered him, separating him from Jamie. A

EXCERPT

gunshot boomed on his right, letting him know that the young wizard was still standing. He sharpened his senses, and over the howls of the wolves, he heard the cacophony of a battle unfolding in the other part of the house, suggesting that Cole and Atticus were still fighting.

"On your left, Commander!" A tiny, high-pitched voice sounded in Damian's head, causing him to flinch. He knew it wasn't Cole, and he had no idea whose voice invaded his mind, but he had no time to think about it. Jumping aside, he spun to the left just in time to see the giant body of an honest-to-God lion rising in the air, its massive paws with hooked claws aiming at him.

He yelped and ducked out of the way, but one of the paws caught his shoulder, sending him tumbling to the floor slick with blood. He skidded on his back, hitting the wall with his bleeding shoulder and arm. His fingers unlocked, and the daggers fell on the tiled floor, their metallic clatter swallowed by the deafening roar of the monstrous animal. A cry of pain escaped his lips as he struggled to get back to his feet. Another roar rolled through the room, and then his brother's furious voice rose over the mayhem.

"Hey, lion! King of assholes!" Cole shouted somewhere at the other end of the room. "Why don't you pick on someone your own size."

The lion snapped around, its thick mane flowing with its move, and now Damian could see Cole standing with the glowing sword in his hand, a giant black wolf by his side. The wolf growled, exposing its terrifying fangs dripping with fresh blood, and Cole laughed in response, his ominous, dark laughter promising nothing good to the remaining shifters for hire.

Using the opportunity to regroup, Damian pushed off the floor, rising to his feet with a strenuous groan. The lion snapped back to him, baring its fangs in a low growl, his foul breath engulfing Damian's senses.

"Procedia Amnia!" Damian shouted, pressing his back against the wall as he summoned his daggers.

Cold perspiration covered his forehead when he realized that if the lion charged him now, he wouldn't be able to deflect the attack, praying for his basic protection spell to hold back the powerful supernatural animal. At the same time, the black wolf jumped forward, and Cole screamed, terror in his voice, and sped toward him.

As the lion leaped in the air again, the boom of a gunshot echoed through the house. Like in a slow-motion video, Damian watched a silver bullet fly through the lion's head, exiting through its eye with a splatter of blood. The animal yelped and fell dead to the floor in front of him, slowly turning into a man. The remaining three shifters assumed their human forms and froze in place, their faces contorted with fear.

Damian searched the room and saw Jamie lying on the floor, his Glock in his hands, his sword on the floor by his side. With a groan of pain, the young wizard threw the body of another dead shifter off his legs and got up, his blood-smeared left arm dangling powerlessly by his side, four deep claw marks running across his bicep.

"A goddamn lion?" he yelled, blood mixed with sweat dripping down his face. "A lion? What the fuck?"

Cole winked at Jamie and snapped his fingers at the wolf. Before Damian had a chance to say anything, the remaining shifters fell dead to the floor, beheaded and torn apart by the mighty jaws of the purebred werewolf.

With a loud roar, the black wolf shifted, taking his human form, and a heartbeat later, Atticus stood next to them, his wide chest rising and falling with heavy breaths. His clothes were torn and soaked with blood and sweat. His body was covered in bite marks and lacerations. Red and brown splatters coated his face and arms, and Damian had no doubt some of this blood was his.

"Damian, we should go upstairs," said Cole, approaching him. He frowned, and a muscle twitched in his tightly pressed jaw. "Atticus and I dealt with a few vampires and demons in the family room. He pointed toward the dark hallway on his right. "There is a staircase to the second floor there, and they were willing to do anything to stop us from going there." He raked his fingers, throwing the blood-soaked hair off his face. "Whatever they're hiding there must be important."

"Let's go." Damian headed toward the hallway, gesturing for Jamie and Atticus to follow them. "Cole, were the vampires yours? Did you manage to capture them?"

"No," replied Cole. "Not mine. I wish I could've asked them a few questions, but unfortunately, I couldn't capture any of them alive."

Stopping in front of a wide staircase leading to the second floor, Damian glanced over his shoulder and pointed at the second floor, gesturing for his friends to follow, remaining behind him. Cole frowned but didn't object.

Damian channeled his magic and opened his second sight, but just like before, he could see nothing. It seemed as though the walls of this strange house were soaked through with some magic that blocked his magical sight. Shaking his head, he slowly moved up, all his senses stretched to the maximum. As he reached the last step, he found himself in front of a doorway leading into a narrow hallway. He was about to move forward when the same tiny, high-pitched voice he'd heard before sounded in his mind again, making him flinch.

"*Commander, be careful! Above you!*"

Damian raised his eyes but could see nothing. Holding his breath, he approached the threshold, but instead of crossing it straight, he stepped slightly to the right, summoning one of his daggers. A dark figure dropped from above, aiming to crush him with their weight, but Damian was ready. In one fluid motion, he jumped to the side and spun around, catching the man, his fingers wrapping around the attacker's throat in a deadly grip.

A low growl rumbled in Damian's chest as he slammed the man against the wall and pinned him with his dagger. The assailant hissed, his eyes glowing with a menacing scarlet light, and his dangerous fangs expanded, betraying his vampiric nature. He grabbed the blade, trying to pull it out of his chest, but cried out and let go, the palm of his shaking hands covered in blisters of burns.

"Hey, Cole," Damian reached out to his brother. *"You wanted to capture a vamp? Here, I got you one, little bro. Don't ever tell me I don't get you any presents."*

Cole walked inside and stopped by his side, his glowing eyes narrowing into angry, scarlet slits. The vampire's jaw dropped as he stared at Cole, his face contorted with fear.

Damian gestured for Jamie to come in and whispered in his ear, "Do you have the silver cuffs with the runes that I made for you? I can't leave my dagger stuck in this moron."

The wizard nodded and pulled out a pair of handcuffs from his pocket, offering them to him. Damian took the cuffs and restrained the vampire, ignoring his groans of pain. The few runes engraved into the cuffs lit up with a brilliant white light as soon as the lock clicked, and the vampire cried out, his head dropping powerlessly to his chest. Then he grabbed Jamie's sword and thrust it into the vampire's chest, before pulling his dagger out. Cole leaned forward slightly and seized the vamp's hair, yanking his head back.

"Don't go anywhere, asshole," he hissed, his voice shaking with barely contained fury. "The King wants to have a word with you."

Damian touched his brother's shoulder to attract his atten-

EXCERPT

tion. *"Cole, my other sight is still blocked. Can you detect any human or supernatural presence?"*

Cole straightened and turned around, staring into the dark, long hallway lined up with closed doors on either side.

"Four heartbeats," he projected. *"Yes... three heartbeats behind the first door on the left and one heartbeat behind the door at the very end of this hallway."*

Damian approached the first door on the left and halted, listening intently. He had no idea what this little voice in his head was, but at this moment he wasn't sure he cared. Whoever it was, it saved him twice in one day. Since the voice remained silent, he assumed it was safe to open this door.

"It is safe," peeped the tiny voice in his mind. *"I would tell you if it wasn't."*

What the hell? Damian gasped, his hand reaching up to his head.

"Hello, Commander—"

Who the hell is talking in my head?

"Don't you know?"

No, goddammit!

"Ew... Language, please—"

What the fuck???

"Damian, are you okay?" whispered Jamie, touching his hand. "You look like you saw a ghost, and your tattoo is glowing a little, by the way."

Damian flinched and glanced at his arm. Under the layer of dirt and dried out blood, the runes and the words in Dragon tongue entwined with the intricate lines of the tattoo were glowing with a soft bluish light. Yakov had given him this tattoo six months ago, but he had never explained what it was and how it was supposed to work. Now it was glowing, and a strange voice was tormenting his mind, yet he had no idea how to deal with it.

I'll kill Yakov when he shows up again... Damian swallowed hard. The time wasn't right for all that.

"I'm fine," he replied to Jamie and added for the pesky, little voice in his head, *"Shut the hell up. I still have work to do here. So, unless you have something important to tell me, keep your goddamn mouth shut. I'll figure out what you are and how you're able to invade my mind later when I get home."*

"Yes, my lord, Commander. I'm as silent as a mouse."

Grrrr...

Damian pushed on the handle, but the door was locked. Without thinking twice, he pulled his leg back and kicked it, placing all his aggravation into a single push kick. The door flew off its hinges and crashed to the floor with a loud bang.

The air conditioner wasn't working, but because he was either too preoccupied with the fight or got used to the smoldering heat outside, he didn't notice it until now. The thick odor of unwashed human bodies and excrements assailed his senses as a hot wave of stuffy air, unfit for breathing, hit him in the face like a sledgehammer. He staggered back, burying his nose and mouth into the crook of his elbow.

A large bedroom with a boarded window was dimly lit by the light of a single lightbulb hanging from the ceiling in the place where a ceiling fan used to be. Three mattresses were thrown on the tiled floor, and three young women lay motionless atop mattresses. Their eyes were closed, and they appeared to be sleeping, their chest moving up and down with shallow breaths. While they weren't restrained, it didn't appear as if they had tried to escape at any time.

Damian sucked in a deep breath and walked inside, taking a knee next to the woman closest to him. Her face was pale, and deep, dark shadows lay under her eyes. Her long dark hair covered part of her face and chest, but as Damian moved it to the side, his heart gave a painful jolt. Multiple puncture wounds on her neck told him all he needed to know.

He got up, pressing his hand over his mouth, and his gut twisted with the realization of what had transpired in this dirty room with unbreathable air.

"Are they drugged?" asked Jamie, his hoarse voice breaking.

"No," Damian managed to say, his eyes darting to the other two women. He couldn't see their necks, but their arms were covered in the distinctive puncture wounds of vampire bites.

"Vampires," whispered Cole. "They're not drugged, Jamie, but they are addicted." He bit his lip, shaking his head. "To the pleasure of a vampire bite. It's worse than any drugs." Then he punched the air with his fist, a haunted expression hiding in his eyes. "Goddammit! How could I miss it? Arizona is my territory! I'm responsible for all this." He pointed at the women.

"We'll figure it out, brother." Damian moved past Cole and walked out of the room, pulling Jamie and Atticus with him. "Let's check who is in the last room, and then we need to call River. These three women are human. They lost a lot of blood and need medical attention and memory adjustments... not necessarily in that order. Cole can take care of the latter. The vampire's glamor will be safer for them than my memory modification spell."

He walked through the dark hallway, everything inside him shaking with suppressed fury. As he reached the last door, he didn't slow down but kicked it open right away. The door flew off its hinges, revealing a large, dark room behind it. Unlike the previous room, there were no mattresses on the floor, and the window wasn't boarded. In the silvery light of the moon, he saw a woman chained to a metal chair with iron chains so thick, they could hold a cruise ship moored during a hurricane.

She was dressed in a black shirt and jeans. Her clothes were partially ripped, exposing ugly welts and bruises on her arms, chest and stomach. Her head was bowed low to her chest, and her short, golden hair was covered in brown stains of dried blood. Slowly, she lifted her head. Her emerald eyes swept from one face to the next, and her full lips twitched in a crooked smirk.

"A vampire, a werewolf, a wizard and... a Destiny Enforcer," she rasped, her voice too deep for a woman. A short burst of laughter escaped her lips, but her eyes remained cold and angry. "It does sound like the beginning of a bad joke."

TEASER: THE BURNS FIRE

(THE FIRE SALAMANDER CHRONICLES BOOK 1)

~Zane Burns, a.k.a. Gunz~
Modern Day, South Florida

The restaurant was nothing special, just another tiny hole-in-the-wall located on one of the countless South Florida canals. There wasn't anything noteworthy about its limited menu either. The only thing special about this place was its relaxed atmosphere. The restaurant had an open porch with three tables facing the canal. But the regulars were never sitting on the porch. They preferred to stay inside, leaving the romantic view to tourists and lovey-dovey couples.

Gunz had discovered this place shortly after he moved to South Florida, and since then he had become one of the regulars, visiting the restaurant at least a couple of times a week. He liked the laid-back atmosphere and easy-going crowd. It was a place where he allowed himself to relax and drop his guard. To a degree.

The inside room of the restaurant wasn't big, just a few tables and a bar. A big screen TV was hanging on the wall

TEASER: THE BURNS FIRE

behind the bar, next to a few shelves with liquor. The air was infused with the smell of alcohol and fried food, and a heavy curtain of cigarette smoke was hanging under the ceiling. The room was relatively dark. Out of six wall lights only three were on, but no one ever asked to turn up the light.

Gunz walked through the room, quickly surveying every corner, and sat down at the bar. Tonight, besides a few regulars, there was no one new. A pretty young woman in her mid-twenties approached him right away. Here, she was everything—the owner of the restaurant, a bartender, a waitress—all-in-one, cross-functional queen of *Missi's Kitchen*.

"Usual, Mr. Burns?" she asked, smiling at him. Her skin, the color of dark chocolate, was smooth like silk and her large gray eyes framed with thick black eyelashes looked unnaturally bright on her face. Her long black hair was braided into countless thin braids and pulled into a ponytail on the back of her head, calling attention to her elegant neck.

"Yes, Missi, thank you," said Gunz.

She put three small shot glasses on the bar table in front of him and filled them with vodka. "I'll be back with your food in a moment," she told him, heading toward the kitchen door.

"Take your time, Missi," muttered Gunz, picking up the first shot glass. "I'm not in any rush tonight." He took a deep breath and downed the vodka without flinching. Placing the empty shot glass on the table, he exhaled and closed his eyes, enjoying the feeling of the harsh burning liquid rushing down his throat.

For a few minutes, he sat quietly staring at the TV. It was set to the local news channel, but he didn't listen to the news, his thoughts far away. Then he sighed and picked up the second shot glass. He gulped the vodka and put the empty glass next to the first one.

"Hard day, Mr. Burns?" asked Missi, placing a plate with a burger and steaming pile of french fries in front of him. "You seem to look broodier than usual."

Gunz smirked. He picked up a hot french fry with his fingers and nibbled on it. "You could say so," he said finally. "Just one of those days... This day a couple of years ago, I lost... someone."

"Your friend?" asked Missi, gazing at him with sympathy in her bright eyes.

"Yeah... friend. Vladislav Kirilenko," he replied absentmindedly, taking the next burning-hot fry from his plate. "I lost him to the world of magic. He's never coming back."

"*The World of Magic*," she repeated in disbelief, her eyebrows rising. "What is that? A fantasy novel? There is no such thing as magic. You're making fun of me, Mr. Burns." She shook her head, a soft smile tugging at her full lips.

Gunz smiled tiredly and picked up the last shot glass, squeezing it in his fist. "Third one for the fallen," he murmured and drank it quickly, returning the empty glass to Missi. "You know, Missi, I've been coming to your restaurant for over a year. Don't you think it's time you stop calling me *Mr. Burns*? I don't think I'm that much older than you. You know that you can call me Zane, or even Gunz, if you prefer to use my nickname."

"I know. I don't like nicknames. You're a man, not a pet," she said lightly, taking away the empty shot glasses and wiping the tabletop with a white towel. "Zane Burns..." She pronounced his name slowly, like she was sizing it up. "Sounds good, but I prefer to call you Mr. Burns. For some reason, it seems to fit you better."

Gunz felt someone's hand on his elbow and a hardly noticeable wave of magical energy swept through him. He snapped his head to the right and found a fake blond sitting next to him. She was devouring him with her eyes, her lipstick-enhanced lips stretched in a sensual smile. Her hand unceremoniously traveled up his arm, following the shape of his biceps, and stopped at his shoulder.

"Yum," she said, gently probing him with her magic. "I'll call you anything you want, hon."

Gunz gave her a frosty once-over, turning his senses up. He had no doubt that she was something other than human. Her fingers softly massaged his shoulder, sending a stronger wave of magical energy through him. For a moment, his mind became clouded with desire and his body responded to her salacious magic with more eagerness than he expected.

Succubus, concluded Gunz, channeling the Fire, burning the poison of her magic out of his body. Her hand traveled down his arm, landing on his inner thigh. He seized her wrist, prying it off his leg and sent some fire toward his hand. Her skin blistered like from the touch of a hot stove and she yelped in pain.

"Who are you? What are you?" she whimpered, trying to free herself from his smoldering grip, but he didn't let her go.

Gunz glanced around, making sure that no one, including Missi, was watching. "I'm a man who is not looking for company," he growled, sending some fire toward his eyes. The bright flames went up in the depths of his eyes, and she gasped. "Especially not the company of your kind." He released her wrist, observing red spots of burns and blisters on her skin. "Leave this place and forget about its existence. You understand?"

She nodded, fear making her every move jerky, and rushed out of the restaurant, nursing her burnt wrist. Gunz sighed, releasing the Fire, and turned back to the bar.

"Hey, Missi," he called and waited a moment as she appeared from the kitchen. "Can I have everything to go, please? And one more before I leave." He pointed at the bottle of Russian vodka that he usually ordered.

She put a shot glass on the bar table and filled it with vodka. "That's unusual," she murmured, her hands quickly packaging the burger and fries into a take-out box. "You never drink more than three shots."

A lopsided smile crossed his face, making a single dimple

appear on one of his cheeks. "I know. Usually three shots are my limit, but today I felt like I needed more." He downed the vodka and got up, grabbing the take-out box.

Missi shook her head, checking him with concern. "Do you want me to call you a cab?"

"Thank you, Missi. I'll walk. Take care." He nodded to her and walked out of the restaurant.

* * *

Gunz walked away from the restaurant and turned into a dark alley. He stopped and rubbed his forehead tiredly. *Maybe Missi was right. I didn't need that fourth shot,* he thought, smirking. It had been a while since he felt drunk and right now the world around him seemed to be unsteady. Possibly it was a combination of vodka with the residuals of the succubus magic. He surveyed the alley carefully to make sure that no one could see him and once satisfied, he waved his hand, unfolding the fire curtain of a portal.

He walked through the fire and ended up in the backyard of his house in Coral Springs. The house wasn't really his. It belonged to his friend, but she was away and wasn't planning to come back any time soon. In the meantime, Gunz had the full use of her house. Dizziness assailed him as he took a step forward. He chuckled and sat down heavily on the steps in front of the back door.

He closed his eyes and leaned his back against the door of the house, still feeling a little buzzed. He was about to get up when he felt a soft touch to his leg. Gunz looked down and noticed a small kitten. It couldn't have been more than a month old. The kitten was trying to climb on his lap, its tiny sharp claws catching the hard fabric of his jeans.

"Oh, hello, little buddy. What are you doing here?" said Gunz. He put the take-out box on the steps and gently picked

TEASER: THE BURNS FIRE

up the kitten, holding it in his hands. The kitten turned on his engine, purring loudly, and licked his hand. Gunz laughed, gently stroking the kitten's thick gray fur with his fingers. "You found the wrong man, little buddy. I'm a dog person—give me a giant German Shepherd any day. Well, occasionally, I don't mind dealing with lizards. But cats…"

The kitten ignored his statement and climbed up his shirt, settling on his shoulder. He meowed into his ear and poked his cheek with his wet nose. Gunz petted the kitten, leaving him sitting on his shoulder, and picked up the take-out box. "Well, you're taking your life in your own paws, buddy… but if you're sure that you want to adopt a man like me then let's get going." He unlocked the door and walked into the kitchen.

Inside, Gunz put the kitten on the floor and opened the refrigerator. He poured some milk in a small bowl and placed it in front of him.

"Sorry, little buddy, I don't have any cat food or litter for you"—he quickly glanced at the wall clock that was showing past one in the morning—"and it's too late for shopping. I'll buy everything you need first thing in the morning."

The kitten ignored him, preoccupied with his milk. Gunz squatted next to him and softly stroked his back. The kitten moved closer to his bowl and growled defensively. Gunz laughed, rising. "I think I'll call you Mishka in honor of my good friend. You sure remind me of him."

He left the kitten in the kitchen and walked to the living room. His body was buzzing with the exhaustion of this endless day and the incident with the succubus didn't sit well with him. Missi's restaurant was normally free of supernatural visitors. He was probably the only one. And the succubus' behavior seemed a bit odd too. Until he used his power, she didn't sense the creature of magic in him. Something didn't feel right.

His cell phone rang, making him flinch. He pulled it out and

TEASER: THE BURNS FIRE

looked at the display. Jim. *One o'clock in the morning? That can't be good.* He clicked the green button, answering the call.

"Hello, Jim," he said and fell silent for a few seconds, listening to Jim. "You want me to come over now? Can it wait till morning?"

He lowered the phone down for a moment and sighed, bringing the shouting device back to his ear.

"No, I'm not drunk. Just a little—," Jim interrupted him urgently, obviously not pleased and Gunz fell silent again, listening to his boss. "Yes, sir, I know the consequences of losing control of my power and I assure you, I'm in complete control."

Gunz lowered himself on the couch, rubbing the stubble on his chin tiredly.

"Yes, sir, I know that my job doesn't have weekends and days off," he said, hoping to calm Jim down. "I'm sorry, sir, I needed to unwind a little... I'm not drunk..."

He had been working with Agent Andrews for over a year and he had never heard him talking like this to him. Something serious was going on.

"Yes, sir, I know what Code Shadow means... I understand the urgency of the situation... No, sir. You don't need to summon me."

Jim didn't have magic and he couldn't use summoning spells, but his partner, Angelique, could. She was a witch and a seer. Gunz hated when they used summoning spells to call him. The persistent pull of the summoning spell on his mind was driving him crazy, giving him a pounding headache afterwards.

"I prefer not to drive right now, so I'll open my portal to your office right away, if you don't mind... Yes, sir, to Angelique's office... I'll see you both in a few minutes."

Gunz hung up the phone and shook his head, biting his lip. Code Shadow. It meant an abnormally high level of supernatural activity, endangering civilian lives. Since he started to work with the secret division of the FBI, dealing with supernatural occurrences, it was the first time that Code Shadow was officially issued.

"Fire Salamander—go," he muttered to himself and waved his hand, opening the fire portal into Angelique's office.

Get your copy of The Burns Fire Online Today!

DEAR READER

Thank you so much for reading The Shadow Enforcer. I hope you enjoyed the book and will join Damian Blake's next adventure in the second book of the series.

If you would like to stay up-to-date on the latest information about new releases, special offers, and more, sign up for my mailing list and get a FREE novella—www.nmthorn.com.

For more information follow me on

Facebook (www.facebook.com/nmthornauthor)
Instagram (www.instagram.com/nmthornauthor)
Or visit my website www.nmthorn.com
Join N.M Thorn's readers group to meet other readers, discuss the novels and the characters, get updates and do anything else related to the series.
www.facebook.com/groups/authornmthorn

BEFORE YOU GO...

Your reviews mean the world to me and are greatly appreciated. If you enjoyed the Shadow Deception, please take a few minutes to leave a review. It doesn't have to be long. It can be just a few words or stars rating.

Please help spread the word by taking this small extra step and leave your review on Amazon and/or Goodreads.

ABOUT THE AUTHOR

N.M. Thorn currently lives in South Florida with her husband and son. Owner of a digital marketing agency by day and a writer by night, she loves spending her times creating new worlds, paranormal planes of existence and anything that could be described as supernatural.

When she is not busy working with everything digital or exploring fantasy worlds, she enjoys spending time with her family, reading, painting and practicing martial arts.

If you would like to share your thoughts, ideas or just send N.M. Thorn a message about the Fire Salamander world, feel free to contact her at: nmthornauthor@gmail.com

facebook.com/nmthornauthor
instagram.com/nmthornauthor
amazon.com/N-M-Thorn/e/B07MY9JZMB

Printed in Great Britain
by Amazon